"James writes smart, taut, high-octane thrillers. But be warned—his books are not for the timid. The endings blow me away every time."
—Mitch Galin, producer of Stephen King's *The Stand* and Frank Herbert's *Dune*

## Praise for the Novels of Steven James

### Checkmate

"*Checkmate* is high tension all the way. The author writes with precision and incisiveness. Fast, sharp, and believable. Put it at the top of your list."
—John Lutz, Edgar Award–winning author of *Single White Female* and *Frenzy*

"In his latest Patrick Bowers thriller, Steven James pens another fast-paced thriller chock-full of great characters, head-snapping plot twists, impeccable research, and a truly fun ride. Highly recommended. Not to be missed."
—D. P. Lyle, award-winning author of the Dub Walker and Samantha Cody thriller series

"A perfectly crafted, hard-hitting, intense thriller that takes readers to the top of the cliff and dangles them over the edge. James is an author that every thriller reader should have on their bookshelf." —*Suspense Magazine*

### The King

"His tightly woven, adrenaline-laced plots leave readers breathless." —The Suspense Zone

"Steven James offers yet another slam dunk in the Bowers Files series!" —*Suspense Magazine*

"Highly engaging, with consuming tension and solid storytelling." —TitleTrakk.com

"If you love edgy, intense, on-the-edge-of-horrifying coupled with great writing, then click and order this one now." —Novel Reviews

*continued . . .*

"*The Bishop*—full of plot twists, nightmarish villains, and family conflicts—kept me turning pages on a red-eye all the way from New York City to Amsterdam. Steven James tells stories that grab you by the collar and don't let go."
—Norb Vonnegut, author, *Top Producer*, editor of Acrimony.com

"Steven James locks you in a thrill ride with no brakes. He sets the new standard in suspense writing."
—*Suspense Magazine*

## More Praise for Steven James and His Award-Winning Novels

"James delivers first-rate characters, dazzling plot twists, and powers it all with nonstop action."
—John Tinker, Emmy-winning screenplay writer

"Once again, James has given us a ripsnorting thriller with a beating heart."
—*New York Times* bestselling author Eric Wilson

"James delivers . . . caffeinated plot twists and intriguing characterizations. Riveting . . . a gripping plot and brisk pacing will win James some fans eager for his next offering."
—*Publishers Weekly* (starred review)

"[An] exceptional psychological thriller."
—Armchair Interviews

"Brilliant. . . . Steven James gives us a captivating look at the fine line between good and evil in the human heart. Not to be missed."
—Ann Tatlock, Christy Award–winning author

"Exquisite."
—Fiction Fanatics Only!

"Best story of the year—perfectly executed."
—The Suspense Zone (2008 Reviewer's Choice Award)

"In a word, intense."
—Mysterious Reviews

"Steven James writes at a breakneck pace, effortlessly pulling the reader along on this incredible thrill ride. A writer to watch for."
—Fiction Addict

## THE BOWERS FILES

# CHECKMATE

### THE BOWERS FILES

## STEVEN JAMES

A SIGNET SELECT BOOK

SIGNET SELECT
Published by the Penguin Group
Penguin Group (USA) LLC, 375 Hudson Street,
New York, New York 10014

USA | Canada | UK | Ireland | Australia | New Zealand | India | South Africa | China
penguin.com
A Penguin Random House Company

First published by Signet Select, an imprint of New American Library,
a division of Penguin Group (USA) LLC

First Printing, December 2014

Copyright © Steven James, 2014

SIGNET SELECT and logo are trademarks of Penguin Group (USA) LLC.

ISBN 978-0-451-46734-8

Printed in the United States of America
10  9  8  7  6  5  4  3  2  1

*To my wife*

"After the game, the king and the pawn go into the same box."

—Italian proverb

# PART I

## Arrowheads

# Prologue

He stood in front of the mirror, unsure he really wanted to remove the bandages.

His plastic surgeon had said there wouldn't be any scarring, had promised him that the incisions on his face would heal quickly, that the stitches would come out on their own.

But still, the surgery hadn't taken place under the most ideal conditions and, although his doctor had an unparalleled reputation, he knew she might have been distracted by everything else that was going on.

He wondered what lay beneath the bandages, beneath the stitches.

A new face.

A new future.

He took a deep breath, reached up, and unfastened the end of one of the bandages that wound around his head.

The surgery had been aggressive and it wasn't the way he would have preferred going about this, any of this. Everything was rushed and the thought of seeing what he would look like for the rest of his life made him a little uneasy.

Slowly, carefully, he began to unwrap the bandage.

His surgeon had told him to wait three to five days.

It had been two.

Though he was relatively self-possessed in many areas of his life, he was anxious about this. There was so much to do before August and he wouldn't be able to do any of it if the surgery wasn't successful.

As he unraveled the bandage he saw that it was tainted with dots of dried blood.

*Unraveled. That's a good way to put it.*

*Everything that was true of your life just over a year ago has unraveled.*

The last few bandages were placed across the incisions and stitches.

Somewhat hesitantly, he peeled them off, until he was looking at his new face, revealed.

It was the strangest sensation, staring into a mirror and seeing the face of a stranger you knew to be yourself.

After depositing the bandages in the trash can beside the sink, he studied his reflection.

Revealed.

Yes, his face was swollen and misshapen, but even with all that, he could tell the difference.

His plastic surgeon really had done an amazing job, especially considering how much stress she'd been under when she performed the surgery.

He had the same bone structure—yes, of course, certainly—and the same general characteristics, but there were enough subtle differences to make it appear that he was someone else entirely.

"We are all strangers to ourselves," he remembered hearing one time, "when the masks fall away."

Well, had the masks really fallen away, or was this just another one for him to wear?

Either way, he was emerging, unfolding, like a butterfly flexing its wings for the first time.

Some people seek out surgery like this to hide the

signs of aging. Others need it to recover from a life-altering accident. Still others so they can start over, start fresh.

That was him.

A second chance to get things right.

After all that'd happened in the last year, after all the publicity—which, truthfully, still hadn't quieted down—after all that, well, it would be much easier if there was a way to go online and pull up the information that was out there and press Delete.

But it doesn't work that way with the Internet.

In cyberspace there's no way to erase your past.

He ran a finger along his jawline and then over the ridge of one of the incisions.

So you have to erase yourself.

A few follow-up appointments with his plastic surgeon would probably be a good idea, but the logistics made that difficult and he expected that he would only be seeing her one last time.

He would ask her about the best post-op care, make sure he knew how to avoid infection, and then be on his way.

Touching the mirror, he traced the outline of his face on the cool glass.

*Here is where you are now. Here.*

*Now.*

Erased.

And revealed.

His wife had divorced him last summer.

He had lost all of his friends during the trial.

Yes, it was time to make a break with the past.

But first, a visit to his surgeon.

Turning off the bathroom light, he headed for the basement, where he'd kept her since the surgery.

Both her and her boy.

When he opened the door at the top of the steps he could hear the child crying.

He decided he would take care of him first—that way the boy wouldn't be frightened when he saw what was happening to his mother.

Unpocketing the knife he would be using, he flicked out the blade, closed the door behind him, and descended the stairs.

To write the first chapter of his new life.

# 1

Eight weeks later

Monday, July 29
Tarry Lawnmower Supply
42 Wayside Road
Dale City, Virginia
8:54 a.m.

Lawnmower posters decorated the walls. Toy riding lawnmowers sat on the receptionist's desk beside the out-of-date computer, ink-jet printer, and an in-box overflowing with receipts, orders, and invoices.

The receptionist was armed.

We knew that.

And she was a good shot.

We knew that too.

After all, the purpose of this building was not to supply and distribute lawnmowers, but you wouldn't know that from studying its website or from simply entering the front lobby.

You wouldn't even know it from watching the semis arrive and leave from the building's loading dock out back as they made deliveries or "picked up orders."

The trucks were driven by undercover agents. We didn't even leave something like that to a private security firm.

No.

Not here.

All a necessary illusion.

Even though the receptionist knew us, Ralph and I were aware that she would be asking for our creds, so we held them out as we approached her desk.

I scratched at my rib cage. Because of a shooting at DEA headquarters last week, everyone here today—including Ralph and me—was wearing body armor. Lightweight, but still a little uncomfortable.

The agent who'd been shot was alright, but it'd put everyone on high alert. Having to wear one of these to work was an annoyance, but for those of us in the business it was more common than most people might think. In keeping with the secrecy of this place we normally didn't wear them over our shirts, but I had a light rain jacket on today so my shirt was under my vest.

"Good morning, Debra." I saw the framed picture of her nine-year-old daughter, Allie, beside the computer monitor. "How's that little girl of yours?"

"Mischievous. Playful." She carefully studied my credentials, but seemed a little distracted, agitated. "Always into something—you know how it is."

Actually, I knew almost nothing about bringing up girls, at least not from personal experience. Though I did have an eighteen-year-old daughter, I wasn't the one who'd raised her.

Tessa's mother and I had married three years ago, and her dad had never been in the picture. Then, less than six months after our wedding, Christie died of breast cancer, and Tessa and I started the long, arduous task of trying to recover together, trying to re-form a family with just the two of us.

For a long time it hadn't gone very well. Now, however, things were finally on the right track. I was remarried, and it seemed like those days of watching my late wife die were in another lifetime.

I was still caught up in my thoughts about my family when Debra handed back my creds. While I waited for her to finish with Ralph's, I glanced out the window. Rain drizzled beyond the bulletproof glass, providing a welcome respite from the northern Virginia heat wave we'd been experiencing.

Ralph drained the last of his forty-four-ounce gas station cup of Mountain Dew. I had coffee with me from home, where he'd picked me up.

Guatemalan Antigua.

Never trust gas station java. You can't even trust most coffee shops if you truly enjoy a cup of good coffee. I'd roasted these beans over the weekend. Normally I would have downed it in the car, but today I'd been waiting to savor it.

Now I tasted some.

*Yes.*

*Excellent.*

Although . . . thinking about it . . . I might have gotten by without grinding the beans quite so fine.

Special Agent Debra Guirret finished and, satisfied, waved us over to a door behind her desk. Ralph flipped down the numbered keypad beside it, punched in the entry code, and then we passed through the security checkpoint and started toward the elevator bay.

Debra had been working the front desk here at the headquarters for the Bureau's National Center for the Analysis of Violent Crime, or NCAVC, for the last six months, ever since moving to the area from Baltimore after her divorce.

This building contained the offices of the FBI's profilers and housed the archives for ViCAP, the Violent Criminal Apprehension Program, which was the world's largest repository of investigative material on solved and unsolved homicides, sexual assaults, and missing-persons cases.

Needless to say, this was not a place whose location we wanted to announce—thus, the lawnmower distribution–center facade here in this isolated industrial district near Quantico.

Despite what might appear on the news, and despite the fumbling attempts of the NSA to keep whistleblowers' revelations about their hacking attempts and covert surveillance programs under wraps, when the Bureau sets out to keep a secret, it does a surprisingly good job.

Admittedly, Director Wellington took a bit of pride in that—although we would see how things moved on from here since she recently announced that she would be leaving the Bureau in the fall to start her campaign for Virginia's First District congressional seat.

Ralph and I walked side by side down the hall, my friend's hulking frame filling the space beside me. Even though I was a little taller than he was, he probably had me by fifty pounds. Solid muscle. Before joining the Bureau, he had served a stint as an Army Ranger and before that he'd been a high school All-American wrestler. Not a guy you'd want to mess with.

Glad he was on our side.

We arrived at the elevators.

"So." I pressed the Up button. "It's what, five days, now?"

"Six and counting. She was way early with Tony—

course, that was twelve years ago. So who knows? She's all into this natural-childbirth deal: doesn't want to be induced—any of that. And so we wait." He sighed and rubbed his hand across his shaved head. "I'm getting too old for this."

"You're only forty-one, my friend."

He grunted in vague acknowledgment. "Just wait till you hit forty."

I still had three years to look forward to that milestone.

The elevator doors opened and we entered.

"You still thinking Shanelle?" I asked him.

"Brin's going back and forth between that and Tryphena."

"Tryphena?"

"It's Greek. Means 'delicate.' Brin came across it the other day somewhere in the Bible, thought it was pretty."

"It is. It's nice."

"It's growing on me."

As the NCAVC director, he had an office on the third floor. He punched the 3 button and the doors closed.

I had a workspace set up just down the hall from him, but my actual office was at the FBI Academy, where I taught environmental criminology and geospatial investigation. It wasn't easy, but I tried my hardest not to undermine the material taught in the other classes, where the instructors covered the importance of searching for means, motive, and opportunity, none of which I was a big fan of.

Or the focus on DNA—which recent studies had shown could be faked with a little know-how and ingenuity, not to mention the existence of multiple genomes in the same person, which, as it turns out, is much more common than we used to think.

Or profiling—and that always promised a spirited conversation when I brought it up with my wife of two months, who was one of the Bureau's top profilers.

The elevator doors slid apart, and we found our way to Ralph's office at the end of the hall.

He had his own unique, personalized "filing system" and his desk contained countless stacks of papers strewn in an array of meticulously organized clutter. Ever since being appointed to this position a year ago, he'd shown an astonishing ability to find anything he needed when he needed it, a chore that might have taken someone else hours. "Added security," he told me once with a hint of pride, "and it doesn't cost the Bureau a dime."

Added security.

I liked that.

Maybe I could use that line to explain the condition of my side of the bedroom closet at home.

A photo of Ralph's family floated across his computer's screen. Brineesha—his diminutive, pretty, no-nonsense African-American wife and Tony, their twelve-year-old video game–playing, skateboarder son. Ralph had tried to get him interested in wrestling, but Tony preferred soccer, a sport Ralph complained reminded him of France.

Ralph did not like France.

He shuffled through the sheaves of paper and retrieved the file on a missing-persons case the NCAVC was consulting on.

I had taken my rain jacket off and was situating myself in the chair facing his desk when I received a text from Jerome Cole.

Jerome was one of the agents responsible for driving the eighteen-wheelers that delivered the lawnmowers to the back of the building. His text: He wanted me to meet with him in the lobby.

When I looked up, I saw that Ralph also had his phone out. He glanced my direction, then turned his cell's screen so I could see it.

"Mine says he wants to meet me in the lobby," I said.

"And mine says the loading bay."

"Wonder what's up."

He was already on his feet. "Let's go find out."

Maybe it wasn't strange that Jerome wanted to speak to the NCAVC director in the loading bay, but it was odd that he would ask to meet with me in the lobby at the same time.

From here the stairs were closer than the elevators so we took them down to the ground floor.

Ralph gestured for me to follow him. "We'll check the loading bay first. It's on the way."

When we arrived, five other people were already there, milling around.

An array of several dozen riding lawnmowers stood parked in neat lines throughout the expansive room.

A semi was backed up to the dock and, from what it looked like, someone had just unloaded a mower that sat behind the truck.

Two more people emerged from the hallway and entered the loading bay.

"What's going on?" Ralph didn't sound angry, but his gruff voice naturally rumbled off the walls. A couple of the agents mentioned texts they'd gotten. One still had her phone out.

As I walked toward the truck, I was able to glimpse the face of the driver in the side-view mirror. Dark glasses. A well-worn ball cap. Hard to tell through the rain, but it didn't look like Jerome.

"Hey," I called. "Hang on."

No reply. The truck was idling.

He glanced my way, but only for a second. He didn't step out of the vehicle, but instead reached out with his left hand to adjust the side-view mirror. When he did, I saw he was wearing a wedding band.

*Jerome isn't married.*

Unholstering my weapon I started for the loading dock. "Step out of the cab. Hands where I can see them."

He shifted into gear and started rolling forward.

I spun toward the group of profilers and technicians, my attention on that lawnmower sitting on the loading dock.

"Clear the bay," I shouted. "Now!"

Looks of confusion.

"Go!"

I leapt off the loading dock and started sprinting through the rain toward the truck, but I'd only made it seven or eight meters from the building when the explosion ripped through the loading bay behind me, the force of the blast sending me hurtling toward an SUV parked nearby.

Impact.

Then stars.

And then everything went black.

# 2

Ringing.

A ringing in my head.

Sharp. Distinct. Disorienting.

For a moment it seemed like it was a part of me that'd always been there, lurking just beneath my consciousness, and had only now been set free.

*Yes, and it'll always be there from now on. It'll never stop.*

*Never stop.*

Even though I could tell I was sprawled against the parking lot and lying on my stomach, it felt like my balance was off and I was about to fall over.

I felt rain splattering against the back of my neck. That, along with the noise in my head, a sore right rib cage, the brassy taste of blood from a cut lip, and the dizziness, all told me something that was obvious, but that also seemed necessary to remind myself of: I was breathing, existing, hurting.

Yes.

I was alive.

Somewhere beyond the sharp noise reverberating in my head, I heard a woman scream.

*This is real. This is now. Go.*

Trying to gather my bearings, I clambered to my feet, but still off balance, I almost collapsed and had to lean my hand against the side of the SUV to steady myself.

*Get ahold of yourself, Pat. Do it.*

Finally, the ringing began to subside, but my senses all seemed to fuse together and it was hard to sort out what I was seeing from what I was hearing: the cries for help; the muted gray air billowing ash and dust; the tart, ripe taste of some type of explosive—all became one and then splintered apart again.

Sight. Sound. Taste.

Presence.

I scanned the parking lot. The semi was gone. With cloud cover this thick, there was no way our defense satellites would have caught footage of it leaving and—

The woman screamed again. Louder this time.

I faced the building.

The gaping hole torn through it was spewing out dust and smoke like a great mouth exhaling stained air into the day.

Quickly, I scrambled back onto the loading bay where my friends and coworkers were.

Not far from me, Ralph was lying on his back, unmoving on the concrete. I rushed toward him through the maze of damaged lawnmowers, ceiling beams, and rubble, then stooped and touched his shoulder. "Ralph, you okay?"

He didn't stir.

Only as I knelt beside him did I feel the sharp slivers of pain on my right side along my rib cage, where there'd been a vague ache since I first came to.

It wasn't vague anymore. I looked down. Four jagged shards of metal were sticking through my body armor into my side, the largest protruding maybe five or six centimeters, the smallest, two or three.

It wasn't possible to determine how deeply embedded into my side the pieces were, but when I tried to pry one loose, I found that it was pretty firmly lodged in there.

Pulling my vest off would have ripped them out. At least right now the bleeding was controlled and I didn't anticipate that any of the wounds were life-threatening.

*Okay. Deal with that later.*

"Ralph?"

Nothing.

A tremor of fear caught hold of me.

He had to be alright.

*He is.*

*He's okay.*

I felt for a pulse.

It took me a moment to find it, but I did.

*Good.*

*Okay, good.*

First-aid training kicked in: check airway, breathing, circulation, and look for blood loss.

None visible.

I repositioned his head to make sure his airway was clear.

When he didn't awaken I shook him gently, trying to revive him. "Ralph, you with me here?"

He still didn't move and I felt a deepening sense of uneasiness.

*Come on, man.*

*Come—*

I tried reviving him once more and this time he groaned, coughed roughly, and opened his eyes.

"You alright?" I asked concernedly.

"Yeah," he muttered, then rubbed one giant paw against his forehead. His gaze found my blood-soaked shirt. "You?"

"I'm okay."

He indicated toward the metal protruding from my side. "You sure?"

"Yes."

There's no such thing as a "bulletproof" vest. Though body armor is designed to dull the impact of most center-mass shots from the front or back, objects can penetrate them on the sides where the vests Velcro shut. I shuddered to think of what that shrapnel would have done if I hadn't been wearing this thing.

Though I tried telling Ralph to rest for a minute, he would have none of that and started getting up.

In the end, I helped him to his feet and we turned our attention toward the rest of the loading bay.

Half the ceiling was gone.

Rain fell around us, creating a thick residue of ash that was turning muddy around our feet.

Despite the rain, the tinge of the explosion still lingered in the air, but there was another smell lurking beneath the acidic residue of whatever explosive had been used. I recognized it from arson cases I'd worked.

Flesh.

Burnt flesh.

And then I saw why.

An arm, scorched and blackened and ripped off at the elbow, lay about four meters in front of me on the concrete.

But that wasn't the only body part I saw.

It looked like a war zone, like the footage you see in the aftermath of suicide bombings in the Middle East—in those rare cases when the news coverage hasn't been scrupulously edited and tidied up, and the footage actually shows what happened.

Amid splashes of blood, shredded body parts lay scattered across the floor and on the riding lawnmowers that were tipped over and blackened from the blast. Based on the burn patterns on the concrete and the positioning of the debris and the wreckage, the explosion had apparently come from the lawnmower that'd been left behind by the semi driver.

I felt a tight grip of grief and anger.

I've been with the Bureau for just over ten years and before that I worked as a cop and homicide detective. You'd think that after all these years of investigating homicides and consulting on some of the most shocking crimes in the country, I'd be able to look at scenes like this with emotional distance or detachment.

But that's never happened. I always think of the pain, the loss, the finality of it all.

The woman who'd been screaming was silent now and was staring vacantly at the rubble, muttering to herself. She was an analyst named Pamela Neumann and didn't appear to be seriously injured but was obviously in shock.

She'd drawn her purse close to her and was clutching it like it was some sort of anchor back to the normal world, before any of this happened.

A weak cry came from the other side of the loading bay: "Help."

Stu Ritterman, one of our ViCAP techs, sat leaning against the wall in a part of the building that lay just out of the rain. Since several riding mowers were in the way, I could only see him from the waist up.

"Go." Ralph had his phone out and was calling dispatch.

"Get a BOLO out on the semi." As I hurried toward Stu I relayed the license plate number to Ralph and confirmed that he had an accurate description of the truck.

When I was halfway to Stu I realized why his cries were so feeble.

Both of his legs were gone: one blown off just below the knee, the other halfway up his thigh. His femur bone protruded gruesomely from the meaty stump where his leg had been. Beneath him, a widening pool of fresh blood was spreading across the concrete.

He was trying, but failing, to put enough pressure on the stump to stop the arterial bleeding.

I whipped off my belt and encircled his thigh with it; then I slipped him my wallet to bite into. "This is going to hurt," I said.

As I cranked on the tourniquet I thought Stu might pass out from the pain, but somehow he managed to stay conscious.

It probably would have made it a lot easier on him if he'd blacked out.

*It's too late. He's lost too much blood.*

*No!*

*You can save him. You can.*

The bleeding finally slowed, then stopped. After removing his belt from his waist, I started on a tourniquet for his other leg.

A heavy scraping sound behind me caught my attention. I glanced back in time to see Ralph single-handedly heave aside a huge ceiling beam that had fallen onto Wendy Foster and was pinning her shoulder to the ground.

I couldn't tell if she was alive or not.

Focusing my attention on Stu again, I tightened the second tourniquet, but realized that besides stopping the bleeding, there wasn't really anything I could do for him.

The truth hit me.

Harsh and cold and real: I was not going to be able to save this man.

He let the wallet drop from his mouth.

Based on the amount of blood he'd already lost, I anticipated that he was only going to be able to survive for another couple of minutes.

What do you say to someone who's dying? Do you ask him if he's made peace with God? Do you try to comfort him? Lie, and tell him he's going to be alright?

What's more important: hope or truth?

Sirens in the distance.

"The paramedics are on their way." I put my hand gently on his forearm. "Hang in there."

It felt like a lie disguised as encouragement and I hated that I'd said it, since it implied he would be able to hold on until the EMTs arrived, that they were going to be able to do something to save him when they got here.

He winced in pain with every labored breath.

I'm no expert on talking to God, but I gave it my best shot, praying urgently that Stu would pull through.

As I did, I tried to believe that it would make a difference, that I would see a miracle unfold before me here today, but I couldn't seem to gather up that much faith.

Stu's eyes rolled back.

"Hey!" I slapped his face to keep him conscious. "Stay with me!"

It worked for the moment, bought me a little time. I wanted to assure him that he was going to be okay, that he was going to make it, that the paramedics were going to take care of him, but I knew it was too late for any of that.

I knew it, and I think he did too.

There comes a time when deception does no good—I realized that now as I gently positioned him on his back and used one hand to support his head.

Stu was married; I'd met his wife at a barbecue over at Ralph's house a couple of weeks ago.

No kids. Married less than a year.

I knew that if I asked him the question I had in mind it would be a way of telling him that it was too late, but it was all I could think to do for him at this point.

I didn't have much time to waste debating things, so I just went ahead and said it: "Is there anything you want me to tell Sherry?"

The look on his face made it clear that he knew what I was saying, that my question was an acknowledgment of the inevitable.

His voice was strained as he answered. "I'm sorry."

"No, it's okay, you don't have to—"

"No." From the grimace on his face it was evident that it took a lot of effort for him to reply. "Tell her. I'm sorry. About Iris."

I had no idea who Iris was, but I couldn't keep myself from speculating that Sherry might not be too thrilled to hear her name.

"I will."

Stu didn't respond.

Would never respond.

Over the years I've had four people die in my arms, and each time it's happened there has been a terrible moment when their eyes stopped focusing on me and their gaze just drifted off toward a vacant place in the distance that doesn't exist.

It was a frightening, terrible shift.

Life to death.

That quickly.

One woman in Wisconsin whom I tried to save after a serial killer had attacked her—had cut her in ways no one could have survived from—closed her eyes in the end, and that was better because I got the impression that she'd found some sort of peace.

But that's not what happened now.

Stu's eyes simply glazed over.

And stayed open.

He went limp as the ambulance sirens drew closer, but not quickly enough, almost as if they were mocking the moment of his death.

*Ha! See? We're not there yet.*

*We're not going to get there in time.*

*And what are you going to do about that?*

Though I had a hard time believing that it was going to make any difference at this point, I started chest compressions to keep the blood that Stu hadn't already lost circulating through his system.

And that's what I was still doing when the paramedics arrived and took over for me.

# 3

I stood there beside the EMTs and silently watched as they worked on Stu.

His eyes were still staring blankly at the ceiling and beyond it, beyond everything. The paramedics transferred him to a gurney to get him to the hospital as quickly as possible, but by their demeanor, they didn't appear to hold out much hope for him either.

As they rolled him toward the ambulance, I studied the scene.

Habit.

I couldn't tell immediately how many people had been killed by the explosion, but glancing around the loading bay I reviewed where everyone had been standing when the blast went off. I let the map of the area unfold in my mind.

Time. Space.

Geospatial orientation.

What I do best.

But right now, right here, it seemed like a rather macabre way to put my expertise to use.

There'd been nine of us present in the immediate area. I mentally reviewed everyone's name, pictured where they'd been in relation to the epicenter of the blast, and figured that at least three people were in the immediate vicinity of the lawnmower that blew.

So, status:

Ralph was alright.

Pamela appeared to be okay.

Wendy had been injured by the ceiling beam, but her wounds didn't look catastrophic.

Stu hadn't made it.

And, from what I could discern, neither had Rebekah, Norrie, Justin, or Wade.

A few others who must have been in the adjacent hallway were being treated by the paramedics and appeared to have only minor injuries. Debra Guirret, who looked like she'd been crying, was talking urgently with one of the injured men. I couldn't tell if she was trying to console him or if he was trying to console her.

EMTs from the numerous ambulances that had driven up were scrambling to help the injured and attend to the survivors. Another ambulance was turning into the parking lot.

Dust.

Rain.

Rubble.

Charred bodies.

Yes, the medics were inadvertently disturbing evidence to get to the people who were injured, but there's a time to preserve a crime scene and there's a time to help the injured. A pristine scene or a human life? There's no question these guys had their priorities straight.

A paramedic who'd apparently seen the metal in my side was hurrying my way, carrying an orange tackle box–type kit of first-aid supplies.

My phone rang and my wife's face came up on the screen, her soft smile and Asian beauty standing out in stark contrast to the brutal carnage around me.

I answered. "Lien-hua."

"Oh, thank God, Pat."

"You heard?"

"I was afraid you . . ." She let her voice taper off into a silence that spoke volumes. "So you're alright?"

"Yeah. So's Ralph." I signaled to the paramedic to give me a moment. He was staring at the metal shards sticking through my vest.

Lien-hua would have been here this morning too if she hadn't had a physical therapy appointment for a tib-fib fracture in her right leg from being hit by a car a couple of months ago. Someone had canceled and she'd set it up Friday afternoon.

Just the thought that she might have been in the loading bay too, that she might have been among the dead, chilled me so much that I felt my hand tremble.

The paramedic set down his first-aid box and popped it open.

"Listen, I have to go," I told Lien-hua. "I'll call you back in a little while." My daughter had spent the night at a friend's house. "Let Tessa know I'm alright."

"Okay."

A pause.

"Talk to you soon," I said. "I love you."

"I love you too."

As we said those parting words and ended the call, I thought back to what Stu had told me to share with his wife, that he was sorry about Iris.

Not that he loved Sherry.

He'd been more concerned with her knowing that he was sorry than with her knowing that he cared about her.

*Maybe that was his way of saying he loved her—maybe his apology was him telling Sherry how much he cared.*

*But how will she respond when she hears that?*

*Stop worrying about it. That's none of your business. Just give her the message. That's what he wanted.*

I turned my wounded side to the paramedic, whose name tag read T. Foster.

"What's the *T* for?"

He saw that I was looking at the name badge. "Todd."

"What can you do for me here, Todd?"

The adrenaline was draining from my system and the more it did, the more I began to notice the pain caused by the shards of metal sticking out of me.

As Todd inspected my side, his expression told me the shrapnel was probably more serious than I'd thought. "We need to get you to a doctor, sir. If we remove your vest it's going to pull those loose. They're secured pretty well right now and I don't want to take them out here in the field. They're going to bleed pretty . . ."

"Yeah. I hear you."

"You're going to need stitches."

Stitches meant needles.

Needles meant pain.

Did not like needles.

Metal shards—no problem. I could cope with that. Needles, on the other hand—not my thing.

"Dispatch is saying everyone here is a federal agent." He sounded somewhat impressed.

The word was going to get out to the public soon enough. "That's true."

"I want to make sure these don't move around during transport." As he gently placed some bulky four-by-four dressings around the pieces of metal and wrapped my torso to keep them in place, a phone in the pocket of one of the bodies only five or six meters from me began to ring.

I didn't recognize the tune of the ringtone, but it was lively, cheery.

*Someone who knows the victim well is calling. Someone special.*

In a tweeting, microblogging, texting, instant-messaging world, the news about the explosion at the NCAVC had no doubt hit cyberspace within minutes of the attack. Family members and friends of those who worked here would undoubtedly be calling more phones momentarily.

Concerned texts, voicemails, left for those who were already dead.

These days it happened all too often in morgues and at crime scenes—phones ringing or vibrating in the pockets of corpses. The living contacting the dead and leaving innocent, oblivious messages.

*"Can you pick up some milk on the way home?"*

*Call me when you get a chance. Luv u!*

*Hey, girl! How was the date with Jake? Huh? Txt me.*

I've gone through more than my share of those messages while following up on clues after a homicide. It's gut-wrenching.

The ringing stopped.

I hoped the Bureau could get word out to the victims' families and friends before those people tried contacting their loved ones, but I doubted it. The wheels almost never turned that fast.

I was about to tell Todd that he should take care of someone else, that I was fine, but when I looked around I realized that everyone who was injured was being treated already.

Right now, there wasn't really anything else for me to

do here on-site. Evidence recovery wasn't my job and there were people better trained to do it than I was.

The Bureau's Evidence Response Team, or ERT, was certainly en route by now.

Todd finished gently wrapping the bandages around my torso, but before heading to the ambulance I excused myself. "Give me just a sec."

Using my phone, I took video of the scene and photographed the site from different angles, trying to record as much of the undisturbed parts of the room as I could. When the ERT got here they would do the same thing, but the sooner you can get photos of a crime scene, the better.

After touching base with Ralph and finding out that we still didn't have any word on the location of the semi, I joined Todd in the ambulance. His partner took the wheel and we left for Tanner Medical Center, a twenty-minute drive, give or take, depending on traffic.

These days it just about takes an act of Congress to get my daughter to answer the phone, but she typically replies to texts within seconds, so rather than call, I texted that I was fine and asked her to give me a shout. Then I reviewed the photos of the scene and tried my best to recall if I'd ever seen that semi driver's face before.

++++

Less than fifteen minutes ago the man responsible for the explosion, the man who liked to think of himself as a storyteller, as a bard for the ages, had abandoned the semi in the parking area of the Exxon station near the Marine Corps Base Quantico, crossed through the strip of woods to the car he'd left on the road bordering the trees, and started driving south.

Now he was on I-95, with a seven-hour drive in front of him: five and a half to Charlotte, North Carolina, where he would take the photos, then on to Columbia, South Carolina, where he would be spending the night.

Right before the explosion he had seen Special Agent Patrick Bowers outside the loading bay. Bowers should have been in the lobby on the other side of the building.

That's how it was supposed to work.

The others were supposed to be in the bay, he wasn't.

The bard doubted that Bowers had recognized him, not after the surgery, not after seeing him only briefly and only in the reflection of the truck's side-view mirror.

But still, Bowers might have been killed by the blast.

He turned on the radio, found a news station that was covering the breaking story of the explosion, and, although it was still probably too early, he listened to see if they would list the names of the deceased.

If Bowers was dead, things would still move forward and there would be a sad irony at the scene when they discovered Jerome Cole's body. But if Bowers had survived, he would find himself caught up as the major player in the most elaborate story the bard had ever penned.

# 4

"Where are you?"

My daughter hadn't even given me time to address her when I answered my phone.

"Actually, I'm . . ." I didn't really want her to worry about me, so I wasn't too excited about explaining that I was in an ambulance on my way to the hospital. "I'm in Springfield," I said truthfully.

"They're saying five people were killed."

I wasn't certain about the number of fatalities. In situations like this, when everything is in flux, misinformation can spread rapidly through the media, but, including Stu, five did sound right.

*Five of your coworkers.*

*Five of your friends.*

"It was bad." My voice was hushed.

"But a terrorist attack? At the NCAVC?"

"Yes, listen—"

"And you're okay? How's Ralph?"

"He's good. I got a couple little cuts, but I'm alright."

"What? Cuts?"

"A couple. Little ones."

"Are they spurting?"

"Spurting? No, they're not spurting." Despite myself

ed at the bandages holding the shards of metal in place. "Like I said, they're little cuts."

"Should I meet you at the hospital?"

"Who said I was going to the hospital?"

"I've known you for, like, four years, Patrick. Whenever you get hurt you underexaggerate how bad it is. You nearly get buried alive, you say it's no big deal. You get shot, you tell me not to worry. You wouldn't have even mentioned these so-called *little* cuts unless they were bad enough to send you to an emergency room. So which one are we talking about? St. Mary's or Tanner Medical Center?"

"Tanner." I hated it when she did that. "Are you still at Melody's?"

"Yeah. Her mom's on her way back home—I wish I'd driven over here. Anyway, when she gets here we're gonna swing by our house so I can pick up my car. I'll meet you at the hospital as soon as I can."

"I'm not sure how long I'll be there."

"Text me when your ambulance arrives."

"I'm . . . hang on. I didn't tell you I was in an ambulance."

"You just said you weren't sure how long you'd be *there*, not how long you'd be *here*. So I'm taking it you're still en route. Are you?"

"Yes, but I could be driving myself," I countered.

"Ralph picked you up this morning and he wouldn't chance you getting blood all over his car. Lien-hua wasn't there so you're not using hers. You're in an ambulance."

Logic.

A girl after my own heart.

"I'll text you," I said.

"I'll see you at the hospital."

As I was lowering the phone, I paused and scrolled

back to the text I'd gotten from Jerome Cole's number just a few minutes before the explosion.

I tried calling him, but it went directly to voicemail.

Jerome hadn't been in the loading bay, hadn't been driving the semi.

I phoned Ralph, asked if they'd located him yet.

"No one's answering his cell or his landline. But all those texts that told us to meet in the loading bay came from his phone. I sent a team to his house. The HRT guys are there right now."

The Hostage Rescue Team is the Bureau's most elite tactical-response unit. They're far better trained than any SWAT team—more on par with Navy SEALs—and they're called in for any terrorist attack on U.S. soil.

He went on, "They're concerned the place might be booby-trapped. They're checking for explosives before going in."

*Those text messages came from Jerome's number.*

"Are we tracing his cell?"

"Angela and Lacey are on it."

If anyone could locate Cole's cell phone—whether it was turned on or not—it was Angela Knight at our Cyber Division. She'd named her computer Lacey, and at first we'd humored her by going along, but over time all of us had gotten used to referring to Lacey as if she were a real agent.

It always took a bit of explaining when new agents joined the team.

"Great," I said. "Call me if you hear anything."

We hung up.

I took a moment to process what had just happened: the explosion, the corpses, Stu dying in front of me while I tried helplessly to save him.

It's always a struggle for me, but I try not to dwell on

've seen, on the bodies I've found, on the trag-
witnessed. Instead, I try to remember the people I've caught, the rapists and pedophiles and killers I've
helped put away.

I tell myself that justice will prevail.

I have to. Otherwise I couldn't keep doing what I do.

But I find it hard to forget the faces.

The victims always rise to the forefront. I've talked
with other law enforcement officers about this, other FBI
agents, even Interpol and Scotland Yard investigators.
And for most of us it's the same. The public remembers
the killers—the Jeffrey Dahmers of the world, the Ed
Geins, the Ted Bundys and Gary Ridgways, but for us,
it's the victims.

Their dead, staring eyes. Their quiet, gray lips.

And the questions that linger there in the stale air
around the visages of the dead: *Why couldn't you have
gotten here sooner? Will my death make any difference?*

And now Stu's face would be joining the others.

It was definitely going to take a while to work through
today's events.

I didn't think Jerome Cole had anything to do with this
attack, but there was too much going on right now for me
to sit around a hospital exam room, getting stitches.

*The metal shards are stabilized.*

*The lacerations are sealed off, not bleeding.*

*The vest protected you from the worst of it.*

After I looked up his address, I informed the ambulance driver that we were going to be taking an alternate
route to the hospital.

"Turn left up ahead. I'll give you directions from
there."

# 5

Jerome Cole's house was in a subdivision about a mile from the Potomac River.

By the time we arrived, the HRT had already cordoned off the neighborhood and they weren't even letting emergency personnel past the barricades they'd set up at the end of the street.

"Okay," I told the driver when we reached the news crews who were stationing themselves as close as they could to the crime scene tape. "This is good."

We parked.

With my torso bandaged and scraps of metal still visibly wedged into my side, I was a little conspicuous, but I wanted a status report and there wasn't time to swing by Walmart to refresh my wardrobe first. Todd had a Windbreaker with him, stored on a shelf there in the ambulance. "Let me borrow that, okay?"

"Sir, we really need to get you to—"

"I know, I know. So, the Windbreaker?"

"I'm—"

"Thanks." I snagged it. "I'll get it back to you."

Because of my wounded side, slipping the jacket on wasn't easy and I had to clench my teeth when I threaded my right arm into the sleeve, but I managed.

It reminded me of the first case I'd worked with Ralph, back when I was a detective in Milwaukee and he was with the Bureau, helping us with an investigation into a series of kidnappings and mutilations in the region.

I'd been shot in the left shoulder and had borrowed his FBI Windbreaker at a scene similar to this. Later, when he encouraged me to apply at the Bureau, he'd told me that the jacket looked good on me.

And now here I was again.

Injured.

Bloodied.

In a borrowed jacket.

Full circle.

I stepped out of the ambulance.

The rain hadn't let up. If anything, it'd gotten heavier, steadier, the day deepening around us, becoming as bleak as dusk.

The HRT had snipers stationed around the area and an incursion team had the house surrounded. There was a communication and command center nearby, just beyond the barricades.

I found Brandon Ingersoll, the leader of the unit. I've worked with him a few times over the years and we've practiced target shooting together at the firing range at Quantico. "What do we know?" I asked him.

"So far we're clear." He spoke with brisk, truncated syllables, militaryesque, although from what I knew he'd never served in the Armed Forces. Thin, but with tight sinewy muscles, he was intimidating even though he was only about five-eight. He eyed the paramedic's Windbreaker I was wearing. "What's with the jacket, Pat?"

"I didn't have my raincoat with me. Managed to borrow this one. Time frame?"

"So far, so good. We're almost ready to send in a team."

When I turned to face the house, pain flared through my side. It was really starting to hurt, especially when I moved.

Or breathed.

So that wasn't exactly ideal.

*Cope. You'll be at the hospital soon enough.*

When I asked Ingersoll if he'd heard from Ralph he told me he was still back at the NCAVC. I was glad. If there was anyone there who could take charge, secure the scene, notice what needed to be noticed, and manage the situation, it was Ralph.

"Any word on the semi?"

Ingersoll shook his head. "Not that I know of. No."

A voice crackled through his radio. "Sir, we're in position. Do we have a green light? Over."

Ingersoll checked in with a few of his men, verified that his snipers were in position, then replied to the incursion team, "Roger that. Full breach."

I watched as the guys surrounding the house moved forward stealthily but without the slightest hint of hesitation or apprehension.

The HRT doesn't do anything halfway and when they went in, they went in heavy, but there were no booby traps, no explosives. I could hear the men on the other end of the radio announcing that one room after another was clear.

When they reached one of the bedrooms on the second floor, their voices became softer, until finally all that came through the radio was a stretch of uncomfortable silence.

Ingersoll asked his men what they saw, but the only response was the chatter of a couple of HRT members there in the room.

*"Check him. See if he's still breathing."*

*"There's no way anyone could still be—"*

*"Check him."*

*"Yes, sir."*

More silence.

*"He's gone."*

*"And it's Cole?"*

*"Yeah."*

*"How can you—?"*

*"It's him."*

A moment later, one of the HRT guys called through the radio, "We need to find Bowers."

Ingersoll looked at me quizzically, then replied, "He's right here with me."

"What? Well, send him in with the ERT."

"What is it?"

"It'd be best if he saw this for himself."

That was all I needed to hear. Ignoring the pain in my side and moving my right arm as little as possible so it wouldn't exacerbate the wounds, I crossed the street and headed for the house.

# 6

I joined Natasha Farraday, an ERT member who'd transferred in from St. Louis a few years ago, on the front porch. Late twenties, Caucasian, slight build, and a Tuesday-night yoga companion of Lien-hua, she was good at her job, and I couldn't have chosen a better agent to be here on this case.

I'd first met her while working on one of the most gruesome investigations of my career last year in DC, when two killers provoked some primates to chew off the face of one of their victims while the woman was still alive.

It's disconcerting to find yourself remembering your coworkers based on the dead bodies you first met them beside, but unfortunately it goes with the territory.

Two of Natasha's team members were there as well. She greeted me, then asked, "They want you to come in with us?"

"Yes." It's common to have a detective or special agent accompany the ERT onto the scene. In fact, keeping us away could be counterintuitive to the investigation. Forensics teams are experts at gathering evidence, but interpreting it is another matter altogether, and the sooner you have someone on-site whose expertise is doing that, the better.

Not to mention the fact that today there was something at the scene that had led the HRT guys to ask for me by name.

"I heard you were at the NCAVC," Natasha said.

"Yes."

"I'm really glad you're okay, Pat. And Lien-hua too."

I couldn't help but think about those who were not okay. "Yeah. Let's just figure out who did this."

"I'm with you."

With my injured side, bending over was difficult, but after tugging on booties over my shoes and snapping on latex gloves so I wouldn't contaminate the scene, I let Natasha lead me and the rest of her team into Jerome Cole's house.

Though I knew him through work, this was my first time in his home.

The living room: a white shag carpet, a charcoal leather couch and matching reclining chair. Two floor lamps, a glass-topped coffee table. A flat-screen television was mounted on the far wall. Two houseplants hung in the south-facing window. As a bachelor, Cole had chosen not to decorate the room with many pictures and it had an austere, almost spartan feel.

The words I'd heard on Ingersoll's radio just a few moments ago replayed in my head. I'm pretty good with remembering details and now I heard the conversation word for word:

*"Check him. See if he's still breathing."*

*"There's no way anyone could still be—"*

*"Check him."*

*"Yes, sir."*

*"He's gone."*

*"And it's Cole?"*

*"Yeah."*

*"How can you—?"*

*"It's him."*

I both wanted to know what had happened to Jerome and did not want to know. You can't erase the things you see at crime scenes from your mind. They get rooted in there in a place that's impossible to run from. Whatever I ended up seeing in that bedroom, I expected that the images would stay with me for a long time. Maybe forever.

We came to the stairs leading to the second level. One of the HRT members was at the bottom of the steps. He looked pale.

"Upstairs," he said softly. "He's . . ." It sounded like he had more to say, but instead of going on, he hurried to the bathroom down the hall. As Natasha and I started up the steps I heard him vomiting.

I thought about Jerome, about seeing him at work. Early forties. Short-cropped blond hair. Left-handed. A jogger. Liked to tell the same jokes over and over.

I tried to prepare myself for what I was about to see.

Sometimes killers leave messages scrawled in blood on the floor or on the wall. In one case that I'd worked, the offender had left the word "Sow" shaped from the victim's intestines.

We reached the hallway at the top of the stairs.

Two HRT guys in full tactical gear were at the end of the hall near what I presumed to be the master bedroom. Neither spoke. Instead they both just stepped quietly aside as Natasha and I approached.

And entered the room.

# 7

Jerome lay on the sheets, clothed, his hands outstretched and tied to the bedposts. His legs weren't bound, but both of his knees were broken and had been chopped into, apparently with the hatchet or axe of some sort that lay beside him on the bed.

It was the same with his ankles.

And elbows.

And wrists.

He'd been beaten severely and it looked like his jaw was broken, or at least profoundly dislocated. Two arrows had been driven into his eye sockets and the shafts rose stiff and rigid from his blood-covered face. The fletching appeared to be made out of real feathers and the shafts looked old, like antiques or replicas of Native American arrows.

A book lay open—pages down, spine up—on Jerome's chest.

But not just any book.

One of the two volumes I'd authored.

This one, *Understanding Crime and Space*, had grown out of my research for my Ph.D. in Environmental Criminology back when I was new at the Bureau.

Natasha's team began snapping photos and filming video of the scene.

I took it all in.

Some people seem to be able to ignore the dark side of human nature, to live their lives in denial of the evil that our race is capable of doing to each other. I've never been able to do that, never been able to close one eye to the truth.

But, personally, I'd rather be disturbed by the world, as terrifying and unnerving as it can be, than comforted by putting my head in the sand. They say the truth will set you free, and that may be true, but it can also be devastating when you look at it unflinchingly.

They also say the truth hurts.

And they are right.

No one in the room spoke.

I mentally flipped through the five steps you take when processing a crime scene.

(1) *Orient* yourself to the location: the lighting, the exit and entrance routes, the geospatial orientation of the site in time and space. (2) *Observe* as carefully as you can what you have to work with. (3) *Examine* the forensic evidence. (4) *Analyze* the data by keeping the context in mind. (5) *Evaluate* all the material you've collected and form a working hypothesis that will lead you into the next investigative route.

I figured that the last three steps would grow out of our visit here: Natasha and her team would be collecting and examining any forensic evidence, the Lab would analyze whatever they collected. After that, everyone on the case would evaluate what we had and figure out where to go from here.

Right now I would focus on those first two steps: orientation and observation.

Unlike in the movies, killers in real life are not omniscient. They can plan, yes, they can prepare, but they cannot tell the future, and they can't always guess exactly how the authorities are going to react.

And so it's there, in that disconnect, that we catch them.

I studied the room.

The shade-drawn window faced west toward the road. The digital clock on the bedside stand glowed red with the correct time. Based on the blood spatter, it appeared that the wounds Jerome had sustained had all been inflicted while he was on the bed.

The closet door stood slightly ajar. "Was this open or closed when your team came in?" I asked the Hostage Rescue Team members.

"Closed. We checked it to clear the room," one of the men said.

I peered inside.

The shoes were all lined up in pairs. The clothes hung neatly, organized by color. No blood. Nothing in disarray.

Once Natasha was done photographing the dresser, I went to it and opened the drawers one at a time. The clothes were stuffed in, unfolded.

The top of the dresser was empty. I checked for patterns in the thin layer of dust on it to see if anything had been removed, but didn't see any.

"Were the lights in the room on or off when you entered?" I asked the guy I'd just been speaking to.

"Off. Why?"

"With the orientation of the trees along the side of the house, the streetlamp outside wouldn't have cast light in this window."

"How do you know that?"

"I saw it when I was approaching the house."

"You took note of where the streetlights and trees were?"

"Yes."

"Why?"

"Because light is part of a scene. Also, I heard your team over the radio, clearing the rooms. I knew we were looking at one from the second floor. The location of the windows told me we'd be in here."

I turned to Natasha. "Listen, I don't think he did all this in the dark. If the time of death was last night and he wasn't simply using a flashlight, and no one else has been in here, then the offender may have turned the lights off before he left."

"We'll make sure we look for prints on the light switch," she said.

It was standard, but still, articulating it, reiterating it, didn't hurt.

"And the shoes," I said.

"The shoes?"

"The clothes in Jerome's dresser drawers are just tossed in there, yet the closet is almost obsessively neat."

"You think that the killer tidied up in there before he left?"

"I don't know. That or maybe he rummaged through the dresser. Let's do what we can to find out."

In a few minutes Natasha and her team would be looking under Jerome's fingernails for DNA in case he scratched his attacker or attackers. Now she was taking the temperature of the body to try to narrow down the time of death.

I asked her, "Do you have the photos you need? Can I look at the book?"

"Yes."

Carefully, I turned it over to see what section it had been opened to.

Pages 238 to 239, in a chapter about the critiques of my approach.

Nothing was highlighted or circled, but seven numbers were scrawled in the right-hand column:

**6'3"   2.53   32**

I didn't know what that meant, but I could evaluate it in a minute. For now, I noted that this section of the book was about how all the data for developing geographic profiling models and distance decay algorithms were based on solved cases.

Obviously we only had data from investigations we'd wrapped up. So it made sense, but it created a problem, since during each of the past forty-five years, the percentage of solved violent crimes has rarely tipped over the fifty-percent mark.

That doesn't even take into account all of the crimes that go unreported.

So the section was about unsolved and unsolvable cases.

Had this book randomly been left open to these pages? Possibly.

But I doubted it.

"Has anything been moved?" I asked the Hostage Rescue Team guys who stood near the doorway.

"No, sir," the shorter man replied.

Using my phone I photographed the pages.

Since the book hadn't been randomly discarded on the body, but carefully squared up and positioned there, it would make sense that it was turned to these specific pages for a reason as well.

Questions scampered through my mind: *Did the offender follow Jerome home? Was he waiting for him when he arrived here? How did the killer—or killers—know that Jerome drove the truck for us, that the lawnmower business was a front? Why these pages? Is he taunting us? Mocking us? Saying his crime will remain unsolved?*

"Have you ever seen anything like this?" Natasha asked, drawing me out of my thoughts. She was staring at the arrows driven though Jerome's eyeballs.

"No."

"Who would be capable of . . . ?" Her voice trailed off into a grim silence.

I said nothing.

In truth, we are all capable of evil. That's the thing. We're all made of the same material. Though some people might be predisposed toward certain types of behavior, no one is predestined to act on his desires.

We choose.

And all of us have it within ourselves to choose evil.

Who's capable of something like this?

Well, the unsettling truth, the fact that no one really wants to admit: any one of us is capable of it, given the right circumstances.

Or the wrong ones, depending on how you look at it.

I didn't bring that up, but just said, "What can you tell me about time of death?"

"The ME will have to narrow things down, but based on lividity and body temp I'd say Jerome died early this morning—probably somewhere between two and four a.m. We can tell by the blood spatter and the amount of bleeding around the wounds that they—"

"Were not postmortem," I said.

"That's correct."

"Cause of death from the arrows?"

"Could be from shock—depends on if he was dead when those arrows were driven in there. It appears that whoever did this knew what he was doing, how to make Jerome suffer but keep him alive."

One of the ERT members bumped into me, causing my arm to brush against my wounded side.

Pain streaked through me and I had to stop and take a couple deep breaths to calm myself.

I rested my arm against the wall, trying to hide the pain from the other people in the room.

"You okay?" Natasha asked.

"Yeah."

Just a few more minutes, then I really needed to be on my way.

To get my mind off the pain, I focused my attention on the numbers that had been written in the column. I showed the people in the room the book's page. "Do these mean anything to you?"

People shook their heads. Everyone was quiet.

I evaluated the number sequence:

**6'3"   2.53   32**

The first set of numbers was written as a height—my height, actually—but what about the others?

Weight? Age?

The volume of something?

A mathematic equation of some sort?

I tried to think of both the hidden and the obvious, playing with the numbers, adding, subtracting, multiplying them, looking for a pattern, but nothing seemed to click. Nothing hidden came to mind.

So, what about the obvious?

*It's seven numbers.*

*A phone number?*

I tapped it into my phone. No one picked up and it went to a generic voicemail. I identified myself as a federal agent and left a message for the person to call me back, then I phoned Angela to have Lacey tackle the number pattern. "Online searches, street addresses, equations, phone numbers, anything."

"Gotcha." Angela was chronically overworked. Though she did her best to hide how stressed she was, I could hear exhaustion in her voice. And this week, with everything that was going down, it was only going to get worse.

"And," she added, "I'll have her check different iterations of those numbers and Jerome's phone records, his credit card statements, birthdays, anniversaries of those close to him—see what we can pull up."

"Great. Talk to you soon."

After we ended the call I got right back on the line, this time with Ralph. "We need to find out when Jerome was last seen alive. And let's locate an expert on Native American weaponry. I want to know what the difference between a hatchet and a tomahawk is."

"Why?"

I summarized the scene, then explained, "With the arrows, if that thing's a tomahawk we need to figure out—"

"What kind of message he was trying to give us."

I would leave the specifics of that up to Lien-hua and the other profilers. "Right."

End call.

Careful not to disturb any evidence, I spent a few more minutes looking around the room, but finally pain and common sense got the best of me and I left Natasha and her unit to process the scene.

Todd Foster, the paramedic who'd somewhat protestingly lent me his Windbreaker, was still outside the HRT's barricade, waiting by the ambulance with his partner.

I returned the jacket to him, and after texting my wife and daughter to let them know that I was on my way to Tanner Medical Center, I climbed in and we took off.

# 8

Lien-hua was waiting for me at the emergency-room entrance when we arrived. She was three years younger than I was, and I'd been impressed with and attracted to her from the first moment we met just under two years go. "How are you?" she asked urgently.

"I'm okay. Is Tessa here?"

"She texted that she was on her way, said something about Melody dropping her off so she could pick up her car."

Melody Carver was pretty much the total opposite to Tessa. Boy bands instead of death metal. *Cosmo* instead of Kierkegaard.

But they'd become friends at the end of the school year and had been hanging out during the summer. Tessa isn't the world's most social girl and, frankly, I was glad she'd made at least one friend since we moved here from Denver last winter.

The paramedics had called ahead with my name and condition and there was a young doctor of Middle Eastern descent waiting for us. I've been here once or twice and I knew him.

When Habib saw the bandage around my vest and the metal jutting out of it, he just shook his head. "I'm not sure if I should say it's good to see you again or not, Agent Bowers."

"Let's call it good, Habib. And I told you last time, you can just call me Pat."

"Well, let's see what we have here."

After removing the bandages and before getting the vest off, he had to pry the metal free and, to put it lightly, that did not feel warm and fuzzy. He gave my side a cursory inspection, then, after packing the lacerations to keep the bleeding down, ordered a chest X-ray to make sure that the shards hadn't punctured a lung.

The X-rays went surprisingly fast, and, thankfully, they didn't show any lung damage. Habib motioned for me and Lien-hua to follow him. "Well, let's stitch you up. Come along, then." He started down the bright white, too-clean hall. "Come."

After leading us to an exam room, he left us alone while he went to get some supplies.

It wasn't even noon yet, but it felt like a week had passed since I'd kissed my wife good-bye and left for work earlier this morning.

Sometimes the most eloquent things are shared when you're not saying anything, and now she put her hand on mine and we sat together in silence, the unspoken language of the moment enveloping us.

It felt like a necessary interlude, a chance to process some of the emotions from the morning, to separate ourselves at least a little from the pain of loss.

Death comes to us all, almost always unbidden, almost always unwelcome, and almost always too soon. I've been to more than my share of crime scenes, autopsies, and funerals and it never gets easier. It just never does.

Even being at hospitals like this brings harsh memories to mind.

In my classes at the Academy I'm always on the lookout for the new agents who are the most troubled by death.

Those are the ones I want working out in the field rather than behind desks somewhere, because as soon as we forget what's at stake in our cases—the value and dignity of human life, the primacy of justice, the pursuit of the truth—we've taken the first step toward letting the criminals win.

I want it to be hard for our agents to do this job, hard for them to sleep at night. The curse of empathy is the most necessary one of all for effective investigators.

At last Lien-hua broke the silence and quietly asked me to tell her about my visit to Jerome's house. After I'd filled her in, she said, "Arrowheads and a tomahawk?"

"Well, we're checking to see if it was a tomahawk, but that's what it looks like, yes."

"We need to look at the personal narrative he's working from—the significance of the book, the series of numbers, why he would torture Jerome like that."

Motives.

Not my deal.

I'm more interested in why the offender was here at this time, in this specific place, and what that might tell us about the environmental cues and his cognitive map to show us where he might be based out of, rather than trying to guess what was going through his mind as he planned for or committed the crime.

"And the scene," she went on, "the posing; it's about appearances to him."

"Staging" refers to altering a crime scene after the fact to make it look like it was a different crime than it was; "posing" is altering the scene so that it sends a specific message to law enforcement or meets a specific need for the offender. It's not always easy to tell the difference between staging and posing. Sometimes, it can only be seen in hindsight, after you know the specifics of a case.

"Yes," I said, trying to affirm her approach. It was not the time to argue about our different perspectives on criminology.

"The numbers," she reflected, "could they be referring to pages in the book? For example, pages 63, 253, and 32, or maybe 6, 32, 5, 332—some combination like that?"

"That's a good thought. I'll look into it when we get home, see what material those pages covered."

"You don't think . . . I mean, with your book being left there, and opened to pages about critiques of your approach . . . and . . ."

"What?"

"Basque?" Her voice was hushed.

"Well, if it is him, he has certainly changed his MO."

Richard Basque was a serial killer I'd apprehended early in my career back when I was a detective with the Milwaukee Police Department.

Last year while he was serving the thirteenth year of his sentence, his lawyers convinced the courts to hold a retrial because of some testimony discrepancies and controversial DNA evidence. Subsequently Basque was found not guilty and released.

But being found not guilty by our courts didn't make him any less guilty for the crimes he'd actually committed, and since he'd been freed his body count had only continued to rise.

His typical MO: abduct young women, then methodically cut out their lungs and intestines and eat them while keeping the victims alive for as long as possible. We knew he was responsible for the deaths of more than twenty people and suspected him in the deaths of at least twenty more.

Last spring he'd gone after Lien-hua and Tessa and they'd both nearly been killed—Lien-hua from being stabbed in the chest, Tessa from drowning. I fired at him—three shots center mass—and he fell into the Potomac. We never found his body.

And neither did we find the Kevlar vest of one of the FBI Police officers he'd killed earlier that night.

Since then, whenever I had the chance, I'd been scouring case files of missing persons and homicide investigations from around the country, searching for any sign that Basque was still out there somewhere, still active, still killing, but so far I hadn't found any evidence that he was still alive.

However, until we found his corpse, his case remained open and I was doing my best to stay current and informed on the search for him.

"Setting explosives?" I said, picking up my train of thought where I'd left off. "And the connection to Native American weaponry? He's never done anything like that before. And torturing Jerome without, well . . ."

"Without eating him."

"Yes. It's not like Basque."

"I agree. But what you told me the killer—or killers—did to Jerome . . . if it's not Basque, then we're looking at someone who's just as . . ."

She paused to think about the right word to use and I ran through some in my mind: *twisted, deranged, demented*.

It surprised me a little when she said, "Someone just as possessed by evil."

"That's a good way to put it."

Habib returned with a suture kit, bandages, and several syringes. A young, wide-eyed nurse who didn't look much older than Tessa stood beside him.

My attention was on the syringes. "Um, I should be alright," I told him. "Maybe you could just stitch up the—"

"I need to numb the area where I'm going to put the stitches in. You know the routine."

"He's not a fan of needles," Lien-hua explained, more to the nurse that we didn't know than to the doctor that we did.

"Just give me a sec." I took a calming breath and carefully lay on my left side so he could work on my right one.

Not long after we'd met, Lien-hua had tried to probe into my childhood to find the reason for my aversion to needles, asking me if I'd maybe had a bad experience with them once.

"Who's ever had a good one?" I'd replied.

Habib removed the now-bloody bandages that he'd put in place earlier.

He steadied the needle against my side.

The young nurse tried to be helpful and told me reassuringly, "This will only prick a little."

"Oh. Thanks."

I tried to focus on happy, cheery thoughts until it was over. Rainbows and cheeseburgers and Lollipop Mountain.

Didn't work.

Never does.

To numb the whole area Habib needed to stick me four times for each laceration. I tried not to keep track, but when someone pierces a needle through your flesh it's hard not to notice.

After the area was prepped, he started cleaning out the largest wound and I heard Tessa down the hall, telling the receptionist that she was the daughter of the FBI agent who'd just been brought in and that she was here to see me.

"You'll need to wait here until I can—"

"Patrick?" Tessa hollered into the hallway. It sounded like she was opening doors, checking each room on her way toward us. "Where are you?"

The receptionist tried calling her back, but that was going to be useless.

"In here," I said, loud enough for my voice to carry into the hall.

A moment later my daughter appeared at the doorway to the exam room as Habib tugged the needle through to stitch up the cut.

"Oh. Ew." She closed her eyes. "I think I'm gonna be sick."

"Hi, Tessa," I said. "It's good to see you."

She opened her eyes again but squinched up her face in disgust. "You said on the phone they were little cuts."

"They are. I mean, it's just that the stuff that had cut me—"

"Was still sticking out of you."

"Yes."

"That's just not right."

"Have a seat."

"Okay."

There was one extra chair in the room and she tilted it toward the wall where she wouldn't have to watch the doctor work, took a seat, then touched back a stray wisp of her midnight black hair. Shoulder length—just long enough to hide behind when she wanted to. She'd recently added a dark blue streak along the right side that looked surprisingly good on her.

Today she wore skinny jeans and a faded gray long-sleeve T-shirt with the skull-shaped logo of Trevor Asylum, one of her favorite thrasher bands, on the front of it. Pierced nose. Eyebrow ring. A bevy of bracelets. Deep blue fingernail polish that matched the colored streak in her hair.

The sleeves of her shirt covered the scars on her arm from her cutting days, as well as the raven tattoo she'd snuck out and gotten while I was occupied with a case when we were in San Diego together last year.

Tessa was a paradox to me. She was, at the same time, one of the most resilient and one of the most emotionally scarred people I've ever met. She'd grown up without a dad, watched her mom die of breast cancer, and then, when she finally did meet her biological father, she was present when he was killed in a shoot-out.

She had a sea inside of her with deep currents she'd never shared with anyone. I tried to keep the door open for her to talk to me, but there are some things I imagined she would never feel comfortable sharing with anyone.

Though I hadn't brought her up, over the past couple years I've come to care about her like a real dad would, with a love that, as Lien-hua once put it, is at the same time one of the fiercest and the most tender things in the world.

Before I met Tessa I wouldn't have had any idea what that meant.

Now I did.

For someone as into Gothic horror stories as Tessa

was, real blood made her queasy. But after all she'd been through, all the suffering she'd seen, it made sense.

She glanced again at Habib, then tried directing her attention at the wall, but there was a picture of a human body's circulatory system, and she finally sighed and found a place near the sink to stare.

Habib suggested that she might want to find a seat in the waiting room.

"That's my dad. I'm not going anywhere—unless I have to puke, I mean, then I might have to find a bathroom somewhere or something."

The nurse opened her mouth slightly as if she were going to offer a comment, but in the end she just went back to assisting Habib in cleaning the wounds and in dabbing up some blood that was seeping through the stitches he'd just finished sewing.

Tessa let out a long breath. "I'm seriously glad you're not dead, Patrick."

"That makes two of us."

"Three of us," Lien-hua added.

"And you too, Lien-hua," Tessa said. "Maybe you should be thankful you were hit by that car and had physical therapy this morning."

"Maybe I should."

"Being in that accident might have saved your life. I mean, in a butterfly-effect sort of way."

"That's a good way of looking at it."

Habib worked on the stitches and I might have winced if there weren't three women in the room who were gauging my reaction to see how I was doing.

Lien-hua, Tessa, and I didn't chat much as he finished stitching up the last wound. It seemed like a mutual understanding that we would talk through things later, rather than here in front of the doctor and the nurse.

After Habib was done, he confirmed that my tetanus shot was up to date, then reviewed instructions on how to avoid infection.

"I think we've been through this before," he said.

"I think we have."

Because of the nature of the lacerations, he hadn't used dissolvable sutures and he told me they would need to be removed in six or seven days. Then he gave me one prescription for antibiotics and another for pain medication. I'm not one for taking pain meds unless absolutely necessary, but I thanked him. I figured I'd go with the antibiotics, and I could always grab a couple of Advil if I needed to.

I got a call from Ralph that the ERT had cleared the bodies to be removed from the NCAVC site and that they were being brought over here to the morgue at the medical center.

Tessa must have overheard him because she bit her lip and rubbed two fingers together nervously.

Thankfully, the paramedics wouldn't be bringing those bodies in through the front doors, but rather through another hallway to the morgue on the lower level, so it wasn't likely we were going to run into anyone rolling a corpse in.

For Tessa's sake I was thankful.

Well, for my sake and Lien-hua's as well.

We were making our way through the waiting room toward the front doors when I saw Sherry Ritterman, the wife of the man who'd died in my arms, sitting in one of the chairs near the window.

He would have been brought over earlier and I wasn't sure why she was here in the waiting room—unless the doctors had somehow managed to revive him.

Before losing consciousness he'd enjoined me to tell Sherry he was sorry about Iris.

And, not having any idea who Iris was, I couldn't even begin to guess what kind of reaction Sherry was going to have when I told her that.

She noticed me, rose, and then approached us, calling for me to wait.

# 9

"Pat." Sherry's makeup was smeared and ran in tired, sad streaks from her bloodshot eyes. "I heard you were there with Stu when he died."

*Yes, and I did all I could. I swear,* I thought, but I didn't tell her that.

"Yes," I said. "I was."

She waited. Either she couldn't think of anything to say or she expected me to go on.

"He was brave." I hoped that would be enough.

She sniffed back a tear, but said nothing.

This did not feel like the right time or place to tell her what Stu had said about Iris.

I said, "I'm so sorry for . . . all that's happened."

*It's not your business why he was apologizing about Iris. Your business is just telling Sherry what he said. That's all. You're just a messenger.*

"He wanted me to tell you something, Sherry."

"What?" Her tone was touched with longing and profound sadness. "What did he say?"

"He told me that he . . ."

The look in her eyes was what did it.

It was a look that yearned for some hope, some meaning, some comfort. Her husband had died this morning and—

"Yes?" she said imploringly. "What was it?"

"That he loves you." The words just came out. "That he's always loved you."

*Pat, what are you doing? Tell her what he said about Iris. That's what he wanted. That's what—*

Her eyes moistened. "He said that?"

"Yes," I lied. "He wanted to make sure you knew how much he cared about you. That you never doubted that."

She wiped away a tear and said nothing.

"He loved you," I reiterated.

"Okay." The word was so soft it was hardly audible. "Thank you."

Before I could think of anything else to say, she returned to the window and leaned, weeping, into the arms of a woman I didn't recognize—a friend maybe, a relative perhaps.

Just being here made my heart break.

"C'mon." I led Lien-hua and Tessa outside.

The rain had stopped, although the sky was still overcast. The sun was trying to find its way through the clouds but was failing.

"Lien-hua and I need to swing by the NCAVC and check in with Ralph," I told Tessa.

"You're not thinking about going back there to work," she scoffed. "Patrick, I mean, come on, you gotta be kidding me."

Though I would have been glad to work at the scene, I knew that Director Wellington would never allow an agent who'd been to the emergency room to return to the field that soon—if nothing more than to avoid bad publicity and to placate the Bureau's lawyers. However, Lien-hua might be able to help with the case there at the NCAVC building.

"No, I expect I'll be stuck doing paperwork at home for the rest of the day. But why don't you follow us in your car, and then if Lien-hua needs to stay there I can catch a ride home with you."

She contemplated that and finally shrugged. "Sure. I guess. Whatever."

Tessa left for her VW bug and I walked with Lien-hua to her Infiniti Q60 Coupe. My wife knows her cars and she likes them fast and classy.

"Why did you lie to Sherry?" she asked me.

"What do you mean?"

"Why did you lie about what her husband said?"

I paused, stared at her disbelievingly. "How did you know?"

"I know your baseline, Pat, where you look when you're telling the truth, your posture, your mannerisms, when you typically pause. You've never been a very good liar."

There are times when being married to such an observant student of human nature does not play to my advantage.

"To try to protect her," I said.

"Protect her?"

"Yes."

"From what?"

"The truth. From what her husband actually said."

A pause. "'The truth is the one thing no one needs to be protected from.' You told me that once, remember?"

It was a saying my advisor for my Ph.D. program came up with, and I'd shared it with Lien-hua soon after we first met. "I remember."

"So?"

"I can't tell Sherry what Stu said, Lien-hua. If I did . . . I'm afraid it would bring up bad memories. And that's the last thing she needs right now."

We climbed into the car.

"But you will?" Lien-hua asked.

"Tell her?"

"Yes."

I hesitated. "Yes. I will. When the time is right."

She started the engine and pulled onto the road. "And Tessa as well. You were only telling her part of the truth."

"You mean about me doing paperwork and you staying at the NCAVC building if they needed you?"

"Yes."

"That was true."

"But only partly."

"How's that?"

"That wasn't the main reason you told her to follow us, is it? You didn't want her at home by herself. I mean, whoever attacked Jerome Cole left a copy of your book there." She didn't have to say any more.

"It's better if she's not left alone this afternoon."

She was quiet.

Habib had sent in the prescription for the antibiotics, but I contacted the pharmacy to verify that they'd be available for pickup on the way home. When I hung up Lien-hua said to me, "Pat, I need to ask you to do something for me."

"What's that?"

"Don't ever lie to me."

"I wouldn't lie to you."

"Listen to me: even if you think it would be for my good. Even if you think you would be protecting me by doing it. We don't hide things from each other and we don't deceive each other. Understand?"

"I understand."

"Okay. And you promise?"

This time I wasn't so quick in replying. "I promise," I told her at last. But I wondered if I would really be able to offer her only the truth if it came to the place where I could offer her hope instead.

# 10

The meeting with Ralph at the NCAVC building took less than five minutes.

He asked about my stitches and after I'd assured him that I was alright, he moved right into the case. "Some state police found the semi at a gas station about five miles from here. The security cameras at the station didn't catch anyone leaving the cab. The guy parked the truck so the driver's door was next to the woods."

*He knew the position of the cameras.*

"Sight lines," I said.

Ralph nodded. "Yeah. He knew what he was doing. He must have slipped out, gone through the forest. Volunteers from the base and a couple dozen agents are scouring the woods as we speak, but there's a road nearby and it's very possible he had someone pick him up or had a vehicle waiting there."

"Check for prints on the side-view mirror," I said. "I saw him adjust it and he wasn't wearing gloves."

"Good. I'll get the ERT on it."

"What about Cole's cell phone?"

"Destroyed in the cab of the truck. Oh, and Angela and Lacey are all over those numbers you found in the book in Cole's bedroom. You'd mentioned it might be a phone number?"

"As a possibility, that's all."

"I'm not sure what they've pulled up nationally from other area codes, but locally the guy with that number is a grocery bagger. Twenty-year-old kid. We brought him in for questioning, but he looks clean."

"Okay," I said. "Lien-hua suggested that the numbers might refer to page numbers in the book that was left at the scene. I'll check that out tonight."

"Great."

Lien-hua asked him, "What do we know about the semi's route to or from the building?"

"Our guy managed to avoid all the traffic cams in the area—and I know what you're going to say, Pat."

"That I don't believe in coincidences."

"Exactly."

"He scouted it out," Lien-hua surmised.

"And he chose a rainy day, when our satellites couldn't pick up anything."

*A weather report? Did he really think that far ahead? Would that have even entered his mind?*

"What about our exterior surveillance cameras at the back of the building?" I asked Ralph. "Surely we have footage of him when he left the semi to unload that lawnmower."

"Nothing helpful so far. I have a team reviewing the video, but the guy wore that cap for a reason."

"And he knew just where to look? Where to tip his head to avoid getting caught on camera?"

"It appears so. Yes."

*Did Jerome give him the locations of the surveillance cameras at the back of the NCAVC building—and, if so, why would Jerome have even noted where they were in the first place? If not, how would the offender have known where to turn his head to avoid being caught on the security videos?*

Too many questions, too few answers.

And it was probably going to be that way for a while.

The ERT was busy on the site and, as I suspected, Ralph told me to head home and write up my report, but then surprised me somewhat by telling me that he wanted me at a nine o'clock briefing with him in the morning at FBI Headquarters. "I saw you taking photos before you left in that ambulance."

"Yes. And video."

"Alright, pull everything you have together, upload it to the online case files. And look over what we have regarding the scene at Jerome Cole's house, see if there's anything you noticed there that you can add to what Natasha and her team come up with. I'll see you in the morning at HQ."

He paused and took a deep breath as if he were preparing himself to do something he didn't want to do. "Director Wellington will be there and, because of the possibility that this was a terrorist attack and more government agencies might be targeted, we'll have AD Sheridan from the Counterterrorism Division, the director of the Joint Terrorism Task Force, probably some DOJ reps, maybe even someone to report back to the National Security Council."

"Ralph, I don't belong in a crowd like that. Bureaucrats and politicians? I'm just an instructor at the Academy."

"You're a lot more than that, Pat. In any case, with your book left there on Cole's body, there's a connection to you in all this. And you're the only one who saw that guy in the semi. Director Wellington specifically requested that you attend."

I tried to hold back my enthusiasm.

My friend laid one of his gorilla hands on my shoulder. "Go home, man. Fill in the gaps we have in the files. I have a press conference to prepare for. Get some sleep tonight. I want you rested and ready in the morning. We all know how much you like briefings."

"Yeah, about as much as I like needles."

"And about as much as I like the metric system."

"Or France."

"Or France."

"I'm staying," Lien-hua informed him. "To help work up the profile."

He nodded brusquely. "Good."

As I was walking to the car, Debra met up with me. "Pat. I heard about Jerome." She appeared absolutely devastated. "How he was tortured."

Even though he delivered to the back of the building and didn't come past the reception area much, she knew him. We all did.

"Yeah." Man, she really did not look good. "You should go home," I suggested. "Spend some time with Allie."

Debra didn't answer right away. "She's at her dad's this week."

"Right." I wanted to reassure her but I wasn't sure what else to say. "We'll catch the guy who did this."

There I was, making promises to people again.

"Yes," she said. "I know."

Then I left with my daughter to swing by the pharmacy on our way home.

++++

3:04 p.m.
Charlotte, North Carolina

The bard parked his van in the slot closest to the elevator in the northwest corner of the Schaeler Parking Garage near the intersection of 4th and Tryon.

The Bureau still hadn't released the names of those killed in the explosion, so he didn't know whether Special Agent Patrick Bowers had survived.

He hoped that he had.

Stepping outside the parking garage, the southern summer air hit him full force.

Upper nineties. Humid.

He walked to Independence Square at the intersection of Trade Street and Tryon, the most famous intersection Uptown.

Charlotte was a city in love with the future. Some people have called it the next Atlanta or the emerging capital of the South, but those descriptions missed the point. Charlotte wasn't striving to be the biggest city or even the most influential city in the South. Instead it was carving out its own unique space as a center for science and the arts, for thinkers and dreamers.

It was a city that wasn't ashamed of its conservative religious roots, but neither was it afraid to welcome the neoliberals flowing in from the Northeast. It was a city with a broad heart, open arms, and a spirit bent on being ahead of the curve.

He was here to snap photos of the four statues on the four corners of the intersection, to get them in this light, at this time of day, before driving down to Columbia, South Carolina, to spend some time with Corrine.

Each twenty-four-foot-tall, five-thousand-pound sculpture signified a chapter of Charlotte's history. From the first time he'd visited this corner two months ago, he'd been interested in their symbolism and how they portrayed the history of this city and this region.

He faced the first one.

Commerce—the statue of a prospector panning for gold. Back in 1799 gold was discovered near Charlotte, and for fifty years North Carolina was the gold capital of the United States. The region was dotted with literally hundreds of gold mines, a few of whose abandoned shafts and tunnels still ran under sections of the city.

In the statue, the man was emptying his pan of gold over a likeness of the former Federal Reserve Chairman Alan Greenspan to celebrate the city's banking and finance interests.

That was, admittedly, odd, but Charlotte was the second-largest banking center in the U.S., trailing only New York City, and at the time the statues were dedicated in 1995, Greenspan ended up being the natural choice to represent that part of the city's identity.

The bard centered the statue on his phone's screen, snapped the photo, and then turned to the next corner.

Transportation—an African-American man holding a sledgehammer that resembled those used to build the railroads of the region. The eagle that most people miss seeing when they look at the statue represented air travel.

He took the picture.

Next: Industry—a female mill worker, to pay homage to the textile industry, which created the boom that resulted in the banks being established in the area. A child beside her knees stood for the children who also worked in the mills before child-labor laws were passed to protect them from abusive work conditions.

Snap.

And, finally, number four.

Future—another woman. The other three statues were all turned toward her and she held up a baby to signify Charlotte's dreams of the future. She was emerging from dogwood flowers—the state flower of North Carolina.

A hornet's nest appeared in the branches, a reference to the time when Cornwallis called the people of Charlotte a nest of hornets because of how persistent and relentless they were in defending their land.

The bard clicked the final photograph.

During his time in the city he'd spent countless hours in Uptown Charlotte, doing research in the Carolina Room of the library's main branch. Because of his familiarity with the city, he knew that, since the iconic sixty-floor Bank of America Corporate Center was identified as the primary terrorist target in Uptown, police officers stood guard around the base of the building all day—a security measure that had been instituted sometime after 9/11.

Today, in light of the attack on the NCAVC, the sidewalk surrounding the Bank of America skyscraper was closed off.

That was smart, but, really, it wasn't this building that they needed to be worried about. The real threat was somewhere else nearby, and when everything played out this weekend, the story was going to be even more memorable than an attack on a skyscraper ever would've been.

Using his phone, he uploaded the photos to the site he was using to record his story. The page wasn't live yet, but when everything came to completion, when the dust had settled, these pictures would prove to be the key to everything.

The drive to Columbia was another hour and a half. He would go down there, meet up with Corrine, and spend the night with her before bringing her back up here tomorrow.

After returning to the parking garage, he checked the back of his van, made sure that the eye bolts he would be cuffing her to were secured to the floor, then left Uptown and merged into the congested, sluggish traffic heading south out of the city.

# 11

I spent the afternoon and evening filling out paperwork and going back over the collected data about the bombing and about Jerome Cole's death.

I uploaded everything I had to the online case file on the Federal Digital Database—dragging and dropping the photos and video, adding them to what the ERT had posted, inserting and merging my report with the ones that were already there.

As I did, I reviewed what we knew.

(1) No trace evidence had been found that might indicate who tortured and killed Jerome or how many people might have been present when it happened. The light switch had been wiped clean. No prints.

(2) Every major media outlet was leading with the story, and tips were pouring in to the hotline that had been set up. When you have something this high profile, it's not unusual for hundreds of tips to come in every hour, and in this case our team was overwhelmed trying to follow up on them all.

(3) Jerome was last seen having dinner at a friend's house. He'd left there around eight, and one of his neighbors remembered him returning home, driving up his driveway "sometime before nine." We didn't know

yet if the killer was waiting for him in his house when he arrived.

(4) Field agents were working with local law enforcement to canvass Jerome's neighborhood to see if anyone had noticed a car parked nearby or saw anything unusual leading up to his murder. They were also scouring the business district near the gas station where the semi had been found, looking for anyone who might have seen the guy leaving the truck or driving off in another vehicle.

(5) Twitter went crazy in the aftermath of the bombing, mostly in support of the FBI.

Using algorithms the NSA had developed, we located all the microblogs and messages—mostly from overseas and known Islamic extremist groups—that were in support of the bombing.

A joint team of our agents and NSA personnel were following up on the source of all those tweets.

So far, however, no groups had claimed responsibility for the attack.

(6) There was no shortage of Colonial- and Revolutionary War–era weapons buffs out there, but so far the team hadn't found anyone who could offer us the kind of expertise we needed on tomahawk design. Two agents were still looking, still making calls.

(7) No prints on the semi's side-view mirror. So far, no DNA, prints, fibers, or trace evidence in the truck. Whoever did this knew how to leave a clean crime scene.

It appeared that he was aware of what we look for and how to avoid detection, leaving only what he wanted us to find: the hatchet, the arrows, the book, but nothing else that would lead us directly to him.

But lack of evidence is evidence. It tells you something important about the offender's preparation, sophistication, and background. Our guy had done his homework, he was forensically aware, and he'd thought things through.

Whoever committed the crime was organized and careful, not impulsive. The location of the semi, of Cole's house, of the gas station all spoke to the timing and location of the crimes.

But how all that fit together was still a mystery to me.

We were missing a lot of puzzle pieces.

But we would find them.

I studied the numbers that'd been written in the book left on Jerome Cole's body, trying to find connections between them and my previous cases, poring over the pages in the two books I'd authored, trying to discern what the numbers might have been referring to.

$$6'3'' \quad 2.53 \quad 32$$

After an hour without coming up with anything, I rubbed my tired eyes, then glanced absently at my phone to see if there were any messages from Lien-hua.

Nothing from my wife, but Tessa had texted me from her bedroom, asking when I would be ready to eat.

As I tapped my cell's screen to text her back, I paused midmessage and stared at her phone number.

My thoughts began to rush ahead of me

I scrolled to the numbered keypad.

*What if it isn't a phone number, but a mnemonic of one? What if the letters on the numbers spell something?*

Quickly, I worked up a chart, then scrutinized it.

| 6 | 3 | 2 | 5 | 3 | 3 | 2 |
|---|---|---|---|---|---|---|
| M | D | A | J | D | D | A |
| N | E | B | K | E | E | B |
| O | F | C | L | F | F | C |

Though I was able to identify a few words and phonetic combinations just by glancing at the columns, I wanted to make sure I didn't miss any possibilities, so I went online to see if I could find a site that would calculate—if that was even the right word—words from phone numbers.

It took me less time than I thought it would. The site I found was apparently for businesses that wanted to create memorable phone numbers that spelled certain words.

When I plugged in the numbers, thousands of combinations came up, but only a couple dozen contained actual words.

Of those, ten caught my eye:

|          |          |
|----------|----------|
| Meal-Deb | Neck-Feb |
| Meck-Dec | Neal-Dea |
| Necked-2 | Me-bled-2 |
| O-e-bled-2 | 6-faked-2 |
| O-fake-DC | Me-ale-3-a |

I wondered if the ones containing the words "fake" and "bled" would lead us anywhere—especially the one that spelled "me-bled-too."

*What about "o-e-bled-2"? Could it be a phonetic version of "Oh, he bled too"?*

*Does "Neal-Dea" refer to someone in the Drug Enforcement Agency?*

*Or what about "Feb" and "Dec"? February and December?*

*A timeline? A deadline?*

All possibilities.

I uploaded the info to the case files, and a few moments later Tessa emerged from her bedroom.

"Ready for some lasagna?" she asked.

I knew that my vegan daughter was thinking of veggie lasagna. And probably a spinach and kale salad to go with it.

"I was thinking BLTs."

"Don't even tease."

She'd never given up trying to convince me to switch to a plant-based diet, but today I was ready for her. As we walked to the kitchen, I nonchalantly said, "I heard on the BBC last week that the latest research shows that plants actually make attempts to communicate with each other."

"There's also research that they respond to sound and feel pain."

"There you go."

"So you're saying what? That even I eat sentient beings? That's your point?"

"Yup."

"And meanwhile you eat bacon."

"Yup." I took some of it out of the fridge for my sandwich. I love a nice BLT with crispy bacon. Somehow that added crunch just makes the sandwich work.

"And what does the most recent research on pigs show?"

A pause. "What do you mean?"

"You know, that they're more intelligent, self-aware, cognizant of, and sensitive to their surroundings than dogs are."

"Oh, and let me guess: Despite that, people still imprison them in tiny cages for their entire lives and then mercilessly slaughter them in barbaric ways." We'd been through this before. I knew the routine.

"Well said. And here's the irony: You can make a pretty good living doing that to pigs, but try doing it to a bunch of golden retrievers and see where that gets you.

I mean, just let a couple Dobermans kill each other like Michael Vick did and you get to spend nineteen months in jail."

"Well, from what I remember, it wasn't just letting a couple Dobermans—"

She went on undeterred. "Torture and slay a few thousand piglets a day and become a millionaire. Do it to a single puppy and you could end up behind bars, even though pigs suffer more anguish from squalid and confined conditions than dogs do. Yeah, that makes a ton of sense."

I stared at the bacon for a moment, not really caring how sad the pig was who'd provided it for me, but then I glanced up and saw the look on my daughter's face and slid it back in the fridge.

We ended up eating LTs, which just seemed to me like a lame salad in between two pieces of toast.

Afterward, she went to her room to work on packing for college, which she was leaving for in two weeks, and I turned my attention to the hatchet/tomahawk question while I waited for Lien-hua to get home.

Bypassing consulting with an expert for now, I read what the team had pulled up so far and added some on-line research of my own.

I found out that in Colonial times, hatchets were used to trade with Native Americans. Depending on where you look online, the term "tomahawk" apparently came from the Algonquin or Powhatan and referred to a tool used in cutting.

So, originally, tomahawks were the same as hatchets, but eventually, in the Revolutionary era, when they started to be used in warfare and as combat tools, their design changed and they became more lightweight, while hatchets remained heavier to serve their main purpose of splitting wood.

One was used to chop through logs.

The other was used to chop through people.

Based on its design, the object that had been left in Jerome Cole's bedroom was a tomahawk.

Though it was made to kill, in this case it'd been used to brutalize him, to torture him in a way that was meant to let his death be a slow one.

I was evaluating that when Lien-hua parked in the driveway.

# 12

I met her at the door and when I gave her a kiss I could tell she was distracted, no doubt still mentally caught up in the case. I figured it would be best to allow her to get some things off her mind, so after confirming that she'd already had supper, I just went ahead and asked her where we were with the profile.

"The attack on Jerome was very emblematic," she said. "The posing, the weapons used—there was a lot done at the scene that didn't need to be done. But at least it helps us establish a baseline and a groundwork for understanding his signature."

In our business, "signature" refers to the unnecessary acts that offenders perform at the scene, especially after the crime—positioning the body, covering it, wrapping it, specific ways of tying ligatures or ropes, sexual or physical contact with the body after death. Also, ritualistic or compulsive behavior that has some type of special meaning to the offender.

She went on, "Even the wound patterns were ritualistic—with the use of that tomahawk or hatchet."

"Tomahawk, it looks like."

"Yes, well, I can't imagine how much pain Jerome went through before telling the offender what he wanted to know, but those wounds are—excuse the term—overkill. But they were. It went beyond just someone torturing him to get information."

"Both of Jerome's wrists, both of his elbows, both ankles and knees. There was a grim symmetry to it. Completion. Closure."

"A grim symmetry," she said, "that's a good way to put it. And, as you noted in your report, the crime scene was organized. Also, the lack of physical evidence and no defensive wounds on Jerome tell us the offender was experienced. He apparently overpowered Jerome quickly—or he may have known him and that's how the killer gained access to the house without forced entry. Cause of death, as it turns out, was from shock."

She thought for a moment. "Based on the sophistication of the detonation mechanism and the type of explosives used at the NCAVC, we're looking for someone with an above-average IQ. A history of working with explosives would be helpful, but studying some of the videos out there on the Web could compensate for lack of experience. No evidence that souvenirs or emblems were taken, but that's just a preliminary finding."

Killers often take some kind of token or souvenir of the crime so they can relive the experience over and over. Often serial killers will give the emblems to their wives, daughters, or girlfriends—hair clips, rings, watches. Every time the killers see those things they can be reminded of their crime. And they can feel that sense of power over life and death all over again.

"And he came prepared," I said, "bringing the tomahawk and two arrows with him."

"Yes. It might have been to make a statement or simply just as a ruse to throw us off. The consensus of the group is domestic terrorism, something with Native

American rage against the federal government for wrongs of the past—but I'm not on board with that. I suppose it depends on what definition of 'terrorism' you're using, but . . ."

"What? What are you thinking?"

"Why would domestic terrorists leave your book behind?"

"Good point."

That reminded me of what I'd come up with regarding the mnemonics from the numbers we'd found at the site of Jerome's murder. I showed the list to Lien-hua.

She examined the words and phonetic phrases, then said, "If Basque is involved, what about the combinations with 'meal' and 'neck'?"

Though she'd brought up his name earlier, I hadn't really been seriously thinking that he might be connected to any of this. However, I had to admit that it certainly wasn't out of the question.

"We'll have Angela and Lacey analyze all the combinations," I told her, "see what they can figure out."

Lien-hua tilted her head to the side and I heard her neck crack. She rolled her head to the other side and it popped some more.

I offered to give her a back rub to help her unwind. At first she declined.

"I'll make it a good one," I promised.

"Well, how can I pass up an offer like that?"

We went to the living room and I sat behind her on the couch.

I started with her neck and shoulders.

Even though recovering from her broken leg had slowed her down and put her kickboxing training on the back shelf for the time being, she'd still kept in shape and

I could feel the strength of the toned muscles in her shoulders.

"It's been a long day for both of us," she said softly.

"Yes."

I moved my hands down her back, kneading her muscles, massaging them.

Beneath my touch I could feel her beginning to relax.

So many people never find the love of their life. They search and search and come up empty and some eventually give up the search for good. But I had a lot to be thankful for. First I'd found Christie, and, more recently, Lien-hua. It seemed like two distinct lifetimes that both contained far more happiness than I deserved.

When Lien-hua and I got married she took my last name. I didn't ask her to; in fact, since she'd never been married before and had an established career and reputation of her own, I expected her to keep her maiden name, but she told me she wanted to make sure everyone knew she was with me now. "If I didn't think it was forever, I wouldn't do it."

"It is," I'd told her.

"For forever?"

"Yes."

"I'm glad I found you, Pat."

"I'm glad we found each other."

Back before marrying Christie, I'd never really thought much about the cultural norm of a wife taking her husband's last name, but I had appreciated the significance of the gesture from her and, more recently, from Lien-hua.

*It is.*

*It's forever.*

I let my hands glide down to the small of my wife's back. After a few minutes her breathing became calmer but also more intense, finding a soft rhythm in sync with the movement of my hands.

"As far as the profile," she murmured, "there's just a lot we don't know."

"Shh . . . We don't need to talk about the case."

But she did: "I think it's too early to jump to any conclusions."

"Now you're starting to sound like me."

"That's not such a bad thing." She reached around and took my hands, brought them forward so that my arms encircled her. Then she leaned back and let herself melt into my embrace. After sitting there for a moment she said softly, "C'mon, let's go to bed."

"It's not even nine yet."

"I didn't say, 'Let's go to sleep.'"

"Now you're really starting to sound like me."

She was concerned about my injured side, but I assured her I was alright. Admittedly, the stitched-up wounds did limit my mobility somewhat so the lovemaking was a bit constrained, but there are some things you can work around when you put your mind to it.

Afterward, Lien-hua lay beside me, snuggled up to my left side, her head resting lightly on my chest.

We lay there for a few minutes, a husband and his wife. One. For forever.

When she spoke, her voice was soft. "Pat, what haunts you the most?"

"What do you mean?"

She propped herself up on one elbow and gazed at me with those incisive ebony eyes. "I mean, the pain you've already seen or the pain you will see?"

I thought about it. I'd seen a lot of pain over the years. After all, evil is alive and well on our planet. I'd seen it flex its muscles and I would see that again. "The pain I won't be able to stop," I told her at last.

She let that sink in.

"What about you?"

"I suppose maybe it would be the pain I will see. The unknown is often more frightening than the known. When I consider some of the cases we've worked, as bad as they were, the future might be even worse." She paused, perhaps thinking of something specific. "It's hard, this thing that we do. I don't think a lot of people would understand."

"We end up carrying a lot."

"We end up carrying more than we should."

She lay down again and held me.

And I held her.

All I could think of was the phrase that had passed through my mind a minute ago about evil flexing its muscles.

It wasn't long before my wife's breathing became light and steady as sleep took over.

I had a feeling sleep would not come to me quickly tonight, however.

And when I closed my eyes, I found out I was right.

# 13

They say your dreams are the result of your subconscious sorting through the events of the day, processing what has happened, trying to make sense of it.

I'm not sure about that, but I think that typically people make a mistake when they try to read too much into dreams—but they make another when they discount them as meaningless.

Just like feelings, dreams are information about what's going on deep inside you and because of that they can be useful, even though they might be difficult or even impossible to decipher.

For me, turmoil in my waking life usually meant turmoil in my dreams—which meant there was almost always at least a little turmoil in my dreams.

And now, tonight, harsh images invaded my dreams, tugging and ripping at them like razor wire snagged somehow in my thoughts, catching hold of the memories of the waking world, cutting into them, turning them against me.

In my dream I'm kneeling beside Stu Ritterman, trying to quell the bleeding coming from the stumps that used to be his legs.

It's spurting and I can't stop it. The tourniquets do no good.

Dreams might draw from reality, but they also twist it, morph it, and so now I see that his arms are gone too, lying on the concrete of the loading bay. Someone is screaming, and then Stu's eyes are glazing over and it's no longer him but Ralph who's lying there before me. I'm trying to tell him that he's fine, that he's okay, and then Stu's wife is there—Sherry is standing beside me.

Or Brineesha. It's hard to tell.

It's a dream.

The woman who's standing there is screaming and holding her purse in front of her, but it's been ripped open and its contents are spewing out.

Then she moves it aside and I see that it's really her abdomen that's ripped open.

A dream.

Ripped open.

Her intestines are unlooping, unfolding, and she's still screaming, trying to push them back in, trying and failing.

Then I see for certain that it's not Sherry but Brineesha— yes, Brineesha is standing there. The viscera become a baby, limp and dead, that falls from her stomach and drops heavily to the floor, with a moist and solid thud.

I hear a voice whispering from both above me and below me, four words over and over, a prayer: *"Deliver us from evil . . . Deliver us from evil . . ."*

A prayer.

That God is not answering.

No one is delivering me from evil. Instead it feels like I'm being drawn deeper and deeper into it.

There's no place to hide. No place to run. And the petrifying dream has become the only thing I know here, deep in the folds of the night.

++++

Columbia, South Carolina

The bard waited in Corrine Davis's home. He had the ropes, the gag, the blade with him.

Standing beside the window in the deeply shadowed room, he watched as headlights swept across the front lawn and angled up the driveway toward the house.

The garage door rattled open.

In the light of the streetlamps, he recognized the car as it pulled up—a rust-colored Hyundai Veloster: Corrine arriving home. On Monday nights she typically worked late and then went out for drinks with her friends from the office. He knew that. He'd been studying her.

Forty minutes ago when he was driving to her neighborhood, the names of the deceased had been announced on the radio.

Patrick Bowers was still alive.

So.

Good.

There would be a sense of unity, of the past and the present meeting in the events that were going to unfold in the next five days.

Corrine pulled forward into the garage and the door slid shut behind her.

As the bard went upstairs toward her bedroom, he heard the door leading from the kitchen to the garage pop open, but it was dark on the stairway and the angle wasn't right for her to see him from the kitchen.

He was safe.

He was out of her line of sight.

On the second level, he traversed the hallway, eased the bedroom door open, then slipped inside and returned the door to the position it'd been in so she wouldn't be able to tell that someone was in her room, behind the door, waiting for her.

Last summer during his trial, the prosecution had said that he treated people like pieces of meat, that he would just as soon slit your throat as ask you how your day had been. No conscience, no regret, they had claimed, a complete lack of empathy for others.

Then the media had latched onto the fact that he showed no reaction when the names of his victims were read in court. Which, as it turned out, had taken a while.

After the trial, while the bard was in solitary confinement, he'd had plenty of time to think about what the prosecution had said and, in a very real sense, he found himself agreeing with them.

No conscience. No regret. A complete lack of empathy for others.

In truth, they were right: He didn't know what it was like to care, to love, to become emotionally attached to something or someone. He had never known intimacy, never felt loved or unloved, never understood what people meant when they said their feelings were hurt.

The bard didn't take pleasure in seeing people suffer. He didn't take pleasure in anything, not really. He couldn't recall a time when he'd felt happy, felt joy, felt a sense of accomplishment and satisfaction.

Not one time, not ever.

It wasn't like that for him.

"Pleasure" was not a word that had entered his heart's vocabulary.

He was attracted to women and used them to fulfill certain needs, yes, but his feelings toward them didn't extend to anything beyond that.

In order to successfully navigate his way into a marriage, he had faked love for his wife. Additionally, he had treated his work associates with enough fabricated compassion to become successful in his career, but it had all been an artifice he'd constructed to function in a world full of people who looked with suspicion on those who had no concern for the welfare of others.

True love, if it existed anywhere, was not something the bard had ever known.

It didn't make him feel incomplete. He didn't miss it. Didn't have any sense of longing for it.

When he told his stories, it wasn't for pleasure; it was for posterity. His victims were simply characters in the tale, nothing more. Nothing less. And sometimes the players in the tales he was telling had to suffer.

Just as it is with every story worth telling.

So, yes, the prosecution had been right. He would just as soon slit your throat as ask you how your day had been. That much they'd gotten exactly correct.

In the faint light that made its way through the shaded bedroom window, he could see the orientation of the mirror on the vanity to where he stood and he noted that he wouldn't be visible to Corrine until she was standing directly in front of the mirror.

As the bard thought of her, he looked at the wedding ring he was wearing and recalled his wife, how she had divorced him during the trial. In most prisons they let you keep your wedding rings as long as they're simple bands and not costly, and that'd been the case in the facility where he'd been incarcerated. So why did he still wear his? A reminder of his old life? He wasn't sure. He was—

A slight creak told him that Corrine was on the stairs. Then footsteps padding down the hall.

He waited.

As they came closer he could hear her talking, obviously on the phone.

She pressed open the bedroom door and the bard flattened his back against the wall behind it. As she swept past him, just a few feet away, he caught the scent of her perfume, light and airy and touched with the fragrance of sweet, sweet flowers.

She flicked on the bedroom light.

Leaning slightly to the side, the bard peered out from behind the door and looked at her. Late thirties. Light blond hair. Medium height. A slim figure.

Attractive.

Yes.

He found her attractive.

Corrine didn't see him, remained completely unaware that someone else was in the room with her as she spoke on her cell: "Uh-huh, I know. I heard. I'm so glad we landed the account, anyway . . ."

Her back was to him.

"So, yeah, I'm flying to Miami in the morning. No. As far as I know it's just me . . ."

Having her on the phone was not ideal. If he made a move now, while she was talking to someone, she might cry out and they might hear her.

It would be best if he waited for her to get off the line.

She kicked off her shoes, then loosened her hair and shook it free.

Yes, attractive.

"That would be so sweet of you," she said into the phone. "Oh, and did you hear about Ellie and Matthew? I know. Can you believe it? Twelve years and then . . . Yeah, no kidding . . ."

He waited for her to hang up.

Fortuitously, he didn't have to wait long.

She approached the mirror and reached up to take out one of her earrings. "Well, I gotta go. See you when I get back. Right. Bye."

The bard slowly swung the door away from himself until it was nearly closed again.

She was lowering the phone to set it down when she caught sight of him watching her in the mirror.

Startled, she gasped and spun to face him. "Who are you?" Instinctively she drew her hands up in front of her. A small way of hiding. The bard had seen it before. Right now there was more shock than terror.

But the terror would come.

"Corrine. I know your brother. I thought it was time we met."

He tossed the ropes onto the bed and, just as she began to scream, he was on her, clamping his hand over her mouth and dragging her toward the nearest bedpost.

No conscience. No regret. A complete lack of empathy for others.

Yes.

He would just as soon slit your throat as ask you how your day had been.

Yes.

True enough.

He found her attractive and he had all night ahead of him.

*Let's see where things go from here.*

# PART II

## Mortalis

# 14

I'm not sure how long I lay in bed, lingering between the dream world and the real one, but when I finally did stir from my sleep, sunlight was streaming through our bedroom window.

I did my best to let the troubling images that had plagued me through the night slip away, but they lingered and it seemed as if the harder I tried to make myself forget them, the more they burrowed into my memory.

Once again I saw the dying man, the dead child. Heard the screams. Felt the terrible, wrenching heartache.

Yes, I knew none of it was real, but that didn't offer me much comfort because less than twenty-four hours ago five people I knew were alive, and now they were dead even though no one had actually died—not for real—in my dreams.

Reality is the greater nightmare, the one you can't just wake up from and forget.

I checked the time and realized I would need to be leaving within the next half hour if I was going to make it through DC's rush-hour traffic to the J. Edgar Hoover Building in time for the nine o'clock meeting.

As I sat up in bed the stitches tugged at my side, hurting more sharply than they had last night.

I eased onto my back again.

I'd left the bandages on to keep blood off the sheets, but now when I checked, I found that some of the dressings were stained dark from seepage during the night.

And the sheets hadn't escaped unscathed either.

I heard Lien-hua in the bathroom attached to our bedroom.

"Morning," I called.

She poked her head through the door. "Hey, you. How are you feeling?" She was brushing her hair. Rich. Black. Damp from a shower. I hadn't even noticed her slipping out of bed, and now I wondered how long she'd been up.

"Honestly," I said, "I've had days when I felt more ready to take on the world."

She came into the room wearing a black bra and panties.

Seeing her in that, I wished we didn't need to take off this morning and could spend a little time reenacting last night's rendezvous.

After wiggling into a pair of pants, she said, "You didn't sleep much last night."

"I'm sorry if I kept you up."

"No need to be sorry." She held up a shirt, studied herself in the mirror, then chose a different one—silky and shimmering blue—and slipped it on. "So, was it more your dreams or those stitches?" She was well aware of how my cases often wouldn't leave me alone, even when I slept, so her question didn't surprise me.

"Dreams."

"Do you want to talk about them?"

"I'd rather do my best to forget 'em."

"Fair enough."

"I should get moving." Careful to keep from twisting too much, I stood. "So, what's your plan for this morning?"

"We're meeting at the Academy—the profilers are. Call me when you're out of your briefing with Margaret. I want to hear how it goes. And don't tussle with her."

"I wouldn't dream of it."

"Uh-huh."

"Just call me Mr. Tact."

"Well, then, come here, Mr. Tact." She drew me close, gave me a kiss. "I gotta go. I love you."

"You too."

Moments later she was on her way.

Realizing the obvious—that we were both going to be gone this morning, I made a call to put something into play, then I cleaned up, replaced the bandages, and tugged on some clothes.

Normally when Tessa doesn't have school, she'll sleep in until around noon, so I didn't expect her to be up yet, but I found her sitting at the kitchen table, finishing a bowl of organic granola in soy milk and a plate of chocolate cake—her one vegan vice, since it's made with animal products. Yes, there were plenty of vegan cake options out there, but she'd just never warmed up to any of them.

A cup of steaming coffee sat beside her elbow.

"There's more in the pot." She yawned and I caught it from her, yawned myself.

I filled a mug. "Thanks."

"I'm not going to ask you about your side because you'll just tell me it's fine no matter how much it's hurting. But let me ask you this . . ."

"Yes?"

"You have the choice: either a leech sucking on your eyeball or your side all stitched up like this, what would you choose?"

"Seriously? A leech sucking on my eyeball?"

"It just came to me."

"I'd have to say my side."

"Really?"

"Yes. Definitely."

"Well, then, that's good to hear." She sighed. "So, basically, I got zero sleep last night. There was . . ."

She yawned again.

So did I.

"Did you ever wonder why yawns are contagious?" I asked, somewhat hypothetically.

"No one really knows," she muttered. "Emotional bonding maybe, social empathy, but that's all conjecture. Kids younger than four don't typically catch yawns. Autistic people usually don't either. Dogs can catch yawns from people—more often from their owners than from strangers. So that's pretty weird. And disgusting. The last thing I'd want is for a dog to yawn in my face."

My daughter: Passionate animal lover. Ardent dog hater.

"That's very informative," I told her.

"What can I say? I'm a wellspring of useless trivia. Anyway, I didn't hardly sleep at all. You know. A lot on my mind."

"I know the feeling. Is there anything I can do for you?"

She shook her head. "Naw."

I glanced at the time. "Listen, I have a meeting at HQ. I'm not sure when I'll be back."

"I'll be here."

"Packing?"

"Yeah." She didn't sound too excited about it. "I guess."

She was getting ready for her freshman year at the University of Maryland, College Park, where she'd registered after she decided to bail on her previous choices of English and Deep Ecology and major in Criminal Science instead. Though it wasn't far from DC, we all agreed it would be best if she stayed in the residence hall rather than at home.

Admittedly, I had mixed feelings about her following in my footsteps— on the one hand, I was excited about the idea of someone as sharp as she was entering the field, but on the other, her emotional stability was a matter of concern, so who knew how that was going to pan out?

"Don't watch the news, Tessa."

She gave me a curious look. "What?"

"I don't want you watching the news."

In typical paradoxical fashion, Tessa was as insatiably curious about crimes as she was troubled by blood and dead bodies, often asking me about my cases even though she knew I couldn't give her any details about the investigations. But the more she watched the news, the more disturbed she became.

And the more curious.

A vicious cycle.

She took a bite of chocolate cake. "It's someone from your past, isn't it?"

"We don't know who's behind this."

"Ah, I get it." She swallowed her mouthful of cake. "So, let's see how I do here . . ." As she went on, she vaguely imitated me. "Don't assume. Never trust your gut. Go with the facts over your instincts. And try to prove yourself wrong rather than let your presuppositions color your judgment."

"Couldn't have said it better myself."

"Well, it's all from you from over the years. I mean, I conflated the axioms, but . . ."

"Right."

She polished off another bite of chocolate cake. "I heard there was evidence left at the site of Jerome Cole's homicide that pointed to a connection with you."

"Where did you hear that?"

"The news."

"See, this is why—"

"So?"

"I can't divulge anything about the case."

"But according to CNN, an undisclosed source close to the investigation confirmed that the—"

"Tessa—"

"Yes?"

She looked at me innocently.

*What's the point, Pat? If that's what the media is reporting she'll find out soon enough.*

"Okay. Yes. It's true. One of the books I wrote was left there at the scene. That's all I can tell you."

"So, when should I expect them?"

"Expect who?"

"The agents or cops or whoever you're going to assign to watch the house when you and Lien-hua are gone. I mean, that is what's coming, isn't it? If this has something to do with you, if this killer—or killers; okay, I'm not assuming, I'm just saying—if this killer, he's shown interest in you, then you're going to have someone watch me when you're not around."

"As a precaution only, not as—"

"You know what? That's one of your most annoying quirks."

"What is?"

"Saying something is a precaution. It means you're worried about someone but you don't want to admit it."

"If I was worried I wouldn't leave you alone. Not even

for a minute. I don't think you're in any danger. I just want to be prudent."

"Prudent."

"Yes."

"Gotcha."

The conversation, which had started off on a positive enough note, had turned a sharp corner and I wasn't exactly sure where to take things from here.

"Alright," I said, "well, when I know more of my schedule for the day I'll text you. Okay?"

"Sure."

"Tessa—"

"I said sure." She slid her unfinished breakfast to the side and trekked off to her room.

I waited until the door closed behind her before gathering my things and going outside to the car.

The agents I'd called in right after Lien-hua had kissed me good-bye had made it here and were stationed across the street watching the house.

A precaution.

Prudence.

That's all it was. Just until we found out more information.

I pulled out of the driveway and hopped onto the interstate to head to downtown DC.

++++

Through her bedroom window, Tessa watched her dad leave.

Yup. A dark sedan was parked on the other side of the street. The side windows were tinted and the sunlight glinted slightly off the windshield, but she could make out that there was a guy in the driver's seat. It looked like a woman was with him.

They didn't get out of the car, just sat there, observing the house.

Yeah, she'd called that one.

Okay, sure, it meant that Patrick cared about her and that he loved her—but she could take care of herself and she didn't need some middle-aged, overweight, doughnut-eating cops—or federal agents, or whoever—watching over her.

*Don't forget,* a voice inside of her said, *Basque did attack you a couple of months ago. Patrick does have a right to be concerned. I mean, doesn't he?*

Great, now here she was arguing with herself.

She sighed.

*Okay, whatever.*

*So, pack.*

Her room was filled with boxes.

Nearly all of them empty.

Overwhelmed.

Feeling overwhelmed right now.

Walking to the kitchen, she got an empty cereal bowl from the cupboard and returned to her room. She set her iPhone in the bowl so the sound would be amplified— pretty much the cheapest speaker system ever. She had some acute hearing loss in her left ear from when a gun went off too close to it one time and she needed the extra volume.

Lately she'd been on a CocoRosie kick. Not nearly as dark or intense as most of the bands she listened to, but their music was so earthy and moody and real and just *present* that she couldn't get enough of it.

Patrick complained that the singer sounded like a five-year-old chain-smoker, but there was something about Bianca's voice that drew Tessa in—especially songs like

"The Moon Asked the Crow," "Lemonade," and perhaps the most powerfully haunting one of all, "Child Bride."

After starting the music, Tessa stared at her computer for a long time.

Then she glanced back out the window at the sedan parked on the street.

*Screw it.*

She flipped open her laptop and surfed to a cable news network's news feed to keep an eye on what they were reporting about the bombing at the NCAVC.

Then, listening to CocoRosie and keeping tabs on the news, she began sorting through her rather substantial pile of books, deciding which ones to bring with her to college.

++++

The bard used Corrine's keys to swap her car out of the garage and replace it with his van so he could move her into it without any of the neighbors seeing him.

Then he untied her from the bed and carried her down the stairs.

She didn't struggle.

He could feel her heart beating softly, gently, evenly in her chest.

*Thrum-thrum.*

*Thrum-thrum.*

The rhythm of life.

So fragile. So easily disrupted. So quiet and tender and true.

No, she didn't struggle. The drugs he'd given her took care of that.

Last night, as it turned out, he hadn't needed to use the blade, and he preferred it this way because now he could leave Corrine to die a more natural death.

*Thrum-thrum.*

So tender and true.

Inside the van, he laid her gently on the floor and secured her. After taking a photo of her for the online album he was working on, he left for Charlotte, where he
would put the pieces in place for all that needed to happen before Saturday afternoon.

# 15

Director Wellington had her laptop open on the table in front of her and was removing a packet of papers from her briefcase when I walked into the conference room on the second floor of the J. Edgar Hoover building.

Two other people were already there, dressed impeccably. I recognized one as Dimitri Sheridan, Assistant Director of the Counterterrorism Division. He was talking in a hushed voice in the corner of the room with a man I didn't know.

As I approached the table, Margaret peered at me with those cool, unflinching eyes. Straight brown hair. Perfect posture. "Agent Bowers."

"Director Wellington."

"How is your side, where the shrapnel hit you? Did they provide adequate care for you at the medical center?"

"Yes. Thank you."

I waited.

Her turn.

She said nothing.

Six years ago, before I worked a stint in Denver, Margaret and I were both teaching at the Academy. One day I found out about some missing evidence in a case we were involved with and brought it up to the Office of

Professional Responsibility, the Bureau's internal affairs office.

After an investigation, the OPR didn't officially reprimand anyone or declare any negligence, but they did discreetly arrange for Margaret to be reassigned to the Resident Agency in Asheville, North Carolina—which was not exactly a promotion. At least not in her eyes.

However, she was a persistent woman, and to her credit she'd worked her way back into the graces of the upper echelons of the Bureau and, eventually, after a scandal cost her predecessor his job, ended up getting nominated and approved by the senate to be the new Director.

A few months ago she'd asked me to help look into the apparent suicide of her brother, and as a result of that investigation Margaret and I seemed to have been able to bury the hatchet somewhat—a saying that, when it popped to mind right now, only served to bring grisly images of Jerome Cole's crime scene with it.

As long as Margaret did her job and let me do mine, I was fine with things staying just as they were between us.

Finally, she said, "You'll let me know if there's anything the Bureau can do for you regarding the injuries you sustained. Expediting insurance forms—whatever you need."

"I will. Thanks."

"I appreciate you coming in today."

"Of course."

"I'm trusting that your input will be valuable to the investigation."

"Yes," I said. I wasn't quite sure how to respond to that. "Me too."

Then neither of us had anything more to say.

No insults. No offense. No lost tempers. No tussles.

Chalk that up as a good conversation between Director Wellington and me.

I found a seat at the far end of the table near a sweating pitcher of ice water.

As I was pulling out my laptop, the man who'd been speaking with Dimitri came over and introduced himself as Pierce Jennings, the Assistant to the President for National Security Affairs. Early fifties. Eyes of lead, a gaunt face, and a hard-edged jaw. "I'll be reporting back to the National Security Council this afternoon."

"It's a pleasure to meet you, sir."

So, Ralph had been right about the NSC sending a rep to the briefing.

While Jennings found a seat, René Gonzalez, the Bureau's Joint Terrorism Task Force Director, walked through the door. He was a short but commanding man with a thick scar running along the edge of his chin from a knife fight he'd been in back when he was working as an undercover cop in LA.

Yes, this was definitely going to be the highest-level briefing I'd ever sat in on. And I was so thrilled to be here.

*Tact.*

*You're Mr. Tact, remember?*

*Right. Okay. Tact. No problem.*

I could do tact.

I lost myself in reviewing my notes until Ralph settled in next to me and I saw that two other men and one woman had entered the room in the meantime.

There were nine chairs around the table, so it looked like everyone was here.

I expected that Ralph might ask me about my side as Tessa, Lien-hua, and Margaret had, but he only said, "I don't want you whining about those stitches; we've got work to do."

"Right."

He set his arm on the table and I was reminded about the dog bite he'd sustained last spring. One of Richard Basque's pit bulls had latched onto his forearm when we located his residence. The fight didn't end so well for the dog, but it had managed to score a chunk of meat from Ralph's arm before he stopped it for good.

My friend didn't like to talk about it, but as far as I knew, the recovery hadn't been going as well for him as he'd hoped.

Ralph opened up a package of gummy bears. "Have you ever heard of these things? Amazing."

"Ralph, those have been around for years."

"Just discovered 'em. They made it to my top-ten list."

"Mini-weenies with mustard and ranch dressing still number one?"

"Still number one."

A young woman who had "I'm an intern" written all over her face scurried around the table, placing name-plates in front of everyone. She must have done her homework, because without having to ask anyone his or her name, she correctly identified everyone in the room.

According to the nameplates, the two men who'd just come in were from the Department of Justice and the woman was the Assistant Director of Domestic Affairs from Homeland Security.

Nine people was plenty for me to keep straight, but considering how many chief security officers, section chiefs, assistant directors, and executive assistant directors we had just in the Bureau alone, there could have easily been an-other couple dozen people invited to a briefing like this.

The intern came to me last, gave me a hurried smile, and placed my nameplate, which had evidently been printed up special for this occasion, in front of me.

I turned it so I could read it: FBI SPECIAL AGENT PATRICK POWERS.

With the misspelling, it sounded like a superhero name. Tessa would have a field day with that one if she ever found out about it.

I dialed it back around to face the group.

As everyone else took a seat, Margaret stood, cleared her throat, and got things started. "Alright. We're here to review what we know and put a plan together to coordinate our teams in order to apprehend the individual or individuals responsible for these crimes before any more innocent people perish. Let's stay on track and let's make some progress."

Brief. Concise. To the point.

Good.

Off to my kind of start.

Rather than take time to have everyone introduce themselves, she just directed our attention to the nameplates.

After having Ralph summarize what had happened at the NCAVC and review the findings from the autopsy that had been performed last night on Jerome Cole, Margaret turned to me. "In your report you described the driver who dropped off the lawnmower that had the improvised explosive device." She phrased it as a statement, but left it hanging there as a question.

"Yes," I replied. "Male. Caucasian. No facial hair. Age undetermined. Hair color and eye color unknown. He was wearing dark sunglasses, a weathered Chicago Cubs baseball cap, and had a wedding band on the ring finger of his left hand."

"From what I understand"—it was the woman from Homeland Security—"from reading over the case files, you only glimpsed this man for an instant in the side-view mirror of the truck?"

"Yes."

"Through the rain?"

"Yes."

I was about to apologize that I couldn't offer more details when Ralph spoke up. "Agent Powers has a penchant for noticing things."

*Powers.*

*Great.*

*Thanks for that, Ralph.*

Jennings, the NSC's Special Assistant to the President, said, "So, how do you know he wore a wedding band?"

"He repositioned the mirror. That's when I saw the ring."

"So, our guy, he's married." He jotted something down on a yellow notepad. "That's good. That gives us something."

"No," I said. "I'm afraid it doesn't."

"What do you mean?"

"We don't know why he was wearing the ring, only that he was. It's the same for the Cubs hat—it doesn't mean he's a Cubs fan, it simply means he had it on during the commission of the crime. We need to stay focused on what we do know and not drift into speculation about what we don't."

Everyone stared at me. Someone on the far end of the table coughed slightly and I realized I'd been a little too abrupt. "Sir," I added.

Jennings turned to Ralph. "What about forensic evidence at the scene of Mr. Cole's murder?"

"No prints, no DNA, no fibers."

"Nothing?"

"Correct."

"That would be very tough to pull off, don't you think? I mean . . ." Now he gazed at Margaret. "There must be something there."

"Our team is continuing to evaluate the situation and collect any evidence that might be pertinent."

"And video?" he asked me. "Nothing from the external cameras at the facility?"

"No facial features, not even a partial," I said.

"Because of the ball cap."

"That's right."

A stiff pause.

"And you're telling me that he knew exactly where to turn his head as he exited the vehicle and unloaded the lawnmower?" His skepticism was evident in every word.

"Yes."

"Doesn't that sound like an inside job to you?"

"It sounds like someone who knew what he was doing. I don't think we should assume that it was an inside job or, conversely, that it wasn't. I don't think we should assume anything."

"You don't."

"No."

"And what do you suggest we do instead?"

"Study what we have. Hypothesize, evaluate, test, and revise. The offender could have obtained some of that information from torturing Jerome Cole, but avoiding all the traffic cameras and accounting for the orientation of the surveillance camera at the Exxon station all indicate someone who carefully planned this out from the start."

Jennings looked at me severely and jotted some more notes on the legal pad. He seemed far more impatient than the situation called for and I wasn't sure why.

Joint Terrorism Task Force Director René Gonzalez

spoke up, addressing the group in general. "And no one has claimed responsibility for this yet?"

"Actually, sir," one of the DOJ guys answered, "this morning two Islamic extremist groups have—one from Pakistan, the other from Saudi Arabia. However, at this time there's no way to confirm that either was involved."

"And the ViCAP archives . . ." Gonzalez scratched at the scar on his chin. "Were they damaged in the blast?"

"Minimally," Ralph replied. "It looks like nearly all the files were saved."

"Nearly all."

"Correct."

"How did our guy know the pass code to open the loading-dock door?"

"He likely got it from Jerome Cole when he was torturing him," Ralph said.

A blunt silence spread through the room until the Homeland Security rep asked what we knew about the explosives used in the attack.

Dimitri Sheridan, our resident counterterrorism expert, spoke up. "The Lab concluded that it was military-grade Semtex. Limited production. Made at a plant in Louisiana. A team is on-site now, trying to determine the lot number and figure out who it was shipped to."

"I thought Semtex was more of a European explosive." It was the DOJ member again.

"It's starting to be developed in the States—although that's information that's normally kept under wraps."

"Homegrown terrorists," Jennings muttered. "Perfect."

I recalled my conversation with Lien-hua last night and how she'd said the consensus among her profiler colleagues was that this was an act of domestic terrorism, but that she remained unconvinced.

I did as well.

René Gonzalez scratched at his scar again, a nervous tic. "Last night one of our agents located an expert on Colonial-period weaponry. Those arrows and that tomahawk are authentic. According to the fletching on the arrows and the length of the handle of the tomahawk, the guy was able to establish that the weapons came from sometime between 1710 and 1760."

Okay. Now this was something I hadn't heard.

"Authentic?" I said.

"According to this guy, yes. Apparently, there's a whole subculture of collectors out there and he's the one everyone else talks about—I guess he's the one to ask. Anyway, the style of the weapons points to the Catawba tribe. They're from the southeast, originally, near the border of North and South Carolina. They have a reservation in Rock Hill, South Carolina."

After a little discussion about that and a quick video conference call with Cyber to check on their progress, the conversation pooled off into a discussion of who might have released the information regarding the book that was found on Cole's body and the names of the deceased to the media.

No answers there.

The topic turned to the upcoming funerals.

"They're scheduled for Thursday morning at ten o'clock," Margaret noted. "The families decided they wanted a joint service."

Of the five people who were killed in the blast, only one, Stu Ritterman, the man I'd tried to help, would be having an open casket.

Jennings dialed his focus on me. "You were there. You saw this guy in the truck. What are you thinking as far as motive?"

"I don't feel qualified to say, sir."

"You don't."

"No."

"Well," he said. "Terror. Intimidation. Revenge. Maybe all three. I'm just wondering which direction you're leaning."

"I'm not leaning in any direction. We may never know his motive."

"And why do you say that?"

I tried to get out of this gracefully. "Motive isn't my specialty."

"I see. So what is your specialty?"

"Environmental criminology."

He consulted his notes. "That's what you have your Ph.D. in?"

"Yes."

"And this book that was found at Cole's house, you wrote it?" He made it sound like an accusation.

"I did."

"And?"

"And?"

"And," he said testily, "is that what this book is about?"

I wondered once again why he seemed so contemptuous, but he lived in a different world than I did—reporting to the NSC and having the ear of the president. I couldn't begin to understand his . . . well, motives.

"Yes," I replied. "As well as the theory and practice of the related field of geospatial investigation."

"Talk me through that."

*Go on, Mr. Tact.*

Okay, let's see . . . How to do this as expeditiously as possible?

I slid the water pitcher closer to me, dug out an ice cube, and set it on the table. "Let's say this is a location related to a crime—it could be the site of an abduction or where the victim encountered the offender, or perhaps where the body was dumped or the homicide occurred. Now . . ." I fished out another ice cube. "This is another location in the same crime series."

I continued until I had five ice cubes. "According to routine activity theory, people travel along relatively set paths and have their activities in regular nodes—for example, where they might shop, or work, or recreate."

Dipping my finger into the water I drew lines from one ice cube to another. "By studying the relationship of the crime locations to each other, analyzing the timing and progression of the crimes, as well as the road layout, weather conditions, demographics, and traffic flow, and taking into account the way people form cognitive maps of their surroundings, we can extrapolate backward to identify the most likely location of the offender's home base. I look at target and spatial attractiveness, awareness space, distance decay, buffer zones, and journey to crime research."

I looked up. Everyone was staring at the ice cubes that were now melting on the conference-room table. "So, there you go."

"I see."

"Thank you," Margaret said, "for that . . . illuminating visual representation."

"You're welcome."

My thoughts carried me away: *Could the numbers in the book that we found in Jerome Cole's bedroom have something to do with a GPS coordinate? An address? The Catawba reservation?*

"So, where do we go from here, Agent Powers?" Jennings asked me.

The question jarred me back to the meeting. "I'm sorry?"

"I said. Where. Do we go. From here."

"Well, there is a line of inquiry we're pursuing." I shared some of the mnemonic words and phrases that could be produced using the numbers that were found written in the book that was left on Jerome Cole's body.

The group seemed to think that the phrase "oh-he-bled-too" was the one we needed to take the closest look at.

"Oh, that's just great," Jennings mumbled. "This thing is a public relations nightmare. And now we've got this psycho leaving coded messages for us."

"No, sir," I said. "It is not."

"It's not what?"

"A public relations nightmare. Public relations has nothing to do with this. It's a nightmare for families who've lost loved ones. It doesn't matter what the public thinks of any of this. The only things that matter are protecting innocent lives and catching the offender or offenders as quickly as possible."

Everyone stared at me.

I saw Ralph shaking his head at me: *Don't do this, Pat. Just let it be.*

Jennings narrowed his eyes. "How long have you been with the Bureau, Agent Powers?"

I tipped my nameplate face forward onto the table. "Actually, it's Bowers. Ten years. Sir."

He pursed his lips. "I have a conference call with the president at noon and I need something to tell him other than that we have no motive, no suspects, and no trace evidence."

It didn't seem like he was speaking to anyone in particular and I was about to answer for the group when Margaret beat me to it. "Tell him that we are pursuing all available leads," she said tersely.

"Yes. You can be sure that I will." It sounded vaguely like a threat.

He gathered his things, rose, and before leaving, announced that he needed to get back to his job—as if this meeting had been an annoying detour from anything meaningful or productive about his day.

Margaret set her jaw and I had a feeling she was going to have a follow-up discussion with our new National Security Council friend here.

Good for her.

She announced that we were going to take a short break and meet back promptly in ten minutes. However, instead of tracking down Jennings to speak with him, as everyone was filtering off to the restrooms or the break room down the hall, she asked Ralph and me to stay behind for a moment.

I felt like a student being called to the principal's office. When we were alone with her, I said, "Listen, Margaret, I'm sorry, but I wasn't about to let Jennings make this out to be just a public affairs—"

"That's not why I asked you two to stay."

"Oh."

"René Gonzalez and the Joint Terrorism Task Force will be point on this thing, but I want you two working closely with them."

"Of course," Ralph said. I echoed the sentiment.

"If you have any problems getting what you need when you need it from any of these agencies here, you come straight to me." She took the surprising step of confirming that we had her personal cell number, then addressed Ralph. "I understand your wife is past her due date."

"We're expecting our little girl any day now."

"Congratulations."

"Thank you."

"So, will you be alright working this case?"

"I'm sorry?"

"You won't be distracted from the investigation? I mean, by the pressing needs of your family?"

"We all have lives outside the Bureau," he said somewhat evasively.

"Yes, we do."

I was reminded of a time last summer when she'd offhandedly remarked to me that she volunteered on weekends at a shelter for abused women, helping to watch their children for them. The revelation had been somewhat eye-opening. Before that I hadn't really pictured her doing anything other than working for the Bureau.

"So." She eyed Ralph. "I can count on you, then?"

"Are you seriously asking me that question? After all the years we've worked together?"

She hesitated, then said, "You're fine to give this case your full attention?"

"I'm fine. Director."

"I can assign another person to—"

"I said I'm fine, Margaret."

"Well, then." She punctiliously straightened her papers into a flawless stack. "I'm glad to hear that we understand each other."

"Yes. I think we do."


In the hallway, I waited for him to comment about the exchange with Margaret, and when he didn't say anything I finally asked him if he was cool.

"Oh, I'm peachy."

We grabbed a drink at the water fountain. I expected some colorful comments about Margaret, but Ralph said nothing more. Finally, just to get it out in the open, I stated what I guessed we were both thinking. "I can't believe she said that."

"It's Margaret," he muttered, as if that explained everything.

What he said next took a moment to register; at first I thought I might have misheard him. "I just hope I can."

"You can?"

"Avoid being distracted."

"From the case?"

"Or from my family. I mean, how can I really give either one my full attention? It's impossible, you know. We're always torn. We always feel like we need to do more."

I could empathize with that, but I wanted to encourage him. "You're a good dad. A good husband. And probably the most dedicated agent I've ever met."

"How are we supposed to balance it out—wife, kids, all that—in a case when there's this much at stake?" He didn't usually open up like this, and I really didn't know how to respond. He continued, "I mean, how do you do it? With Lien-hua and Tessa?"

"I guess I just do the best I can."

"Yeah. But it's never quite enough, is it?"

*No, it's not,* I thought.

"It's all we can do," I said.

# 16

After the break, the team spent the next two hours going through the case files in depth.

Ralph seemed preoccupied, probably still distracted by thinking about how to balance out his work obligations this week with his commitment to be there for Brin.

I tried not to let our conversation distract me, but it wasn't easy. I never wanted to sell Lien-hua or Tessa short on my affection or attention, but right now, if you included Jerome, we had six bodies—six dead coworkers—and we needed to find whoever was behind it before more people were killed.

The truth is, I have no idea how to balance work and family, not when I throw myself headfirst into things like I tend to do.

Uncomfortable thoughts.

I slid them aside.

It was nearly twelve thirty before we finally broke for lunch. I offered to grab a bite with Ralph, but he declined, so I walked outside to stretch my legs, get some fresh air, and find a place where I could slip in for a quick meal.

At home, with Tessa looking over my shoulder, I didn't get burgers very often so I found a popular hole-in-the wall restaurant two blocks from the Capitol and ordered my favorite: a medium-rare cheeseburger sans mustard and pickles.

When I tried Lien-hua's number she didn't pick up and I figured she was probably in a meeting. I left a message for her to call me back when she had a chance.

At my table, I texted Tessa that I was expecting to be home around six. Seconds later she texted back that she was packing and that she'd ordered lunch for the two people in the car watching the house. *Burritos. Delivered. I used your credit card. The one in your desk drawer, the one I'm not supposed to know about. See you tonight.*

Ah.

Well.

Our inevitable discussion about that was certainly one to look forward to.

After returning to HQ, I worked the first part of the afternoon in a cramped office, poring over the case files with JTTF Director Gonzalez, evaluating the photos, watching the NCAVC footage, analyzing every detail that we could to try to determine the identity of the truck driver.

Nothing.

The man who bagged groceries had been questioned and released.

The investigation into the Catawba Reservation and the number sequence didn't bring up anything, but we did discover that two arrows and a tomahawk had disappeared from an exhibit at the Mint Museum in Charlotte, North Carolina, last week.

There's no such thing as a criminal who leaves no trace behind. As some of the authors in my field have pointed out, offenders always leave a trail as they move through the geospatial universe, just as we all do, being at specific places at specific times.

So now.

Timing: seven days ago.

Location: Charlotte.

Agents from the Field Office down there were reviewing the museum's security-camera footage from the day the artifacts were stolen. Apparently, there were two exterior cameras and several interior ones, so it was taking some time.

Since Debra Guirret, the agent who'd acted as the NCAVC receptionist, was the person most familiar with everyone's schedules and personnel files, she'd volunteered to look for evidence that anyone might have been noting the locations of the security cameras in the loading-bay area.

A step in the right direction.

Ralph was stuck in a series of meetings with the Counterterrorism and DOJ guys, and I received a text from Lien-hua that I should give her a call at three, so I went back to work.

As I did, her question from last night came to mind, the one about what haunted me the most, the pain I've seen or the pain I will see.

"The pain I won't be able to stop," I'd told her.

In my life I've found that pain has two blades. One is sharp and slices fast and deep, right to the heart.

The other is dull and mangles as it wounds.

I've felt both of them over the years—sometimes from the same event. When my wife died, even though she'd been in a coma and her death wasn't a surprise, the first thing I felt was disbelief, that it couldn't actually be real.

Then the pain came.

Piercing and scissorlike, a pain that stabbed through my hope for her recovery, of the miracle I had secretly prayed for but that had not come.

God mocking me.

A blade slicing right through me.

And then, after the funeral, the mangling pain arrived. It grabbed hold of me, climbing into me as if it were looking for a new and permanent home.

It rooted itself there, in my heart, for months, driving me further from the things I cared about, positioning itself between me and Tessa, the person who needed me the most and the person I was the most unsure how to love.

And it wasn't until the day in North Carolina when Tessa reached out to me, the day she'd been attacked and might very well have bled to death if I hadn't been able to get to her when I did. It wasn't until then that I was able to start healing.

With her.

Together.

And we made it by etching out a new family unit from the ruins of the one that had been torn apart by Christie's death.

Tragedy can either send us spiraling off into our own private oblivion or it can draw us closer to other people. Either way, we rarely heal on our own. We *Homo sapiens* are a strange breed. Almost no one learns the lessons that matter the easy way. It's almost always the hard way.

Distracted by my thoughts, I didn't notice that it was already nearly three fifteen when my phone rang—Lien-hua's ringtone.

I picked up. "Sorry. Time got away from me."

"No problem. So, tell me—how did your meeting go, Agent Powers?"

"Powers. Great. So you've been talking to Ralph."

"It's possible." There was the hint of a smile in her voice. "Actually, he called a few minutes ago asking if I knew where Brin was. I guess he's been trying to reach her. She must have her phone turned off."

"You know how she is, always leaving it somewhere."

"Yeah. So, at the meeting, any tussles?"

"Not with Margaret."

"But?"

"But this guy named Pierce Jennings," I said, "he's with the National Security Council. Let's just say I doubt he's going to invite me out with his buddies to grab drinks after work tonight."

"Ralph mentioned the ice cubes on the table."

"Seemed like a good idea at the time. Hey, did he tell you about our little conversation with Margaret afterward?"

"No."

I summed it up.

"So," Lien-hua said, "she actually called his commitment to the Bureau into question?"

"It sounded like it to me. He was not a happy camper."

"I would guess not."

It seemed like mentioning our exchange about the dilemma of giving a hundred percent to both your family and the Bureau when there was something as serious as this case at stake wouldn't be a good idea, so I kept it to myself.

"Did your team come up with anything?" I asked her.

"Not so much. Now they're looking into hate groups against Native Americans, antigovernment movements and militias . . . None of that really fits, though. From what I've heard, neither of the Islamist groups who've claimed responsibility were involved. They make claims like this all the time to try to recruit supporters."

I told her about the Catawba tribe's weaponry and the connection to the museum in Charlotte, and she considered that carefully.

"So, where does that leave us?"

"Well, we still need to find the connection between all of that and the numbers scribbled in the column of the book left at Cole's house."

"He's taunting you, Pat."

"Yeah."

Typically killers fall into three camps: some simply run, some taunt, others do all they can to cover their tracks.

In order to hamper authorities in discovering the identity of victims, some killers will cut off the head, hands, and sometimes even the feet of their victims. Some murderers prefer to remove the teeth. That way, forensic odontologists can't match dental records.

Once I apprehended a killer in New York who'd kept the teeth of his victims in a jar in his bedroom. All of them had tool indentations that matched a pair of pliers in his toolbox.

He later admitted to pulling his victims' teeth, one every hour, while he kept the people restrained in his basement. He liked to hear their screams while he sat upstairs and wrote his science fiction novels. "They were my muse," he said at the trial. "I did my best work during those hours."

But our guy here, he wasn't trying to hide anything.

He was laying it all out there for us.

*Basque?*

That didn't seem to fit.

But if the book at the crime scene meant anything, we were looking for someone with a connection to me or my work.

*Someone else from your past?*

I didn't know.

It would make sense, but no one popped to mind.

"He didn't want me dead," I told Lien-hua.

"What?"

"At the NCAVC, Ralph's text, and the texts to the other people working there at the time, asked them to meet Jerome in the loading bay, but I received a text to go to the lobby."

"Where the explosion wouldn't have harmed you."

"That's right."

"So that, taken into account with the book at the site of Jerome Cole's homicide—you're at the center of this, Pat."

"Good," I said. "Then it'll make it easier for me to catch whoever's behind it."

She didn't reply.

"Lien-hua?"

"I'll see you tonight," she said at last.

"Yes. I'll see you then."

# 17

The bard drove to the abandoned textile warehouse just off South Graham Street in Charlotte, North Carolina, and parked his van around back.

Opening the vehicle's side door, he retrieved the things he would be needing.

For now he left Corrine inside the van.

He faced the building

The textile plant hadn't been open in twenty years, but because of the chemicals that were used here leaching into the soil, the environmental cleanup would have been too costly to make it worthwhile to develop the land—even if a person planned to tear down the building and start from scratch.

So in the end, the EPA's requirements made development financially unattractive and the property remained polluted as decades slipped by—the very thing the EPA didn't want to happen.

The bard had made the purchase through a front company with money he'd hidden away before his arrest. Eventually, the authorities would be able to trace things back to him, but by the time anyone made the connection it would be too late.

He'd bought the property a month ago and had spent

quite a bit of time in it since then. And, no, he wasn't interested in tearing down the building and putting up something else.

Instead, he was interested in what lay beneath that warehouse.

It'd taken dozens of hours of research in the UNC Charlotte library's special collections room and the city's public library, trying to pinpoint whether or not this building would serve his purposes and, at last, perhaps with a stroke of luck, he'd found the Southern Railway 1904 property map, and the 1906 map drawn by Charles G. Hubbel that showed the location of the Saint Catherine Mine and the others in this area of Charlotte.

Nitze and Hanna's 1896 "North Carolina Geological Survey Bulletin" had helped, especially when he compared it to the 2005 geospatial map that had been drawn up to record the location of the shafts of the Rudisill–St. Catherine Mine system as a precaution for land developers in Third Ward and the Wilmore area.

Finally, there was even an October 29, 1960, article in *The Charlotte News* that outlined the location of some of the shafts.

When he had explored this property, everything had come together.


A rusted fence topped with razor wire encircled the old textile plant. He unlocked the padlocked chain on the swinging gate, and then locked it again behind him.

Once inside the warehouse, dirty sunlight oozed through the grime-encrusted windows that lined the walls of the three-story-tall, mostly empty building.

The floor throughout the plant had been broken up, and the uneven slabs of concrete lying at odd angles throughout it looked like rough, jagged teeth gnawing up through the ground. A medium-size backhoe sat in the corner.

When the textile plant closed it must have been hastily vacated, because there was still dusty and dead equipment scattered throughout the place. Tables, conveyor belts, and folding machines were pushed up along the east wall.

Nine gaping holes, each about ten or twelve feet wide, had been dug into the earth. The maps weren't quite as accurate as the bard had hoped, so he'd needed to poke around a little before he found what he was looking for.

The holes were of varying depths, but the largest one appeared to have no bottom.

That's the one he was going to use today.

In fact, that's the one he'd purchased the property for in the first place, the one he'd been trying so hard to find, first on the maps when he was looking for this property, then digging with the backhoe, trying to locate the shaft.

At first he'd thought he might want Corrine to be unconscious while he moved her to the place where she was going to die, down there in the dark, but in the end he'd opted for drugs—not enough to knock her out, just enough to make her submissive and controllable.

Still, it was going to be a chore getting her down the shaft.

But with the ropes and harnesses, it was doable.

He set the items down, returned to the van, unshackled her, and led her toward the building.

And she went with him. Silent. Compliant. Like a lamb to the slaughter.

# 18

All day, as Tessa sorted halfheartedly through her books, packing for college, she had been monitoring the news, but it hadn't really been very informative.

The streaming-news Internet sites brought on an endless string of "experts" who each seemed to know less about what had happened than the previous ones did.

As the day wore on, she realized how thankful she was that she'd never met any of the people who died in the attack. It would have made things a lot harder if she knew them, as Lien-hua and Patrick had.

Just before three forty-five, Tessa heard the doorbell ring above the sound of her music.

In the living room, she peered out the peephole in the front door and saw a guy standing on the porch, holding up some credentials to identify himself as a federal agent. When she pushed the living-room window's curtain aside and looked at the sedan, she saw just one person inside it.

Oh. So they were checking in on her. Great.

She swung the door open with one hand and slung her other hand to her hip. "Well?"

"Well?"

"What do you want?"

"Do you need anything, ma'am?" He pocketed his creds.

"No."

"Okay."

He was young, mid-twenties. Though he was dressed in immediately forgettable khakis and an overstarched oxford and wore a rather unfortunate tie, he somehow made it work. He had a ruffled look. Strong features. Slightly rakish. Breezy walnut hair.

"Aren't you supposed to be keeping a low profile?" she said, a little less impatiently now that she'd had a moment to take him in.

"Well, with the burritos you had delivered to us, I figured you knew we were here."

Burrito Express was the only Mexican place in the area that delivered. They had plenty of vegan options. She knew their number by heart.

"How were they?"

"Spicy."

"I ordered double habaneros." She couldn't hold back the glimmer of a smile. She hadn't ordered them any drinks. "Did you go with the black bean one or the pinto?"

"Pinto."

She sized him up. "Not too spicy for you?"

"I like things spicy."

"Really."

"Yes, ma'am."

"And your partner?"

"Not so much."

She glanced at the sedan where the woman was sitting. "I think you two need to work on your spy craft. That, or maybe just stick a sign on the sedan that says, FEDERAL AGENTS INSIDE."

He scratched at the side of his jaw. "Yes, ma'am."

She waited. "Well?"

"Well, we're here if you need anything."

"Yeah, I think I'm getting ahold of that. How old are you?"

"Excuse me, ma'am?"

"I asked how old you are and you can stop calling me ma'am. It makes me feel like I'm old enough to be your mother. Just call me Tessa."

"Alright, Tessa."

"So?"

"So?"

"How old are you?"

"I'm twenty-four."

"Fresh out of the Academy, huh?"

"Well. Eight months."

"That counts as fresh. Do you have a name?"

"Beck."

"That first or last?"

"First. Beck Danner. Special Agent Beck Danner."

"So, what do you want me to call you? Is that what I'm supposed to call you? If I need something, I mean? Special Agent Beck Danner?"

"First names will be fine. Just call me Beck."

"Alright, Beck. Now go back out there and keep me safe."

"Yes, ma—"

She held up a finger.

"Tessa."

"Better."

She closed the door, but watched through that peephole as he ambled down the driveway back to the sedan.

++++

Brin was fine.

Half an hour ago Ralph had been worried about her and had left Headquarters to go check on her. He called to let me know she'd only misplaced her phone again.

One small mystery solved.

That was always nice.

But it wasn't much, considering all that we had on our plate.

After finishing up at HQ and battling my way through rush-hour traffic, I arrived home at six thirty, a little later than I expected. Lien-hua was already there, having skipped yoga in favor of working on the case here at home.

She'd released the two agents who were watching the house this morning. However, I called in to make sure there hadn't been any problems. A young man answered. "This is Agent Danner."

"Patrick Bowers. I was wondering how things went today."

"Yes, sir. Your daughter never left the house."

"Thanks."

A slight pause. "She ordered lunch for us."

"Yeah, she told me. So, no problems, though?"

"No problems at all."

"Good."

We hung up.

Tessa was quiet as we ate supper. There was nothing particularly unusual about that, but when I'd left this morning she'd been upset that I'd asked for a detail to be assigned here to keep an eye on things and I guessed that my decision to do that might still be bothering her.

When she finished her meal she didn't leave the table. "So, when you're at work tomorrow, are they gonna be back?"

"Who?"

"The agents outside."

Ah, so she was thinking about them after all. I braced myself for an argument. "Yes, and I don't want this to be—"

"The same ones?"

"I would imagine so. Probably. Why?"

She shrugged. "At least now I know what kind of burritos they like."

"Oh."

"Or at least one of 'em."

"Well, don't use that card that you're not supposed to know about. And what did you do, fake my signature?"

"When the guy delivered the food he just had a swipey-swipe—one of those little white box thingies on his phone."

"A swipey-swipe little white box thingy? And this from a girl who aced her ACT?"

She shrugged. "It works. I signed it 'Pat' for you—good thing you have such an androgynous name."

"Right. So you're cool with me calling them in?"

"I mean, if you have to."

It was nice to know that she was finally starting to listen to me without me having to put my foot down.

"I'll be in my room," she said on her way to the hallway. "Text me if you need me."

# 19

When Corrine Davis opened her eyes, she noticed nothing different from when they had been closed.

"Hello?" she called.

The word reverberated around her, a hollow, vacant echo.

She heard no reply, just the faint drip of water somewhere in the thick, pitch-black darkness surrounding her.

Water on water.

Every few seconds, another drop.

She blinked again, trying to discern the difference between the blackness of having her eyes closed to the blackness of having them open, but noticed nothing.

"Is anybody there?"

No response.

She was seated, leaning against a hard surface. She felt behind her—cool and unforgiving and damp. A rock wall.

Somewhat hesitantly, she passed both hands in front of her and found nothing there.

One more time, she tried closing her eyes and then opening them, tried looking in each direction, but there wasn't even the slightest amount of light to help her discern where she might be.

Now she yelled louder, "Hello?"

The word came back at her as if it were mocking her: *"Hello . . . Hello . . . Hello . . ."*

Corrine reached her hands in front of her again, then to each side.

Nothing.

She felt a growing pang of anxiety.

*Okay, okay, okay.*

*Calm down now.*

*Figure this out.*

The last thing she remembered was that man leading her from the van.

That man.

The one who'd been waiting for her in her bedroom. The one who'd tied her to the bed, who'd photographed her there like that, who'd laid that blade against her throat and told her that he would end her life if she made a sound.

The one who'd slept next to her, one arm under her head, the other draped across her chest, holding her as a lover might, while she was helpless to get away, too terrified to scream—too terrified to sleep.

That man.

Who'd said he knew her brother.

Now, as she thought of that, her heart churned with apprehension.

*Calm down, Corrine.*

The van. She was there—she remembered that—handcuffed. For how long? He'd drugged her and she had no idea. Hours? Days? But no, it couldn't have been days, could it? She was hungry, yes, but not starving.

*Calm down.*

*You're wearing clothes. Shoes. Jeans. A shirt. At least there's that. At least—*

*Calm.*

*Down.*

She was an executive vice president for The Berringer Group, an internationally known accounting firm. She was not the kind of woman to panic. No, no, no, she was not. She could handle this and she was going to figure it out.

*You're fine, you're fine, you'll be fine.*

However, despite her attempts to reassure herself and to feel in control of the situation, she didn't feel like she was in control of anything.

Her breathing was becoming ragged.

So, where was she?

She felt the ground.

Rock, with a small layer of loose dirt on top of it.

"Hello!" She screamed it this time and she couldn't tell, not for certain, but it didn't sound to her like she was in a cellar. The echo was too narrow and drawn-out, went on too long.

*A cave or a tunnel of some kind.*

Blinking meant nothing. The world of darkness inside her and outside her—it was all the same. With no light and without some reference point, it was as if she were lost inside of herself with no way to look out.

Pressing against the wall and feeling with one hand above her to make sure her head didn't hit anything, she slowly stood, then reached up hesitantly and found a rock ceiling not far above her head.

She turned and, patting her hands in front of her, discovered that the wall was relatively uniform, not like a cave, but with no sign that concrete blocks had been used either.

Some sort of tunnel.

Musty.

Cool.

Water dripping nearby.

Somewhere in the dark.

She felt her way along the wall for a couple feet, but then realized that without some sort of reference point, she might easily get lost. She needed a way to identify where she'd started so she could map out in her mind where she was.

*Drip.*

She knelt, scavenged for a rock that she could use to mark her spot, and eventually found one about the size of a softball. After memorizing its shape, she placed it against the wall to mark where she'd been when she awakened.

*Drop.*

*Keep your hand on the wall and count your steps. Check one direction, then the other.*

Touching the wall, she cautiously moved forward, tapping her foot to make sure there was no drop-off.

*Drip.*

Water on water.

Somewhere nearby.

Punctuating every passing moment.

Slowly, carefully, and counting every step, Corrine began to try to orient herself to the tunnel that the man who knew her brother, the man who'd pressed that blade to her neck and had held her through the night, had left her in.

# 20

My mentor once told me that every dead end shows you more clearly the pattern of the labyrinth, that each one you encounter gives you one more piece of information that'll help you as you methodically fail your way to success.

That's how he put it: failing your way to success.

And very often that's exactly what an investigation feels like. You reach dead end after dead end, but as you eliminate possibilities you begin to narrow down the possible outcomes.

Failure.

That leads to success.

At least you hope it leads there.

First thing in the morning, Lien-hua and I went to work at the Academy. Beck Danner was watching our house. Budgetary concerns meant that from here on out only one agent could be there to keep an eye on things, but apparently he and his partner were going to alternate shifts.

Before I left, I told him he was welcome to use the bathroom in our house if he needed to.

This morning everyone was following up on tips. We

had a conference call with Margaret and Jennings so he could keep the president appraised of the situation, although as time went on, it seemed more and more like this was an isolated case and not part of an ongoing terror campaign against the government.

The morning passed in the examination of evidence, the analysis of the data, the reevaluation of the information we had.

Investigations don't move forward at an even pace but rather in jumps and starts. Setbacks and revelations come in waves. Doors open, even as others swing shut. And as you move forward everything is in flux.

Keeping all of the working parts moving in the right direction and making sure everyone has the most up-to-date information are always some of the biggest challenges.

These days it's much easier to do with live updates and text notifications from the online case files, but still, all throughout the morning I felt like I was playing catch-up.

After two hours, we turned our attention to the video footage of the people who'd been present at the museum the day the artifacts disappeared, comparing their gait, posture, and build with that of the unidentified man who had unloaded the lawnmower at the NCAVC building.

There were no cameras directed at the Colonial weaponry exhibit, so we focused on the footage of people entering and leaving the building during its operating hours, but none appeared to be carrying any eighteenth-century arrows into the parking lot.

I was interested in the events immediately leading up to the explosion at the NCAVC. Agent Guirret and two others were working their way through the list of employees, speaking with everyone, seeing what we might be able to turn up.

Failing our way forward, we evaluated the evidence we had and tried to thread together the movements of the offender before the attack occurred.

++++

Here's what Corrine had found out: She was in a tunnel that varied somewhere between six and eight feet wide and rose about six feet high. Rocks up to the size of melons were strewn along the ground, but from what she'd been able to discern, the path was mostly flat.

One tunnel.

No connecting passageways.

In some places, thick wooden beams supported the ceiling or propped up the walls. In others, all she could feel was the cool rock or sections of grainy dirt that crumbled beneath her touch.

She'd ventured a hundred steps in one direction and fourteen in the other—only fourteen because that's when she found the water.

It spanned the width of the tunnel and there was no way to tell how far back it went, but when she tossed a few small rocks in front of her to gauge the distance, the stones ended up hitting a wall that, based on the sound, couldn't have been very far away, before dropping into the water.

Though the cool air of the tunnel chilled her, she wanted to know how deep the water was, so at one point she'd removed her shirt and dipped her arm in until the water was up to her shoulder. She didn't feel the bottom.

Since this seemed to be the end of the tunnel, she wondered if maybe there was a shaft that dropped before her and had somehow filled with water.

*But how did he get you in here? Did he lower you down somewhere and then carry you here? Is it possible he did something to fill that shaft with water? Maybe to keep you from crawling down to another tunnel?*

She wished she could remember more, but she'd been too out of it, and the memories of the trip into the tunnel had still not come back to her.

She tried to get some sleep, dozed a little, but she had no way of knowing how long she'd slept.

While she was awake, her eyes did not get used to the dark—there is no getting used to complete and total blackness.

Without light, without routine, without anything to accompany her apart from the slow, steady drip of water, she had no sense of the passing of time.

In time, the dripping sound became a companion to her. She began to comfort herself with it as the monotony wore on her. She became dependent on it, like an addict. If it were ever to stop, she would feel like a friend had deserted her.

It was almost like her life was split in two—the days before she woke up here in this tunnel, and the eternity of darkness that had begun when she opened her eyes and found herself in this place of no light.

How much time had passed now?

It was impossible to say.

She took to counting the drips of water and taking her pulse and using that as a way of reconnecting herself to the world somewhere far above her, where the continuity of time and the passage of moments meant something.

She wondered what she would be doing if she were up there.

Would she be in bed? At work? At the gym doing her spinning class?

Certainly, by now, she would have been missed. After all, she never showed up for her flight, she hadn't made it to Miami, and her boss and colleagues would no doubt be wondering what had happened to her. There would have been texts to her, yes. E-mail, phone calls, sure. But would anyone suspect foul play? Would they call the cops? She wasn't sure. Maybe.

Hopefully.

And her disappearance would undoubtedly make the news—considering who she was the sister of.

*But what good would that do? How are they ever going to find you?*

Corrine had never been scuba diving, but she had been snorkeling in Hawaii on a business trip two years ago. She knew that the farther down you swam, the more pressure you felt on your ears. But as far as she knew, it wasn't the same with venturing underground.

So she might just be a few feet beneath the earth's surface or, if the man who'd abducted her had found a way to lower her, she could be hundreds of feet underground.

*But either way, you have to find a way out. You missed your flight. People will be looking for you.*

But how would they ever think to look here, wherever here was?

Corrine realized the water nearby could serve as a reference point for her. She could go as far as she wanted in the other direction, and then come back this way until she reached the water's edge. When she did, she would know that she was fourteen steps from where she'd woken up.

As far as getting by, as far as surviving, she needed air, food, and water.

And warmth.

She needed that too.

The tunnel was large enough that it didn't seem like

running out of air was going to be a problem. But she would need food and she definitely needed water.

Yes, she could drink the water at the tunnel's end—but since she had no idea how contaminated it was, the thought disturbed her.

The dripping water was out of reach, but when she'd explored earlier she'd found a trickle of water coming from the ceiling about fifty steps away, so she could use that if she needed to.

She had no food.

And no way, apart from moving, to stay warm.

A number of years ago a friend of hers had hiked through the Wind River Range of Wyoming and had told her about hypothermia, about how you shiver at first and then lose circulation in your fingers and toes, the nonessential parts of your body, so that you can conserve heat in the parts that matter most—the heart, the lungs, the brain.

Yes, at first you shiver.

And then you stop shivering and that's a bad sign. It's your body telling you it's giving up.

There's mental disorientation. Lack of clear thinking. Poor decision making. Maybe even hallucinations.

She needed to keep moving, to keep her core temperature up, because once you started on the spiral into a lower core temperature, you would be on your way toward serious trouble.

*Okay.*

So, try the other direction, away from the water. It would give her the information she needed about the length of the tunnel and it would help keep her warm.

*Stay dry. Keep moving. And find a way out.*

With one hand on the wall, she tapped her foot before her and left to see how far this tunnel actually extended.

++++

Tessa checked her messages and saw that her friend Melody had asked her where she was. She thumb-typed: *At the house. My dad has this guy watching me.*

*A guy watching you?*

*An FBI agent.*

*Oh. Old?*

*Twenty-four.*

*How do you know?*

*Asked him.*

*Ha! Is he cute?*

*He's . . . Yeah.*

*You go, girl.*

*It's not like that.*

*Uh-huh. :)*

All morning as Tessa had packed, she'd tried not to think about Beck Danner, but her thoughts kept finding their way back to him—which sort of annoyed her, since there was no way in the world she would ever be able to hook up with him.

But still.

He had this kind of raffish thing going on.

And he was sitting out there in the car the whole time.

Okay, it was true—she had a thing for older guys. Not *way* older or anything, not like Patrick's age, but guys in their early twenties.

Twenty-four?

Sure, you know? She would be nineteen in a couple months, so twenty-four wasn't really *that* much older.

Her interest in older guys hadn't gone over so well with Patrick. As a former cop and now an FBI agent, he was insanely overprotective. She realized that because of what he'd seen in his job, he couldn't really help it, but still, it was irksome. He'd actually ordered background checks on some of the guys who'd asked her out.

Admittedly, a few times things had gone awry when she was alone with older guys, but that was all in the past.

*Beck.*

It was kind of a cool name.

*Stop it. He's probably married or at least seriously into someone. Just forget him. Just pack.*

She paged through her 1935 copy of *Vidocq: The Personal Memoirs of the First Great Detective*. She had Edwin Gile Rich's translation, since she wasn't proficient enough yet in French to read the book in its original language.

What other literature was inspired or impacted by the book? Only Hugo's *Les Misérables,* Balzac's *Vautrin*, Dickens's *Great Expectations*, and, of course, the detective stories of Sir Arthur Conan Doyle and Edgar Allan Poe. And yet most people had never even heard of the French detective and master of disguise.

It bugged her that she hadn't been able to pick up French as fast as she had Latin.

She'd traveled to Mumbai once with Patrick when he was teaching at an international conference on emerging technology and investigative procedures. While he taught, she explored the city. It was humbling. Most Indians knew at least three languages—Hindi, English, and a regional language like Tamil or Telugu. Many knew five languages.

Even though she was learning French and could— most of the time—read it, she really only knew Latin and English. Two languages. Better than most Americans, but still pretty lame.

Yeah, take *Vidocq* to college, finish reading it there.

She turned to the books of the Christian mystics that her mother had given her—*Dark Night of the Soul* by Saint John of the Cross, the anonymous volumes *The*

*Cloud of Unknowing*, and *The Way of a Pilgrim*. There was a collection of the works of François de Fénelon—maybe the most insightful of the mystics. And of course, Brother Lawrence's *The Practice of the Presence of God*.

Finally, she picked up the volume containing the works of the woman her mother had named her after, Saint Teresa of Avila. She paged through the book, translated by Kavanaugh and Rodriguez, and found one of the prayers of her namesake. Last winter she'd scribbled a date next to it indicating when she first read the prayer:

> *If suffering for love's sake*
> *Can give such wondrous delight?*
> *What joy will gazing on you be!*

What would it be like to love God like that? To have that kind of faith? A faith that looks on it as an honor to suffer for the sake of love, a faith that's astonished and overwhelmed with anticipation at the prospect of seeing her beloved's face?

Tessa really had no idea.

For Saint Teresa, suffering for the sake of her Savior meant delight, and seeing his face meant everlasting joy. In her poem "Ayes del Destierro," or "Sighs in Exile," she wrote those shocking lines that only a saint could pray:

> *Ansiosa de verte,*
> *Deseo morir.*

> Longing to see you,
> Death I desire.

How could anyone love God more than life itself? *Your mom did, remember?*

*True.*

But—

The doorbell rang.

*It's him! It's Beck!*

*Okay. Hold that thought.*

Tessa went to the front door's peephole.

Yeah. It was him.

She swung the door open.

"Hello, Tessa."

*Nonchalant, be nonchalant.* "Hey."

"Listen, I was wondering if I could use the bathroom—your father told me it would be okay."

"Um. Sure." She stepped aside and motioned for him to come in. "It's down the hall." Then she added, "Just past my bedroom."

"Thanks."

As he passed her, she caught the scent of cologne. Outdoorsy. Bold. He hadn't had it on yesterday.

He walked down the hall, past her bedroom door that was slightly open, and found the bathroom.

As she waited for him to return she felt her heart pounding anxiously in her chest.

A few minutes later she heard the toilet flush and then water running in the sink.

That was it.

That quick.

But it seemed like forever.

Beck emerged. "Thanks. It's a long time to sit in the car."

"No kidding. If you want to sit in the living room here, I mean, that's okay with me. If that'd be easier— that's all I'm saying."

"Thanks. But I should probably stay in the car."

"Right. Yeah. That makes sense."

"I'll let you know, though, if I change my mind."

"Sure."

Then she got the door for him and he returned to his sedan to protect her.

Once he was outside, she closed the door and just leaned her forehead up against it.

*Seriously? You asked him if he wanted to do his stakeout thing in the living room?!*

But then another voice: *It's not a stakeout. It's protection duty. He could do that better in here anyway. It made total sense that you would invite him in.*

It was weird: She wanted to be with a guy but she also wanted to be independent enough not to need a guy—sort of like this desire to be entangled in a relationship but also free from all entanglements.

Both desires.

Tugging in different directions.

Words came to her as they sometimes did. Fragments. The genesis of a poem or an essay: *A soul is only set free when it becomes constrained by the bonds of love.*

It sounded like something her namesake would write.

Returning to her bedroom, she dug out her journal and jotted down the words, and as she did she realized that the deepest, most fervent love entangles us in a way that frees us. Saint Teresa found the truest freedom only in her submission to her Savior.

Tessa heard more words roll through her mind and recorded them in her journal as they did: *We want the benefits of intimacy without the risks of transparency. So our lives are always made up of games of hide-and-seek. We want to be found and yet we want to hide from the consequences of being found. Intimacy is the license that you give to someone else to hurt you the most.*

And also to set you the most free.

She'd tasted that freedom for the first time last winter,

following in the footsteps of the faith of her mother. And, strangely, it seemed like she had found what her soul was searching for, but that she was still, in a sense, searching for what she'd already found. To have found God and still be caught up in the pursuit of him, what A. W. Tozer called the soul's paradox of love.

Like Saint Teresa, her soul paradoxically longed for the Savior who had already shown her his love.

While her heart longed for a guy who would do the same.

# 21

Afternoon slipped by.

The Lab hadn't been able to come up with any forensic evidence that might lead us to the offender. The straightened shoes in the closet that I'd thought might be significant didn't appear to be. If Jerome Cole's killer did tidy up, he left no trace evidence behind—not even in the rumpled clothes in the dresser drawers. We still didn't know if it was one person working alone or a team of people who had pulled off the attack.

Jerome's neighbors didn't remember seeing anyone suspicious in the area. And despite dozens of tips regarding the identity of the person driving the semi, no one had actually seen him exit the truck.

Three false confessions so far. Publicity seekers. Goes with the territory.

Lien-hua left to go to a late-afternoon physical-therapy appointment.

The team worked, I lost track of time, and then it was evening again.

Eventually, at six I headed home. At the house I told Priscilla Woods, the agent who was there, she could take off.

Lien-hua's physical-therapy appointment must not

have gone too well because when she arrived twenty minutes later, she was grimacing and favoring her leg even more than usual.

I had some supper waiting for her, which we ate in silence. Figuring it would be best to give her some space, I left her to take a quick shower. After cleaning up I looked through my files one more time, seeing if our guy had left us any other footprints in time and space.

I was particularly interested in the timeline that we knew about Jerome: when he had come home, where he was last seen, and what that might tell us about the person or group of people who'd attacked and murdered him.

Debra discovered that someone had accessed the security archives on Sunday evening around six. It wasn't clear who it'd been, but if that was Jerome, why would he have done it, and why then? Did his killer somehow get his federal ID number and log in to find the information? We were still searching for answers.

I recalled the victim's phone ringing in the NCAVC building. It made me think of who might have been calling, and I decided it might be wise to map out the incoming and outgoing calls of the agents who were on duty that day to see if that led us anywhere.

I was deep in thought when Lien-hua called to me from the bedroom. I found her in her pajamas, getting ready for bed, and realized several hours had passed since I'd sat down to look over the files.

*You need to do a better job of keeping track of time, Pat.*

Even before Lien-hua and I had gotten married we'd started a tradition of lighting a unity candle, not just to signify our commitment to each other, but to celebrate that unity, to hold on to the moments, the brief, precious moments we had with each other.

Since April we'd gone through three candles.

As I changed for bed, I lit the lavender one on her dresser.

"Brin's thinking about a new name," Lien-hua told me. "Tryphena. It means 'delicate.'"

"I heard."

"What do you think of it?"

"I like it, but I have to say, just the thought that someone like Ralph would name his daughter 'delicate' does strike me as a little incongruous."

"Nice Tessa word there: incongruous."

"Thanks."

"She's a brave woman."

"Tessa?"

"Brineesha."

"For . . . ?" I was a little lost here. "What? Marrying Ralph?"

"For having another baby, Pat."

I wasn't sure if she was referring specifically to the difficulties Brin had gone through when Tony was born prematurely and almost died, or if she was just referring to raising a child in general.

A decade ago, long before we met, Lien-hua had been engaged but had broken it off after she found out her fiancé had been lying about the extent of a "friendship" he had with a woman at work. And although Lien-hua had been in two other long-term relationships since then, she'd never had any children.

In the past we'd spoken about the possibility of us having kids of our own. She'd said that it'd never been in her plans, and I hadn't been sure if that was her way of saying that she didn't want to have children or her way of saying that she was changing her mind about it. When I'd asked her to elaborate she'd simply said, "It's a hard world to bring a child up in," and left it at that.

Yes.

It is a hard world to bring children up in.

And it was also true that Brineesha was a brave woman—both for marrying Ralph and for having another baby.

When Lien-hua and I climbed into bed, we spoke for a few minutes about what had happened over the course of the day and how we'd only managed to find more and more ways to fail our way forward.

Tomorrow morning at ten, we would be attending the funeral service for Jerome Cole and the five other agents who'd been killed in the attack.

So, once again death was on my mind as I closed my eyes to go to sleep.

++++

It had been thirty-two hours since the bard had left Corrine in the old Rudisill Mine tunnel. She was probably still alive, but it was hard to say.

Despite himself, he couldn't stop thinking about her.

He wanted to visit her, but he also understood that it would be best to leave her alone, let her die quietly in that mine. However, he might at least stop by, if nothing else to get photos of her body.

Now he was in his fourteenth-floor apartment and, just like so many of the lofts in Uptown Charlotte, it was relatively new.

Charlotte had always been a fast-growing city, with one generation leveling the buildings and then constructing new ones on top of the rubble of what the generation before them had left behind.

Other than the relatively small Fourth Ward historic district, pretty much the only thing that'd survived from the past, the only real markers of history, were the settlers' cemeteries in the area.

The irony: The gravestones of the dead served as a constant reminder of the fate of the living who were too distracted to notice them while they built high-rise apartments for themselves to live out their brief lives in just down the street.

He knew that Fourth Ward neighborhood. He'd rented another place there just in case this apartment became compromised.

Now he went online and pulled up the maps of the train route. Freight trains don't run on a precise schedule, so he'd taken pains to make sure he could track its progress as it went through signal territory from Spartanburg, South Carolina, to High Point, North Carolina.

However, he did know that because of its two thirty-five departure time, it would be traveling through Charlotte sometime between three fifteen and four o'clock on Saturday.

He was expecting it at about three thirty, which would be perfect, actually.

A six-thousand-foot train. One hundred cars. Three engines.

When he first started preparing to tell this story, he'd discovered that the railroad line that ran alongside the open-air Bank of America Stadium was a Knoxville Southeast Railway line, mainly used for freight, although a few passenger trains used it.

Now he confirmed the manifest.

Yes, the number of hazmat tankers it was carrying hadn't changed. And neither had the contents.

It hadn't been difficult for the bard to find a young man who was skilled enough at hacking to get into the Knoxville Southeast Railway dispatch office and get past the firewalls.

It had been harder, however, trying to decide if he should let the young man live.

In the end he'd decided against it.

Now he had the code that he needed and he was in the system.

When he came to the information regarding M343's Saturday route, he paused and thought back through the past three months.

So much had changed.

And not just his face, from his plastic surgery. Everything.

A hundred days ago he was in prison.

He'd had his "lawyer" bring him a tube of toothpaste. But it wasn't just toothpaste inside that tube. There was just enough of it on the end to fool the guards if they squeezed it to make sure it contained toothpaste.

But there was something else in the tube.

Mikrosil.

It's a paste that hardens and can subsequently be used to lift intricate patterns off solid surfaces. It comes in a tube similar to toothpaste. In his previous career that's how he'd come across it.

The bard had injected it into the lock of his cell to form a key.

Then he'd removed the elastic waistband from a pair of underwear, slit it down the middle with the handle of a toothbrush that he'd sharpened by rubbing it against the concrete floor of his cell.

He waited until the guard who was his size was stationed outside the door.

After all, he needed a change of clothes.

The bard picked the cuffs they kept him in, used the key to get out of his cell, then looped the elastic band over the man's head in a clove hitch, yanked it tight around his neck.

And tugged.

The elastic band was narrow enough so the skin on the guard's neck folded over it and it would have been pretty much impossible to pull loose even if the bard hadn't been yanking it tight.

There was no sound.

The man died quickly, quietly, with very little fight.

The clothes fit well enough.

Though the bard had planned as carefully as he could, he had several things to take care of before Saturday afternoon.

(1) Stay in touch with his contact so he could remain informed on how things were progressing in DC.

(2) Check the pressure sensor on the tracks.

(3) Look in on Corrine and see if she had died yet so he could take photos of her body for the website he was going to use. And, perhaps, spend a little time with her while he was there.

Before returning to the mine, however, he had business to attend to back in DC: a funeral he needed to show up for. Needed to take pictures of.

And while he was up there, he could pay a visit to the person he'd left locked in a secluded basement in the city—a guarantee that the final act of his story would be told even if he wasn't in the area.

Now he pulled up the app that he was using to disguise the origin of his texts. He verified the wording of the message in Latin that he would be sending tomorrow to Agent Bowers.

Then he went to the parking garage beneath his apartment building, found his van, and took off to drive through the night to DC for the joint funeral service of the six people he had killed earlier that week.

# 22

Ralph, Lien-hua, Brin, and I parked in the graveyard close to the place where they were having the service so Brin, who was now more than a week past her due date, wouldn't have too far to walk.

The sky above us was a stark summer blue, marred only by a handful of cumulus clouds. Bright, optimistic sunlight betrayed the occasion and mocked the tears of those standing around their dead.

The mourners gathered in their drab suits or black dresses—the clothes we keep in the back of our closets and don't pull out until we have to bury someone we know.

Our grieving clothes.

In a world as full of finality as ours, we all need them. Because the truth is—and this is the truth that we don't like to bring up, that we pretend isn't there, the one that lurks behind every conversation, every smile, every pat on the back—one day soon we'll either be saying a final good-bye to everyone we know or they'll be saying one to us.

Wearing their grieving clothes.

Now, here in the graveyard, I wondered what we

might look like from the air—a dark huddle around these open graves.

*Like insects—*

*Scuttling little insects gathered around a burrow that will one day be their home.*

Tessa doesn't do well at funerals and, since she hadn't known Jerome or any of the people who were killed in the explosion, we left her at Ralph's house this morning so she could stay with his son, Tony.

Special Agent Priscilla Woods was parked on the street outside, watching the house.

My daughter had studied Latin back in middle school and has been reading the Vulgate—a Latin translation of the Bible—and before I left, she pointed out to me that in the second verse of the seventh chapter of Ecclesiastes it says that it's better to go to a funeral than to a party.

It seems like a morbid and disheartening thing to say, especially to record in the Bible, but on the ride here I'd thought a lot about it and I could see some wisdom in those words.

Going to a funeral forces you to acknowledge your mortality, to ask the questions of life and meaning and beliefs that matter most: *Why am I here on this planet? Does my life matter? Does the afterlife exist? Where will I go when I die? Will I ever see my loved ones again? What is the meaning of it all? Does God care? Is he even there?*

At a party you distract yourself with pleasure, you drink and laugh and indulge yourself past those questions. At a funeral they're right there out in the open, hitting you full force like a fist in the gut.

Clarity.

Percipience.

That's what funerals can teach us. That's what the final good-bye offers those willing to let the questions in.

Keen awareness. The ability to finally understand.

Or at least to finally understand how important understanding is.

I've never been to a funeral where there was so much security.

Killers often attend the funerals of their victims, so we had video surveillance set up for everyone who was at the wake and at the graveside service. Only friends and family were supposed to be allowed here in the graveyard itself, but still we had facial-recognition software running to make sure no one had come who wasn't supposed to be there.

I noticed nothing unusual, saw nothing suspicious.

Director Wellington attended, as did the rest of the people who'd been at the briefing at HQ earlier this week: the Department of Justice and Homeland Security reps, Sheridan, Gonzalez—all of them.

Even Jennings, the National Security Council member, showed up, although he seemed to be more interested in checking his texts every couple of minutes than in interacting with the grieving family members.

When I saw Sherry Ritterman, I remembered telling her that her husband's last words concerned how much he loved her.

She'd seemed touched by what I'd said, and from what I could tell, hadn't been able to see through my lie.

No, this was not the time to correct it.

She was staring blankly at the open grave beside her where her husband of ten months was going to be buried.

Lien-hua glanced my way and I wondered if she was thinking of what I'd said when I'd promised that I would never lie to her, that I would always be honest with her, even if I thought the lie would protect her.

Truth or hope?

It's not an easy decision when you have to choose between the two of them.

At the far end of the graveyard, news-crew vans and bystanders were lining the street, ready to feed a waiting world whatever tidbits they could from this ceremony. Whoever had pulled off this attack and beaten, tortured, and killed Jerome Cole had a worldwide audience.

I had no idea what to say to the surviving family members of the agents who were killed.

When my wife died two years ago, some of my friends gave me advice on how to get through it and some didn't seem to know what to say.

In the end, the ones who'd ended up helping me the most weren't those who tried to give me answers, but those who just walked with me quietly through the questions without necessarily offering me any solutions.

Today, when I met the family members of the deceased, I told them the perfunctory things we always say: that I was so sorry for what had happened, that I was here for them if they needed anything. I added that I was going to do everything in my power to bring the killer to justice.

But I knew it wasn't enough. It's never enough.

Even though I wanted to somehow comfort them, no other words of comfort came to me. But maybe silence was what they needed.

I hoped that was the case.

As the service was about to begin I took my place beside Lien-hua.

Brineesha had her arm in the crook of Ralph's. She was a devout woman and clutched a well-worn Bible in her free hand.

Even in her loose-fitting dress she was obviously well along in her pregnancy and, although she was petite and not nearly as tall as Ralph, by her poise she appeared to be his equal in every way. Which she was.

None of us said anything, but the steel in Ralph's eyes spoke volumes.

The minister pulled out a Bible that, compared to Brin's, looked like it had never even been cracked open. "Our scripture for today comes from 1 Corinthians 15:54 and 55." It seemed to take him longer than it should have to flip to the right page. Finally, he read, "When this corruptible shall have put on incorruption, and this mortal shall have put on immortality, then shall be brought to pass the saying that is written, 'Death is swallowed up in victory. O death, where is thy sting? O grave, where is thy victory?'"

I'd heard those words at funerals before and, honestly, they seemed more like wishful thinking than anything else.

Where is the sting of death?

Well, right here, in the hearts of the surviving family members and friends.

Where is the victory of the grave?

Spread out now, all around us. The grave always wins in the end.

Most of his homily was benign and easily forgettable. He spoke of how in times like this we'll be tempted to question God's goodness or his power but that we needed to hold on to our faith, to trust in the power of hope, the power of the future, rather than be overcome by thoughts of the inevitability of the grave.

But then he said, "That is what it means to live as a believer. That is what it means to find victory in apparent defeat. These men, these women came from different backgrounds, from different faiths, but they all shared a common goal: Creating a better life for their families, for their country, for other Americans. They served us all bravely and we can learn from their example of service. They are gone but not forgotten. They will live on in our hearts and in the love that we offer to others."

No, I didn't buy it.

Clichés and worn-out half-truths.

These people wouldn't live on in the love we share with others—they were dead. Simple as that. Yes, for a little while they would be remembered, but soon enough they would be forgotten—the destiny that awaited us all. Soon enough their names would disappear into the sands of time and more people would fill the void they'd left behind.

Just like taking a handful of water from the ocean. The waves roll in and roll out again. And a moment later, in the cosmic sweep of time, no one notices the water is missing.

Sure, I understood where this pastor was coming from. He was trying not to offend anyone and just give us all a feel-good message, but I wished he would just be straight with us: The last thing people have power over is death, regardless of how many positive thoughts and common goals they may have. And if God doesn't have power over the grave, then let's just admit it: there's no hope for us overcoming it either. No matter how long we might "live on" in someone's heart.

Afterward, Brin, who was not one to shy away from a confrontation when it dealt with something she believed in passionately, told the minister, point-blank, "You forgot the rest of the passage."

"Excuse me?"

"The rest of the passage. You only read the first part."
She didn't even need to open her Bible, but said the
words from memory: "The sting of death is sin; and the
strength of sin is the law. But thanks be to God, which
giveth us the victory through our Lord Jesus Christ."

She waited.

"And?" he said.

"And it's not the common goal for a better world that
makes a difference, it's the Lord who does. The victory
doesn't come from us showing love to each other but
from God showing love to us."

"Yes, well," he said at last. "I wanted to be inclusive.
Now, if you'll excuse—"

"Really? Inclusive?"

"That's right. Inclusive."

Ralph's eyes narrowed: *Careful about that tone of voice,
buddy. That's my wife you're talking to.*

Brin went on undeterred. "Jesus died for all, sir.
What's more inclusive than that?"

"That's your viewpoint."

"If it's only my viewpoint and not the truth, then I am
to be pitied above all people. Read the first part of the
chapter. Reverend."

Then she took Ralph's arm, spun, and led him away.

As Lien-hua and I followed them to the car it struck
me that the minister, though he may have had the best
intentions in mind, had edited the truth by not taking
into account the broader context of what was being said.

*The very thing you did when you lied to Sherry Ritterman.*

The pastor had tried to give hope without offense by
softening the truth. But when you do that with the truth
you only end up with a lie wearing fine clothes.

If your goal is to offend no one, you'll never tell the
truth, at least not the whole truth.

*Remember, Pat: The truth is the one thing no one needs to be protected from.*

Yes, I needed to tell Sherry what Stu had really said. I would clear things up, not for my conscience, but because the truth, even when it hurts, heals.

However, as we climbed into Ralph's car, I found myself wondering who this minister was and why Brin seemed to know her Bible better than he did. Something didn't seem quite right about it. Who had hired him? Which family knew him? It was something I decided to look into.

We'd left the graveyard and were about five minutes from Ralph and Brin's house when the text message came through on my phone.

# 23

Ralph was driving and I was beside him, with Lien-hua and Brin in the backseat.

The women were talking quietly about the funeral. It sounded like Brin had moved past her issues with the sermon and she and Lien-hua were listing the people they'd seen there that they knew, discussing follow-up calls they might want to make to some of the family members who were grieving.

Ralph had just turned onto his road when my phone vibrated.

I tapped the screen and a text message came up from an unknown caller:

*Cur homo mortalis caput extruis at morieris en vertex talis sit modo calvus eris.*

"That's weird," I muttered.

"Whatcha got?" he asked.

"Somebody sent me a message in Latin."

"Who's it from?"

"I have no idea."

The most obvious answer would have been Tessa, but this was from 426-2225, which wasn't her number.

No area code came up.

I tapped at my screen to put a call through to the

number but no one answered. No voicemail. After letting it ring a dozen times I hung up and called Cyber to have them trace the number.

The conversation in the backseat faded as our wives' attention shifted toward what was going on in the front.

I copied the Latin text and pasted it into an online translator, but the translation it brought up didn't make any sense: *Why a mortal head up but such is only going to see the top, you will be bald*.

Ralph's house was right up ahead and he began to slow down.

"What did you get?" Lien-hua asked me.

"It's nonsense." I read it to them.

"You should have Tessa help you with it."

That was not a bad idea.

We pulled into the driveway.

But first things first.

While the others filed into Ralph's house, I went over to touch base with the agent who'd been assigned to watch the house.

I thought it would be Agent Woods, but apparently Danner had relieved her, and as I approached the car he rolled down his window. An empty burrito wrapper lay on the floor next to him.

I asked him how things had been. "All good. Quiet," he told me. "I knocked on the door once, checked on them. They were watching TV."

"Thanks. Hopefully, we won't have to call you back again."

There was a tiny pause. "Yes, sir."

Inside the house, Tessa and Tony were in the living room. Tessa had the remote control on her lap and the wide-screen TV that stared out across the room had been paused in the middle of *Star Trek Into Darkness*, one of

Tony's favorite movies. I imagined that they'd been watching it as a necessary distraction from having to think about where their parents were.

*Better to go to a funeral than to a party.*

Maybe it depends a little on how old you are.

"Hey," Tessa said to me.

"Hey."

"Did it . . . did it go okay?"

"Yes."

Brin and Lien-hua disappeared into the kitchen to round up some lunch and I said to Tessa, "I wonder if you can help me with something."

"What is it?"

"Come on. I'll show you."

She handed off the remote to Tony, who went back to his movie. Then she followed Ralph and me to the room that had been set aside as the nursery.

"Yes?" Tessa asked inquisitively. "What do you need?"

"A translation. I tried plugging it into one of those online translators and what came up didn't make sense."

"Yeah, well, those things are pretty much useless unless you're just trying to find out how to ask someone where the bathroom is or how much the sombrero costs." She held out her hand. "Let me see what you have."

"It's Latin."

"Perf."

I gave her the phone and she settled into the rocking chair beside the crib. Some baby clothes sat neatly inside it. The pink hat that Brineesha had knitted for the baby lay on top of them.

Tessa studied the phone's screen. "Well, it starts with *cur*, so it's a question—why? *Homo* is 'man,' *mortalis* is an obvious one—even if you don't know Latin you should be able to translate that."

"Mortal, deadly?" I said.

"Yeah. *Caput* is 'head . . .'" It sounded like she was thinking aloud. "'Why, mortal man . . .' *Extruo* is 'to build up, pile up, raise . . .' So: 'Why, mortal man, do you raise up your head . . . ?'"

She paused and I wasn't sure if she was expecting us to reply, but I didn't interrupt, just waited for her to go on.

"Okay, so that's the first part, then *at morieris en vertex* . . . In Latin the word *at* means 'but' or 'while' or 'on the other hand'—anything along those lines. *Morior* can mean 'to expire' or 'fail' but also 'to die.' And *en* is a command—'look!' 'Behold!' . . . So I'm thinking it's, 'When, behold, you will die.'"

She scrunched up her face and studied the phone. "And then there's *vertex*. It's usually the crown or the peak or top of something, but that just doesn't really make . . ." She mumbled a few comments about *talis* and *calvus* and *eris* and the random subjunctive construction of some sort. Then, finger-swiping to a Latin vocabulary website, she looked up a couple of definitions.

"Okay, here's what I'm thinking about the second half: 'When, behold, you will die and the top, or crown of your head, will become as bald as this'—*calvus*, that's bald—'as this' . . . what?"

"What do you mean?"

"I mean, it's referring to something bald and dead, you know, like a skull, but it's just implied. It's not implicitly stated."

"So," Ralph put the whole thing together: "'Why, mortal man, do you raise up your head when, behold, you will die and—'"

Tessa cut him off. "'End up as bald as this skull.' I mean, you can condense it some; that's basically what it's saying, contextualizing it into English."

Ralph pulled out the bulletin from the funeral, wrote her translation on it, and examined it.

I wondered what that text might mean to the investigation.

*You will die? Is it referring to one of the people we buried today? Someone else entirely? Another victim?*

The message could easily be taken as a threat against me.

We really needed to find out who sent that text.

"So what's it from?" Tessa asked. "This phrase, I mean?"

"I don't know," I said.

"But it's a case, right? It has to do with this bombing?"

"Tessa, I don't know."

"Oh, come on. A mystery note in Latin about death and an awareness of the finite nature of human existence arrives right after the funeral of those killed in the explosion? And it just so happens to be sent to one of the FBI agents who actually survived the bombing? The guy whose book was left at the scene of a homicide that's related to the case? Seriously? You don't have to be C. Auguste Dupin to figure that one out."

Most people might have said you didn't need to be Sherlock Holmes to figure it out, but Tessa hated Holmes, was convinced that Sir Arthur Conan Doyle plagiarized and based Holmes on Poe's detective C. Auguste Dupin. But that was a rant for another day.

"Tessa." I gestured toward the door. "Give us a minute, okay?"

"I already know what it says. Why can't I listen in?"

"This is official FBI business."

"So it *is* a case."

"Tessa, you have to . . ." I paused. She probably knew Latin as well as, if not better than, anyone in the Bureau. It made sense to use her expertise as long as she was here. Besides, she'd already worked through the translation. "So, you haven't heard it before? You don't recognize it from any readings you've done?"

"No." She looked deep in thought. "It sounds like something a medieval philosopher might have written."

"Why do you say that?"

"Well, the grammar is all weird and loose. It's not smooth like it would be if it were written by a Roman, by someone who really knew the language well. Besides, in all my reading I've never come across it. And there's no question mark, which is a little odd."

"Lunch is served," Brineesha called from the other room.

"Alright," Ralph said. "We grab a bite to eat and then Pat and I look into this, see what we come up with."

"Pat and you?" Tessa's tone made her disappointment clear.

"Yes. Pat and me."

# 24

After Brineesha said grace and offered up a prayer for those who'd lost loved ones in the attack, we passed the food around. No one really seemed to have an appetite, not even Tony or Ralph.

The meal was uneventful and we decided to wait until later for dessert.

After we left the table, Ralph and I went to his basement for a little privacy.

He and Brineesha had a one-room apartment down here, where Brin's mom had stayed with them before she died late last summer.

Lien-hua spent some time here recovering after she was attacked by Richard Basque in April. Brin was a nurse, so rather than stay at my house, it had made sense to have Lien-hua stay where Brin could help her if necessary. Also, the basement had access from the driveway so she hadn't had to deal with the stairs.

Using my laptop, I looked for anything relating to the Latin phrase—even excerpts of it—but didn't come up with anything.

Ralph took the opposite approach and searched for Tessa's translation online to see if it was a quote from somewhere.

Nothing.

*It might not appear anywhere. It could have just been written by someone to taunt you.*

Yes, that was a possibility.

I heard footsteps on the stairs. Tessa's gait. "Can I come down?"

"What is it?" I said.

"Did you solve it yet?"

"Not yet, but—"

"I've been thinking about it. I might have something for you. Can I come down or do we have to do this whole talking-to-each-other-up-the-stairs thing?"

I looked at Ralph, who shrugged. "Come on down," I told my daughter.

She joined us in the basement. Ralph had his weights set up in the corner of the room and she took a seat on the weight bench.

"The language of the Church is Latin," she said. "Maybe it's something from one of their catechisms or the Vatican archives . . . or . . ." Her voice faded out as she got caught up in her thoughts. "With the whole skull deal maybe it's an inscription on a sculpture or something. You might want to have your team search medieval books or writings from the Church. . . ."

My cell rang.

Angela's ringtone.

"Hold that thought." I answered the phone. "What do you have, Angela?"

"Nothing is coming up for the phone number that the text came from."

Why didn't that surprise me. "So whoever's behind this has found a way to send texts from numbers that aren't his?"

"Unfortunately, that's not too difficult. For less than

ten dollars you can download apps that'll do it. I'll search for mnemonics and look a little more closely to see if I can decipher the origin of the text."

"Good. Thanks."

When we hung up Ralph said, "Anything?"

"Not yet." I turned to Tessa. "You were saying?"

"It might be lyrics from a song or a refrain from a poem. Could even be something contemporary."

"Wouldn't they show up online?"

"Maybe," she acknowledged. "But it could be that someone translated the phrase from English into Latin and that would mean they might have used a slightly different word order or syntax. So, the lyrics might not have come up if you searched for them with those specific words."

"It would be some pretty dark lyrics, don't you think?" Ralph said.

She shrugged. "Not really."

"Any idea on bands?" I asked her.

"I mean, House of Blood or maybe Death by Suzie might have some lyrics like that, but I know most all of their songs, so . . . probably not. Maybe Boomerang Puppy—they actually have a whole song in Latin. The phrase isn't in it, but who knows? It could be there's a song out there that I don't know about. I'll do some checking."

She already had her phone out. "And we need to send out an inquiry into the Latin underground."

She'd gone through this with me before. Over the last decade there'd been a resurgence of Latin on the Web: discussions, videos, podcasts, all in Latin. An essentially dead language was being revived and revitalized by Latin geeks online.

"Tessa, let's say someone didn't know Latin as well as

you do and was translating from the English into Latin, or vice versa. Can you come up with some other phrases—"

"That could have been translated that way."

"That's what I'm thinking, yes."

"So, you're officially asking me to help you with a case?"

"It's not exactly a case, it's just—"

She patted her hand against the air to stop me. "Sure. Let's just pretend it's important."

Some time ago I'd given her the nickname Raven, partly because of her interest in Poe and partly because, with her black hair and untamed imagination, she made me think of a free-spirited bird. And now the nickname slipped out. "That's not what I mean, Raven, I . . ."

"No, it's cool. I get it, Agent Powers."

"Agent Powers, huh?"

She shared a look with Ralph.

I let them have their fun.

Tessa retreated upstairs to look into the Latin underground, and I called Angela back to have her team do image searches on skulls, album and CD covers, different translations of the Latin—and to contact the Vatican just in case my daughter was right about their catechisms or archives.

"Whoever sent that text to you knew how to cover his tracks," Angela told me. "I wasn't able to find out exactly where it came from. It was routed through a carrier in North Carolina, but the GPS seems to have come from the DC area."

"So North Carolina or DC?"

"There are digital signatures that point to both. That's what I'm saying. That's why it stuck out to me."

"Interesting."

"And that's not all. Lacey has been busy. Remember

the list of words that the numbers in the column of the book might spell out mnemonically?"

"Yes."

"And one of them was Meck Dec?" She sounded like I should know what that was referring to.

"Yes."

"That's our link."

"What's our link? Meck Dec? What does that mean?"

"The Mecklenburg Declaration."

"I've never heard of it."

"I hadn't either, but Lacey dug it up. Before the actual Declaration of Independence was written, a year earlier, back in 1775, the people in Mecklenburg County, North Carolina—where Charlotte is located—well, they wrote up their own declaration of independence and had a local tavern owner deliver it to DC. The stories are a little conflicted from there on out, but apparently he completed his trip but the declaration was rejected. He returned to Charlotte and became something of a folk hero. Captain Jack. You know, like in *Pirates of the Caribbean*. But he was a tavern owner, not a quirky, fey yet gorgeous pirate."

"Gotcha." I'd almost forgotten how much Angela, who is single, is in love with Johnny Depp. "So what happened to this declaration?"

"It was destroyed in a fire, although there was an alleged copy of it printed in 1819 in the *Raleigh Register*."

"Alleged?"

"Some of the phrases are so close to what's found in Jefferson's Declaration of Independence that some people think he plagiarized it, others think the version printed was a fake. In any case, in Charlotte they take it all pretty seriously. They even celebrate May twentieth, the day it was signed, as Meck Dec Day."

So.

That gave us three investigative threads that led to North Carolina: the stolen Colonial weaponry; the numbers scribbled in the book, if they really were referring to the Mecklenburg Declaration; and the origin of the text message.

She said, "I'm going to forward you the list of words that can be made from the phone number you sent me. I think one of them will catch your eye."

"Which one is that?"

"Trust me. You'll know it when you see it."

She ended the call and a few seconds later her list of words arrived.

Of the ones that actually contained some meaningful combination of letters, I found *gam-back, ham-cab-5, I-coca-a-5,* and more, but it only took a second or two for my eyes to land on the one that made the most sense.

4-26-2225

*I-am-back*

I showed it to Ralph.

"What are you thinking?

"I'm thinking it's time to call Margaret. We may need to take a road trip to North Carolina."

# 25

"Are you sure you're up for this?" Margaret asked me when I phoned her. "I mean, with that injury of yours?"

"I'm fine."

"Just a moment." She stopped talking and then, when she came back on the line she said, "There's a flight for Charlotte that leaves at four."

"What? Today?"

"Yes. Can you be ready?"

"Um, sure."

"I was hoping you would say that, because if Joint Terrorism Task Force Director René Gonzalez concurs, I would like both you and Ralph down there."

"And you want us to leave now, today?"

"If that's where everything is pointing, why not?"

Good point.

However, I wanted to make one thing clear before I went anywhere. "Since Jerome's killer left a clue that connects me to this case, and now this text message was sent to me, I need to make sure Tessa is safe when Lien-hua is at work. We have a couple of agents who've been rotating watching the house. I want them to be put on detail until I get back."

"I'm sure that can be arranged." She told me that she

would contact the unit chief in charge of the scheduling at the Academy to assign another instructor to cover my classes until further notice; then she asked to speak to Ralph.

I handed him the phone. "Margaret has something to ask you."

He spoke to her briefly, then told her he would call her back.

I told Lien-hua what was going on, making sure it was okay with her if I went down to Charlotte. I sensed a little hesitation in her reply. "Sure."

"If you don't want me to, I can just tell Margaret that—"

"No, no. I do. Tessa and I will be fine. But I think you need to be the one to tell her."

"Sure. Of course."

When I shared my plans with my daughter she said, "So, does this mean those agents have to keep watching the house?"

"When Lien-hua isn't around, yes. Are you going to be able to live with that?"

"You're gonna owe me big-time for this."

"I'll make it up to you."

While I waited in the living room, I could hear Brin and Ralph discussing things in the kitchen. Though I wasn't trying to eavesdrop, they weren't quieting their voices and the conversation was easy enough to make out.

"You need to go down there." It was Brin.

"I need to be here for you."

"They were your people. The ones who were killed."

"And you're my wife. And this is my daughter we're talking about. I want to be here when our little girl comes into the world."

"Honey, I don't want to be a distraction from you catching whoever—"

"You're not a distraction, Brin. It's . . ." He let his voice trail off. "You're more important to me than my work."

"I know that, but that's not what's at stake here."

Despite how Ralph called the shots everywhere else in his life, Brineesha was known to call one or two of them at home. Ralph was, to put it mildly, strong-willed, but when Brin put her foot down even he didn't try to slide it aside, so I really wasn't sure how this was going to play out.

"When you were a Ranger you were sent on missions and you couldn't have just opted out of one to be home for the birth of your baby. You were gone for six months one time. This'll probably be just a couple days."

"And that's one of the reasons I left the military, remember?"

"Okay," she said. "A compromise. Go down there. See what you can find out. You'll only be, what? A forty-five-minute, maybe an hour-long flight away? I was in labor with Tony for nearly ten hours. If I start having contractions, I'll call you and you can get back up here in plenty of time to see your daughter be born."

He was quiet, and when I heard him speaking again I could tell he was on the phone. "Yeah, Margaret, it's Ralph. I go to Charlotte under one condition . . . Uh-huh . . . I fly back whenever I need to, day or night—if Brineesha goes into labor—so I can be here for the birth of my baby girl . . . Yes . . . Right. The Bureau picks up the bill. That'll work. That's it, then. Alright."

A moment later he emerged from the kitchen and announced to me, "Pack your things, bro. We're going to Charlotte."

# PART III

## Broken Blades

# 26

They played together as children, Corrine and her brother did.

The two of them lived with their parents on the edge of town near a field that spread out wide and wild into the Maine countryside. In the summertime they would go there, lay in the meadowed grass, and watch the clouds build and billow and form high overhead. And they would talk about what they wanted to be when they grew up.

She dreamed of being a movie star and living a life of glamour and wonder and beauty and fame.

He wanted to be a forest ranger—not a baseball player or a fireman or anything like that. No, he liked the woods, camping, time by himself.

And so they dreamed their summers away, there in the meadow with the skittery sound of grasshoppers hidden around them in the waving grass.

In retrospect she wondered if she should have noticed something.

*How could you not wonder? Now, looking back—*

How could anyone not wonder?

When you find out the evil someone is capable of, when you see what he is capable of becoming, how can you not wonder if you should have noticed a sign of it beforehand?

Surely there was something that would have given away what was going to happen? Something small, perhaps: the way he spoke to other children or the way he treated their puppy or the look in his eyes when he got into trouble.

But no, there were no clues to make anyone suspicious.

He was a normal boy.

Just a normal boy.

She remembered when she was twenty-four and first heard the news that he'd been arrested, that he'd been found at a crime scene where several women had been murdered.

And not just murdered. Cannibalized.

Yes, she remembered that day.

And for some reason her first reaction had not been shock.

It should have been.

That's the thing.

For someone in her situation, for a young woman to find out that her older brother was accused of such things, it should have shocked her.

But it had not.

And ever since then, she had wondered why that was.

If accusations like that about someone so close to you didn't shake you to the core, then surely you should have seen it coming.

Signs.

She should have seen signs.

But she had not.

No one had.

When the crimes became known, when the verdict was read, the media had pressed her with questions about her upbringing, about her parents, trying to pin down a reason for her brother's actions—abuse, neglect, a brain injury of some type; anything so they wouldn't have to admit that he was a successful, popular, well-adjusted guy who just started abducting, murdering, and eating people.

Psychiatric problems? Had he taken medication? Been depressed when he was growing up?

No.

He'd been a good boy. A good son. A good brother, playing quietly with his sister under the still summer skies, daydreaming about what they would do someday when they were grown and all their dreams would come true.

No, he hadn't been a troubled child. And that's what frightened people the most, because if that happened to him, then the same thing could perhaps happen to anyone.

And yes.

That was it.

That's what made everyone so uncomfortable.

The people who knew him had trusted him.

Everyone in the family had loved him.

She had loved him.

Did love him.

He was her brother.

Their parents were gone now, both dead. Natural causes. All their other relatives had disappeared into anonymity after the trial. Corrine was the only one left.

She knew that he loved her. She had never doubted that.

She'd been married briefly when she was in her late twenties, and after the divorce she'd decided to hang on to her married name. It didn't keep all the reporters and bloggers away, but it did help her establish a small sense of anonymity.

Corrine Monique Davis.

Formerly, Corrine Monique Basque.

The sister of Richard Devin Basque, the killer, the cannibal, who had started off his criminal career by torturing and slaughtering and cannibalizing women who reminded him of her.

The sister he loved.


And now.

Here she was.

In a long, narrow tomb, trapped in this tunnel that dropped off into nothingness two hundred steps from the water. She had almost fallen off the edge, almost lost her balance when she found no ground for her foot as she mapped out in her mind the length of the tunnel.

Then when she raised her hand above her, she found one final beam where the ceiling ended. It must have been how the man had gotten her into this tunnel.

The walls ended too.

A shaft.

*To the surface? A shaft that leads to the surface?*

She'd felt an immediate surge of hope, but it was short-lived because when she tried leaning out and looking up, all she saw was stark blackness. No light. Not even a tiny dot of daylight in the distance.

*Maybe it's night? Maybe there'll be light coming down if you wait here long enough?*

She reached out in search of a rope, in search of anything, but there was nothing there. Just blank, eternal darkness.

She screamed until she lost her voice, begged the silent, unfeeling emptiness to help her.

And she prayed.

How long had passed now since she'd prayed last?

It didn't matter.

There was no reply.

No help came.

A stone tossed into the shaft told her it was a long way to the bottom.

A very long way.

The tears came in waves—she would be fine for minutes, for hours, for what seemed like days, and then she would find herself wracked with tears again.

But they didn't offer her any comfort.

She'd started to shiver more, and though she was walking back and forth to keep moving and to stay warm, she was getting tired and she was afraid to sit down and sleep.

Afraid that she might stop shivering.

She was thirsty but, still leery of drinking the water at the tunnel's other end, she opted to let drops from the ceiling partway down the tunnel land on her tongue. But it didn't quell her growing thirst.

The only option she had right now was to persevere, to hold on, to keep moving, and to trust forces bigger than herself to bring her help before it was too late.

She wasn't sure if she should wait here by the shaft. It seemed like the best option for being found.

*But what if that man comes back?*

*Maybe you should go back by the water.*

*No. What if someone else comes looking and misses you because you're too far away?*

She tried evaluating things, but her thoughts seemed muddy and thick. One moment it was clear that the obvious choice was to stay here, then the obvious choice seemed to be to wait by the water.

*But why? Why by the water?*

*You could swim. You're a good swimmer. You could swim to safety, find where the water goes—*

*What are you even thinking, Corrine? That's crazy.*

Finally, she decided on the sensible thing, the logical thing: to wait by the shaft where she could see if someone was coming down to save her.

Her thoughts returned to her brother.

To summers with him as a child.

And as she sat there alone, shrouded in darkness, she wondered once more, just as she had so many times over the years, why—if Richard loved her—had he gone on a killing spree, brutally taking the lives of women who resembled her.

# 27

Ralph and I landed at the Charlotte Douglas International Airport and entered the famous atrium decked out with a row of old-style rocking chairs lined up along the glass wall that overlooked the tarmac.

Live grand-piano music resonated through the air. The hustle and hum of busy people living busy lives paused here, found a respite near the food court and the rocking chairs that offered a taste of Southern hospitality.

Before exiting past security I went to grab a cup of coffee at Chierio's, an indie coffee shop in the C terminal, something I always did when flying through Charlotte. But today, to my disappointment, I found that it was gone and a Starbucks occupied its place in the concourse.

"So," Ralph said, "I'm guessing you're gonna pass on the java?"

"You know me all too well."

"No mermaid coffee."

"No mermaid coffee."

"Tessa's right. You really are a coffee snob. And to think I'm the one who got you started drinking the stuff. Can I ever forgive myself?"

"'Snob' is such an unflattering word."

He nodded toward a store nearby. "Buy you a Snickers?"

"That'll do."

As we waited in line at the Avis rental counter, Ralph, who was crunching his way through a duty-free almond chocolate bar nearly the size of a tablet computer, said, "Remember the last time we were in Charlotte?"

"Tracking Sevren."

"Yes."

"Yeah, I remember."

Sevren Adkins was a killer who'd left clues at his crime scenes about who his next victim would be. Eventually that investigation had led us to uncover a conspiracy that had its roots in the Jonestown Massacre in Guyana, South America, back in the seventies.

The mnemonic of the origin of the Latin text message formed the phrase *I am back*.

But, no, that didn't work. Sevren was dead.

A copycat?

Possibly.

Something to keep in mind.

Because now death had brought me back to this city.

It's strange how the past threads its way into our lives, affecting the trajectory of our moments, sometimes bringing unexplainable unity to the way the present unfolds.

Even with the priority of this investigation, the Bureau wasn't interested in "unnecessary case-related expenditures," so we had only one rental car between us and we were staying at a midpriced hotel fifteen minutes from Uptown.

Once we had our car, a compact that Ralph could barely squeeze behind the steering wheel of, we navigated through the early-evening traffic.

As he drove, he shared what he thought the people

who'd laid out the road system, with the right-hand lanes ending so frequently and abruptly in exit-only lanes, should do to themselves. His suggestions included a few unique and rather memorable anatomical suggestions that, though impossible, were, if nothing else, quite inventive.

Traffic held us up and we didn't arrive at our hotel until after seven, too late to swing by the FBI Field Office, so we grabbed supper next door at a small, locally owned fried-chicken place. "Tessa's not here," Ralph reminded me. "That means you can have chicken without any meat guilt."

"What about deep-fried Southern-grease guilt?"

"I won't tell Tessa if you don't tell Brin."

"Deal."

When we'd finished, I had a mango smoothie to help assuage my grease guilt. Ralph chose a packet of gummy bears.

Afterward, as I stowed my suitcase in the hotel closet, I said, "When I first met you in Milwaukee, back when I was a detective, you told me that you used pillow mist."

"That's right."

"I didn't believe you."

"I know."

He dug through his things and produced a small spray bottle. "You should have." He held it out, offering it to me.

"I think I'll pass."

He chose the bed nearest the television and spritzed his pillow. "Your loss, my friend, your loss. There's nothing like a nice-smelling pillow to welcome you to dreamland."

"Did you just say 'welcome you to dreamland'?"

"Just seeing if you were paying attention."

We spent some time reviewing the case and then laid out our plan for the morning: visit the Field Office and orient ourselves to what they were working on, drive past the locations in Charlotte that seemed pertinent to the case, and then connect with the curator of the Mint Museum at eleven thirty, a meeting Margaret had set up for us while we were flying down here.

Earlier, on our way to the airport, I'd called Gonzalez and asked him to look into the minister from the funeral, and now he texted that the pastor was a friend of Jennings, the National Security Council rep, and that Jennings was the one who'd coordinated with the families to have him speak.

I found that informative, but I couldn't see how it had any immediate bearing on the case.

At last, Ralph and I called it a night.

I've stayed in hotel rooms with my friend on a couple of occasions, and I was thankful he didn't snore.

Or at least that's what I thought, but I soon found out he'd developed a new habit since I last traveled with him.

I tried adjusting the air conditioner/heater unit under the window to cover up the sound, but the thing apparently had two settings: tepid and arctic.

In the end I went for arctic.

With my unscented pillow folded around my head and an extra blanket over me so I wouldn't shiver from the frigid air blasting at me from only a few feet away, I tried to get some sleep.

++++

The bard was back in Charlotte. It'd been a long day, but it had been worth it to visit the graveyard. He'd gotten the photos he needed. He'd seen Lien-hua and Patrick Bowers, and also Agent Hawkins and his quite-pregnant wife.

He'd also made sure his captive was secure in that basement on Pine Street.

Yes, at an address that the Bureau would, eventually, find to be quite informative.

A productive trip.

Now he retired to his bedroom. Tomorrow he had to go to work in the morning; then in the afternoon he could check on Corrine and confirm the Semtex placement.

He contacted his person in DC and offered a reminder of what would happen if things did not go as planned.

"You have a job to do," he said. "And you understand what will happen if it's not carried out?"

"I . . . understand," came the soft reply.

++++

Though Tessa had searched all afternoon and evening, she hadn't found anything online about the Latin phrase, and now, with her dad and Ralph gone to Charlotte, she doubted she was going to get any more chances to help them out.

Which pretty much sucked.

She hadn't admitted to them how important it was to her that she help them, that it was her way of trying to deal with what was happening this week. It was something positive she could do in the face of something so devastating.

Ever since her mom had been diagnosed with cancer, the idea of death, of real people dying in real life, had been hard for her to deal with.

Blood.

Corpses.

Funerals.

All deeply distressing.

Not that anyone likes those things—of course not—but for her it was different. She'd already seen too much suffering and death. Her mom. Her dad. Media photos from the cases Patrick worked.

Obviously, he never let her see his case files, but the pictures that made the rounds on the cable-news shows and the Internet were grisly enough.

She almost felt guilty being thankful at a time like this, but she *was* thankful—thankful that he and Lien-hua hadn't been killed when the bomb went off. That would have been too much for her. That would have sent her plummeting off a cliff she never would have recovered from.

Given everything that had happened, despite herself, she found her thoughts revolving around death and loss: her mom dying of cancer, her biological dad being shot last year.

She needed to process all this, needed to sort out the jagged images that were caught in her mind.

Making sure she didn't wake up Lien-hua, she snuck out for a smoke, but that didn't seem to help.

Back inside her room, she pulled out her journal and picked up a pen.

She could type faster than she could write, much faster, but there's something about having a pen in your hand that forces you to think carefully about every word.

Typing gives birth to bloviated writing, fat and wobbly and sloppy.

You see it all the time on the Web. Thoughtless, mindless prose, unwieldy and unfocused.

Blog. Blog. Blog.

Even the word sounded fat and imprecise.

But with a pen, you actually experienced each word as you shaped it, stroke by stroke, curve by curve. One letter flowing to the next, each word a nonpareil experience.

But when you type, every letter is shaped the same beneath your fingers, a flat or maybe concave square little world.

Tap. Tap. Tap. Type. Type. Type.

Only writing longhand allowed you to enter the breadth and unique form of every letter, every word.

She flipped to a blank page in her journal.

*Write. Clear your head. Get death off your mind.*

She thought of her mom, and of growing up in Minnesota—springtime in a budding, unfolding world, the smell of moist soil underfoot, a warm rain erasing the remnants of winter.

But even her memories of spring led her back to thoughts of death when a very specific afternoon came to mind, a day when she and her mom were taking the laundry outside to hang up on the line that stretched between two poles in their backyard.

And she wrote:

> *One day they found a dead bunny in the yard. It wasn't fun to pet and they couldn't leave it there or it would attract the wrong kind of flies.*
>
> *So they buried it beneath a spreading tree and said a prayer, and the little girl watched her first dead body get lowered into the ground on a sunny day when all she'd wanted to do was hang up the laundry with her mother and play tag in the tall, leaning grass.*

As she stared at the words, a cord seemed to stretch across the canyon of pain inside of her, connecting the sting of those memories with the present-day vague sense of grief that had draped over her life in the years since her mom had died.

The Latin phrase that'd been texted to Patrick came back to mind, as well as the translation she'd come up with: *Why, mortal man, do you raise up your head when, behold, you will die and end up as bald as this skull?*

Yeah, that was actually a pretty good question. Why, indeed?

She hadn't been able to find the quote anywhere.

Sure, the Web was a great repository of knowledge, but it wasn't the only one.

Last summer she'd gotten a Library of Congress card. They're only given to researchers—and sometimes students who can prove they're doing research "of a significant and enduring nature." She'd convinced them to give her one and was thankful because it allowed her to get into the main reading room, which was off-limits to the general public. They were good for a year, so she was golden.

Yeah, tomorrow she would visit the Library of Congress while Patrick was gone and Lien-hua was at work.

Who knows? Maybe Beck would need to come along with her, to protect her.

*Or maybe it'll be that woman, his partner.*

Well, if it was Beck, Tessa told herself that she would just have to find a way to put up with it.

As if that was going to be a problem.

# 28

The exercise room at the hotel consisted of a single, dated treadmill and a stained, yellow yoga mat discarded haphazardly beneath the window.

I opted for a jog outside.

With my wounded side, I had to be careful not to swing my right arm too much, which made running a little awkward, but I managed.

A wooded park nearby, enshrouded in early-morning mist, gave me a quiet place to run.

After half an hour I turned around, and on the way back to the hotel I explored a side street where I found a park with a children's playground. One bar looked about the right height and I would have loved to pump out a few sets of pull-ups, something I try to do as often as possible to stay in shape for rock climbing, but there was no way the stitches were going to stay intact if I tried something like that.

A discarded toy helicopter lay beside a rusted metal swing. The chopper was splattered with mud from a recent rain and was half-covered with dirt. I'm not sure why, but I picked it up and found that its blades were broken.

It would never fly again.

And it took me back.

Memories.

A boy.

Taken.

I was working as a detective in Milwaukee. One day a woman lost track of her five-year-old son on the Summerfest Grounds. She was nearly hysterical by the time I arrived. "He's okay," she was saying over and over. "He has to be okay."

But the boy wasn't okay. I was the one who found him two days later. He was still alive. The man who took him, a high school English teacher, had kept him locked in his guest bedroom and videotaped the things he'd done to him.

That boy would never be okay again.

And I was the one who had to tell his mother.

I wish I didn't know so much about crimes.

For some reason it didn't feel right to leave the helicopter there, so I took it with me.

Back in the hotel room I found Ralph doing push-ups. I had no idea how long he'd been at it. I've seen him lay out a set of seventy-five in a row before, so when I realized he was finishing a set of twenty and was sounding winded, I imagined he'd been working out for a while.

"What's with the helicopter?" He took a break, lifted his right arm, stretched his triceps.

*A reminder of a time I was too late.*

"A souvenir from my run." I set it on the bedside stand.

After we'd both cleaned up and changed clothes, we left for the Field Office.

++++

The bard drove to work.

A month ago he'd taken a position that allowed him access to the local museums as well as other businesses throughout the city that he'd used while he was looking into the location of the mines. It'd made it easier to get the artifacts that he'd needed for his night with Jerome Cole.

Really, the job was perfect—only a couple of days a week, flexible hours, and it got him into places he never would have been able to enter otherwise.

He kept a low profile.

Didn't cause any trouble.

He was a good, quiet, faithful employee.

No one at work had any idea about his extracurricular activities.

++++

We took Exit 3 to get to 7915 Microsoft Way, where the Charlotte Field Office was located.

"By the way," Ralph said, "did you think it was a little cold last night in the hotel room? I was freezing."

"Hmm . . . We'll have to take a look at that tonight."

"Yeah. I don't want to miss out on any of my beauty sleep."

"Now, see, you just lobbed one over the net for me and I'm not even going to spike it back at you. No snide comment coming your way."

"You're a smart man."

"I'm a beacon of self-control in a factious world."

"It sounds like you've been spending too much time with Tessa."

"That just may be true."

As we drove toward the five-story building, the sunlight glared off its dark windows situated in the reinforced concrete sides. An imposing, spear-tipped steel fence ran around the property.

The FBI has its own police force and now, even though the officers here were expecting us, the two men in the guardhouse took their time verifying our creds and, in light of the bombing at the NCAVC on Monday, even checked under the car for explosives.

After parking, we met up with Special Agent in Charge David Voss in a conference room. He was a tall, spindly man who made me think of a human spider. Glassy eyes behind retro glasses, late thirties. I figured he must either have been an incredibly bright guy or someone who was shrewd at politics to snag his position at his age. Maybe he was both.

After introductions, he said to Ralph, "I got word from Director Wellington that you were coming." It seemed like a needless thing to say.

"Yes," Ralph replied.

"I'm here to do whatever I can to help you."

"Glad to hear that."

Voss gathered up the leaders of three of his units—Cyber, Evidence Response, and Counterterrorism.

Fortunately, the agents had prepared for our arrival and were already relatively familiar with the case. Together Ralph and I filled in the blanks for them.

When we'd finished, Ralph said, "So, where are you guys at? What do we know?"

"Well," Voss replied, "we have a team looking into historical markers and locations that deal with the Mecklenburg Declaration. So far, nothing. We're consulting with the Charlotte Historical Society to see if we can find out about a connection between the Catawba tribe and the Mecklenburg Declaration."

Ralph nodded. "Good. And the museum footage?"

"Still reviewing it."

I flipped open my laptop and connected to the room's projection-screen system for a video conference with Joint Terrorism Task Force Director René Gonzalez, the man Margaret had put in charge of the investigation.

Once he was on-screen he said, "Angela hasn't been able to find anything pertinent regarding that Latin phrase or the English translation relating to sculptures or CD covers. The Vatican has assured us that they're going to do whatever they can to help, but so far they haven't come up with anything either."

*Maybe the sentence isn't from anywhere. Maybe the text was written up specifically for you.*

"What do we know about the Semtex?" I asked him.

"Two hundred pounds were taken."

"What?" I gasped. "I thought it was only twenty."

"Yeah, well, so did we. An extra zero got dropped out of the initial reports. And from what we can tell only a few pounds would have been needed at the NCAVC to cause that extent of damage. We could be looking at a much bigger attack on the horizon."

"A shipment that size of Semtex was lost and we didn't hear about it on the news?" Voss said skeptically.

"It's not exactly something the Army was excited to publicize, but, believe me, I'm looking into it."

"With that much Semtex"—it was Voss again—"how much damage could you do to . . . say, a skyscraper?"

Ralph answered this time, drawing from his background as an Army Ranger. "If you knew what you were doing and where to place it, and, of course, depending on the size of the building and its structural integrity, you could probably bring one down."

After we'd all had a chance to take that in, I asked Gonzalez what else we knew.

"The Semtex was shipped last Monday. It was supposed to go to Fort Bragg, but it never arrived."

"What does that mean, 'it never arrived'?" I said. "It didn't just disappear en route. What are we talking about here?"

"Yeah"—Gonzalez scratched with irritation at his scar—"that's pretty much what I said. I'll let you know more as soon as I find anything else out."

After the video conference, Voss adjourned the meeting and Ralph and I went with him to his office. Once the three of us were alone, Ralph said, "Talk to me about your joint task force work with the CMPD."

Charlotte is a little different than many major cities in that its police department covers the whole county rather than just the city proper. They ended up with the somewhat cumbersome name of the Charlotte-Mecklenburg Police Department, or CMPD for short.

Voss was slow in responding to Ralph's question. "You know how these things can be."

"Tell me how these things can be."

He glanced at the clock on the wall, then back at Ralph. "I'll put it this way: They're not the most cooperative department I've ever worked with."

"And how many is that?"

"Three. Before I came here."

The FBI works with hundreds of state and local law enforcement agencies across the country, as well as dozens of other government agencies. There are more than seventeen thousand different law-enforcement entities in the U.S., many with overlapping jurisdictions. And, despite how things are portrayed in the movies, in real life the Bureau usually has a positive working relationship with local law enforcement.

It didn't sound like that was the case in Charlotte, though.

"What can we do here to help you?" Voss asked us.

"Let's start by taking a look at your city," I replied.

My phone is a beta version of one in development for the National Geospatial-Intelligence Agency, a branch of the Defense Department. Because of my involvement with geospatial applications in law enforcement, they were letting me use it so I could give them feedback on the user interface.

The phone was able to project a three-dimensional hologram based on aggregate geospatial data from our defense satellites, a program known as FALCON, or the Federal Aerospace Locator and Covert Operation Network.

It was a bit like virtually flying through a city on Google Earth, but you could manipulate the images with your hands—throw them into a digital trash bin, enlarge and shrink the objects floating in front of you, zoom in, zoom out. It was pretty slick, and from what I'd heard, it wasn't going to be that long before this technology would be commercially available for the general public.

I pulled up the 3-D map of Charlotte's Uptown, then tapped the button to project the hologram of the city. It hovered half a meter above the table. I adjusted it until it was about a meter wide, then zoomed in on Uptown.

"I've never seen anything like that," Voss muttered.

"Yeah, it's one of his favorite toys," Ralph told him. "I'm asking for one for Christmas."

"Better be good. Santa's watching."

I wasn't sure if Voss was trying to be funny or not. The guy was hard to read.

"Right," Ralph said uncertainly, as if he were trying to discern Voss's intent as well.

Zooming out, I rotated the hologram, turning the city before me, and it took only a moment to notice that the center of Charlotte was laid out in a grid but the residential areas had winding, meandering streets.

With Voss's help we identified the Mint Museum's two locations—one Uptown, and one on Randolph Road, where the theft had taken place. We also looked at possible travel routes to and from the museum and noted which streets might have traffic cameras.

After I'd closed up the phone, Voss said to me, "So, they say you don't believe in motive."

"Who says that?"

"I heard it around."

Well, news travels fast.

"That's not quite the case, but here's where I'm coming from."

And then I told him the truth about motives.

# 29

"All of us are motivated to do things," I said, "but trying to accurately guess what someone else might've been thinking prior to committing a crime is fruitless. Many times we don't even understand what motivates the actions we take ourselves. How can we claim to know someone else's motivation when we can't even pinpoint our own?"

"I'm not sure I follow."

"Take hate crimes, for instance. A man can scribble racist graffiti on a wall and be charged with felony criminal mischief and maybe face a sentence of one or even up to seven years. But if a judge or a jury decides that it was a hate crime the offender might get ten to thirty years in prison, depending on local and state statutes. But how do you know hate motivated it? That's speculation and it could send someone away for decades. That's not justice."

"You have to trust the system, Pat," said Ralph.

Needless to say, we did not see eye to eye on this issue.

This wasn't really the time to debate the merits of punishment in the pursuit of justice, but I didn't need to worry about it since Voss took us in another direction.

"But isn't establishing motive the first step in figuring out a crime?"

"If it's a step at all," I said, "it should be the last one. We should be in the business of collecting and analyzing evidence, not involved in trying to guess what someone was thinking before he might have or might not have taken a specific action. You can never confirm a motive, you can only speculate as to one. Whatever the motive for the crime, offenders ask themselves four questions, even if they're not aware that they're doing so."

"What are those?"

"How much do I want this thing? How much am I willing to risk to get it? How much will I benefit if I get it? How will I get away with this action without getting caught?"

He mulled that over for a moment. "So evaluating risk and rewards."

"Exactly."

"But all this stuff about geography . . ." He gestured toward the phone. "How is that going to help us here?"

"I want a couple of agents working up a full comparative case analysis to see if there are more crimes linked to this case besides the robbery of the Catawba weaponry here in Charlotte, the homicide of Jerome Cole, and the attack on the NCAVC."

"And don't forget the shooting at the DEA headquarters last week."

"So far there's no evidence that's related," Ralph corrected him. "But the Semtex is."

"That's right," I said. "We track its movement—its travel route, the exact timing and location of the robbery as well as why it wasn't made public earlier. We find those things and we might find the link we need."

"But those are all very different crimes," Voss noted. "What are you suggesting we look for?"

"Based on what our guy did to Cole, we know he's violent and he's forensically aware, and this is not likely his first offense. He might have been arrested before and learned from his mistakes."

"So, physical or sexual assaults? Torture?"

"Yes, and even petty crimes, misdemeanors, moving-vehicle violations on the day of the robbery, traffic-camera footage—anything. We need to see if he left any other footprints in time and space for us to find, mistakes that might lead us to where he is now."

I'd taught a lot about comparative case analysis at the Academy and a good example of failure in the realm of police investigation actually had to do with an investigation here in Charlotte. "It happened here with Wallace." I sometimes talk to myself and think aloud and now I didn't realize I'd spoken the words until Voss said, "What do you mean?"

"I'm sorry?"

"You said it happened here with Wallace."

"Henry Louis Wallace back in the nineties."

"Oh." Voss nodded. Apparently he recognized the name after all. "The Charlotte Strangler."

"Yes."

"Nine women," Voss said, "all African-Americans murdered within a two-year span."

Wallace had also confessed to killing a prostitute here in Charlotte, as well as another ten women while he was stationed at military bases around the world, but I didn't bother to correct Voss.

"Raped too," he added.

"Most of them were, yes. But law enforcement failed

to link the cases. Two of the women lived in the same apartment building, two had worked at the same Bojangles' restaurant, two at the same Taco Bell, five had known connections to that restaurant manager's friends and relatives."

"And that was Wallace?"

"It was. He killed the last three women within a three-day span. If the police had taken a closer look at the travel routes, awareness space, and links between the previous victims, they could have pinpointed Wallace as a suspect earlier."

"And saved those three women."

"It's possible," I acknowledged.

"So, focus on finding links between locations and victims?"

"Exactly. Who knows your city the best? Here among your agents?"

He looked at me curiously. "I'm not sure I understand."

"This guy who killed Jerome Cole, he's been leaving clues that relate to Charlotte's history. You can only learn so much from staring at maps and holograms. I want to drive around the city. I need someone to guide me."

He considered that. "Well, I mean, we've been consulting with this one guy over the last couple days. He does tours of the city—you know, history tours, that sort of thing. We found him through the Chamber of Commerce. He's not an agent, but he seems pretty well-informed about Charlotte and, like I say, we've been talking with him, so he's familiar with working with the Bureau."

"That'll work."

"Name's Guido Lombardi."

Ralph blinked. "Your local expert on Charlotte, North Carolina, is a guy named Guido Lombardi?"

"Yes. Why?"

"Just . . . No reason."

We made the arrangements to meet Guido at the Chamber of Commerce office Uptown and then, after Voss assured us one more time that he would do all he could to help us, Ralph and I took off to meet the man who was going to escort us around the city.

# 30

"My job is to keep an eye on you," Beck told Tessa.

She was standing beside his sedan. A few moments ago he'd stepped out when he saw her approaching and now he was scanning the neighborhood. Alert and vigilant. It made her feel safe.

"Well, far be it from me to keep you from fulfilling your duty," she said.

*Wait, don't sound too excited to have him tag along. It'll seem like that's what you want.*

*But it is.*

*Well, you can't let him know that!*

Slightly conflicted, she said, "I think I'll be safe from the bad guys while I'm in the Library of Congress."

Lien-hua was at the Academy, where the NCAVC team had set up shop after their building was attacked, so Tessa was here alone with Beck.

"Will it distract you if I sit at a table near you?" he asked. He hadn't shaved that morning and he had this slightly scruffy look going on.

*Um. Yes.*

"Why would that distract me?"

"Good. Then I think I'll come in with you."

"I'm afraid you're out of luck there, Agent Danner."

She dug through her purse and fished out her Library of Congress card. "You can't get into the main reading room without one of these."

He pulled out his creds. "I think I'll be alright. If they give me a hard time I'll just tell 'em I'm your research assistant."

"My assistant, huh?"

"Whatever it takes to keep you safe."

*Oh, man, why does he have to keep saying things like that?!*

She put her Library of Congress ID card away and just went for it: "In that case, do you really think we need to take two cars? I mean, does that really make sense—having to find two parking spots?"

"Hop in." Beck walked around to the passenger's side and opened the door for her. "I'll drive."

++++

Guido wore black jeans and a pink polo shirt. Medium height, brown hair, early forties, an easily forgettable face. When he greeted us he shook my hand a little too enthusiastically. "Good to meet you, good to meet you. I'd be glad to show y'all around."

"Okay," I replied.

Ralph handed him the keys to our rental car. "You drive. The curator of the Mint Museum will be meeting us there at eleven thirty—at the Randolph Road location. That means you have eighty minutes to give us the history of Charlotte. Let's get started with downtown."

"Actually, we don't call it downtown," Guido gently corrected him. "We call it Uptown, or maybe Center City."

"Ah." Ralph's tone was impossible to read. "Good to know."

"You see"—we were walking to the car—"interestingly enough it was a bit of a controversy. Back in the seventies the city went through the process of trying to decide what to call it. Finally landed on Uptown because, even though it's not so evident now, it was originally located on a hill. It was a trade route for the Native Americans. It's where the settlers used to—"

"Excuse me," I interrupted him as we arrived at the car. "A trade route for Native Americans? Catawba?"

"Yes, yes. Very good." Guido sounded impressed. "And Cherokee. That's how it came to be called Trade Street."

"That's where we start." Ralph swung his door open. "Take us up Trade Street."

# 31

The drive into the heart of DC had passed quickly. Now Beck walked alongside Tessa as they approached the Library of Congress.

"A lot of history here in this city," he said.

"You know, I'm not a big fan of history."

"You don't like history?"

"I mean, I like the stories. But names? Dates? Come on. And when you ask a history teacher why it's so important, they always give you the same answer."

"Let me guess: 'We study history so we can learn from it, so we don't repeat the same mistakes again.'"

"Exactly. But how does knowing the dates of the Chicago fire help us learn not to make that mistake again? Most teachers don't use it as an example of how you need to be careful with lanterns while you're milking a cow."

They reached the steps.

"That's just a theory, about the cow, isn't it?"

"Either way, what does it have to do with daily life? And it's not like you're ever gonna need to know the names of all the presidents—like someone randomly asks you who the twenty-second president of the United States is and you're like—'Grover Cleveland, who was also the twenty-fourth,' and then—"

"Is that true?"

"What?"

"That Grover Cleveland was the twenty-second and the twenty-fourth president?"

"Yeah."

"So you remembered."

The two of them got in line to enter the building.

"I remember a lot of stuff, but that doesn't mean any of it is useful. Point is: No history teacher I've ever had teaches history from that perspective. They never say, 'Okay, here's what happened during Grover Cleveland's presidency and here's what we can learn from it and apply to our lives today so we don't make the same mistakes he did.' Doesn't happen. Instead they end up feeding you facts—dates and names—instead of application. The very reason they use to justify their jobs—using the past as examples and warnings for the present—is the very thing they almost universally fail to do."

They passed through the doors, entered the building, and got in line to step through the metal detector.

Beck was quiet.

"What is it?" she asked.

"I always liked history."

"Oh."

"It was my favorite subject in school, actually."

*Tessa, you are such an idiot!*

"Really, um . . . You know, I get that. When you think about it, it's . . . I mean, it can be sort of . . ."

He grinned as he showed his creds to the Capitol Police officer, then removed his gun and set it on the conveyor belt. "Gotcha."

"What?"

"I was kidding. I hated history."

"Really."

"Really."

"So," she said, "we have something in common, then."

"I guess we do."

They headed through security to the restricted-access reading rooms while Tessa told herself she was not, not, not going to be distracted by having this guy sit at a table beside her.

++++

Guido showed us the four statues on the corner of Trade and Tryon and told us a little about what each one represented as he gave us an abbreviated history of the city—from the early days of textiles and gold mining to the development of the banking industry.

Then he emphasized transportation, with the railroads cutting through the city. And, more recently, the Charlotte Douglas International Airport, which had become the country's second-largest hub for American Airlines since its merger with US Airways.

Four statues: Commerce, a gold prospector; Transportation, a railroad worker; Industry, a mill worker; and Future, a woman holding up her baby.

"This is known as Independence Square, and it's where they signed the Mecklenburg Declaration."

"The Meck Dec," I said.

"You know your Charlotte history."

"I'm starting to take an interest in it. Talk to me about the layout of Uptown."

"Well, there are four districts that used to be the voting precincts, we call them wards. Just remember that Third Ward is growing fast, lots of construction, and Fourth Ward is the historical district. That'll get you by."

I considered what he said in light of the three-dimensional view of the city that my phone had revealed earlier.

A bus passed us and Guido pointed toward it. "The bus routes radiate from the transit center Uptown; the light rail goes southwest and northeast. An extension is under construction. That might be helpful. What are y'all looking for exactly?"

"Anything that helps me understand your city," I said.

"What about segregation?" Ralph asked our guide. "I've heard about issues here over the years."

"Well," Guido said, "just like most major U.S. cities, people here tend to live next to folks who look like them. There used to be desegregation busing, but that ended in the Reagan era. Actually, in the public arena—politics, media, business—Charlotte is pretty well integrated. The most segregated hour of the week is Sunday morning during church."

"Yeah, well," Ralph replied, "Charlotte's not alone there."

"We've come a long way, but there's still a long way to go." Then he abruptly switched topics. "The city continues to grow. People are moving back Uptown again. The trend started maybe a decade or so ago. Lofts going up all over the place."

One was being built about a block away from us and scaffolding covered one side of the unfinished building. They were at nine stories now. I wondered how tall it was going to be when it was finished.

Guido drove us past some of the famous public art Uptown, as well as the statue of Captain Jack, then guided us past the Tudor homes of Myers Park, where he told us the old money was.

A young mom was pushing a jog-stroller along the

winding sidewalk, taking advantage of the cooler morning before the crushing heat of the day took over.

Then Guido took us to the famous intersection where Queens Road curls around itself and meets up with . . . well, Queens Road. "We're named after Great Britain's Queen Charlotte of Mecklenburg-Strelitz," he told us. "She was married to King George III. And, of course, to this day Charlotte is known as the Queen City."

Capitalizing on the Queen City motif, there were crowns on most of the major street signs as well as the streetlamps in Uptown. Even the taxis had crowns emblazoned on their sides. Guido explained that most of the skyscrapers were built to appear to have crowns on top. "Most famously, the Bank of America building."

Just as it was with so many things, now that he'd pointed it out, it was obvious. The spires on top did look like a crown.

We drove past Bank of America Stadium, where the Panthers, Charlotte's NFL team, play. "Tomorrow is Fan Celebration Day," Guido informed us. "The season doesn't start quite yet, but you'll have tens of thousands of fans packed in there to meet Panthers players and watch them scrimmage."

I could almost see the wheels in Ralph's head turning. He was a huge gridiron fan and I imagined that he was trying to figure out a way he could meet some of the players.

South Mint Street wrapped around the stadium. "It's called Mint Street for a reason," Guido told us. "It's where the mint used to be. That makes sense—I mean, that's obvious. They've since moved the building and now it's the Mint Museum over on Randolph, where you're heading, but this whole area was involved in gold mining."

"Yes," I said, "tell us about the gold mining."

"Well, gold was discovered in 1799 by Conrad Reed, a twelve-year-old boy who lived about twenty miles from here. He found a gold nugget that weighed more than seventeen pounds. His family didn't know what kind of rock it was and ended up using it as a doorstop for three years before someone was able to identify it."

Ralph just shook his head. "That's crazy."

"Well." Guido was obviously in his element expounding all this to us. "In the coming years North Carolina became the richest gold-producing state in the Union, bringing with it an influx of foreign mine workers, until the 1849 gold rush in California, during which many of the miners from North Carolina moved out West. They say there are still places where the old mines stretch underneath Uptown, over in Third Ward."

Ralph looked at him disbelievingly. "You're saying that the city was built right on top of these abandoned gold mines?"

Guido shrugged. "I guess. I mean, it wouldn't be feasible to fill up three- or four-hundred-foot-deep shafts—not to mention all the horizontal tunnels. It's a lot easier to cap 'em and go ahead with your building project. You hear about the mines, but I've never actually met anyone who can tell you where one of 'em is located, so I guess you gotta take it all with a grain of salt." Then he added, "By the way, our city streets really are paved with gold, because gold dust was in the tailings that were used to make the roads."

He swung us past Little Sugar Creek before pulling to a stop in one of the city parks near Uptown. "This might be interesting to you gentlemen. You see that culvert over there?" He indicated an overflow tunnel that was obviously there to keep the stream that disappeared into it from flooding during times of severe rain.

"Yes," I said.

"Well, a few years ago, News Channel Thirty-Six sent a reporter down there with a cameraman. Walked right in. No gate blocking the entrance. Nothing. There are storm sewer tunnels that run all under Charlotte, more than three thousand miles of them."

"Three *thousand* miles?" Ralph exclaimed.

"That's right. You can get just about everywhere— light comes down from the manholes and the grates. This reporter, she even found that her cell phone worked down there in most places. She could track exactly where she was with her GPS. And the maps of the tunnels are all online. She planned her entire four-mile trek through the storm-drainage system using the county's website."

Most cities have better-protected storm-sewer systems. It was staggering to think how vulnerable a metropolitan area would be with its drainage tunnels this easily accessible.

"Thought you might find that interesting." Guido smiled.

"I do," I said softly.

Yes, Guido was definitely the right guy to be taking us around. He really did know his city.

I checked the time—just after eleven. "Let's head to the Mint Museum."

"Actually," he said, "there are a few things I need to take care of. Can you drop me off at the Chamber of Commerce?"

"Is there enough time?"

"There should be just enough."

"Sure," I said. "No problem."

++++

No one came.

Corrine Davis had listened and waited and strained her

eyes for any indication that someone was coming down the shaft, but no one did.

Besides catching some of that dripping water on her tongue, she hadn't had anything to drink since she woke up in this tunnel. She'd been fighting off her thirst for as long as possible, but now it got the best of her.

*Go to the water on the other end of the tunnel. You can always swim to—*

*You're not going to swim in the water, Corrine!*

But she needed to drink. She needed that for sure.

With one hand trailing along the wall, she started back toward the far end of the tunnel where the water lay.

# 32

After dropping Guido off, Ralph and I found our way to the Mint Museum's branch on Randolph Road. As we pulled onto the property, I mentally reviewed what Guido had told us just before he climbed out of the car.

In 1837 the building opened as a U.S. Mint, the first one outside of Philadelphia. It served as a mint until the Civil War, when it became a Confederate headquarters, and then eventually a U.S. military post and assay office. Following the First World War, it sat vacant for over a decade. In the 1930s it was purchased by a group of citizens to become the first art museum in North Carolina.

A couple of college-age guys were tossing a Frisbee back and forth in the sprawling, well-kept lawn bordering the parking lot.

Inside the lobby we were greeted by an octogenarian sitting behind the reception desk. She wore a badge: HELLO! I'M A VOLUNTEER! HOW MAY I HELP YOU?

In a voice softened by the years, she told us that her name was Ethel. "And is this your first time to enjoy the exhibits here at the Mint Museum?"

"Actually," I said, "we're here to see the curator, Ms. Sharma."

"Oh. I'm afraid she isn't in yet, but you're welcome to wait out here until she arrives."

"Where's your exhibit on Colonial and Revolutionary War weaponry?"

She pointed toward a sign on the counter with the entrance fees listed.

Ralph held up his creds. "We're federal agents on an investigation."

Her eyes widened. "The stolen weapons?"

"Yes."

"I must say, I had no idea. You're taking this very seriously."

"Yes, we are."

He pocketed his creds.

"And you're really with the FBI?"

"Yes, ma'am."

"Are either of you profilers?"

Ralph nodded in my direction.

"You're a *real* profiler?" she asked me.

"I'm an environmental criminologist. I do use something called geographic profiling. I investigate crimes by studying their timing, location, and progression, but—"

"So, a profiler?"

"Well, not exactly. You see—"

"Yes," Ralph said. "He's a profiler, just like on TV."

"Really, I'm—"

Ralph chugged my shoulder. "Oh, you're too modest. Dr. Powers."

"Wow," Ethel enthused. "Yes. I watch all those profiling shows on television. I'm quite a fan."

She didn't exactly strike me as the target demographic for crime dramas.

"I'll bet the doer is a male, right?" she offered help-

fully. "Caucasian, between twenty-five and thirty-five
with low self-esteem?"

"Maybe," I said. "I don't know."

"So the doer, or the perp—or wait." She caught herself. "You're FBI? You say UNSUB, right?"

*I prefer not to.*

"Some of my coworkers do."

"Let's see," she continued, unfazed, "keeps to himself,
has problems controlling his anger. Probably abused as a
child—they're almost always abused as children. And tortured animals too, I'll bet. Puppies from the neighborhood. Or maybe stray cats—those are always a good
choice because strays often aren't missed."

"You're good at this, Ethel." Ralph pulled out a business card. "If you ever get to DC and want a tour of
Headquarters, give me a call." He scribbled a phone
number on the back of the card.

She beamed. "Oh, my."

"Now." He pointed toward the door. "Can we . . . ?"

"Oh, certainly, yes, yes. I'd suggest you start on the
second level. Um . . . may I watch?"

Ralph leaned close; spoke in a private, secretive voice.
"You know profilers. They need their space. Have to
work alone. Enter the mind of the UNSUB. That sort of
thing."

Ethel nodded knowingly. "Just like on television."

"Exactly."

Give me a break.

When Ralph and I were out of earshot, I said, "Why
do you do that?"

He smiled. "She let us in, didn't she?"

"I can't believe you gave her your card. Whose phone
number did you put on there?"

"Margaret's."

"Well, then, I guess I can forgive you."

We found the Colonial weaponry exhibit. The museum staff had removed any placards that related to the missing items and, unless you knew what you were looking for, there wasn't any way to tell that the exhibit wasn't complete. Some artifacts were behind glass. Most were not.

We saw no surveillance cameras directed at us, so Ralph left to orient himself to the location of cameras elsewhere on this level of the museum, and just after he stepped away, my phone rang. Tessa's ringtone. I was a little surprised; a text would have been more up her alley.

I answered. "Hey. What's up?"

"I think I might have something for you." Her voice was low and whispery. "On the whole Latin-phrase thing."

"Why are you whispering?"

"So I don't get caught."

"Caught?"

"Just listen: it's a painting of a skull. From what I can tell it's supposed to be there in Charlotte at the Mint Museum in the Randolph Road branch."

"That's where I am right now."

"I know." She sounded slightly exasperated. "I texted Lien-hua. She told me to call you, that you'd be there."

"Wait. Back up for a sec. What did you mean when you said you didn't want to get caught?"

"I'm in the Library of Congress's main reading room," she said hurriedly. "You're not supposed to have cell phones in here. I'm sorta hiding behind the stacks."

"And you're there because . . . ?"

"To help you. So, like I was saying, I found a reference to it in a book. There's a painting with a skull that looks like it's on a shelf. Ask for it. It's got that Latin sentence as an inscription. I think it might be what you're looking for. The date on the painting is 1480. They should know the one. Look, I gotta go, Beck's coming."

The line went dead.

I wondered if my eighteen-year-old daughter was going to get thrown out of the Library of Congress for helping the FBI with an active investigation. It wouldn't be the strangest thing that's ever happened to her.

Ralph returned as I was putting my phone away. "That was Tessa," I told him.

"What's up?"

"She found a painting with the Latin inscription. If the information she has is correct, it's here in the museum."

"Well, then." He started up the steps. "Let's see if Ms. Sharma has arrived yet."

# 33

When Ralph and I got back to the lobby we found the curator standing beside the reception desk, speaking with Ethel, the resident expert on profiling. "Like I was telling you," Ethel said, "they're with the *FBI*." When she saw me, she gazed at me with keen fascination.

The curator was a trim, meticulous-looking woman in her mid-fifties. She had wire-rimmed glasses perched carefully on her nose and wore a summery chartreuse blouse.

After introductions, she said, "I heard about what happened to our artifacts. That they were used to . . . That they were used in the commission of a crime. I want to do everything I can to help you find the person who did this."

"Good." I described the painting to her, referring back to what Tessa had just told me. Ms. Sharma nodded immediately.

"Yes. That piece is in our European art exhibit, but that's not currently on the floor. We rotate the exhibits, you see, to keep things fresh. Right now it's in storage. Follow me."

On the way I asked when they had moved this painting to storage.

"Right about four weeks ago. I remember it was the day after the fireworks—so July fifth."

"And this is the only painting that has that inscription?"

"As far as I'm aware, it's the only one that exists."

So our guy either saw it here before it left the floor, somehow uncovered it here in storage, or, perhaps, stumbled across a reference to it like Tessa did at the Library of Congress.

It wasn't much, but it was something.

A trail through time and space.

That's what we were looking for, and now that's what was starting to emerge.

The modest-size climate-controlled storage room was slightly cooler than the rest of the museum. When Ms. Sharma led Ralph and me inside, she requested that we each put on some gloves that were on a table near the door. "In case you have to touch anything."

The gloves were white and dainty and, using my phone, I discreetly snapped a photo of Ralph wearing them in case I needed to pay him back for any future Agent Powers comments.

It took Ms. Sharma less than a minute to find the artwork with the inscription.

Just as Tessa had said, it was a painting of a skull that appeared to be sitting on a small shelf.

"So, this is a wood panel painted with oil." Ms. Sharma sounded proud of the piece. "It was painted in grisaille, that is, shades of gray, to make the skull look like a three-dimensional object."

The shading and the way the artist had rendered light really did make the skull appear three-dimensional. I didn't know the first thing about the history of art or the techniques used to make paintings appear 3-D, but the effect seemed remarkable for a painting from 1480.

There was no signature, no indication of who the artist might have been, and when I asked Ms. Sharma about it, she told us that his identity was unknown. "It's from a fifteenth-century Flemish master. That's all we know. The piece was donated to the museum from a private collection in 1978."

Skulls always trouble me somewhat. It might be easier to deal with them if they didn't look like they were smiling. It's almost as if they're laughing at us, almost as if they know a joke that we, the living, don't want to know the punch line to. And in this case the punch line wasn't very funny, but was summed up in the Latin phrase that appeared beneath the skull:

> *Cur homo mortalis caput extruis at morieris en vertex talis sit modo calvus eris.*

A plaque stored next to the painting included the official translation of the inscription, and it was remarkably close to Tessa's. It read, WHY DO YOU, MORTAL BEING, RAISE YOUR HEAD? YOU WILL DIE, TOO, AND WILL BE AS BALD AS THIS SKULL.

*Nice work, Raven.*

"Such paintings are known as *vanitas*," Ms. Sharma explained, "from a verse in the Book of Ecclesiastes in the Bible: 'Vanity of vanities, saith the preacher, all is vanity.'"

"May I pick it up?" I asked.

"Um . . ." Her hesitation made it clear she wasn't excited about the idea. "Yes. But please, please be careful."

I gently picked it up, and when I flipped it over Ms. Sharma gasped.

A phone number was written in black marker on the back of the painting's wood panel: 783-4745.

"Who . . . who would have done that?" Ms. Sharma said, aghast that someone had damaged the piece.

Ralph pulled out his cell and tapped in the number.

I answered the stunned curator, "We're going to do all we can to find out."

My friend spoke for a moment on the phone, introducing himself as a federal agent, then shook his head and hung up. "Doesn't sound like the woman with that phone number has any idea about a painting. I'll have Voss's guys follow up."

"We're going to need to process this at the Lab," I told Ms. Sharma. "Ralph?"

"I'll get a team over here."

*It's not about the number. It's about something else.*

*The spellings.*

*The codes.*

While he stepped away to make the call, I set down the painting and went online on my phone to pull up the site that allows you to translate phone numbers into words. I plugged in the numbers but didn't recognize any of the words that they brought up. Some contained the words "Sue," "dish," or "fish" but nothing recognizable beyond that.

Lacey could run them.

*Did he write it on here while it was on display?*

"Is this painting protected by glass when it's being exhibited?" I asked her.

"Yes."

Okay, so he marked it up while it was back here.

*But how did he access this room?*

I studied the ceiling, the walls. No visible security cameras.

"Are there any surveillance cameras in here?" I asked Ms. Sharma.

She shook her head. "No. Maybe we should have more, we just never thought that . . ." She was staring at the painting, her face blanched. "But there is one near where this piece is displayed while it's on the floor. Maybe that'll help?"

"Maybe."

*So, if someone were to come in here, what route would he have taken?*

I left the room. The hallway passed two doors on the way back to the lobby.

Trying the first, I found that it was a small bathroom with no windows, no way to slip into or out of the building.

The second doorway led to the employee break room.

Ralph returned. "Some of the local ERT guys are on their way over. I'll have the Lab get started on handwriting analysis too, see if it matches those numbers written in the book we found at Cole's place."

"Good." It would be tough to match such a short sample, but it was worth a shot.

Our team had reviewed the museum's video footage and nothing indicated that any of the patrons who visited the building on the day the weaponry was stolen had taken it.

Yet it was gone.

*An employee?*

*A volunteer?*

*July 5th . . .*

"Is there another entrance to the building?" I asked Ms. Sharma.

She shook her head. "Nothing besides emergency-exit doors—but alarms go off if those are opened."

*This just doesn't make sense.*

"What time did you realize the weaponry had been stolen?"

"It wasn't until the end of the day, when we were doing a final walk-through to make sure no guests were still in the building. I need to contact our board of directors. You don't think there might be more pieces that have been vitiated?"

"It's possible."

Needless to say, that did not encourage her.

*Someone got those weapons out of this building and someone wrote that phone number on the back of the painting.*

"Do you get tour groups through here?" Ralph asked.

"Sure. All the time."

"What about on the day the items were stolen?"

"I'd have to check."

"You don't know a guy named Lombardi by any chance?" he said. "Does history tours of the city? Guido Lombardi?"

She shook her head. "I don't know that name. Should I?"

I turned to Ralph. "Find him."

"On it." A moment later I heard him talking with the police dispatcher.

*No, it can't be Guido. That would be too easy. Things never turn out to be that easy.*

If the offender wasn't one of the museum guests and it wasn't one of the staff then it had to be . . .

*The video that the team looked at only covered operational hours.*

I asked Ms. Sharma, "What about beforehand? Before the doors opened? Were there any shipments that day? Deliveries? Moving things to or from storage?"

"I'm not sure, but that is when it would happen. We don't allow any deliveries during business hours. We don't want it to disrupt the experience of our guests."

While Ralph spoke with dispatch, I entered the employee break room to have a look around.

A couple of vending machines—one for snacks, the other for soda—and a small table surrounded by three chairs. A counter. Sink. Microwave. A coffeemaker that needed cleaning. Federal health safety codes and employment-policy statements were posted prominently on the walls beside flyers announcing upcoming functions and events at the museum's two branches.

No security cameras, which, taking into consideration privacy concerns for staff, was not that much of a surprise.

We were on the first floor, but there was an elevator at the end of a short hallway. It was conveniently located to take deliveries up from the storage room to the museum's other levels.

"I'd like a list of all your volunteers and employees," I said to Ms. Sharma. "Anyone who might use this room."

"I really don't think this could have been done by any one of our staff."

"Well, we're going to need to eliminate that possibility. Do your board members have access to these rooms?"

"Well, yes, but they are our *board members*."

"I'll need their names as well. You have a volunteer working the front desk today—why is that? Why a volunteer?"

"We try to invite as much participation from our community partners and volunteers as we can. Do you really think other pieces might be damaged?"

"We'll have to check to make sure."

I closed my eyes and pictured the layout of the building, the parking lot outside, the location of the security cameras, the footage I'd seen the other day of people entering and leaving the facility. "I'd like to see the footage of the employees arriving before the museum opened that day."

Ralph came into the room. "Lombardi never showed up at the Chamber of Commerce. I need to take off to help coordinate the search for him."

"I'm going to stay here and check out the surveillance video prior to when the doors opened for the public, see if there's anything there that'll help us out."

"We're gonna need another car."

"Yes," I said, "we are."

"Alright, look, I'll have someone pick me up and I'll get the paperwork started to requisition the Field Office to get me a vehicle. You keep the rental. I'll locate Guido. As soon as we find him, I'll give you a call."

"Right."

I went to Ms. Sharma's office to pull up the surveillance-camera footage from before the museum opened on July 23rd, the day the artifacts disappeared.

# 34

It took me about fifteen minutes to find what I was looking for.

But it wasn't an employee entering the premises that caught my attention.

Instead, it was a delivery man from a vending machine company. He arrived ten minutes before the doors officially opened and was allowed in by one of the staff members. He left again only a few minutes later, pushing a hand truck with the same number of crates of soda as he'd pushed in.

So, he hadn't actually delivered any, just rolled them in and then rolled them back out.

The dolly was tall enough so that he could have hidden the arrows and the tomahawk along one side of it. With the elevator he could have accessed that floor and without any guests here yet to see him or cameras to catch him, he could have gotten the weapons down to the break room.

The museum's software for analyzing video wasn't very good so I sent the file to my phone. When I zoomed in I was able to make out four initials on the side of the delivery van: NVDS.

A quick online search brought up the name of the company: National Vending Distribution Services.

Their regional shipping center was located about half-way between here and Matthews, North Carolina. The map app on my phone told me it would be a fourteen-minute drive with current traffic conditions.

Perfect.

It's usually best to show up unannounced for these kinds of discussions so I decided not to call ahead.

Before leaving, I used my laptop to pull up the video we'd gotten of the exterior of the NCAVC of the man who'd been driving the semi that delivered the lawn-mower that blew up.

We had no visuals in either case of the man's face, and, while I couldn't be certain enough to confirm it was the same man, his height and build did appear to be consistent for a possible match.

There are some people who are invisible in a workplace—like the maid from a few years ago who took care of my room at a hotel in Miami. On the first day of the conference she wasn't wearing a name tag and the detective I was working with on the case asked her what her name was, then later thanked her by name. She stared at him, bewildered, and you could tell she'd rarely had anyone do that, remember her name like that.

That incident stuck with me.

I was the one who was supposed to notice things and she'd slipped right past me, just like so many people have over the years. Custodians, same deal. Migrant workers. Cabdrivers. Homeless people. Delivery men. They pass namelessly through so many people's lives.

And if you're someone who's trying to steal some-thing from a museum, that's what you would want: to pass through unnoticed.

I sent the footage of the delivery guy to Angela to have Lacey take a closer look.

"I was just going to call you," she told me. "The phone number you gave me that was on the back of the painting, well, I had Lacey analyze it, searching for any instances of any phone number mnemonics, and I found one that relates to Charlotte—or at least it might."

"What is it?"

She spelled it out for me: "R-U-D-I-S-I-L. Apparently, there were gold mines in the area and one of them was named that—or at least that's an alternate spelling of the name. Normally it appears with two *l*s—I even came across a couple of other spellings as well. In any case, I thought that with the Charlotte connection it might be what we were looking for."

"If it's the name of a gold mine, it very well may be. See what else you can find out about this mine."

"Actually, I did," she replied. "Unfortunately, there's not much online. I'm guessing that maybe the layout and specific location would appear in old land deeds, local surveying maps—that sort of thing—but we're talking about information from a century or two ago. I doubt those documents would ever have been scanned in or posted on the Web—if they even exist anymore."

"Alright. Well, let me know if you come up with anything."

After the call, my thoughts returned to the delivery guy who'd arrived before the museum opened.

Someone had opened the door for him.

I replayed the video, paused it when the employee's face appeared. "Who is that?" I asked Ms. Sharma.

"Bryan Anders. He works the front desk on Tuesdays."

I called Voss at the Charlotte Field Office and asked him to get a couple of agents over here to review the footage from before July 5th when the staff rotated the exhibits. "We're looking for someone who stared at that painting long enough to memorize the Latin, write it down, or someone who might have taken a picture of it."

"Do we have video of that floor?"

A few minutes ago Ms. Sharma had mentioned to me that we did. "Yes," I told him. "I'm having the curator draw up a list of the board of directors, staff, and volunteers. I want someone to talk with each of them. Start with Bryan Anders. I'll have her e-mail them to you. I'm taking off here in a minute."

"Where are you going?"

"The National Vending Distribution Services warehouse. There's a certain delivery man I'd like to have a word with."

# 35

Before heading to the car from the Library of Congress, Tessa and Beck stopped to grab some sandwiches for lunch.

The sign on the window read:

**Bill's Psychedelic Café**
**Your place. Your pace.**
**Come. Relax. Enjoy.**
**Exist in Bliss.**

As they entered the neo-Bohemian, vegan-friendly restaurant, she thought of her comments about history and how they so easily could have offended Beck.

She didn't want to take the chance that she might start ranting against something that he actually did like and decided she needed to be a little more careful next time around.

So when she saw the guy dressed in surgeon's scrubs who was adding some sugar to his coffee, she kept her mouth shut.

But still, it was hard not to be annoyed and, despite herself, she sighed.

"What is it?" Beck asked her.

"Nothing."

"I don't know you very well yet, Tessa Bowers, but I can tell it's not nothing. Go on. What are you thinking?"

"It's just . . ." She'd kept her mom's last name, so her full name was actually Tessa Bernice Ellis, but she didn't correct Beck when he naturally thought her last name was Bowers. "What's the deal with doctors doing that?"

"Doing what?"

"Wearing their scrubs in public. Okay, so are they showing off that they're so busy they can't spend thirty seconds slipping off their scrubs, but they can sit for half an hour sipping a latte, reading the paper? Do they have any idea how idiotic they look wearing scrubs in public? It would be like me wearing my pajamas in here."

"I don't know that they look all *that* idio . . ."

She was staring at him beneath two raised eyebrows.

"Okay," he admitted. "They do look idiotic."

After they had their food, Beck chose a place in the back where no one would be behind him and he could monitor the restaurant and assess any potential threats, just like Patrick would have done.

Not long after they'd started eating, Tessa caught him looking at her.

"What is it?" she asked self-consciously.

"I was just . . ." Beck seemed embarrassed. "That's a pretty necklace."

"Yes. It is." She held the stone loosely in her hand. "It's my birthstone. Tourmaline. Patrick gave it to me for my seventeenth birthday."

"Huh," he said.

"What?"

"Well, most people, when you compliment them about something—maybe, 'Nice shirt' or 'That's a cool sweater,' you know, stuff like that—they say 'Thank you,' but when I said your necklace was pretty you just said, 'Yes. It is.'"

"Uh-huh."

"That's not . . . It's just not the common response."

"Thanking you wouldn't have made any sense."

"Why not?"

"Because I have no control over how the necklace looks and unless I set the gem, it's not me that you're complimenting, but the person who actually did the work. Why on earth would I thank you for complimenting something that someone else should get the credit for?"

"You know, I've never really thought about it like that before. I have to say, you have a unique way of seeing the world, Tessa Bowers."

"You know, it's no big deal, but my last name is Ellis. I kept my mom's maiden name."

"Sorry, I—"

"No problem. So, 'unique' as in 'fresh and intriguing,'" she asked, "or as in 'weird and anomalistic'?"

"Fresh and intriguing."

"Well, thank you, Beck."

"You're welcome."

As he ate and scanned the room, he sometimes let his eyes linger on her for just an instant longer than he needed to.

And that was just fine by her.

++++

We hadn't eaten yet, so I was grabbing a quick lunch at a drive-through on my way to the distribution center when my phone rang.

When I answered, Lien-hua jumped right in: "Pat. Listen, Corrine Davis never showed up for her flight on Tuesday morning."

"What?"

"She was supposed to fly to Miami, Florida, from Columbia, South Carolina, for a business meeting. She didn't make it to the airport and no one's seen or heard from her since Monday night. The story hit the news cycle this morning and they're not letting it drop. Do you think it's possible her brother took her?"

Corrine was the one person, the only person, I'd ever known Richard Basque to care about.

I'd spoken with her a few times over the years and gotten to know her a little when we contacted her a couple months ago after we failed to find Richard's body, when I shot him and he tumbled backward into the Potomac. She'd been cooperative and promised to let us know if he got in touch with her, but we hadn't heard anything from her.

I processed things. "It wasn't him."

"How do you know?"

"I know Richard. She's the last person he would ever go after."

"But when he first started out, didn't he kill women who looked like her?"

"Yes. I can't explain it, but he cares about her. That much I know."

According to Freud, pretty much every motive can be explained by someone wanting to have sex with someone else. So Freudian psychologists would have probably had a field day psychoanalyzing Richard's relationship with his sister, no doubt finding all sorts of hidden sexual meanings in his choice of preferred victims.

But neither Lien-hua nor I went there.

She wasn't Freudian.

Neither was I.

Without jumping to conclusions, I had to acknowledge the obvious. "The timing points to her disappearance as being related to this case. We need to add the search for Corrine to the mix."

"I'll talk to Gonzalez, get a team down to Columbia to work with local law enforcement, look into her disappearance."

"Good. And I want to know who saw her or talked to her last before she disappeared. Check her phone records. Let's see if we can pin down a time and place where she was still accounted for."

Then I told her about the search for Guido and the possibility that the vending-machine-supply worker was involved. "I'm on my way to their distribution warehouse now."

"Keep me informed."

"I will."

"Is there anything else I can do for you from here?"

"Hmm . . . maybe look into traffic cameras near Corrine's house. There might be something there—you know, an unaccounted-for car entering or leaving the neighborhood around the time she disappeared."

"Good call."

"And why don't you pull up Basque's files. Last year there was an attempt on his life in Chicago during his retrial. The father of one of his victims went after him. Let's see what other threats have been made against him."

"You think someone might be trying to hurt him by going after Corrine?"

"It's worth looking into. Also, any more word on establishing who it was who looked up the location of the surveillance cameras?"

"Debra's on it. I just spoke with her. With Allie at camp this week she's been working on this nonstop. The minute I have anything I'll call you."

Debra had mentioned to me earlier that her daughter was at her dad's this week. Maybe the guy had sent her to camp.

"I'll let you know what I find out at the distribution center," I told Lien-hua.

++++

Corrine knelt and swirled her hand through the chilled water.

She told herself that the sediment would have drifted to the bottom. Yes, this water would be safe to drink.

Trying to put out of her mind how muddy it might be or how polluted it might have gotten from minerals or chemicals that had seeped into it, she used one hand to cup the water and took a drink.

It tasted gritty and coarse and sour and she had to spit out the first mouthful.

*You have to drink. You have to!*

She readied herself, dipped out some more water, and drank it.

*Swim.*

*You could go for a swim.*

*Just take off your clothes and—*

*Stop it, Corrine! What are you even thinking about here?*

*—to safety. You could swim to safety.*

*Think about something else!*

She forced herself to mentally shift gears and ended up moving on from the water to the man who'd left her down here.

*Why is he doing this to you? Is it because of Richard? He said he knows him, but is this his way of getting back at him? Did he know one of Richard's victims? Is this revenge?*

Revenge.

Justice.

The concepts cycled around each other in her mind. Where does one end and the other begin?

Revenge exists. There's no question about that. But does justice? Does it really?

When you look at the natural world there's no evidence of justice; there's only the struggle for life, the inevitability of death.

Life.

Death.

Injustice.

Yet we naturally know that there are things that are right and things that are wrong and that people should be punished for the wrongs they commit.

Punished for their wrongs.

*Like Richard.*

*Like you, for not noticing what he was becoming.*

*Is that what this is now—punishment? Divine justice? Divine retribution?*

She thought of her brother. Was he still alive? How would he react when he heard his sister was missing? Did he even know yet? Certainly—if he even was alive—he wouldn't chance coming to her funeral.

*If your body is ever found.*

*If—*

*Stop!*

She thought again of the man who'd left her down here.

Corrine didn't know what frightened her more: the thought of that man returning or the thought that he might never return.

If he came back, she could only imagine the kinds of things he might do to her.

But if he didn't come back and if no one else was able

to find her, she would eventually die down here, starve to death or die from hypothermia.

Maybe it would be better if he came back.

At least then it would all be over sooner.

*Swim.*

Corrine couldn't shake that thought.

*The water leads somewhere.*

*Down. It leads down.*

*Where else?*

*To another tunnel. To a way out!*

*But how? How could it lead out?*

The voices inside of her vying for attention became more and more distinct. In fact, they became undeniably audible until she realized she was saying the words aloud, arguing with herself about whether or not she should get into the water.

And that frightened her almost as much as the thought of what might happen to her if that man returned.

*You need to get ahold of yourself.*

*Relax.*

But as she passed her hand through the water again she couldn't help but wonder if it was more than just a shaft that had filled with water over the years, and, if so, where the water might actually lead.

++++

The bard had left work an hour ago.

He was at his apartment now, reviewing dosages and delivery mechanisms for insulin. Subcutaneous would be quicker. But using an IV would be a little more surreptitious, if the circumstances allowed for it. So he would have to see how things played out.

Taking a sedative with him was also a good idea, in

case he needed to make sure the character in his story was unconscious while he administered the insulin.

An insulin overdose was not something the medical personnel would be looking for.

At this point he was planning to give her the drug himself, but if necessary he would have his person in DC do it for him. From the information he currently had, there didn't appear to be any rush to make that decision.

As for right now, after he wrapped up some research here, he would go check the Semtex placement in the mine. However, on the way to the Saint Catherine tunnels and shafts he would need to pass through the Rudisill Mine, and while he was there he could visit Corrine.

Yes, he was attracted to her.

He hadn't fully satisfied himself with her the other night.

It would be ideal if she were still alive, still warm, but she didn't need to be breathing for him to meet his needs with her.

So.

*Finish up here.*

*And then head to the mine.*

# 36

The manager, a disheveled, overweight man who introduced himself to me simply as Fletcher, led me to his office at the National Vending Distribution Services warehouse.

"I need to know who's assigned to make deliveries to the Mint Museum," I said. "The Randolph branch. He would have visited there last Tuesday."

"Randolph branch? I imagine that'd be either Ned or Danny. I'd need to look it up."

I waited while he went to his desk, which was surprisingly organized, considering his unkempt appearance. He flipped through a few time sheets, then pulled one out and showed it to me. "Danny Everhart."

The name didn't ring a bell. "You have his personnel files?"

"I can't show you those."

"You let me see them now, you help the FBI out. You make me get a warrant, you slow us down. Which scenario would be better for your company when word leaks out to the press?"

He looked like he might have a rebuff, but then grudgingly pulled out Danny Everhart's personnel file and handed it over.

As I perused the file, Fletcher told me, "He came in

about a month ago. Always shows up for work on time. Never complains. He's a good worker. He'd been in a bad car accident, I guess, a couple weeks beforehand. His face was still all bruised up. Needed a chance, a fresh start. I gave it to him."

"Uh-huh." I flipped through the papers. "It says here part-time. How many hours per week?"

"A couple days, usually. We moved most of our full-time staff to part-time. You know, Obamacare. All that."

"Sure. Has he been in today?"

"Made a delivery earlier to the stadium—they're gearing up for Fan Celebration Day tomorrow."

I looked up from the file. "The stadium uses vending machines rather than concession stands?"

"Most of the time our products are distributed through vending machines. Occasionally, for big events like this, they're hand sold. They're expecting twenty thousand people tomorrow. You need a lot of soda and candy bars for a crowd that size. Is there something I should know about him?"

"No. This address—is it still correct?"

"As far as I know."

In addition to the twenty-third, Everhart had made a delivery to the museum on the first Monday and then the third Friday of July, after the skull painting had been moved to storage.

He could definitely be the guy who'd written the numbers on the back of the painting.

*Could be. There's no guarantee that he is.*

"Thank you."

*You need to see if Voss's guys find any video footage of Everhart observing the painting before it was taken down to storage.*

I spoke Everhart's address into my phone, asked for directions, and took off to see if I could catch up with him at his apartment to have a little chat.

++++

Tessa and Beck returned to the house and parked on the street out front.

Lien-hua's car was gone so she must have still been at work.

"Um." Tessa had been debating whether or not to bring this up again ever since they left the restaurant, and now she decided to just go ahead and do it. "You know, it really is kind of stupid for you to be sitting out here. Seriously, you can hang out in the living room. I mean— if you want to. Unless it's against some sort of rule or protocol or something."

He smiled in a way that she was quickly getting used to. "No, that's not against a rule. I'm not staking out your place. I'm just here in case . . . well, in case anyone shows up who's not supposed to be here."

"Okay."

He shut off the engine.

"I suppose it can't hurt anything to sit inside."

++++

On the way to Everhart's apartment building, I phoned Ralph.

"Anything on Lombardi?" I asked him.

"Still looking for him. He's turning out to be a little hard to track down."

"I've got something else to check into. I want us to find out everything we can about a guy named Danny Everhart: DMV records, credit-card activity, past residences—

everything. A full background. He's the guy who drove the vending machine truck to the museum on the day the artifacts were stolen."

"You think he might be our guy?"

"Maybe, maybe not. But the timing for his visit fits. Also, he had a delivery run there a couple weeks ago. He might have accessed the storage area on either occasion. I'm on my way to talk with him right now."

"I'll contact Gonzalez, get things rolling on the background."

"Also, send a team to the vending-services warehouse, look over Everhart's delivery van, get the ERT out there, see what we can pick up DNA-wise." I told him the address.

"Done."

End call.

Five minutes to Everhart's place.

He lived in an awfully nice part of the city for someone on a part-time delivery man's salary.

I tried to hold myself back from assuming too much, but it was data to add to the mix.

Data leads to discoveries.

Discoveries lead to the truth.

Finding out how long Everhart had lived here and what he did before starting work at NVDS would help. Hopefully, the background Ralph was running would tell us what we needed to know.

++++

Corrine saw colors.

Yes.

For the first time since she had awakened in the tunnel, Corrine Davis began to see shapes and objects swirling around her.

It took her a moment to realize, however, that they were appearing while her eyes were closed rather than open.

The colors took shape, took form.

*You're five and your mommy and daddy are in bed and you're jumping up and down on it, up and down, telling them to* get up *because it's* Saturday! *And they promised you* pancakes!

Giggling.

It's echoing.

Images as clear as day.

*You're nine and you're playing with your brother. You're chasing him through the basement, around the couch, and he's laughing.*

*The laughter courses all throughout the basement and then you're having a pillow fight. He's a normal boy.*

*You're fourteen and you're behind the bleachers at the football stadium at your high school and the guy you have a crush on is drawing you toward him. Then he's kissing you and it's awkward and it's your first time and it's terrifying and electric and—*

*You're twenty-four and you hear the news that your brother was arrested.*

Arrested?

Laughter.

He's a good boy. A good brother.

*You're thirty-eight, at home, and you're turning around. Someone is there in your bedroom.*

Laughter.

That echoes throughout the basement.

But you're not in the basement.

*You're here.*

*Where?*

The tunnel.

The colors are real.

*Open your eyes.*

She did. Reoriented herself. And then Corrine realized it was her. She was the one laughing and she was not in the basement.

*You're losing it, Corrine.*

*You're losing it!*

She was in a tunnel somewhere deep, deep in the earth.

*The water. You can do it. You can swim out of here.*

*Now. Jump in. Swim to safety.*

*Take off your clothes.*

And this time, she listened to the voice.

Corrine Davis bent down to untie her shoes.

++++

As a precaution, the bard never left certain items in his apartment when he wasn't there: the sedative, the insulin, and his laptop. Also, just in case, he set the trip wire on his front door to protect what was in his bedroom. If anyone tried to enter, the whole apartment would blow.

Taking the phone and the sensor to check the Semtex detonator, he stowed his duffel bag with the harnesses and rappelling equipment in his van beside the handcuffs he'd used on the woman, then he climbed in and started the engine.

# 37

I showed my ID to the attendant working the parking garage that lay beneath the apartment building where Danny Everhart lived. Then I found a parking space near the exterior wall, which was not completely closed in, allowing my cell phone to have two bars—but at least it still worked. Before leaving the car, I used it to pull up the background Ralph had run on Everhart.

I didn't recognize his DMV photo and I couldn't tell if he was the guy who'd been at the NCAVC earlier this week. Single. Brown hair. Brown eyes. The healing wounds from his car accident were visible in the photo on his driver's license.

*So the photo's recent, taken since the accident.*

*Find out more about that accident.*

*Timing.*

*Location.*

Through the Federal Digital Database, I sent out a national law enforcement inquiry into moving-vehicle accidents that involved anyone named Everhart.

I was hanging up when I saw a text from Lien-hua that Corrine's friend Isabelle Brittain had been on the phone with her Monday evening from 10:26 to 10:32 p.m.

Traffic-camera footage down the block caught a white van entering the neighborhood about forty minutes earlier. It left the area Tuesday morning.

Checking Everhart's records, I saw that a white 2004 Chevrolet van was registered in his name. A recent purchase.

Oh, this was good.

Exiting my car, I started toward the elevators. Slightly distracted, I noticed how poorly lit the parking garage was and I was thinking about how lighting is such an easy step in crime prevention, when movement caught my attention.

A van, pulling around the bend.

White.

Yes.

An older-model Chevy.

The plate number matched.

The van turned before I could see who the driver was, but it was Everhart's vehicle, alright.

So—follow it or continue up to the apartment?

There wasn't enough evidence to allow us to bring him in for questioning, but there was certainly enough for me to follow his van and have a little talk with him, and if that was him driving, then going to his apartment wasn't going to do me any good.

I needed to make a decision fast because the driver was approaching the exit and I might lose him if I hesitated.

*Go.*

Quickly, I returned to my car and saw the van angle left out of the exit. Recalling the 3-D hologram and Guido's tour, I reviewed the street layout in my mind. There were a lot of one-way streets in Charlotte and that would affect the route the driver would need to take.

I hopped in, left the garage, made the turn, and caught sight of the van up ahead of me at the end of the block.

As I merged with traffic, the thrill of the hunt caught hold of me.

And it felt good.

Whether or not this turned out to be a dead end, I was making my way deeper into the labyrinth. And right now that's exactly where I needed to be.

++++

Out of instinctive modesty, Corrine kept on her bra and panties, but set her shoes, shirt, and jeans beside the water, shoved against the wall.

*Besides, when you swim to safety, you don't want to be naked, do you? When you finally get out of here? How would that look?*

Strange thoughts. Odd thoughts.

But they were real.

Everything was real.

She stood at the water's edge and thought about what she was getting ready to do.

*If you go in, if you do this, there's no turning back. It's going to be hard to dry off again, almost impossible to get warm.*

*Is that what you want?*

*Are you ready for that?*

She sat down and started to lower her feet in, but gasped and pulled them out again as chills shocked her. It felt like jolts of cold electricity shooting up her body.

*You can make it.*

She had no idea how deep the water was: if it was four feet deep or forty or four hundred. It might lead to an-

other tunnel, or it might just be a shaft that sank down
into the earth.

*No, something's not right. Go back to the other end of this
tunnel. Wait for help, Corrine. Wait—*

But she felt compelled.

*Swim,* a persistent voice inside of her said. *You can
swim out of here.*

She dipped her feet in again, then slid forward and
drew in a deep, hurried breath as the chilled water envel-
oped her body.

Electricity.

Cold and alive.

Shivers that coursed up and down her spine.

Hand over hand she moved to the right, feeling
around with her feet.

Nothing.

Complete darkness—

*You have to get out!*

*No.*

*It's a shaft that's filled with water. But it leads to an-
other tunnel. It has to.*

*But wouldn't that be filled with water too?*

On the one hand, it all seemed logical. On the other,
she knew she was not being guided by logic at all.

She felt her way along the edge until she came to the
wall on her right, then along that wall to the one she'd
thrown stones at earlier—all those hours ago or days ago,
she had no idea.

Her feet never touched bottom.

*You can do this.*

Only one thing mattered: getting out of this mine as
quickly as she could.

She made her way all the way back where she'd started,
by her pile of clothes.

*Okay.*

*So.*

*You need to go under. You need to see if this shaft leads anywhere.*

*This is crazy, Corrine. There's no way you can swim to safety.*

Shivers.

A dream.

*You're in a pool. You can swim to the other end.*

"I can make it." She heard the words, realized she had spoken them aloud.

*You're talking to yourself again.*

Yes, but that was okay, it was all okay.

She tentatively dipped her head under, feeling around with her feet, tracing her hands down the shaft, then rose back to the surface.

*Deeper. You have to go deeper.*

She filled her lungs, readied herself, then brought her legs together, drove her arms upward in the water and forced herself under, dropping feet first as far down as she could.

She wasn't sure how far she went, but as her ears popped, her feet eventually did hit the bottom. Desperately, she felt in every direction to see if there was another tunnel, but she couldn't feel anything.

Corrine kicked off the bottom and shot back to the surface.

Gulped in some air.

*There has to be a way out! It must lead out to another tunnel. It has to.*

She went under again, and this time found that there was an opening on her right.

*Go.*

*No! What if you can't make it back out?*

*You will. Of course you will. You're going back home, Corrine.*

She returned to the surface one last time for more air, then went back under. Feeling along the wall, she found the opening and pulled herself forward into the tunnel that led to safety, that she knew, *she knew*, just had to lead to freedom.

# 38

Corrine flipper-kicked her way into the fathomless darkness stretching before her.

As she stroked, she found her hands brushing the tunnel's sides. She went on.

Five strokes.

Then six.

But then she felt the tension rising inside of her from not having enough air.

*Relax.*

*Think about getting out of here, about going back home.*

She struggled forward another two strokes, feeling along the ceiling now. A beam. Just like the ones in the tunnel she woke up in.

*Keep going.*

*No, go back! Now, before you use up your air!*

Everything she'd been through this week seemed to swirl around her: Coming home. Finding that man waiting for her. The van ride. Waking up in the tunnel.

Justice being played out. Being postponed. Denied.

Memories. Of growing up.

Of her brother.

*He loved you.*

*Does love you.*

Hands on the ceiling, she drew herself forward.

And then realized she had gone too far. A gasp of air escaped her lips.

*Go back.*

*Turn around!*

Corrine pressed off the wall, spun around, kicked, swam.

*You can make it.*

Disoriented, she banged into the side of the tunnel. She tried to hold on to her air, but more bubbled out of her mouth. She went two strokes in the direction she thought was correct, but her hand found another beam.

*Pull yourself forward!*

Instinct took over and she tried to grab a breath but gagged on water, and then she was shaking, dreaming, drifting, but she forced herself to keep swimming and when her hands found nothing, no ceiling, she frantically kicked upward.

Up.

And up.

Her hand splashed out.

Air.

She emerged and gasped. Sucked in a breath.

A deep, urgent breath.

Trembling.

Shivering.

Corrine climbed out of the water. There was no swimming out of here. She knew that now, had to have known it all along, but she wasn't thinking clearly, no she was not, not anymore.

Her body must have gotten used to the temperature of the water when she was in it, but now, as she got out, chills writhed uncontrollably through her. Knowing that she needed to get her core temperature warmer fast, she used her cotton jeans to dry off, and then pulled her shirt on.

The jeans were too cold and damp to wear.

*You'll be alright. You just need to warm up.*

The shivers made it hard to stand and she dropped to her knees.

*But at least you're shivering. At least your body hasn't given up.*

And that's how she tried to comfort herself, but she knew that soon enough, now that her core temperature had dropped, the shivers would eventually stop.

The laughter that she heard echoing dully around her didn't sound anything like hers. It was someone else. It must be someone else. Echoing and dying.

But it wasn't someone else.

It was her. And it was always going to be her, deep and alone beneath the earth, laughing by herself until the laughter disappeared for good.

++++

As I drove, I had my cell phone read me the background we had so far on Everhart—and it wasn't much. Yes, there was a spotty work history, a past address in Athens, Georgia, where he apparently worked construction and a series of odd jobs.

It wasn't the inconsistencies that caught my attention, but the consistency of it all. Nothing to raise a red flag.

Which is a red flag in itself.

Real lives are messy and when a background is too neat, it often doesn't hold up to scrutiny. I've seen fake-identity packages before, and that's what most often gives them away.

Keeping my distance, I followed Danny Everhart—or whoever he was—as he drove through Third Ward.

++++

Tessa and Beck were in the living room. He was on the couch. She'd chosen the leather recliner. Only five or six feet separated them.

Neither seemed to know what to say.

*You're almost nineteen. He needs to know that, to know that you're not some little girl. But how do you tell him that? Offhandedly mention that you're packing for college?*

It just didn't seem like the right time, but she wanted to, needed to say something. *He's probably got a file on you anyway. Probably already knows all about you.*

For the moment she steered clear of talking about herself.

"So," she said, "when's your partner taking over for you?"

"Agent Woods is supposed to be here at two—so I guess half an hour or so. But I'll be back tonight at eight."

"Oh."

"That is, unless your mom gets back and doesn't need me here."

"Right. That makes sense."

Even though her real mom was dead, Beck would have no way of knowing that—other than her not being Asian—and Tessa didn't mind him referring to Lien-hua as her mom. She actually did so herself. It made her feel like she was part of a family, something she'd always wanted.

"Um . . ." She was right where she wanted to be—alone in the house with Beck—and her feelings thrilled her but also frightened her. A catch-22.

"Can I get you anything?" she asked. "A root beer? Some chips?"

"I'm good. Thanks."

"Sure."

Silence, silence, silence. Awkward, awkward silence.

Finally, he said, "Um, there is one thing you might be able to do for me."

"Yeah?"

"There's something I've always been wondering and you seem like the kind of person who might be able to help."

"What is it?"

"It's sort of philosophical."

"I like philosophical."

"Okay. Here it is: If a blue box was invisible, would it still be blue?"

"You've always been wondering that?"

"Well . . . Okay, you got me. It's only been a month or so, ever since I was at a party and someone asked me what superpower I would choose if I could have one, and I said I'd like to be able to be invisible. It got me thinking about what color my clothes would be. What about you?"

"Me?"

"What superpower would you want?"

*To actually know what to say to guys so I don't sound like a complete moron.*

"I'd need to think about that."

"Yeah, of course. That's fine."

"But as far as your blue box goes, we could approach it from Plato's forms or from modern quantum mechanics, in which the presence of a conscious observer is requisite for existence."

"A conscious observer? So someone there to watch things unfold?"

"Exactly," she said.

"Let's start there and see where it leads."

"Let's do."

++++

Corrine stopped shivering.

*This is it. You need to end this.*

*The shaft at the far end of the tunnel.*

*All you need to do is jump. Just walk over to the edge and step into the darkness. It'll all be over. No more wondering. No more questioning.*

*You won't be cold any longer.*

*You'll finally be free.*

Justice.

Yes, she should have been able to tell that something was wrong with her brother. She knew him as well as anyone. If only she could have seen where things were heading, all those people might not have died.

*You should have stopped him.*

*It's not your brother's fault.*

*No. It's yours.*

*Finally be free.*

She started to make her way through the tunnel toward where it met up with the shaft that dropped off into the unknown depths of the earth.

# 39

Everhart pulled into a deserted street behind a long-neglected warehouse.

Doing my best to keep my distance, I parked down the road and used the video function on my phone to zoom in and record him. The bruises and swelling were gone, but it was the same guy from the DMV photo.

He unlocked a padlock on the swinging gate on the edge of the property and drove through.

I hadn't finished listening to the background information on him, and now I quickly scrolled through it and found no evidence that he owned the place.

I put in a call to find out who did.

Everhart locked the gate behind him, so if I was going to follow him I would need to get over that fence. I've climbed over razor wire before and it's not very fun.

A stout oak tree with thick, sweeping limbs grew beside the fence near the northeastern corner where it angled along the edge of the property.

*Just climb the tree, get on that limb, and jump down on the other side of the fence.*

*Voilà!*

If I were careful, maybe I could even pull it off without ripping those stitches out of my side.

Yeah, well, probably not.

But was that the right course of action?

I could certainly call for backup; however, at this point Everhart hadn't done anything wrong—unless he was trespassing, but that wasn't really a big deal.

However, it was enough of a reason to follow him.

He was carrying a large duffel bag.

*It won't hurt to have a look around.*

I didn't necessarily need to enter the building, but there were windows surrounding it and I could take a peek inside.

Just a little peek.

He disappeared out of sight.

I've never been good at sitting around waiting for things to happen.

Just not my thing.

I opened the car door and headed for the oak tree.

++++

The bard emptied the contents of the duffel bag onto the table near the shaft.

He spread out all of his climbing equipment—headlamps, a couple of harnesses and rappelling devices, some Prusiks, and an ascender.

He had a small hip pack with the items he needed to use to check the Semtex.

Yes, it would have been possible to do his readings from the tracks that led past the stadium by using the pressure-release mechanism he'd buried up there in the ballast of the track, but doing so from down here allowed him to also visit Corrine.

After putting on one of the harnesses, he positioned a headlamp on his forehead, then grabbed the ascender and Prusiks he would need to get back up the rope. He clipped in for a rappel and, after confirming that he had his folded up blade in his pocket, lowered himself into the shaft.

++++

After all my years of rock climbing, scaling the tree was no problem, but keeping those stitches intact in my side was.

I felt a tight, searing pain as they tugged free.

The blood on the shirt was no big deal. I could change later.

I edged out on the limb and leapt to the ground on the inside of the razor-wire fence.

Before looking in the warehouse's window, I decided to have a peek in Everhart's van to see if there was anything there that might implicate him.

Inside: a computer bag next to a pair of handcuffs.

Okay.

Now that's interesting.

I crossed the scraggly grass growing between the van and the building.

Most of the windows were covered with a film of dirt, but there was one that was cracked. A centimeter-wide triangle of glass was missing.

I leaned close and peered inside.

# 40

Nine wide holes had been burrowed through the concrete floor of the expansive three-story-tall warehouse. A backhoe sat in the corner of the building.

Guido had mentioned the gold mines in this part of the city from back in the early 1800s.

*Everhart is searching for the shafts.*

Immediately I thought of the mnemonic from the back of the painting: R-U-D-I-S-I-L.

Yeah. I liked where this was going.

There was no sign of him, but there was a rope that led from one of the holes out to the leg of an abandoned conveyor belt on the right side of the warehouse.

Two words came to mind: "exigent circumstances."

We're allowed to enter a premises if there are exigent circumstances—which is generally interpreted as when a reasonable law enforcement official would believe that delaying entry to obtain a warrant would increase the likelihood of the destruction of evidence or allow a suspect to cause severe harm to himself or another person.

*Corrine is missing.*

*Handcuffs in the van.*

*That van spent the night in her neighborhood.*

*The likelihood of severe harm to another person . . .*

It worked for me.

I'm not too bad with locks so I pulled out my lock pick set, knelt beside the door, and got started.

++++

Corrine's foot tapped only at empty air. The ceiling above her ended.

*Okay.*

This was it.

The shaft.

It would be so easy.

She just needed to step forward. Not even that, really—just lean, lean out into the darkness.

*Into the future.*

She stood there on the brink of life, of death, and wondered what it would be like to slip into nothingness, or everythingness, if you believed in the afterlife.

*So do you?*

*What do you believe?*

*Do you believe in the eternal? In the soul?*

It struck her that if there really was such a thing as justice, true justice, it would need to be meted out in the afterlife, because all too often it doesn't happen in this one.

*Like with your brother. Like with Richard.*

And if there was an afterlife, then there must be a God. And he would not let people enter into eternity without administering justice for deeds done on the earth.

It couldn't be one or the other. It was both. An afterlife and justice.

Or neither.

Only nothingness.

*Our secrets always find us out, in this life or in the next.*

She took a deep breath.

*If there is justice, there is a God.*

*If there is a God, there is justice.*

Both or neither.

Closed her eyes.

Opened them.

No difference.

The darkness around her.

Within her.

The laughter had stopped.

The shivering had stopped.

*Now, Corrine. Do it.*

*Justice.*

*Everythingness—*

She spread out her arms as if she were going to fly, as if she were going to dive into the sea of eternity.

And heard something in the shaft above her.

++++

The bard paused in his descent.

A moment ago he'd knocked a rock loose and he could hear it now, clattering off the beams crisscrossing the darkness far below him as it plummeted to the bottom of the shaft more than 250 feet past the entrance to the tunnel where he'd left Corrine.

++++

She felt her heart hammering in her chest.

A rock. Someone had jarred a rock loose.

*There's someone here!*

*But who?*

She listened.

Heard nothing more.

"Hello?" She said the word softly, unsure if she was actually speaking it aloud. Her voice was so light and airy it didn't even bring an echo.

No one answered.

Holding on to the support beam beside her, she leaned out as far as she could and peered uncertainly up the shaft.

*Oh.*

There was a dot of light—more than that, a narrow beam that swept through the shaft.

Someone was there.

Someone was definitely there.

*No, no, no. It's just your imagination.*

She blinked, and when she opened her eyes, the light was still there.

*It's someone else. It's not him. It can't be him. It's someone coming to help you.*

"Hello?" she yelled. And this time the sound reverberated upward through the shaft, loud and fervent and strong.

And then she heard the reply, echoing down to her: "I'm coming, Corrine. I'll be right there."

# 41

*Your name!*

*He said your name!*

*He knows your name!*

Though the acoustics of the echo made it impossible to tell if it was the same man who'd brought her here, who else would it be? Who else could it be? Who else knew she was down here?

Her heart went wild with fear.

*It's him. He's back.*

*Step forward. End this.*

*But no.*

*If you do, he wins. You can't let him win.*

*But he'll kill you!*

*Not if you can stop him. Not if you kill him first.*

The thought shocked her. The fact that she would even consider that.

*You have to do it. You have to kill him.*

*You couldn't do that, even if you—*

*How?*

*What? Push him down the shaft?*

*No. If you try to fight him here, you'll lose. He's too strong. Look how easily he overpowered you in your bedroom.*

*But you have to fight him—you have to!*

*No. Someone else will come. Someone will follow him.*

She backed away from the edge.

For some reason she thought of her clothes, of leaving her jeans at the far end of the tunnel by the water where she'd used them to dry off. At least she'd put her shirt back on for warmth.

*Find a rock. Fight him off. Don't let him win.*

*You can do it. You have to.*

++++

I pressed the door open and angled my Mini Maglite's beam into the dim warehouse. "Mr. Everhart?"

No reply.

Dismal, muted light oozed through the dirt-covered windows that flanked me. My flashlight's beam sliced through the dreariness of the abandoned factory, but the inside of this place didn't look like simply an empty warehouse. It looked more like a construction zone.

With a rope leading down into one of the holes.

*The Rudisill Mine?*

*Evaluate, don't assume.*

As I considered that, I couldn't help but think of the time in Denver when the serial killer who liked to be known as Giovanni had tried to bury me alive in an abandoned gold mine in the mountains west of Denver.

*Height. Weight. They're similar to Everhart's driver's license.*

Giovanni?

The age on the DMV records was close.

The face was different, but plastic surgery could have taken care of that.

*It would explain the bruises, the swelling.*

Giovanni had escaped from prison a few months ago. I knew that, but—

*Is it him again? Resurrected now as Danny Everhart?*

The message: *I am back.*

*Giovanni's free. He tells elaborate stories of tragedy and death. He taunts law enforcement.*

The dates of his employment at NVDS fit in with the timeline.

It could work.

A coincidence?

No. I don't believe in them.

Giovanni's real name was Kurt Mason and he'd been a police lieutenant in Denver. A good one too. He'd hidden who he was incredibly well. Truthfully, it was scary how normal he'd acted in his everyday life, how well he fit in. He was a killer without a conscience, a psychopath as twisted as they come.

The pit that lay nearest to me was about three meters wide and just about that deep.

*He knows explosives. He used C-4 in Colorado. He could have set that Semtex up in Virginia on Monday morning.*

The more I thought of Mason, the more likely it seemed that that's who Everhart really was.

I walked to the hole that yawned open just a little wider than the others, the one that dropped out of sight. The climbing rope that disappeared into it had been tied off with a figure-eight follow-through, the end tucked back into the knot in what rock climbers call a Yosemite backup.

Whoever had attached it knew his knots.

*Mason does.*

I'd gone climbing with him twice.

I scanned the warehouse. Still no movement. This was the only hole that had a rope leading into it. The stillness, the jagged slabs of unearthed concrete, the smear of filthy light coming through the windows, gave the place an eerie, unearthly feel, almost like something from the set of a horror movie.

When I peered into the shaft I saw the flick of someone's flashlight or headlamp far below me.

Mason?

An array of rock-climbing equipment sat piled on a table nearby.

*Wait for backup or go in after him?*

I was trying to decide when I heard the scream echo up from somewhere deep in the earth.

# 42

It was faint, as if the shaft were a throat emitting a sad, distant farewell to the world. It might have been a woman, might have been a man. I couldn't tell.

I listened carefully but heard nothing more.

Whipping out my cell phone, I contacted police dispatch, told them who I was and that I needed them to get a unit over here ASAP. I relayed the information that I had: I'd followed a suspect—Danny Everhart, or possibly, Kurt Mason—to this location, saw cuffs in the car, and heard screams from inside the shaft.

"The shaft?"

"A mine shaft. It's a long story. And tell SWAT we need anyone who's been trained in vertical rescue and assist."

"Who is this again?"

"Special Agent Patrick Bowers." Only after giving her my federal ID number did she finally put out the call for SWAT to respond. The average national response time for police officers in urban areas is eleven minutes. I was hoping today they could beat the average.

But until then, I wasn't just going to stand around waiting for them.

I grabbed a climbing harness and slipped it on.

I recalled the last time I faced Mason in that tunnel in Colorado.

He'd abducted a man and sliced his right wrist. The guy was bleeding, dying. While Mason stood behind him, a straight razor pressed against his throat, he had me cuff my hands behind my back. The only reason I was still alive today: I was able to pick the handcuff's lock with the spring from my Maglite.

I thought of that now as I slipped my flashlight into my pocket. In order to have both hands free for the rappel, I put on the headlamp that was on the table.

I couldn't stop thinking of that day in the tunnel—of fighting Kurt and then almost being sealed alive down there when the C-4 that he'd placed in one of the shafts blew.

*Two hundred pounds of Semtex were stolen. Only a few pounds were used at the NCAVC. That means—*

Another scream from somewhere deep within the earth.

*Go!*

There were no ascenders here to get back up the rope, but I figured I could cross that bridge when I came to it. I'd find a way back up. Right now I just needed to get down there and help whoever was hurt or in danger.

Corrine?

Maybe.

No way to know.

I cinched the harness's waist strap tight, then using the carabiner that was clipped to the rappel device, I attached it to the harness.

The device would create friction as the rope passed through it and that friction would slow my descent. I could control my speed by how fast I allowed the rope to move through it.

The light that I'd seen far below me had disappeared.

I felt the rope. It wasn't weighted, so whoever had been on the other end was no longer there.

I clipped in.

Eleven minutes' response time from when I first made the call.

Let's see how the CMPD did.

I tightened my grip on the rope, leaned back, and lowered myself into the shaft.

# 43

The screaming had stopped.

If these gold mines were anything like the mines near Denver, the shafts would drop down hundreds of feet and have tunnels fingering out from them to follow mineral veins in the rock at various levels.

A typical climbing rope is sixty meters long, but they can also come in coils much longer than that.

As I descended, I passed thick, rough-hewn timbers that were wedged horizontally against the sides of the shaft every two or three meters. They crisscrossed past me, far enough apart to provide space for me to rappel and for the miners, long ago, to be lowered down to the tunnels they would be working in.

The farther down I went, the cooler it became until the temperature leveled off in what felt like the mid- to high fifties.

I arrived at a tunnel that led toward the southwest.

Pausing my descent, I directed the headlamp's beam into it.

The quartz rock must have been reasonably stable through here because there weren't any beams propped up along the walls or spanning the ceiling. It appeared that the tunnel had been blasted directly through solid rock.

"Hello? Corrine?" I said. "Mr. Everhart? Kurt?"

The tunnel led out of sight into the thick darkness, swallowing my light after about ten or twelve meters as it curved to the west.

So, explore this tunnel or rappel deeper into the shaft?

I strained my ears listening for any more screams, but heard nothing. Just a vacant, empty stillness all around me.

*They could be in this tunnel around the corner, somewhere out of sight.*

Once again I looked at the rope trailing off beneath me. Since it led quite a ways farther down, it was logical that there would be other tunnels leading out from the shaft.

*Or it could just be that he used a longer rope than was necessary to get to this tunnel.*

Angling the light in front of me again, I studied the tunnel.

No sign of anyone

*Go in here or look for another tunnel?*

From where I was I could see what appeared to be the entrance to another tunnel closer to the end of the rope. I couldn't be positive, but since I had no ascenders, I needed to make sure this tunnel was clear before rappelling farther, or else I wouldn't have any way of getting back up here.

I kicked off the wall, swung into the tunnel, unclipped my harness from the rope, and unholstered my .357 SIG P229.

# 44

Corrine had a rock about the size of a baseball in her hand. It was small enough to hold, large enough to do some serious damage.

She figured that if she swung it hard enough and hit him in the face or on the side of the head, it might knock him down. And if he was on the ground she could use the rock to finish the job.

*Neck, face, forehead. Get him vulnerable then smash his head in. Yes, you can do this.*

But was she capable of something like that? Of taking a person's life?

*Yes.*

*You are.*

Maybe she wasn't so different from her brother after all.

*Maybe none of us are.*

The man was in the tunnel with her now.

It took some time for her eyes to adjust to the light coming toward her, but she had backed up about fifty feet from the shaft to make him think she was afraid and was trying to get as far away from him as possible.

She blinked her eyes against the light. "What do you want from me?"

"I want you to struggle."

With the light shining in her eyes, it was impossible to see his face, but he held a blade in front of him and she saw it glint wickedly in the light.

She gripped the hidden rock and crouched, ready to go at him once he was close enough.

++++

At the edge of his headlamp's beam, the bard could see Corrine cowering on the ground. As he directed the light on her, she closed her eyes and covered them with one hand to shield them from the light.

For some reason she had taken her pants off.

*Well.*

*Alright.*

*It'll save you the effort.*

++++

Corrine clenched that rock and readied herself to do whatever it took to get out of this tunnel alive.

*Get him down. Knock him down.*

*Then finish him off.*

*Kill him, Corrine.* It was almost an audible voice, venom spewing out from her soul. *You can do it. Kill him, kill him, kill him.*

++++

The bard centered his light on her as he moved closer. "Come here, Corrine."

++++

She didn't move, just tensed the muscles in her legs to leap at him once he was close enough and his guard was down.

*He needs to bend down, needs to be right beside you.*

He called for her to stand up.

"No." She eased backward away from him, staying low to the ground, keeping the rock out of sight.

++++

The bard worked the blade back and forth in his hands.

She was maybe ten feet away and she still hadn't gotten up.

He saw her shake with fear.

"We have some unfinished business, Corrine."

++++

Five feet

*Steady—wait, wait, wait.*

++++

He arrived at her side and grabbed her armpit to lift her to her feet.

++++

Corrine sprang at him, swinging the rock as hard as she could against the side of his head.

With incredibly quick reflexes he threw a hand up to block her arm and it took some of the force, but she still connected, and the impact of the blow sent him reeling sideways into the tunnel's wall.

On her feet now, she went at him again, but this time he whipped out his hand, lightning fast, and snagged her arm.

++++

The bard wrenched her arm behind her, pried the rock loose, and tossed it away from them.

"That was good, Corrine, using the resources you had available to you. You don't give up easily. I like that."

He slammed her head against the tunnel's rock wall to take some of the fight out of her. He did it again and she became limp and unsteady in his arms.

One more time.

Then, as she wilted, he entwined his hand in her hair and began to drag her toward the shaft.

++++

Corrine's thoughts became lost within themselves, as if they were curling down, trying to find their footing in a sloping, unsteady world.

Where was she?

The basement?

No.

Yes—

*The tunnel. You're in a tunnel. In the mine.*

He was dragging her by the hair, and it hurt so much. So much!

She tried to wriggle free but couldn't, tried digging her nails into his hand to make him let go, but it did no good.

She cried out in pain.

Then she heard her name, but it didn't come from the man beside her. It was from someone in the shaft: "Corrine? Are you in there?"

"Help!" she screamed.

++++

The bard stopped.

He hefted Corrine to her feet, slipped behind her, and pressed the blade against her throat, then turned toward the shaft.

++++

There'd been nothing in that other tunnel, so I'd returned to the shaft to descend farther.

I heard more cries for help.

It was a woman—I could tell that for sure now.

SIG in one hand, rope in the other, I descended, and the tunnel that the cries were coming from was only a few meters below me.

*She's there. She's close.*

"Don't hurt her, Kurt," I called.

I lowered myself until I was hanging in front of the tunnel, my weapon aimed into it. I locked off the rope to hold my position and directed the light from the headlamp in front of me.

Corrine Davis stood maybe eight or nine meters away, a man behind her. He wore a headlamp and at first I couldn't make out his face. He was holding the blade of a straight razor against her throat, just like Kurt Mason had done with that helicopter pilot Cliff Freeman in the mine west of Denver.

"Drop the blade." I sighted down the barrel at him. "Do it now."

# 45

"Patrick?" There was surprise in his voice. "Nice work, my friend. I didn't expect to see you so soon. This is so close to what happened in Colorado, don't you think? You with your gun, me with my blade?"

The voice matched Mason's, and when I directed my light at his face I could see for certain that he had altered his appearance and it matched Everhart's DMV photo.

*Surgery.*

*Yes, that explains the bruises and swelling.*

Corrine squinted and averted her eyes from my light.

I aimed my gun at Kurt's head, but since he was standing behind her not much of it was visible. Additionally, since I was still attached to the rope, I was rotating slightly and there was no way I was going to be able to make this shot. Even if I'd been standing still, at this distance I didn't trust myself to not hit Corrine.

It was just like Colorado.

*The past.*

*The present.*

*Becoming one.*

Mason said, "Drop your gun down the shaft, Pat."

"SWAT is on its way, Kurt. There's no way you're getting out of here. Let her go."

"It'll take them time to get down here. And there are more ways out of this mine than you know about. Now drop the gun."

*Stall. You need to stall.*

"I'm not going to do that. Set down the razor blade."

*He won't kill her. She's the only bargaining chip he has.*

I aimed.

No, I didn't have the shot. There was no way. But even if I couldn't shoot him, I could stall, I could—

Kurt went on, his voice steady, calculating. "This reminds me of what happened with Freeman—his wrist, remember?"

*Oh no.*

"Kurt, don't—"

Remaining behind her and holding her tightly, he whisked the blade down and swept it swiftly and deeply across her right wrist.

A thin spurt of blood shot out, even as he raised the blade and pressed it against her throat again.

She cried out and used her left hand to stop the bleeding.

*No!*

"There," he said, "now there's a true sense of unity between the two stories. And it brings some urgency to our little face-off here. Drop the gun, Pat. We need to get her to the surface or she'll bleed to death. Do it."

Thoughts wrestled inside me.

*Save her!*

"Okay." I redirected my SIG so it was no longer aimed at him. "Just let me help her."

"Get rid of the gun."

I let go of my weapon and it disappeared beneath me into the darkness, bouncing off one support beam after another as it fell. Time stretched out long and thin before it finally hit the floor of the shaft.

"Please," Corrine begged me. Her hand was covered with the blood that was flowing profusely from her wrist.

"Keep pressure on there," Kurt told her. "It's really important for you to control that bleeding."

He motioned toward me. "Pull up the hem of your pants legs, one at a time. Show me that you're not carrying in an ankle holster."

Sometimes I have a backup weapon. Today I did not. I showed him. "Kurt, there's—"

"Everything out of your pockets. Keys. Phone. Lock pick set. Your Maglite. You still carry that automatic knife with you? All of it. Down the shaft. Everything."

*Think, Pat!*

I couldn't come up with any other way to hurry things up other than going along with him, so I emptied my pockets.

"Now, I need you to come into this tunnel and take off your harness."

*You have to help her anyway. If he lets his guard down, you can go at him. Take him down.*

Pushing off the far wall of the shaft with my free hand, I swung into the tunnel and grabbed one of the support beams, but when I pulled myself over so I could stand on the edge of the tunnel, some of the dirt crumbled away and I momentarily lost my footing.

I tried again, and this time I made sure the ground was sturdy under my feet. Then, passing a little slack through the rappel device, I pulled myself into the tunnel, loosened the rope, eased another step into the tunnel, and unclipped the carabiner.

He was edging slowly toward me, keeping Corrine in front of him, the straight razor's blade still at her throat. "How did you find me?"

Blood dripped off her wrist and dribbled onto the ground beside her feet as she shuffled forward.

"There isn't time for this, Kurt. We need to get her to the surface."

"You stall, she dies. Now tell me, how did you find me? What was it? What gave me away?"

"The museum. The timing. You had to get out of there with the arrows. How? You had them hidden along the edge of the hand truck you were pushing. You brought too many crates of soda in. And you carted it all back out. It's how you hid the arrows from the cameras."

"That's not enough. It can't be."

"And Isabelle Brittain's phone call to Corrine on Monday night. It helped us with the timing. We caught video of your van entering her neighborhood forty minutes before she arrived home. Then you left the next morning."

"Timing and location."

"Timing and location. And you knew about the painting of the skull. I'm waiting to confirm it, but the timing works—you saw the painting before the staff rotated the display. Now let her go. This has nothing to do with Corrine. This is between you and me. Let her alone. You're armed, I'm not. I'll fight you."

"That's not going to happen. There's a much bigger story in play than what's unfolding here with the three of us."

"What story is that?"

He didn't respond.

*You don't have any ascenders or Prusiks. You can't follow him up the rope.*

I thought about the shaft, the beams in it. They were old, yes, but they looked sturdy. They were placed at relatively uniform intervals.

*You can do it.*

Maybe.

*Yes, you can.*

"How did you know about the exterior cameras at the NCAVC?" I asked him. "Jerome?"

He shook his head. "It's never that easy, Pat."

"But you're the one who blew the lawnmower?"

"Yes. I was going to share this with you later, but let's just go for it: Now seven gods use thirty-eight." Before I could even respond, he said, "That's all I'm giving you. Now, we need to switch places. Take off that harness. Leave it on the ground."

Loosening the harness, I stepped out of the leg loops and tossed it to the floor of the tunnel. Questions raced through my mind: *Seven gods use thirty-eight? Who's he talking about? What does that even mean?*

The obvious would be a .38 caliber handgun. The seven gods could be referring to something from history, a myth, other victims, the deeper story he was—

"Come toward me slowly," he said. He was about five meters away.

I started toward him.

"Slowly."

I slowed down, but only slightly. I needed to get that ascender from him and haul Corrine up that rope.

Two meters away.

"Alright," Mason said. "Stop."

There wasn't much room in the tunnel.

"Who are the seven gods, Kurt?"

"It's not what you think. Hands to the side."

"Help me." Corrine looked faint. It was the blood loss. We didn't have much time.

"I will," I told her as I held out my hands and faced

Mason. All the while I was calculating, watching, trying to figure out a way to overpower him without letting him cut her again.

His riddle about the seven gods wouldn't leave me alone.

*Did Jerome tell him the camera locations? The timing doesn't fit. It's—*

He held the blade tightly against Corrine's throat as he edged toward me, his back to the tunnel wall. I flattened my back against the other side to give them room to pass.

"If you make a move," he said, "she dies. You need to know that. You might get to me, but not before I slit her throat."

"I understand."

When I looked into Corrine's eyes, I saw desperation. Truth or hope?

*Give her hope.*

"It's going to be alright," I told her as convincingly as I could. "I promise you. Just keep your hand on that cut. Slow down the bleeding."

Still controlling her, Mason passed me, then backed up slowly toward the shaft until he was standing about a meter from the drop-off with Corrine in front of him.

*Rush him. Maybe if you can get to her, you can push him off the—*

"Back up, Patrick. I don't want you playing the hero here."

I eased away from them until he told me to stop, about ten meters away.

Mason grabbed the rope, pulled up a few arm lengths of slack, then looped it into a clove hitch, which he slipped over Corrine's head and snugged up around her neck.

"No, Kurt," I said.

She cried out and tried to pull away, but he drew her firmly toward him.

I started for them, but he yanked her backward until her feet were right on the loose soil on the edge of the drop-off. "Stay there, Pat. I need to clip in. Not another step or I push her into the shaft."

I froze, tried to evaluate what to do.

There was nothing stopping him from killing her. What did he have to lose? If I caught him he was going back to prison for life.

He slid her forward slightly so she wouldn't fall while he attached his ascending device to the rope above her.

Corrine's eyes were wide with terror.

"Look at me," I said to her. "Right here. You're going to be okay. I'm going to help you, alright?"

She stared in my direction. "He'll come." Her voice was soft but also firm.

"Who?"

"My brother."

"Let's hope you're right," Mason said. He clipped in, attached his ascender to the rope along with a Prusik for his foot, then faced me.

"Untie her, Kurt," I told him. "There's no reason to hurt her."

"There never is."

He tugged lightly on the rope he'd looped around her neck, forcing her back toward the edge of the shaft. With his other hand he pulled out a phone and snapped a picture of her, then pocketed the cell again. "You do remember in Colorado when you got there just in time to save Freeman?"

"I'm telling you, Kurt, don't do this."

"This time, though, you were just a little too late."

He yanked the rope backward, pulling Corrine over the edge, and as he swung out to ascend the rope, she disappeared into the shaft with a final scream that was cut off abruptly when the slack in the rope played out and the knot jerked tightly around her neck.

# 46

I bolted forward, but by the time I got there, Mason was already out of reach above me, smoothly, efficiently ascending the rope.

I looked down and saw Corrine's body convulsing where she hung a few meters below me.

*It's too late.*

*No! You can save her!*

Leaning forward, I tried to get ahold of the rope to pull her up, but it was just out of reach. I held on to a beam with my left hand and reached out to grab it with my right.

The shaft around me washed in light as Mason tipped his headlamp down toward us. I glanced up just in time to see him flick out his blade.

"Make sure you have good footing, Pat."

"Kurt, don't—"

He slit the rope beneath him just as I snagged it with my right hand. Corrine's body weight yanked it through my fingers. Despite the friction burns it was causing, I tried to hold on, but I couldn't.

As she disappeared into the darkness beneath me I saw her flail her arms.

*She's not dead.*

*You might have saved her.*

She fell for what seemed like an eternity, and the sound of impact when she hit the bottom of the shaft was harsh and terrible and sickening.

I directed my headlamp up toward Mason. "You're mine."

"The future ends tomorrow, Pat. And you can tell Agent Hawkins I said so."

He began to ascend.

No, I didn't have a rope, but the beams that criss-crossed the shaft were spaced just far enough apart.

I grabbed the one closest to me and began to climb.

# 47

Pull-ups.

It was just like doing pull-ups

One beam after the next.

In the light of the headlamp I could see Mason maybe five or six meters above me.

*You can catch him. You can do this.*

But he obviously knew what he was doing and had a rhythm going—one hand, then the other, gripping the ascending device that locked off the rope to hold him in place, sliding up the loop of rope for his foot. Then he would stand, slide up the ascender, and start over again.

I climbed faster, trying to gain on him until I came to an impasse: The beam above me was missing. Either it'd fallen long ago or had never been placed there when this shaft was built.

The next one was out of reach. I would need to jump, but if I missed it I was going to fall, and there wasn't anything besides the beam I was standing on to stop me.

I told myself I wouldn't miss.

Taking a deep breath, I crouched, gauged the distance, and leapt.

But I didn't make it high enough.

I barely snagged the edge of the beam, but it was

damp and slippery and my hands slid off. I plunged backward, smacking into the beam I'd leapt off from, hitting it hard on my right side. The impact flipped me around upside down.

Throwing my arms out, I managed to grab hold of it just before I would have rolled off for good, but the momentum carried my legs around and my ankle banged into the side of the shaft, jarring me so much that I nearly lost my grip.

My side raged with pain but I did my best to ignore it.

Using a narrow ledge in the rock wall for a foothold, I scrambled onto the beam and quickly assessed myself. My side was wrenched pretty badly. Where the stitches had been, the cuts were bleeding heavily, but when I passed my hand over my rib cage it didn't feel like I'd broken any ribs.

My ankle was bruised, but I could deal with it. My right hand was on fire from the rope burns, but that was manageable.

I directed my light up the shaft.

Mason had paused and was staring down at me. "Are you alright, Pat?"

I said nothing, just dried off my hands on my jeans and got ready to go after him.

"Good. I'm glad," he said. "I don't want you to miss the climax tomorrow night." Then he turned and began to ascend again.

*Don't slip this time, Pat.*

*Higher. You need to jump higher and hold on to that beam.*

With every second, he was lengthening the distance between us.

I readied myself and then leapt as high as I could.

This time, despite the friction burns on my hand, I

managed to hold on. Gripping the beam, I kicked off the wall and pulled myself up. Even more focused now, adrenaline erasing the pain in my side, my hands, my ankle, I climbed one beam after another. But I could see that I was falling farther behind him.

He was going to make it to the surface.

He was going to get away.

# 48

Kurt Mason reached the top of the shaft and clambered out of the hole.

No SWAT.

No police.

Sirens, though.

Law enforcement was on its way.

He didn't have much time.

No matter how good your grip strength is, it's incredibly difficult to pull yourself up a standard-diameter rock-climbing rope without an ascender; it's simply too narrow.

However, just to make sure and to slow Patrick down, before he headed for the door of the warehouse, Kurt confirmed that Pat wasn't holding on to the rope, then he drew his blade across it.

++++

The rope snaked past me on its way to the bottom of the shaft.

Still ten meters to go.

I climbed.

*Come on!*

Five.

Then three.

And then I ran out of beams.

With the loose dirt near the top of the shaft I expected that getting out would be a problem, but as I made my way over the edge, I found the soil firmer than I thought it would be and it only took me a few moments to get to ground level, where I grabbed one of the angled slabs of concrete and swung myself out of the hole.

"Kurt!"

Nothing.

I spun, studying the ragged ground, the shadows, the abandoned equipment, for any sign of Mason.

Out of instinct I reached for my gun, but of course it was at the bottom of the mine.

Sprinting out the door, I burst into the day.

For some reason my sense of time was warped and it seemed like it should have been night out here, but it wasn't.

Still early afternoon.

Hot.

Summer in the South.

He was nowhere to be seen.

I sped toward the place where Mason had parked his van. The gate was open, the vehicle gone.

*He can't be far.*

Sirens were approaching from a nearby road, but without my phone I had no way to contact the responding officers, no way to tell them about Mason's van.

I ran to the road and looked up and down the street.

Nothing.

Which way? Would he hop on the highway or disappear into the web of residential streets in this neighborhood?

I didn't know.

*He knows how you think. He won't do what you'd expect.*

Even if I could have guessed his plans, my rental car's keys lay at the bottom of the mine shaft, so I couldn't drive anywhere to look for him.

*He killed Corrine right in front of your eyes!*

In anger, I smacked a street sign beside me, then raced toward Summit Street, where the sound of the sirens was coming from.

| | + +

Kurt pulled into a circular driveway in a residential neighborhood about a mile from the textile plant and parked next to an older-model Buick LeSabre.

He shut off the engine.

A small strip of woods helped isolate this home from the others just down the street. And the house had what he needed: a garage.

As a former police lieutenant, he knew that law enforcement would be looking for his vehicle on the nearby streets but wouldn't immediately search for it in driveways. And they wouldn't be able to search in the garages of people's homes, not without warrants.

So, he could buy some valuable time if he could get his van in this garage.

He exited the vehicle and started toward the porch of the house.

A few moments after he rang the doorbell an elderly man appeared in the doorway. "Yes?" There was guarded suspicion in his voice. "Can I help you?"

"I'm going to need you to back up."

"What?"

"Please. Take a couple of steps backward."

"Why?"

"I don't want to get any blood on your porch. It might attract attention when the police go door-to-door."

Confused, the man retreated a step, if only to close the door—but it was just what Kurt needed. He went at the man and cut him swiftly, mercifully, in a way that he would bleed out quickly.

Once inside, Kurt stepped over the man's twitching body and went looking for the car keys to the LeSabre parked out front so he could borrow the vehicle after hiding his own in the garage.

++++

I flagged down the first cruiser.

When the driver saw the blood on my shirt, he leapt out. "Sir, are you alright?"

"I'm fine." I approached them. "I need you to—"

"Stop." He seemed suddenly anxious, wary. "Stay where you are."

My wallet and my creds were at the bottom of the shaft so I couldn't prove who I was, but I rattled off my federal ID number. His partner was out of the vehicle now too. He radioed it in.

"How many units are en route?" I asked.

"Three," the first officer replied, somewhat hesitantly.

"SWAT?"

"He's good," his partner announced. "It's Agent Bowers."

"With SWAT," I went on urgently, "how many units do we have?"

"Well, three is counting SWAT."

"We need more. Let me use your radio." I called dispatch, gave them a description of Mason and his van, and told them its plate numbers. "This guy is armed, danger-ous, and must be approached with extreme caution. He's responsible for more than a dozen deaths. I repeat: Tell your officers to use extreme caution."

The other squads were arriving now. Mentally reviewing the road layout of this Ward from having studied the
3-D map and driven around with Guido, I took into account the typical patterns for fleeing suspects and Mason's obvious familiarity with this city; then I told the
officers how I wanted them to fan out and search the area
until we could get more officers here to go door-to-door.

"And we need eyes in the air," I said to the ranking
officer. "How many helicopters does your department
have?"

"Only one, but state patrol can help us out. They have
some—I mean, they're not all here in Charlotte, of
course."

I'd seen a landing pad beside the FBI's Field Office.
"Call it in. And get the Bureau's chopper on it as well. I
want all major highways covered. Mass transit and air-
ports too. Mason's been using the alias Danny Everhart,
but he's smart and he might have another identity package. I want facial rec at the Charlotte airport."

"Are you sure we need to do all that?"

"Listen to me: This guy killed six federal agents earlier
this week, and a woman just now in that shaft. From what
we know, he has nearly two hundred pounds of Semtex
and he's planning something big. He told me the climax
would be tomorrow. We need to find him and we need to
find him now."

By the look on his face I could tell that the gravity of
the situation was finally hitting him. "Alright."

I doubted Mason would return to his apartment, but
I radioed in the address and told dispatch to get a SWAT
team over there. "He has hundreds of pounds of explosives at his disposal so the place might be booby-trapped.
Do not rush in. Take it slow and evacuate the apartment
building before you make a move."

I turned to the officer closest to me. "Do you have a cell phone?"

"Yes, sir." He produced it from his pocket.

"I'm going to be needing that until I can get a new one." I waited for him to hand it over. "Thank you."

"Um . . . yeah."

I contacted Cyber to see if they could get any satellite footage of the area from the Defense Department's Routine Orbital Satellite Database, or ROSD, and also to get them looking into what "seven gods use thirty-eight" might mean; then I called Gonzalez and updated him on the search.

When I was done he told me, "We need to release Everhart's—well, Mason's—DMV photo to the press."

Normally I don't like working with the media, but in this case it was the right call. "Agreed," I said. "We should set up a tip line. And get a photo of that model van out as well."

++++

FBI Director Margaret Wellington sat in the conference room at HQ and listened as JTTF Director René Gonzalez quickly brought her up to speed on the status of the search for Kurt Mason in Charlotte, North Carolina.

"We need the Hostage Rescue Team down there," she told Gonzalez. "They should be able to make it in just over an hour if they take one of our jets. I want them rather than local SWAT to clear Mason's apartment. They're better trained, and this guy has explosives and he knows how to use them. "

"Yes, ma'am."

"Send Ingersoll and his men. I don't want to take any chances."

++++

After leaving his van in the dead man's garage, Kurt Mason drove Uptown to a parking garage where he left the LeSabre and hot-wired another car. Taking that car, he went to Fourth Ward to regroup in the house he'd rented under another name as part of his contingency plan.

Patrick was smart, but Kurt couldn't think of any way he would track him to this location.

Now he parked that vehicle around back, out of sight behind the house and under a tree to hide it from satellites and choppers.

He grabbed his computer bag and hip pack containing the sensor for checking the Semtex detonator, and went into the kitchen.

When he'd been looking to rent a house, he'd wanted one that was furnished and he'd stumbled onto this gem here in this quiet, relatively crime-free neighborhood.

A perfect fit.

Based on his experience, he knew that law enforcement would initially assume he would try to flee, to leave the area. They wouldn't start with the hypothesis that he was going to stay here in Uptown Charlotte, but even though it might put him at more of a risk, he had things to do in the city and he wasn't about to leave until they were completed.

He'd told Patrick that the climax would be tomorrow night, but he hadn't told him where it would be.

Timing and location again.

It was always about how the two of them came together.

Kurt assessed things: If the authorities hadn't done so yet, they would be searching the neighborhood surrounding the textile mill he'd used, house by house.

They would release his DMV photo.

His face was going to be all over the news.

They would probably already be at his apartment as well. He hadn't left anything there that would reveal what was going to happen tomorrow, but still it was a setback—especially if they were somehow able to look at the photos he'd left in his bedroom.

But with the trip wire that he'd set by the door, if SWAT did try to access the place that wasn't going to turn out very well for them.

He figured that watching the news would give him nearly real-time status on the search for him. But the big question was: Would the FBI send a team into the mine, thinking that there might be more victims down there?

He wasn't sure. They would eventually do so, but they would probably know about the Semtex by now, and, if so, they would take the search through the tunnels slowly and, without any evidence, they wouldn't cancel Fan Celebration Day at the stadium tomorrow.

There were a lot of unmapped tunnels down there. However, he'd lied to Bowers about one thing: There weren't any other open shafts. Just that one. But deceit in the service of utility was always justifiable.

Really, the tunnel from the Rudisill Mine to Saint Catherine, the mine that really mattered, was only one of many. And there was no reason law enforcement would think about the significance of the railroad tracks that crossed above the capped-off Saint Catherine mine shafts.

It would almost certainly take them a couple of days to search all the tunnels and that was more than enough time to see everything through to the end.

But it wasn't just the revelation about him and their search for his location that was going to be foremost in the news—the media would also highlight Corrine's death.

And that would undoubtedly bring Richard out of the woodwork.

Kurt hadn't expected that to happen until tomorrow, after things had played out with M343.

So now he also had to be vigilant and keep an eye out for Basque.

*Lie low.*

*Be smart.*

Patrick had interrupted him before he could check the Semtex in the mine, but he could walk the tracks and do it externally through the pressure-sensor mechanism tonight.

Not ideal, but workable.

So, for right now, monitor the news, and wait things out. Once it got dark he would walk the tracks to verify that the pressure sensors beneath that overpass were calibrated properly and set to the right time to become operational tomorrow afternoon.

# 49

Based on a tip called in about a van in the neighborhood, we found Kurt Mason's vehicle in the garage of a residence just over a mile from the mine.

The owner was dead, his throat slit. The 2005 Buick LeSabre registered in his name was missing. We looked it up, but his vehicle didn't have GPS.

Our defense-satellite footage over Charlotte wasn't in real time and was spottier than it should have been. So even though we had footage indicating that the LeSabre had been driven Uptown, we lost it in the network of streets shielded by the city's skyscrapers.

Local SWAT had evacuated Mason's apartment building but were waiting for Ingersoll's HRT unit to arrive from Quantico before attempting to access his place.

ETA: thirty minutes.

The CMPD and North Carolina State Highway Patrol choppers were looking for the LeSabre, but I guessed that Mason would have switched vehicles again by now.

Based on what Voss had told Ralph and me about his difficulties working with the CMPD, I thought our joint work with them might be a hassle. However, they were as professional and on top of things as any law enforcement agency I'd ever worked with, which made me wonder if maybe Voss was the problem here rather than the Charlotte police.

The media had a photo of Mason that we'd pulled off footage from the NVDS security cameras. We released that along with his DMV photo. A team was tracking down his associates from work and people from his apartment complex whom he might have contacted since he fled the mine shaft, as well as those who'd written to him or visited him in prison.

Calls went out to his relatives and his ex-wife.

Angela and Lacey were looking for any credit cards or phone bills in Mason's name or with the name of Danny Everhart, but the last I heard they hadn't located any.

Through it all, one image kept coming back to me: Corrine tipping backward into the shaft with that rope cinched around her neck.

The look on her face.

Terror.

"He'll come," she'd told me right before she died.

"Who?" I'd asked.

"My brother."

And then Mason had said, "Let's hope you're right."

*Is all this a setup to draw Basque out? Is that where all this is leading? Does that have to do with the climax Mason told you is coming?*

I could almost hear the unspoken cry of Corrine's heart as Mason jerked her back into the shaft, words that she might have said to me if she'd had a chance: "You said you'd help me. Why didn't you help me?"

And I had no *satisfying* answer.

In that tunnel, right before he killed her, Mason had taken Corrine's photograph.

I had Cyber search to see if he'd posted it anywhere online.

So far, nothing.

*Find him, Pat. For Corrine, for Jerome, for the others, for everyone he's ever killed.*

I was antsy. I wanted to be in on the search so I joined one of the teams in the air, riding in the Bureau's helicopter.

We circled Uptown and I analyzed the street layout while staying in radio contact with Voss and Ralph.

My ankle throbbed, my right palm was blistered with rope burns, and my side hadn't stopped bleeding. I needed stitches again, so my pilot arranged for us to land on the pad of one of the hospitals so I could get that taken care of.

Five minutes until we were scheduled to land.

Until then, I held my left hand against my side to stem the bleeding as I scoured the area below us and considered where things were at.

Mason hadn't confirmed that it was Jerome who'd given him the camera locations, but he had told me something about seven gods using thirty-eight—whatever that might mean.

The team was looking into it.

I liked the feeling of the chase and, for me, anger always played a role in it. But now the rage I felt over what Mason had done unsettled even me.

To catch these guys you have to meet them where they're at, and that often means going to a very dark place. You have to ask yourself how far you're willing to go in this job.

And you need to be careful not to lose your way in the process.

I've seen it happen with other agents, other cops.

We want to remain pure, but darkness always sticks to

you when you venture into it to find the people who traffic in causing pain to others.

Your soul does not come away unscathed.

Lien-hua and Tessa knew the darkness was there, but they didn't know how far I've let myself be drawn into it while trying to catch the people I track.

Secrets.

I keep them.

I have to.

In order to protect the people I care about most.

There's always that lure of the forbidden, that gravitational pull of your base, primal desires tugging you downward toward doing the very things that frighten you the most.

Something we all need to fight against.

Or we'll get lost for good.

In my early days as a detective, the woman I was seeing at the time asked me why I did what I did. At first I made light of her question, but when she pressed me, I ended up landing on a phrase that has stuck with me over the years: to keep the demons at bay.

My biggest struggle isn't achieving justice. It's holding myself back from what I would become if all the constraints were removed, what I'm tempted to become every day when I see the evil that humans are capable of doing to each other.

We throw around the term *unthinkable*, but most of the time what seems unthinkable has already been done somewhere, by someone who is following the dark threads deeper into his own desires.

And justifying it as he does.

No, right now it didn't feel like I was doing a very good job with the whole keeping-the-demons-at-bay thing.

In the mine, Mason had told me that he was glad I'd be around for the climax tomorrow night.

Well, we'd found the mine shaft. We knew where he lived. We would find him.

And whatever he had planned, I was going to stop it.

The pilot brought the helicopter around to the Charlotte Regional Medical Center, positioned it over the landing pad, hovered there for a moment, and then took us down.

# 50

Over the last half hour I'd texted my daughter several times to call me, and I'd left a couple messages for Lien-hua, and now I finally caught up with my wife on the phone as I made my way to the emergency room.

I shared all that had happened in the mine. "I couldn't save her, Lien-hua. I couldn't save Corrine."

"From what you just told me, no one could have."

"But maybe if I would have done something differently, if I would have rushed Mason, tried to knock him down the shaft or . . ."

"He would have killed her. You know that."

*She's dead anyway. At least then we would have taken him out. At least then he'd be gone too.*

I almost said those words, but then realized how uncaring and detached toward Corrine's death they might seem. And that's not how I felt about her death. Not at all.

Lien-hua continued, "You're not going to help anyone by beating yourself up about what happened. You need to let it rest. I know it's hard, but you have to."

I didn't want to argue with her, but I wasn't ready to agree with her yet either. Just thinking about Corrine made me ache deep in my chest.

"What did you find out this afternoon?" I asked.

"We were looking into people who've made public threats against Richard Basque. Well, it turns out there are a lot them."

"I believe that."

I wasn't sure we needed any of this information now, since we knew Mason was behind this, but we still didn't know if he was working alone. "Upload what you have to the online case files. Maybe it'll help us out as we try to nail down the timeline and piece things together."

"There are people on it as we speak," she said. "Listen, Pat, how much do you want me to tell Tessa? I mean about you trying to save Corrine?"

"I left a couple texts for her to call me, but I haven't heard from her yet. I'll talk with her. Don't worry about it."

"You sure?"

"Yeah."

However, that wasn't going to be an easy conversation. *She's going to hear about it on the news. You may as well be the one to tell her.*

Still, I didn't want to have to tell her how close I was to saving Corrine only to see her get killed right in front of my eyes.

"Well," Lien-hua said, "let me know if you need anything from me."

After a quick good-bye, we ended the call.

In the emergency room, a doctor who wasn't nearly as good at stitches as Habib back in DC patched me up. The thought of syringes piercing into my flesh was not really something I wanted to be worried about right now, so I had him work on my side without numbing the area.

After he was done he warned me to be more careful.

I told him I'd do my best.

"And that hand of yours," he said, "you've got some

pretty bad friction burns. I can give you a prescription for some cream that might help."

All that did was remind me how I'd been unable to save Corrine.

"I should be alright. Thanks."

I hid the limp from my bruised ankle. It would be swollen a little, but I didn't anticipate I would need to wrap it.

As he was finishing up, I received a text from Ralph that Brandon Ingersoll's HRT crew had arrived. They'd found evidence that the apartment had been booby-trapped, so it was a good thing SWAT hadn't rushed in. The HRT was working at figuring out the best way to access the scene now.

With advancements in robotics in recent years, there were robots that could search for bombs, robots that could sniff out explosives, robots that could disarm charges, and more. Although I wasn't sure which ones the guys might have brought down, they had access to them all. They knew what they were doing, and if anyone could figure out a safe way into Mason's apartment, Ingersoll and his team could.

Ralph met me outside the hospital to fill me in and swing me by our hotel room so I could change clothes before we headed to the apartment to have a look around—as soon as the HRT had cleared the site.

"Mason wanted me to tell you that the future ends tomorrow," I told him.

"How does he even know me? I've never worked his case."

"You're the head of the NCAVC. He attacked it. I suppose it makes sense that he would know who you are."

"Yeah." He didn't sound convinced.

At the hotel, he stepped out of the room to give me some privacy. I cleaned up and was changing clothes when I finally heard from my daughter.

# 51

Ever since Beck had left the house two and a half hours earlier, Tessa had been distracted from packing by thinking about him.

She'd been so caught up in her thoughts that she hadn't even been checking her texts. Then, when she finally did, she found a ton from Melody asking how she was, and three from Patrick telling her to give him a call.

So after replying to Melody, she phoned her dad and now listened as he told her what had happened in that mine shaft.

Lieutenant Mason had worked closely with Patrick while they lived in Denver, so she'd known him before he was arrested last summer. He'd fooled everyone into believing that he cared about his family. He'd been especially convincing when his baby died. He seemed as devastated as anyone, but as it turned out, it was all an act.

Just an act.

Patrick asked, "Do you want me to come home, Tessa?"

"No. Obviously, you need to stay there. You have to catch him."

"Until we do, I'm going to want an agent there with you whenever Lien-hua isn't around."

Tessa looked outside and saw the sedan where Beck's partner was stationed.

Her conversation with Beck on Plato's forms and quantum mechanics had been really engaging.

It wasn't pride, it was just reality—sometimes it was hard for people to keep up with her. However, Beck hadn't had any problem doing so. He was scintillatingly smart and wasn't intimidated by her like some guys seemed to be.

And that just made it even harder to put him out of her mind.

Of course she wanted to see him again, but now she stated the obvious to Patrick. "But if Mason's down there, what's the danger up here in DC?"

"He might not be working alone. He's trying to tell a story and I'm caught in the middle of it, which . . . well . . . means you are too. There are still a lot of questions about what's going on. Hopefully, in the next day or two we'll be able to get some answers. Are you good with that?"

"Yeah, whatever. That's fine. You just need to find him. Don't worry about me."

So she wouldn't be distracted thinking about Beck, she switched topics and asked Patrick about the skull painting she'd tracked down in the Library of Congress. "Was it there at the museum? The artwork with the Latin text?"

"Yes. That was good work, finding it. I never thanked you for disobeying the rules of the Library of Congress and calling me."

"Anytime you need me to break some more federal regulations for you, just let me know."

"I'll keep that in mind." He paused. "Hey, I have to get going. Is there anything else you need right now, or are you good?"

"I should be good," she said.

"Text me if anything comes up."

"I will."

++++

I met up with Ralph in the parking lot. He was finishing a phone call with Brineesha and, from his side of the conversation, it was clear that something was up.

When the call ended, I asked if things were alright.

"Brin had a doctor's appointment today. Her cervix is dilated two centimeters. So it's not much, you know, but it's a start." His tone made it clear that the news both excited him and made him anxious.

"Does that mean you have to go back?"

"Not yet. She hasn't started having contractions. I should be good. She's going to keep me updated as things progress."

"Congratulations, Ralph. I'm thrilled for you guys."

"Yeah. Thanks."

I was a little surprised he wasn't checking into flights yet, but I figured he knew what he was doing and would take care of that in due time.

"Oh," he said, "Ingersoll's guys sent THROWERS in."

The acronym stood for Throwable Handheld Remote Operating Window-Entry Robotic Sentries. They were heavy enough to break through the glass of most windows, and once they landed, their legs would unfold and the robot would scamper around taking video footage, almost like the mini "spider" robots in the movie *Minority Report*.

The apartment was on the fourteenth floor so I anticipated the HRT would have probably rappelled off the roof, cut a hole—a clean hole—through the window's glass, and sent the THROWERS in that way.

Ralph continued, "They're still working at clearing the place. We've got a few minutes. Let's snag some supper, then get over there."

After a quick bite, we drove to the apartment building. With the search for Mason, the chopper ride, the trip to the hospital and then the hotel, and now supper and the drive back to the apartment building, the afternoon had gotten away from me and it was already after five.

Ralph and I took the elevator to the fourteenth floor. By the time we arrived, the HRT had finished and the Evidence Response Team was gearing up to process the scene.

Voss was standing near the elevator bay, speaking with some CMPD officers. They seemed to be getting along alright—which I was glad to see. When he asked how I was doing, I assured him I was fine.

"What do you need from me?" he asked.

"A gun. A phone. A car."

"Done."

That was easy. "And a new Mini Maglite. Mine's at the bottom of that shaft."

"Um, yeah. We can do that." The officers he'd been talking to stepped away.

"Great. Who owns that textile-mill property?"

"A Vietnamese industrial company."

"Vietnamese?"

"We're looking into it."

"Did we ever find Guido?"

"Yeah. He was at an ice cream parlor Uptown. There are a couple of agents talking with him, but it doesn't look like he had anything to do with this."

"See if he knows anyone—any historians, any

researchers—who could tell us more about the Rudisill Mine."

"I will."

Brandon Ingersoll had left the apartment at the end of the hall and now joined us. I said to him, "Don't send any teams down into that mine until we know more about the layout of the tunnels. Last year Mason used C-4 to blow a shaft in an abandoned gold mine in Colorado. Now he has nearly two hundred pounds of Semtex. He could have other explosives as well that we don't know about. Taking out this mine system while we have teams of SWAT or HRT guys down there might just be the very 'climax' Mason has in mind."

*But then why would he have said the climax is tomorrow night? How would he know when we were going to send people in there?*

I wasn't sure.

Ingersoll said, "You're thinking he might have booby-trapped the mines like he did his apartment?"

"I wouldn't be surprised. We need to take this slow, think things through. Seal off the mine shaft and that textile mill. But before we send anyone down there we need to finish processing Mason's apartment and find some historian who can inform us about the layout of those mines and, ideally, their structural integrity."

Ralph added, "Once we know what we're looking at, I want your team to study the mine's topography and identify the most likely places where Mason might have left explosives to cause a cave-in."

"Roger that," he said.

"And why don't you put a call out to a mining company, see if they have any engineers who can get over here. Maybe arrange for some ground-penetrating radar to help analyze the area."

Ingersoll nodded briskly, then strode off.

Ralph turned to me. "So, you ready to see where Mason lived?"

"Absolutely."

Together we walked toward the doorway at the end of the hall.

# 52

"So, I'm not too familiar with Mason's case," Ralph told me as we crossed down the hallway toward the apartment. "Fill me in."

"He's not a typical serial killer—if there even is such a thing. It's not about a sexual thrill for him, or power or control."

"What is it?"

"He's a storyteller. Typically, he frames his crime sprees around literature or famous stories from history. He isn't into seeing people suffer. That's not his deal. It's all about context."

"Stories, huh? So a folktale or a myth about seven gods? But what about them using thirty-eight?"

I shook my head. "I don't know. I'm hoping Angela and Lacey can dig something up. In any case, there's a detachment to what he does. When I confronted him last year, I asked him why he did it, why he killed all those people, and he told me it was interesting to watch people die."

"That's cold."

"Yes." It still disturbed me to think about it. "It is. And when he said it there was no emotion, no regret, no empathy."

"So, why did he call himself Giovanni?"

"It has to do with the stories he reenacts, the crimes he commits. It goes back to this book called *The Decameron* by Giovanni Boccaccio. It was written in the 1300s and contains a hundred stories—ten stories told on ten consecutive days while a group of travelers is fleeing the black plague. Basically, the group passes the time telling stories. Well, on one of the days—day four—all the stories are about tragedy and love. He set about reenacting his version of those ten tales. It included some really brutal crimes, and he nearly got away with it. His stories always have a twist and they never have a happy ending."

We arrived at the door. "And this is the guy who killed Werjonic?"

Last year Mason had attacked and poisoned my mentor. "Yes."

Ralph cursed under his breath, then he showed his creds to the officers stationed outside the apartment, and we stepped inside.

Rarely do their lairs look like you'd expect.

Based on the violent or aberrant nature of some crimes, it's easy to think that the people who commit them are somehow different from the rest of us, that the places they live in would reflect that deviancy. And, although that's true in some isolated cases, it's not the norm.

For every Jeffrey Dahmer storing bodies in vats in his bedroom, there are a hundred other killers who have relatively normal homes.

Normal lives.

At least on the surface.

So.

Now.

Mason's apartment.

The place was dimly lit, the thick shades drawn shut,

leaving only a few slits for sunlight to leak in. No bulbs in the overhead lights, just two amber floor lamps in opposite corners of the living room.

Typical furniture.

All so typical.

In truth, every one of us leads a double life. We act one way when the door is open, another when it's closed. We have certain impressions we try to make on others, pretenses we strive to keep up.

In some branches of criminology, deviancy is considered anything you do in the dark. In other words, it's any act that you try to hide from others. So, what kind of person are you when the shades are drawn? That's really the question. "Integrity," as Dr. Werjonic used to say, "has no private life."

But, of course, no one has complete integrity because everyone has things to hide. All of us act differently when no one is watching.

We are, each of us, a contradiction in terms. We're a species that's puzzling to even the most astute philosophers and psychologists. Evil and good wrapped up in flesh and blood and hope and dreams.

We choose, we act, we live within the incongruity of our godlike desires and our animal instincts.

A double life.

And no matter how self-controlled we might be, we all do things we don't want to do, that are antithetical to our beliefs.

And sometimes we enjoy them.

Yes. Sometimes we do.

*You do.*

*You don't always keep the demons at bay.*

*Sometimes you invite them in.*

I pushed that thought aside.

No, it's not hypocrisy to have high ideals and fail to live up to them—it's called being human. Even saints have their imperfections and flaws. The only people who aren't hypocrites are those whose morals are so twisted, whose consciences are so seared, that they don't believe in any ideals higher than those they actually live out.

Like Mason.

Yes, when it comes right down to it, psychopaths are the only people you'll ever meet who aren't hypocrites.

There was a thought to carry you through the day.

With that at the forefront of my mind, I passed through this apartment where everything looked so normal.

Until we came to Kurt Mason's bedroom.

# 53

Photos printed from a high-quality ink-jet printer were taped on the east wall, nearly covering it.

There were hundreds of pictures of Uptown Charlotte, the four statues on Independence Square, the Mint Museum, the open-air Bank of America Stadium, the textile mill Mason had used.

There were photos of railroad lines and highway overpasses and a house that, based on the visible address on it, was Corrine's. Also, a tightly cropped picture of a street address: 669. Just an address, nothing else visible to indicate where it was.

He had photographs of the NCAVC building, Cole's house, his body, the inside of the mine tunnels, and the interior of a break room that I didn't recognize. Corrine tied to a bed. Cuffed in the van.

And there were many more—some obviously related to this crime spree, others that may have been, but at this point there was no way to tell for sure.

The printer sat on the desk near the bed. No computer. One window was missing its glass. I guessed that was the one Ingersoll and his team had used to send the THROWERS in before they accessed the apartment.

I turned to one of the ERT guys. "I want to know if

any of these photos are online anywhere. And all those locations, we need to know where they are and when the photos were taken."

"When? How are we going to tell that?"

"Sunlight. Shadows. Do what you can."

"Why does it matter when they were taken?"

"Because you can't be in two places at once. He might not be working alone." I punched my finger against the photo with the 669 address on it. "And I want to know where this is taken. Every 669 address in the country."

"That's going to take us a while to scan and check."

"Then we better get started."

Ralph and I spent the better part of the evening with the Evidence Response Team at Mason's apartment, analyzing the photos. While we were there we received updates on the case:

(1) There was no evidence that any other pieces of art at the Mint Museum were marred or damaged in any way.

(2) The analysis of the NCAVC staff's incoming and outgoing calls was finished. Nothing really jumped out at me. Nothing suspicious. Mostly relatives calling in, as Lien-hua had done, presumably to see if their loved ones were safe.

(3) Handwriting analysis of the writing in the column of the book and on the back of the painting was inconclusive. The samples could have been written by the same person or two people. At this point there was no way to tell.

(4) Voss's people confirmed that Mason's DNA was in the van he'd driven for NVDS.

A few minutes after hearing about the DNA, an officer delivered a new phone to me, a standard-issue Glock 22, keys to a Field Office car, and a new Mini Maglite.

Well, Voss really did aim to please.

The Glock was a dependable, sensible gun, but I knew I was going to miss that SIG. We've been through a lot together over the years. Even if they could recover it from the bottom of that mine shaft, it would certainly be damaged beyond repair.

I made arrangements to return the phone I'd borrowed earlier from the officer at the textile warehouse. Then, even though it was after hours, Ralph and I met with the team at the Field Office to regroup and finish up some paperwork.

We patched into a video call with Gonzalez and he gave us the details on the Semtex that had been stolen.

It was being shipped from Tallulah, Louisiana, a twelve-hour drive to Fort Bragg. The transport had stopped twice: first in Birmingham, Alabama, and then in Augusta, Georgia, to refuel.

The transfer papers appeared to have been in order when the drivers left the processing facility. We checked the video footage of businesses and gas stations in both areas where they'd stopped and caught sight of Mason's white van near the Augusta gas station. Agents were looking into how anyone would have known when the transport would pull over there, but it might have been as easy as intercepting a radio transmission.

At least now, little by little, we were untangling the threads of the case. Mason's path through time and space was becoming evident.

*Unless that was a partner there.*

I wasn't ready to disregard the possibility that he might have someone working for or with him.

After we'd wrapped things up with Gonzalez and finished our reports, Ralph and I left for the hotel.

It was already starting to get dark when I called Lien-hua.

"Hey, Pat. I'm driving. What's up?"

"You're not home yet?"

"On my way. Maybe ten minutes out. Why?"

"I just . . . I don't know. I wanted you to know I love you."

"Is something wrong?"

"No." I realized that I said it a little too quickly. "It's . . . just all of this. It's got me thinking about how thankful I am to have you—both you and Tessa—in my life."

*And how I don't deserve you. How I've kept secrets from you to protect you, secrets about how the darkness calls to me. A double life.*

"Yes." She sounded distracted but not curt. "I'm thankful too. Listen, I'm in traffic. Can we . . ."

"Yeah, of course. I'll talk to you later."

++++

FBI Director Wellington was at her home on the out-skirts of Washington, DC, trying to relax with a cup of tea, but it wasn't working.

It wasn't just the case that was on her mind, it was how information regarding it was being released to the press and how that was affecting the investigation.

She reviewed what she knew: Earlier this week some-one had leaked details of the attack at the NCAVC build-ing to the press. And now, today, it'd happened again when Agent Bowers's name was released as being the one who'd tried to stop Kurt Mason when he killed Corrine Davis in the shaft.

There weren't too many people who had the information in both cases prior to its official release to the press. In fact, only five came to mind: Bowers, Ralph Hawkins, Brandon Ingersoll, René Gonzalez, and Pierce Jennings, the National Security Council representative.

She knew and trusted Hawkins, Ingersoll, and Gonzalez. Bowers annoyed her sometimes, but he was principled and hated working with the press. He wouldn't have leaked anything to them.

Kurt Mason liked to get his stories out there to the world, so it was always possible he had shared the news himself. But Margaret had her doubts that it was him.

Right now, Jennings seemed like the most likely candidate.

However, before she could confront him or before telling anyone else about her suspicions, she needed more information.

With this case on her plate and with Mason still missing, she was already planning on working all day in her office tomorrow, even though it was a Saturday.

So, as she sipped her now-cold tea, she decided that while she was there she would find out as much as she could about Mr. Pierce Jennings.

# 54

"I know the story," Beck said.

Tessa looked at him curiously. "What story?"

"About what happened to you last spring. About when Richard Basque attacked you."

She was quiet.

The two of them were alone in the living room. At eight o'clock he'd taken over for his partner. With all that was going on, Lien-hua had still not made it home from work. Tessa had invited Beck inside. He'd accepted the invitation and they'd been in here talking since then.

"You were brave," he said. "You fought him off."

"I wouldn't say I exactly fought him off. He locked me in the back of a police car and then ran off the side of the road into the Potomac. I basically drowned. If it hadn't been for my dad getting there when he did, I wouldn't even be alive."

"He's pretty legendary at the Academy. Your dad is. You know that, right?"

"I . . . I mean . . . I guess. Since you graduated in January I guess you never had him?"

"Just missed him."

After a brief pause she said, "So, you know my story. What's yours?"

"My story?"

"What did you do before going to the Academy? Where did you grow up? What was it for you—sports or video games? Did you ever have to fight off any serial killers?"

But she was thinking, *Do you have a girlfriend? What kind of women do you like to date?*

She didn't say that. Didn't dare.

He was slow in responding.

Yes, they were moving into personal territory now.

She didn't know if he would reply or not.

He did.

"Well, I grew up in a small town in Illinois. My parents had a dairy farm. For me it was sports—basketball mainly. Never got into video games too much. Never met up with any serial killers. I studied criminology and political science in college."

"That's what I'm going into—well, close. Criminal science."

"Really?"

"Yeah. Starting in a couple weeks—University of Maryland, College Park. Why did you join the FBI?"

"When I was a boy I always liked reading mysteries and spy novels. I wished I were a part of them, that I could step into them, you know? I guess this is the closest I could get to living all that out."

"Huh. Ever dream of spending your life filling out paperwork?"

"And, see, that is a point well-taken."

Silence, but it didn't seem awkward like it had earlier in the day when it'd settled between them during their conversation.

"I'm gonna grab a smoke." She gestured toward the door. "Wanna join me?"

"I'll come with you, but I don't smoke."

"Yeah, I know, I shouldn't either. It's just one of those things. It's like I get stressed and, well, I have these self-destructive tendencies. I was into self-inflicting for a while."

They passed outside into the deepening twilight. "Self-inflicting?"

She pulled up her sleeve to show him her scars. "Cutting." She tugged the sleeve back down. "You should feel privileged. I don't show too many people my scars."

"I do."

"You do?"

"Feel privileged."

"Right."

She shook out a cigarette, but then on second thought she realized it might turn him off and that was the last thing she wanted to do, so she slid it back in and put the pack away. A neighbor must have mowed recently because she could smell the freshly cut grass.

The sound of crickets was alive in the deepening shadows of the neighborhood.

Beck stood beside her on the lawn.

"Let's try something," she said. "Sometimes, when I'm making up a poem, I'll kind of brainstorm one line after another, like I'm having a conversation with myself. Only this time, I want you to be the other part of the conversation. So I start a line, then you add one, and I go after that."

"Oh. I don't know. I'm not very creative."

"Just try."

"I'm not really—"

She touched his arm lightly. It wasn't on purpose, it just happened. "Humor me."

She lowered her hand.

He didn't step back. "Okay."

"I'll start."

"So, I'm just supposed to . . . ?"

"Follow up on what I say. We'll do it on scars. You'll be fine. Just say what comes to mind."

She thought for a moment. "I have this dreadful scar on my heart from the wound of my friend."

He took his time answering. "And I have this terrible scar on my soul from the wound of my enemy."

"I believe mine will heal faster," she said, "because it is from a friend."

"And I believe mine will heal faster," he replied, "because it is not so deep."

"Where does the truth lie?" she said.

*Oh, man. Do not look into his eyes. Do not . . .*

But she did.

She shouldn't have, but she did.

*Where does the truth lie?*

Scars.

So many scars that needed healing.

He might have looked away. He might have averted eye contact, but he didn't.

Time hesitated, wrapped them in its arms. Everything was about to pass. Everything was about to be lost.

She took a small step toward him through the dusk-damp grass. She was lost in his eyes. "I think I came up with it."

"Came up with what?"

"The superpower I wish I had."

"And what's that?"

"To not be invisible."

"To not be invisible?"

*To you,* she thought.

"To you," she said.

Then Tessa leaned up on her toes.

And she kissed him.

# 55

Beck kissed her back. She could feel her heart racing in her chest, running wild, wild, wild, like a colt that had been penned in for far too long and had now, finally, finally been set free.

But the kiss lasted only a few seconds and then Beck was placing his hand gently on her shoulders and easing away from her. "Tessa, I'm . . . I can't do this."

A car turned onto the street.

"I'm not too young," she said. "I'm almost nineteen."

"It's not that. Um, I'm . . . I'm sorry."

"There's someone else—is that it? You're not . . . You're not married, are you?"

The car slowed.

He let go of Tessa's shoulder. "No, no, it's . . ."

"Okay, so you're supposed to be protecting me. Does that mean you can't feel anything toward me?"

It was Lien-hua.

She pulled into the driveway.

"I should probably go."

"Okay, I shouldn't have kissed you," Tessa said, trying to recover, trying to salvage things. "I guess I was . . . I thought you wanted me to. I just thought we were—"

Lien-hua stepped out of the car. "Hey."

"Hey," said Tessa.

"Hey," said Beck.

Lien-hua's gaze went from Tessa to Beck, then back to Tessa. "Everything good?"

"Yes," Beck answered. "Did you need me to stay outside, or . . . ?"

"We should be fine. Thanks." Lien-hua was still looking at Tessa. Perceptively. So perceptively. "I'll contact you in the morning about my schedule," she told him.

*She knows something's up.*

"Okay. Great . . . Well, good night, then." Beck glanced somewhat uneasily in Tessa's direction. "Good night, Miss Ellis," he said to her.

"Good night, Agent Danner." Her words were thick and distant and felt heavy in her throat.

Without looking back, he went to his car, slipped inside.

Started down the street.

Carrying her computer bag, Lien-hua walked toward Tessa. "Did I disturb something?" There wasn't judgment in her voice, but still, Tessa didn't want to answer her.

"No, it's . . ."

*Tell her.*

*No, don't! You shouldn't have kissed him. It's your fault.*

"Are you okay?" Lien-hua asked.

"Yeah."

*No!*

"Um," Tessa said, "I'm gonna go get ready for bed. Cool?"

Lien-hua glanced at her watch as if to say, "Isn't it a little early for that?" But she didn't comment about the time. "Of course."

She was right beside Tessa now and before Tessa could

leave she laid a hand lightly on her forearm. "Are you sure you're alright?"

"I'm . . ."

*Don't cry, Tessa. Do not cry.*

She turned away before Lien-hua could see the tear forming in her eye. Hastily, she made her way through the living room and then escaped down the hallway to her bedroom, where she covered her eyes and dropped to the bed and made sure she stifled her tears enough so she wouldn't attract her mom's attention.

# 56

Back at the hotel, Ralph stepped outside to call Brineesha to see if she'd started having any contractions yet.

While I was alone in the room, I stared at the toy helicopter I'd salvaged from the dirt at the base of the playground this morning during my jog.

That run seemed so long ago.

I thought again of not arriving until too late to find that boy in Wisconsin, before that man who kidnapped him had stolen his innocence from him.

A lost childhood.

A shattered life.

*And you were too slow today too.*

*Too slow to save Corrine.*

Over and over I replayed that moment when Mason jerked her backward into the shaft. I kept wondering if there was something more I could have done.

I crossed the room and picked up the helicopter.

The other day Lien-hua had asked me about pain, about what haunts me the most, and I'd said it was the pain I wasn't able to stop.

*Like today.*

*With Corrine.*

And like on Monday when I couldn't stop Stu from bleeding to death.

I spun and threw the helicopter against the wall.

The toy shattered, spraying shards of splintered plastic across the carpet. And there, right before me, they became lives, shattered lives, just like that little boy's, now strewn across Kurt Mason's path as he moved forward with his plan, the one that he'd told me would have its climax tomorrow night.

The hotel room door opened up and Ralph came in. He saw me standing there with the broken plastic parts lying on the floor in front of me.

"It didn't help, did it?" he said quietly.

"No. It didn't."

He closed the door behind him.

"Listen, I don't know if this is the best time to bring this up, but I just had an interesting talk with Brin. She started having contractions, but she hasn't gone to the hospital yet. She'd rather stay at the house as long as she can."

"So it may be a while?"

"Could be. Or it could be quick—a couple hours. Really, it's different for every woman. But either way it looks like I'm being called back home."

He pulled out his laptop and went online to check flight times, and a few minutes later announced, "So, there's a flight to Dulles at nine fifty-nine and a ten fifteen to National."

It was already nearly nine thirty. "That's not going to happen, Ralph."

"Yeah. Let me check for the morning."

He tapped at the keys. "Alright, we're looking at a seven fifteen to National or an eight twenty-two to Dulles. Let me see if there's room on either of them. I think I'll call 'em—maybe they won't charge us full fare because of the circumstances with the baby on her way. Save the Bureau a few bucks."

We'd flown out of Dulles and his car was there in long-term parking, but if he flew into National he could always make arrangements to have someone pick him up.

He switched from his computer to his phone.

It took a little while before he was able to speak to an actual person. Finally, I heard him asking if that was really the earliest flight they had room on; then he was giving his credit-card information to the person on the other end of the line and confirming his aisle seat on the eight twenty-two flight.

End call.

"I gotta head back, man," he told me. "For Brin."

"Ralph, you don't have to explain anything to me. Believe me, I understand."

"Yeah." He sighed. "Maybe I'm just saying it for my-self."

"Look, when you get some free time in the next couple days—I mean when Brin and the baby are sleeping—you can always work on the case from there in DC on your laptop, or you can make some calls, help coordinate things."

He seemed lost in his thoughts.

"What time do you need to be at the airport?" I asked.

"Well, I don't have any bags to check, just carry-on. I'd say as long as I'm there an hour or so before the flight we should be good."

One of the advantages of being an FBI agent: You can get through security without having to wait in long lines.

"Okay," I said. "We'll leave here at seven just to be on the safe side."

# 57

Louisville, Kentucky

Richard Devin Basque was hunting when he heard the news about his sister.

For the last two months he had restrained himself from acting on his urges. He'd been out to meet women, yes, had even brought a few home with him—yes, he had. But ever since the night Patrick had shot him, Richard had not killed anyone, not eaten anyone, not even forced anyone to come back to his place against her will.

He'd heard about a magician who'd died from cobra venom while trying an elaborate escape in the Philippines last winter and it had made him curious. Consequently, he'd become interested in cobra venom—it was surprising how easy it was to acquire.

Monocled cobra venom and ten vials of antivenom.

Ordered online.

Who would have thought?

But he hadn't used it on anyone yet. It would have made it impossible to eat them afterward.

It was true that he'd been bold in his visit to the Supermax facility in Colorado to help free a prisoner there, and he'd needed cosmetic work done on his teeth since Patrick had shattered some of them when they fought in April, but other than that he'd made sure he didn't leave any tracks that Bowers or his team would be able to pick up.

Now he was at a roadside bar twenty minutes from the place he was staying.

He wasn't sure if he was going to kill the woman he was sitting next to—the woman who'd told him her name was Tiffany—and he wasn't sure if he was going to eat her.

He really didn't know. Maybe it was time to end his streak.

Hunting.

Predator and prey.

He bought her another drink.

Richard was in his early forties but looked a decade younger, with stunning aquamarine eyes that he had learned to use to his advantage. He had some scars from an encounter with a young woman who'd lit his hair on fire, but they only served to make him look more rugged and stalwart. Picking up women had never been a problem for him. Sometimes he chose a disguise. Tonight he had not.

The place was veritably empty: only the bartender, Richard, and the woman.

Prey.

A television mounted on the wall behind the bartender was broadcasting some highlights from a baseball game earlier that night.

"And then . . ." Tiffany was telling Richard a story about how she got her apartment, "I was, like, are you serious? Seven hundred fifty dollars a month? That's it? I'm telling you, you should see the place."

"I'd like to."

She laughed lightly at that. "Maybe I'll let you come over and take a peek." As she reached for her drink she brushed her arm against his. "That is, if you have a little time to kill."

The irony of what she'd said was not lost on him. "Actually, I do have a little time to kill."

Playing things right, he might have taken her hand in his, but that's when it happened.

The sports show went to commercial and the bartender tapped at the remote, surfing through the channels: sitcom reruns, more commercials, news, another game somewhere, some sort of science fiction movie with exploding space ships and—

*Hang on.*

"Hey," Richard said to the bartender. "Flip back a minute. Please."

The guy, early twenties, disinterested, reversed order and paused at the game.

"Keep going."

One more channel—the news.

"Yes. There."

The bartender set down the remote and started absently drying some glasses that didn't need to be dried.

CNN was covering a developing story about a woman who had been killed that afternoon in Charlotte, North Carolina.

But people get killed every day and don't make it onto the news.

This woman, however, was special, memorable, newsworthy. Because of who she was related to.

She was the sister of one of the most wanted men in the country.

Apparently, she'd been missing for the past couple of days.

Richard didn't watch the news much. He hadn't heard. He just—

Her name was Corrine Davis.

His sister.

And they were saying that she was dead, but that couldn't be right.

No, she couldn't be dead. They had to have the wrong person. She was okay.

Corrine was fine.

But then, they were reporting that Kurt Mason had killed her, that he was the leading suspect in an explosion earlier in the week that'd taken the lives of five FBI agents, and that he was also the prime suspect in a related homicide of an agent at his home in the DC area.

Kurt Mason was the man Richard had helped escape from prison. Richard had posed as his lawyer and smuggled the Mikrosil in to him, gotten him the paper clip he'd used to pick the lock on his cuffs.

They'd been in touch twice since that day and Richard knew of Kurt's plan for this weekend.

But nothing had ever come up regarding his sister.

*She's not dead. No. She can't be.*

"What are you . . . ?" Tiffany's voice was stark and strained with concern. "Are you okay?"

He looked at her, then down to where she was staring, at his hand. He'd crushed the beer glass he was holding and the shards were digging into his palm. Beer had splattered across the bar and onto his pants and blood was seeping out around the jagged glass that was embedded in his flesh, but it all seemed so unreal. He hadn't even noticed.

Beer. Blood. Glass in his palms.

*She's dead?*

*Not Corrine.*

*She can't be.*

Patrick Bowers's name came up on the broadcast. That was not entirely surprising, but it was informative.

Richard noticed the bartender peering at him with concern, but also with a hint of admiration. "I've never seen anyone . . . Dude. That's sick."

He handed over the towel he'd been using and Richard wrapped it around his hand.

Tiffany just stared at him. "Are you alright?"

"Yes." His attention was on the television screen, and now he watched as his own face came up—the most recent photo the FBI had of him, taken in April after Patrick had apprehended him at his home an hour outside of Washington, DC. It was the photo that'd been taken right before he escaped from FBI custody.

*Your sister is dead, Richard.*

*Corrine is dead.*

"Randy?" The woman was waving her hand in front of his face, using the name he'd given her. "Are you sure you're . . ."

But then her gaze shifted past him to the television screen.

His picture was still up there.

It took only a moment for recognition to light up in her eyes, and when the bartender saw her staring at the screen, he glanced up there too, then at Richard.

His hand snuck beneath the bar.

Richard stood.

"Hey, buddy," the guy said. "Hang on a sec."

Richard was turning toward the door when the bartender whipped out a shotgun that'd been hidden under the bar. "I said hang on. That's you, isn't it?"

Richard stopped and faced him. "You don't want to do this."

"There's a reward, isn't there?" He was pointing the barrel directly at Richard's chest. Less than ten feet separated them. "I'm guessing there's a reward."

Tiffany was still seated but looked dismayed, confused, overwhelmed.

Afraid.

Richard unwrapped the towel and laid it on the bar. He pried a large piece of glass loose from his palm, licked the blood off it, then set it on the towel.

Both the bartender and the woman watched him in dead silence.

"I'm going to walk out of here now." He pulled another piece of glass loose. "Don't try to stop me."

And another.

Licked the blood off them both.

"Call the police if you want," he said, "but I would suggest you don't try to follow me."

When the bartender spoke he seemed intimidated, even though he was the one who was armed. "I have a gun."

"Yes," Richard said simply, then he turned to go.

*Corrine is dead.*

*Mason did this.*

The bartender called out once for him to come back, but his voice cracked as he did. Richard walked out the front door to his car.

Every FBI agent and police officer in the state of North Carolina was going to be looking for Kurt Mason and, even knowing what Richard did about him and about what he had planned, it wasn't going to be easy to track him down before the authorities did.

Charlotte.

From here it would be at least a seven-hour drive.

No, Richard hadn't killed anyone, hadn't eaten anyone since April.

But that was about to change.

As soon as he found the man who had murdered his sister.

# 58

Kurt Mason, dressed in black jeans and a black turtleneck in order to blend in with the night, eased out of the underbrush near the tracks where M343 was going to come through tomorrow afternoon on its way from Spartanburg to High Point.

He made sure he remained in the shadows.

The stadium loomed above him on his left, and ahead of him the I-277 overpass spanned the tracks.

Tomorrow that overpass would crumble when the concrete foundations supporting it gave way.

Explosives on the tracks would have been far too easy to detect. Instead there was a pressurized sensor that would send the radio signal to the detonator located in the capped-off mine underground nearby.

He'd thought about using Astrolite. The idea of using a liquid explosive that could be sprayed onto the ground and was nearly undetectable was attractive to him, but he eventually abandoned the idea when he realized how hard it was going to be to obtain the material.

Semtex was much more available. Just like C-4, which he'd used before, it was relatively easy to mold, safe to transport, and surprisingly available if you knew where to look.

Kurt had consulted the *U.S. Army Special Forces Handbook* that he'd found on the Internet. The book wasn't as detailed as FM 3-34.214, the Army's *Explosives and Demolitions* manual, but it did include a helpful chapter on rail cuts and derailing trains.

Using the information from the two publications, and taking into consideration the location and layout of the mines, he'd figured out what he considered to be the most effective placement for the Semtex.

The railroads transported nearly two million bulk shipments of hazardous materials every year. More than seventy percent of hazardous materials shipped in North America were shipped by rail. Some trains were made up almost entirely of hazmat cars. They went through our cities unnoticed.

Until, of course, a spill occurred.

A six-axle locomotive weighed about two hundred tons and most loaded tank cars only weighed about a hundred-thirty tons. And there was also a mandate that when a line was transporting hazardous material, there had to be five buffer cars between loaded hazmat cars and the closest engine.

Kurt had taken all that into consideration when placing the sensors in the ballast under the tracks.

There were three engines on M343, and when the lead engine hit the pressurized sensors it would trigger the mechanism and, based on the speed the train would be going at this point in its route, the Semtex that was in the mine shafts that ran alongside and underneath the railroad bed would blow just as the anhydrous ammonia tanker cars passed.

As the shafts and tunnels that interlaced a stretch of ground as large as a city block collapsed, the entire area would fragment, and when those tanker cars full of anhydrous ammonia ruptured, the vapor cloud would be enormous.

It would fill the open air stadium and, with the overpass taken out in the explosion, the authorities wouldn't be able to evacuate the area quickly enough to save the people inside.

The real-life application of National Institute for Occupational Safety and Health, or NIOSH, limits: inhale 150 parts per million of anhydrous ammonia, you'll experience irritation in the eyes and throat. At 300 ppm there's immediate danger to a person's health. The more concentration you have, the more discomfort you'll have until, as you approach 1,000 ppm, victims' eyes will swell shut and they'll struggle for breath. Bronchial spasms start at 1,500 ppm, and at 5,000 ppm, pulmonary edema will cause death within minutes.

The tank cars could each hold 35,000 gallons, but to account for heat expansion they were usually filled to about 85 percent so there would be a vapor space above the liquid.

But still, Kurt was looking at potentially releasing more than three hundred thousand gallons of liquefied, compressed anhydrous ammonia into Uptown Charlotte.

In the stadium, there would be mass panic as people became blinded and tried to breathe but choked on the vapor. Depending on the turnout for Fan Celebration Day and the wind and weather conditions, tens of thousands of people might be inhaling 4000-5000 ppm.

But it'd never been about a big body count to him. However many people died, one or ten thousand, it'd always been about the bigger story that was being told.

It all had to do with those four statues at Independence Square.

Now, Kurt used the handheld sensor to check the transmission signal and dialed the timer to 3:15 p.m. so the next engine after that to cross the track would set off the detonators. No trains other than M343 were scheduled to cross that section of track between 2:30 and 5:00 p.m.

It only took a few minutes to verify the readings.

Yes.

It was set.

All was in place.

Tomorrow afternoon the train would come through, right around the time of the scrimmage game's kickoff. The track would blow. And the story would move on from there to its final act.

# PART IV

## M343

# 59

Saturday, August 3
7:30 a.m.
8 hours until kickoff

I pulled up to the curb in front of the check-in and ticketing counters for American Airlines. For some reason, traffic was heavy and it had held us up a little, but it looked like Ralph would still be good for his flight.

As we exited the car to get his suitcase from the trunk, he got word that Brin was having regular contractions and had started to have a little bleeding. "So you're at the hospital?" he said. "Four centimeters? Why didn't you call earlier?"

"Did you have a flight earlier?" I overheard her say matter-of-factly.

"No."

"Then what good would it have done?"

He looked a little annoyed but had no response to that and instead did an end run around her question. "Okay, so Lien-hua drove you there—is she staying with you?" This time I didn't hear Brin's response, but he said, "Good. I'll be there in a couple hours."

Ending the call, he grabbed his things and said to me,

"We'll keep each other informed. I'll fill you in about our baby. You call me about the case."

"I will."

Without another word he was off.

I hadn't had a really good cup of coffee since we arrived in Charlotte, and this morning's briefing at the Field Office wasn't until eight thirty, so I checked my phone to see if there were any coffee roasters with coffee shops that were open this early.

One came up. It was in a part of town called NoDa, which an online search told me referred to North of Davidson—a little like SoHo in New York City, which refers to South of Houston. Apparently NoDa was a hip, artsy part of Charlotte.

Perfect.

I plugged in the address and took off.

And even though the team wouldn't be meeting for almost an hour, my thoughts were already back on the case. The whole way to NoDa, I was contemplating what "seven gods use thirty-eight" could possibly mean.

++++

Tessa rounded up some breakfast long before she wanted to, especially on a Saturday.

About forty-five minutes ago Lien-hua had left to take Brineesha to the hospital.

Sitting around a hospital waiting room for what might have ended up being all day was not really ideal for a twelve-year-old boy, so Tony Hawkins was going to spend the day at a friend's house.

The guy's dad was a cop who had the day off, so everyone was cool with the arrangement. After the baby was born and Brineesha was feeling better, he would bring Tony over to meet his little sister.

Right now, Ralph was on his way back to DC, Agent Priscilla Woods was outside the house, and Tessa was torn. On the one hand she was excited about the baby—especially considering the story of her own birth—but she was also distracted by her thoughts about Beck.

She had kissed him.

Yes, she'd read things that way, had gotten the vibe that he wanted her to, and she'd gone ahead, and ended up ruining everything.

Turning him off.

Making him back away.

Usually she waited for guys to make the first move, but last night she'd decided to go for it and that had ended up completely backfiring.

And things were even more confusing now, because right before Lien-hua had left she'd said, "He's cute."

"Who?" Without any context, Tessa really had no idea who her mom was talking about.

"Beck. He's cute. And he can't be that much older than you, is he?"

"He's twenty-four."

"Twenty-four?"

"Yeah."

"You asked him?"

"Yeah."

"So, mid-twenties, which in Patrick's eyes would be way too old for you."

"Pretty much."

A moment passed.

"I got a call from him this morning—Beck, I mean," Lien-hua said. "He asked to be reassigned."

"Oh. Well, I'm not super surprised."

But then Lien-hua went on, "I'm just telling you because now his cell number is on my phone." Then she set her phone on the table. "I need to grab my purse from the other room. I'll be right back."

And she left Tessa alone.

With the phone right in front of her.

Lien-hua was familiar with Tessa's history with guys, how hard it'd been for her to find one who was both cool *and* was someone she could connect with—Lien-hua also knew how badly things usually turned out.

Lien-hua had done all the stuff her real mom would have done: encouraging her, hanging out with her, even taking her prom-dress shopping. Of course, prom ended up being a complete disaster when Tessa found a text message on her date's phone from his supposedly ex-girlfriend about them hooking up after the dance. But Lien-hua had even been around to listen to her deal with that.

Though her friend Melody had done her best to set her up with a couple guys since then, Tessa hadn't dated anyone all summer.

Maybe, officially, Lien-hua shouldn't have been doing anything to help her get together with an agent assigned to watch her, but she undoubtedly knew this assignment was short-term and that after it was done there really wasn't any reason the two of them couldn't get together.

Except age, maybe.

But Lien-hua was three years younger than Patrick and, as far as Tessa could tell, had never looked at age differences as that big of a deal for relationships.

So, when Lien-hua stepped away, Tessa had done it—she'd looked up Beck's number on her mom's phone.

Then Lien-hua returned. "Well, I better get going."

"Sure."

She had a slight smile as she retrieved her phone. Then she'd left to take Brineesha to the hospital.

CHECKMATE                        359

Now Tessa had Beck's number, but she wasn't sure where to take things from here.

Should she contact him or not?

Well, either way, whatever she decided to do, she wasn't about to text him at this time of day on a Saturday.

So now she was at home, alone.

That is, if you didn't count Agent Woods in the sedan across the street.

Tessa was planning on visiting the hospital in a couple of hours to see how Brineesha was doing and also to talk to her about the baby, about how glad she was that she was having it.

Personal reasons.

It was important to tell her, and she just hadn't really taken the opportunity yet.

*Better late than never.*

She needed to figure out the best way to move into that conversation.

Until then, she settled down at the table with an orange, a sliced apple, and the last piece of chocolate cake and tried to get up enough nerve to contact the cute twenty-four-year-old FBI agent whose phone number she now had.

++++

Richard Basque snapped his eyes open just in time to avoid colliding with the car to his left. The driver was hitting his horn and flipping him off.

Richard had driven through the night and now found himself bleary, unfocused.

But at least he'd made it here to Charlotte, North Carolina, safely.

Barely, maybe, but he had.

He exited the highway toward the warehouse that contained the mine shaft where his sister had died.

He wanted to see the location for himself. However, he knew it would've been foolish to show his face in public or stand on the edge of the police tape near the cable news vans, so instead he drove down one of the neighboring streets.

Throughout the night he'd monitored the news using his phone and the radio. From what they were saying, the FBI hadn't yet been able to recover Corrine's body from the mine shaft. The Feds were apparently wary that Mason had left explosives down there, and based on what Richard knew about him, that seemed like a very real possibility.

He parked halfway down the next block.

Though he tried to convince himself that Corrine was in a better place, he wasn't sure what to believe about the afterlife.

In order to get sympathy during his retrial, he'd claimed to have found religion in prison. He'd had to do a lot of Bible reading to make things plausible, and it had informed him but had not, in the end, changed him.

Regardless of whether heaven existed, as he sat in the car now, he took this opportunity to say good-bye to his sister. Maybe she could hear him in some way, maybe she couldn't, but in either case nothing was lost by the gesture.

"I love you," he whispered. "I always have."

And he might have been imagining it. He probably was. Maybe it was from lack of sleep, but he thought he heard the words "I know" echo somewhere deep inside of him.

Though his pulse was still racing from his near miss in traffic, he yawned. He needed to find Mason, but he needed to be alert to do that, and right now he was not.

He'd been up for nearly twenty-seven hours straight, and as much as he wanted to start looking for Mason, he figured he'd better clear his head and rest a little first.

Richard drove to a park, found a spot in the shade, shut off the car, locked the doors, tilted the seat back, and closed his eyes.

# 60

The cup of coffee had really hit the spot.

In fact, I'd also taken a cup to go and had it here with me now in the conference room of the Field Office.

Ingersoll and Voss were here, as well as half a dozen agents who were working the case.

I started by telling them about Ralph flying home for the birth of his daughter, then we turned our attention to the search for Kurt Mason. I shared all that I knew about him from apprehending him last summer.

"And he escaped from prison with the help of Richard Basque?" Voss asked.

"Yes. The surveillance video at the prison confirmed it."

"If it was confirmed, why didn't the guards stop it?"

"It was only later that they identified him. He played himself off as Mason's lawyer. He snuck in the materials Mason needed to escape."

"And now Mason went after Basque's sister? Killed her?"

"That's right."

"Does that make any sense to you?"

"No."

"Let's ask Mason why he did it when we find him," Ingersoll said.

"I'm good with that," I replied.

*Unless we take him down first.*

An outcome I was not exactly opposed to.

I finished my coffee while Ingersoll gave us an update on the HRT's analysis of the mine shaft. "According to our calculations, the one Corrine was killed in is three hundred and fifty feet deep. I'm still not comfortable sending my men down there. We need to find out more about the tunnel network and structural integrity first."

We spent several minutes discussing how to do that.

Then, during a video conference with Gonzalez, we laid out our plan for the day.

Ingersoll and his team would be using ground-penetrating radar that was being delivered from a mining company in West Virginia to try to map out the tunnels.

Voss's agents would keep searching the city for the Buick LeSabre, following up on tips, interviewing people who had known "Danny Everhart," and piecing together a timeline of his movements over the last month to see if that might lead us to anything specific regarding Mason's current whereabouts.

We also had agents investigating myths and folklore, especially from the Catawba and Cherokee tribes, that might be related to seven gods.

After finishing up with Gonzalez, we phoned Guido and put him on the line for a conference call.

He'd located a UNC Charlotte professor who supposedly knew more than anyone else in the area about the gold mines. I wondered briefly why his name hadn't come up earlier, but apparently the guy had been out of town speaking at a nanotechnology conference. He was driving back this morning and would be available to meet with someone from our team at the campus library at ten.

It seemed like a promising avenue of investigation, so I volunteered to go.

"A nanotechnology professor who's an expert on the gold mines?" Voss said skeptically.

"He has varied interests," Guido answered. "He's also a member of the Charlotte Historical Society and is on the board at the Mint Museum. His name's O'Brien."

Frankly, if he could help us, I didn't care what department he taught in—nanotechnology, scuba diving, or candle making.

We finished the call, wrapped up the briefing, and then it was time for me to leave to meet with Professor O'Brien.

# 61

On the way to the UNC Charlotte campus, I phoned Lien-hua to find out how Brin was doing.

"She's fine; I'm in the room with her now. There's not much happening and from what they're saying, it could be a while. I've got my laptop with me. I was studying Mason's history. He's the real deal, isn't he?"

"Yes, he is."

Although I'd told her about Mason when I tracked him down last year, Lien-hua and I had been going through a rocky patch in our relationship and had broken things off for a short time, so she wasn't intimately familiar with his case.

She said, "From what I've read about him, it's always about the story he's telling. He sees himself as the author."

"Yes. Of stories about tragedy and death."

"And lovers. It's more than just about death—it's about the tragic consequences of love."

She was the profiler, I was not. And though I'm not a

big believer in her approach, I had learned to trust her insights and acumen, so I just went ahead and asked her the question that had come up during our briefing. "Can you think of any reason why Mason would have gone after Corrine like that? What's he trying to do?"

"Maybe he's trying to find Richard."

"What do you mean?"

"You mentioned it yourself yesterday: Corrine is the only person Richard ever loved. Maybe Mason went after her to draw Richard out. And based on what you said he told you in the mine, he was hoping Richard would be coming."

"That is true."

On one level it made sense, but why anyone would want to provoke Richard Basque like that was beyond me. Especially when you knew what he was capable of and that he would come after you.

She continued, "We don't know why Basque helped him escape from prison, but from what I can see from reading Mason's case files, he's not random and he's not petty. It's not revenge and it's not just publicity— although he does want his story known. There's something big on the horizon."

"I agree with you there. He mentioned a climax occurring tonight."

"Everything is significant and this 'seven gods use thirty-eight' thing is at the heart of it."

"Yes, but we still have no idea what that means. Angela and Lacey pull up anything?"

"No," she said. "Not yet."

The conversation pooled off as we both sorted through where things were at. Finally, I broke the silence. "Say hi to Brin for me. I have a meeting at ten with a prof at the university here who might be able to help shed some light on this mine system Mason was using."

"Great. I'll talk to you soon."

++++

Kurt Mason stepped outside the Fourth Ward home where he was staying.

The day looked like it was shaping up to be a hot one. Humidity was down, which worked in his favor.

Streaks of high, shredded clouds were scudding across the sky like they were in a hurry and had somewhere important to be. He was hoping that as the day wore on there would be a breeze down here in the city too.

A northeasterly one, ideally.

With the size of the vapor cloud, even a little breeze would carry it a quarter of a mile—which was all he really needed.

The train yard where M343 would be departing from was an hour and fifteen minutes by car. The train wasn't scheduled to leave there until two thirty-five, which gave Kurt more than enough time to get over there now, disable the air brakes on the two tankers that he had in mind, and return here to the house to be present when everything went down this afternoon at the stadium.

When a train sits in the yard, its air brakes are engaged so it won't roll, but Kurt had found a way to override that and still leave the train stationary and pass the engineer's and conductor's on-site inspection.

He went inside to get the things he would need to close the angle cocks of those two train cars.

++++

Richard Basque woke up.

He wasn't sure where Kurt Mason might be hiding,

but he did know one thing that the FBI did not: the alias Mason was using.

According to the news reports, the Feds knew about "Danny Everhart," but there was no mention of this second identity. Getting the name out there to the public would have helped their search for him, so if they had it they would have released it.

For Corrine's sake, Richard wanted to take care of Mason, to make him suffer.

However, he understood that everything he had planned was not in the service of justice or of balancing the scales. After all, it was naive to think either of those two things was attainable.

Balancing the scales?

Really?

It's simply not going to happen.

How many true statements balance out one lie? How many kind words make up for one cruel one? How many kept promises balance out one betrayal? And those are the simple questions—what about making up for rape or murder? It's just not possible.

Richard was all too aware of this. After spending thirteen years in prison, a good portion of it in solitary confinement, he'd had plenty of time to think through issues of justice and morality.

As far as justice goes, an eye for an eye might help make the punishment fit the crime, and that might be as close as we can get to it in this life, but even that wouldn't erase the pain in the lives of the people affected, and no form of retribution would ever make the wrongs go away.

A life for a life doesn't bring back the dead.

Nope. There is no balancing the scales.

It just doesn't work that way.

Not in real life.

There would be no bringing back Corrine.

There would only be avenging her death.

It wasn't much, perhaps, but it was at least a step in the right direction.

Using the iPad he'd brought with him, Richard went online and began his search for the identity Kurt Mason had told him about in their last conversation three weeks ago.

If he couldn't find the information he needed, he knew one person in the city who could.

# 62

Tessa arrived at the hospital.

The parking was insane because a construction crew was setting up shop across the road from the parking lot. They were pouring concrete and fixing a patch of sidewalk that'd been jackhammered away. It looked like they also had some sort of water line they were working with.

After she found a spot and parked, she walked to the family birthing wing.

Since she anticipated being here most of the day, she'd brought along her journal and a couple of books to pass the time.

Agent Priscilla Woods had driven behind her to the hospital.

The woman seemed overly paranoid and uptight and it made Tessa a little uncomfortable. Agent Woods had been planning to come in with her, but Tessa asked her to call Lien-hua, who explained that she could leave.

So at least there was that.

Ralph's flight was supposed to be landing within the hour.

Although Tessa wasn't too excited to be at a hospital, at least the reason she was here was a good one.

The arrival of her friend's baby.

There wasn't a reception desk per se, just a nurses' station with three people working it. Hanging on the walls were paintings of baby animals—lambs, colts, puppies, and kittens. Tessa found it a little sophomoric, but whatever.

The nurses directed her to Brineesha's room, where she gave the door a slight tap and Brineesha called her in.

She pressed open the door.

Entered.

Inside the room: muted lights, soft pastels, a hospital bed for the mom, monitors, a bassinet for the baby, and a flat pull-out couch-thing that Tessa assumed was for the dad to rest on if he had to stay overnight. A television. A window.

Brineesha had an IV. She was propped up in bed, reading a Tosca Lee novel, and had a sheet pulled up to her waist. The pink hat she'd knitted for her baby was lying on the bedside counter, ready for the newborn.

Lien-hua liked flower arranging, and when Tessa saw the bouquet on the counter near the window, she figured it was probably Lien-hua's handiwork.

Lien-hua was seated at the far side of the room on one of the backless swivel chairs that the doctors and nurses use when sitting down to check their patients. She had her notebook computer balanced on her lap.

When Tessa saw Lien-hua, she couldn't help but think of what had happened earlier when she'd accidentally-on-purpose left her phone behind with Beck's cell number on it.

Tessa still wasn't sure what to make of all that.

"Hey," she said to the two of them.

"Hi, Tessa." Brineesha sounded a little uncomfortable, which made perfect sense. Lien-hua greeted her as well.

"So, how's it going?" Tessa asked Brineesha.

"Well"—she pointed to her stomach—"we're mostly just watching and waiting at this point. They keep asking if I want an epidural, but I'm trying to do this with . . ." She cringed. "As little . . . intervention as poss—"

She stopped midsentence and clenched her teeth, tightened her fists, and then drew in a deep breath and let it out slowly in short bursts.

"Okay," Tessa said. "That was enough right there to make me never want to have a baby."

"The end result makes it worth it." She was still cringing when she said that. "At least most of the time."

"In Tony's case?"

"Definitely worth it."

"I'll let him know you said that."

Brineesha offered her a faint smile. "Please do."

Tessa found a seat on the couch. It was stiff and uncomfortable and she was glad she wouldn't have to be the person who was forced to sleep overnight on it. "Did your water break yet?"

"No," Brineesha replied. "It's not like in the movies where your water breaks and then your contractions start—well, it can be. But it's more common for things to happen the other way around."

"Gotcha."

Being here really wasn't easy. It made her think of her real mom and her own birth and how it almost never happened.

# 63

Overall, the campus was pretty much deserted, but there were obviously some summer camps or programs running, because a group of students who looked younger than Tessa were walking in a clump between two buildings. Some of the kids were carrying band instruments.

Insects twittered at me from the blooming pink and white crape myrtle trees lining the sidewalks as I walked toward the library.

A student kick-coasted his way past me on a longboard.

Even though it wasn't quite ten yet, here on a summer Saturday, the doors to the library building were open and the woman at the front desk asked me, "Are you Agent Bowers?"

"Yes."

"Oh. Good. Professor O'Brien told me to let you know he'd meet you in the special collections area. Top floor."

In contrast to the rest of campus, which seemed to be recently built or renovated, the elevator was annoyingly old-school and slow, pausing and beeping at every floor.

When the doors finally opened, I found my way to the research room, where O'Brien was waiting for me.

I guess I was expecting an elderly, professorial man in a tweed jacket with patches on the elbows—something along those lines—but he was the opposite of an aging academic.

O'Brien appeared to be just a few years older than I was. He wore stylish glasses, with a black T-shirt and stone-washed jeans, and looked like he would fit in better in Silicon Valley than here as a scholarly professor in the South.

But, then again, he did teach nanotechnology.

"Agent Bowers?"

"Yes." He had a firm grip when I shook his hand. "It's a pleasure to meet you."

He'd emptied a box of historical documents onto the table and now swept his hand toward them. "I just got here a couple minutes ago and I haven't had a chance to look any of this over, but I found some papers that might at least get us moving in the right direction."

Though I wanted to get started, I gave in momentarily to my curiosity. "I have to ask—you teach nanotechnology and you're a history buff?"

"Interesting combo, huh? Both ends of the spectrum. And why here, right? And not somewhere like MIT?"

"The thought did cross my mind."

"This university used to be known for its architecture program, but we've been shifting focus toward emerging technologies—nanotechnology in particular. Most recently in the medical and law enforcement arenas."

"Nanotech in law enforcement?"

"My department has developed a way of injecting nanobots into the bloodstream. These can be used in the medical realm, of course, to track, treat, and diagnose diseases. However, nanobot beacons can also be used to monitor the location of the patient within the hospital or the community."

I'd heard about this type of thing but wasn't aware of any actual breakthroughs in the area yet. "GPS on the molecular level."

"Something along those lines, yes."

I could see where this was going. "And that's where the law enforcement application comes in: Inject the nanobots into a person on house arrest, or maybe a registered sex offender, and ankle bracelets become obsolete. And there's no way to cut it off, since the GPS is in your blood."

"Exactly."

I tried to think like a criminal. "What about a blood transfusion?"

"No. You'd still have enough of them in you. They wouldn't all be flushed out."

"And this is in development now?"

"Development's done. Patents pending. We're working right now with different agencies to start distribution."

Interesting.

I brought the conversation back on topic and pointed to the documents on the table. "Okay, talk me through what you know so far."

"Well, the Rudisill Mine was closed and sealed up for good in the late 1930s." He unfolded a road map of the city and pointed in the general vicinity of the shaft I'd descended into.

He drew a line on the map with his finger. "It ran along a mineral vein over here for about a half mile, extending up in a northeasterly direction, where it met up with another mine, the Saint Catherine Mine, which traverses under the current railroad tracks. They were the two most profitable mines in the area."

I wished I had my cell phone with the 3-D hologram function, but it was at the bottom of the very mine system we were examining.

Before Kurt Mason had killed Corrine, he'd told me there was more than one way out of the mines. However, so far, despite teams searching the neighborhood, we had no evidence of other entry points or open shafts. "So, the two mines intersected?"

"From what I can tell, yes."

"Do we know about the layout of the mines? The tunnels and so on?"

He shook his head, then tapped the map. "But this whole area is riddled with shafts and tunnels."

As I looked at the maps, I noticed he'd taken some of the land plats from specially labeled boxes, and I had a thought. "Who else has access to this information? To these resources?"

"Students. Staff. Visiting faculty." He indicated a sign-in sheet near the front desk.

I looked over the list from the past two months. There were dozens of names of people who had signed in.

No Masons.

No Everharts.

After studying the list, I photographed it with my new phone and e-mailed the images to Voss along with a note asking him to have his team run the names. Maybe Mason had someone else helping him. Maybe we could catch a break.

When I returned to Professor O'Brien, he was emptying out the contents of one of the boxes.

"So," I said, "at this point we know the general location of the two major mine systems but we have no diagrams of the tunnels or the exact locations of the shafts."

"Correct."

The other day, Angela had mentioned that the maps of the mines themselves, if they even existed anymore, would most likely be in land deeds or surveying maps that had never been scanned into computers or uploaded onto the Internet.

Which meant we were going to have to go about this the old-fashioned way: looking at actual sheets of paper.

I gazed at the table. This was going to be a lot of work. "Well, we need to see if there are any maps of the remaining shafts or tunnels that might still be out there under Charlotte."

O'Brien rubbed his chin thoughtfully. "It's possible there might be some original source material over in the Carolina Room at the library Uptown. I've been through their archives before, but I might have missed something."

"We can always check there if we need to, but let's look over what we have here first."

The two of us took seats on opposite sides of the table and began analyzing the centuries-old land deeds, looking for one that might show us the actual layout of the Rudisill or Saint Catherine mines.

# 64

Tessa listened as Brineesha spoke with Ralph using the room phone, since she'd misplaced her cell somewhere at home that morning before coming to the hospital with Lien-hua.

Apparently, Ralph's flight out of Charlotte had been delayed, but he'd finally landed here in DC.

From what Tessa could discern from listening to one end of the conversation, he was on his way to the hospital right now.

After they'd hung up, Lien-hua asked Brineesha, "So Ralph's going to be here soon?"

"Should be any minute."

Tessa found it a little odd that he wouldn't have called immediately when he landed, but it was certainly possible he might have waited until he saw how traffic was before touching base.

It would be way too awkward talking through any of what she had to say when Ralph was here.

She deliberated the right way to do this but finally

realized she should just get on with it, or Ralph was going to arrive and she would miss her chance.

"How well did you know my mom?" Tessa asked Brineesha.

"Not all that well, I'm afraid."

"Did she ever tell you the story about when I was born?"

"No."

"Did Patrick?"

"Uh-uh."

She'd never gone through any of this with Lien-hua and she didn't know if Patrick had ever shared the story with her, although she doubted it. Despite being overly protective, Patrick did respect her boundaries and he knew this whole thing was a sensitive issue.

Lien-hua sat quietly and listened.

So did Brineesha.

Oh, this was going to be even harder than Tessa thought.

"She was single when she had me," Tessa said to her. "You knew that, right?"

"Yes."

"And she . . . um . . ." She just went ahead and said it: "Before actually deciding to keep me, she'd decided not to."

A pause. "She was going to get an abortion?"

"Yeah. I mean, she was in college, she wasn't married. She didn't really have . . . It's kind of a long story, but basically, yeah. She decided to end the pregnancy."

To *"get it taken care of,"* Tessa thought, but kept that to herself. It was such a crass and unfeeling way to put things, especially when you were the one who was going to get taken care of.

Brineesha had a contraction, but it passed relatively

quickly and when it had, she asked Tessa softly, "What changed her mind?"

"She was at the clinic and she was waiting to get seen. She started paging through the magazines that were sitting there on one of the end tables, and she kept noticing ads with kids in them, maybe with moms having to get grass stains out of their clothes, or kids eating cookies, or for life-insurance policies—I don't even know. But she started thinking about me being around. The good and the bad—whatever. I know it sounds dumb."

"It doesn't sound dumb."

"Well, one real estate ad had this picture of a little girl who was maybe five years old or so and she was trying on her mom's high heels and necklace. I don't know what the text said exactly, but my mom ripped that page out of the magazine and the part that's left just says, 'Homes are not just.' Whatever else it was supposed to say, that's what did it—seeing that ad, thinking about having a baby around, having me around. I'm only alive today because of a real estate ad."

Brineesha was silent.

"After my mom saw that ad, she left the abortion clinic and went ahead and had me. I found the ad in her things one day. When I first learned about it, I hated her for it. Just the idea that she was going to . . . well . . . She was twenty weeks along."

"Oh."

"Yeah. At that point . . . Well, you're a nurse. You know what they have to do to the baby in order to . . ."

"Yes. I do."

"But the thing is, she changed her mind. It took me a while to stop judging her, you know, for wanting things to be easier, for not wanting to have me, but I have a lot of respect for her for taking . . . I guess for taking what wasn't the easy route. So, I know your situation is totally different—I mean, you have Ralph and everything—but I just wanted you to know . . . well, just that I'm excited for you. That's it."

After a long moment letting Tessa's words settle, Brineesha said, "I can't begin to imagine how hard that must have been to find all that out—and to forgive her. I think you're as brave as your mother was."

Tessa had never thought of herself as being brave about any of it and wasn't sure how to respond. She was sorting through what to say when there was a knock at the door.

Ralph had arrived.

So, now Tessa had gotten one big thing off her chest, but she still had one more thing that she needed to tackle: getting up enough guts to at least clear the air with Beck.

++++

Spartanburg, South Carolina

Kurt Mason parked beside the strip of woods parallel to the rail yard where M343 was resting expectantly on the tracks.

He slipped into the underbrush and made his way through a thick mesh of kudzu to the other side of the hedgerow, where a six-foot-high metal fence ran along the edge of the railroad company's land.

It was obviously more of a property marker than a fence designed to keep people out, and after making sure the coast was clear, Kurt was able to easily climb over it.

The rail yard appeared to be deserted, but he had learned that even during off-hours they were often manned, so he was cautious as he approached M343.

From his research, he knew that on a train, air is compressed in the locomotive. It goes through an air hose, through the whole line. In addition to the dynamic brakes, the engineer uses that compressed air to slow down the train, car by car, backward from the engine.

But there's also an end-of-train device, or EOT, and in emergencies when you need to brake fast, you can engage that and the train will begin braking from the rear toward the head end at the same time.

By closing the angle cocks, Kurt would disrupt that airflow so only the cars up to that point would brake. And if he was able to do it both near the head and the rear of the train, those cars in between would not have any brakes. They wouldn't derail, but they would keep the rest of the train from slowing down.

So that's what he was here to do.

Every tank car has top and bottom shelf couplers, which basically means that they won't pop loose, and if one car derails, the car attached to it will as well. Railway companies considered it safer than having a coupler come loose during a derailment and puncture the head shield of the tanker behind it.

And that meant those tankers would all go down together.

Which was exactly what Kurt wanted to have happen.

After making sure the coast was clear, he closed the angle cocks behind one of the buffer cars near the head of the train and then returned to the woods to stay out of sight as he picked his way back nearly a mile through the undergrowth to close another angle cock five cars in from the end of the six-thousand-foot train.

# 65

Over the past hour and a half, I'd pored over countless surveying maps from railroad and mining companies from the last two centuries and even located a few land deeds and shareholding documents of gold mines from the area.

And, frustratingly, I didn't really have a whole lot to show for all that effort.

Here's what I knew: The Rudisill Mine was larger than the Saint Catherine and was mined over the course of more than a century. When gold was discovered there in 1825, the area was still outside of the city. Charlotte grew up around it as people began to settle closer and closer to the mine.

According to some documents, Saint Catherine had shafts that sank down 450 feet, while the deepest Rudisill shaft was 350 feet. However, according to one map, a shaft in the Rudisill mine actually dropped 650 feet.

Based on the effort that Mason had gone through to locate and access the mine shaft and his words to me about the climax happening tonight, I figured that the secret to what he had planned was there, somewhere, in the Rudisill–St. Catherine Mine system.

Solving crimes isn't so much a process of gathering information as it is sorting through data and trying to discern which facts are pertinent and which are just static, or, worse, distractions.

And that's something I was uncertain about now: what, of all the information spread out before me, was static, what was distraction, and what was essential information.

Professor O'Brien found a newspaper article from 1906 that showed the location of some Saint Catherine mine shafts near the railroad underpass close to the Bank of America Stadium. There were numerous tunnels slithering out in a southwesterly direction toward West Summit Avenue, but it wasn't clear what depths they were at or where they met up with the Rudisill tunnels.

I spent some time searching through the library's digital card-catalog system, trying different search terms and combinations to see what I could come up with. Eventually I found a 2005 map titled "Old Gold Mines in Charlotte, Mecklenburg County, North Carolina: A Potential Geologic Hazard for Development."

Okay, that caught my attention.

Call number NC C8 3:061 05-05. The map's authors were Jeffrey C. Reid, Michael A. Medina, and Andy J. Goretti. There were two places listed for where the map might be located and neither was here in the special collections area.

The first was on the fourth floor in the Atkins North Carolina documents section, but when I searched there I didn't find it. So I went to the other location listed, in the maps room on the second floor.

And that's where I located it: a large laminated map nearly a meter wide and just as long.

I read the abstract:

> *Abandoned gold mines were geospatially located in the southwest of the Charlotte city center using historic documents and rediscovered engineering geology reports. The mines and mine workings comprise the Rudisill-St. Catherine's trace of gold mining that ceased nearly 100 years ago.*
>
> *Geospatial compilation of these features can be of considerable assistance to planning large excavations and foundations as the Charlotte city center expands to the southwest and replaces the current warehouse district that is built over these old mine workings.*
>
> *Today there is limited evidence of previous gold mining except for street names. However, historic reports and rediscovered engineering reports show excavations of considerable extent that underlie warehouses, commercial structures, major transportation corridors and numerous property parcels.*
>
> *The rediscovered engineering geology reports identify areas as large as a city block that are so honeycombed below ground from mining to be a concern in land transfer.*
>
> *Site-specific geotechnical and/or engineering studies are likely to be required on individual property parcels. Mapped features in this study should be considered approximate.*

The map showed the location of sixty-three shafts in a line that stretched from just west of the stadium in a northeasterly direction, then down past the intersection of Mint and Summit to the southwest.

There were overlays of some of the horizontal tunnels, but details of the tunnels' actual layout was limited. One of the shafts was directly under the parcel of land where the old textile mill was.

*Mason found this map.*

*That's how he located that shaft.*

If Ingersoll and his team were able to use that ground-penetrating radar in conjunction with the information on this map, they should have the data they needed to detail the layout of the Rudisill–St. Catherine Mine system.

Though it wasn't perfect, this was something that I definitely wanted to get to Ingersoll right away.

O'Brien agreed to keep looking through the documents that we'd pulled up and then, in the afternoon, head over to the main branch of the library Uptown to see what he could find there.

"Perfect," I said.

He gave me his cell number in case I needed to contact him.

Every library has certain books and materials on reserve that you're not supposed to check out, and this map fell in that category. Right now, however, we needed it on-site, so I came up with my own checkout policy—I would walk out the door with it and return it when the team didn't need it anymore.

Good enough for me.

It sounded like a policy Tessa might have come up with.

I rolled up the map, tucked it under my arm, and assured the librarian working the front desk that we would take good care of it.

As I was walking to the car, I checked my texts and saw

that Ralph had made it to the hospital and that Brin's contractions were becoming more frequent. *Baby this afternoon!* he typed.

I texted back asking if he and Brineesha had decided on a name yet, and he responded that they were still going back and forth between Shanelle and Tryphena.

Shanelle: Gracious beauty.

Tryphena: Delicate.

I liked them both; I wasn't sure which one I preferred. Trying to decide between them, I climbed into my car and left for Third Ward.

++++

Kurt Mason finished with the second angle cock. He disappeared into the woods again and started to make his way to his car so he could return to the house in Charlotte, where he would monitor the train's progress on his laptop by surreptitiously logging in to the Knoxville Southeast Railway dispatch center.

++++

Ingersoll met up with me outside the warehouse.

I spread out the map on the hood of one of the cruisers parked nearby and we studied it carefully.

"This is good," he said. "We're still taking radar readings. The ground isn't ideal for the equipment, but along with this map, it should give us enough info to start clearing those shafts. If all goes well I'd say we'll be able to get rolling by this evening."

"Great."

I called Voss to check on things and found out he was at police headquarters, working on some joint task force issues. Since I was still wondering if he might possibly be more of the problem here in dealing with the CMPD than the solution, I phoned the police chief and, without mentioning any names, made sure there were no issues I needed to be aware of.

It sounded like, at least for the time being, things were on track.

After the call, I headed to the Field Office to update the case files with what I'd learned at the UNC Charlotte library.

# 66

A few minutes ago I'd grabbed a sandwich in the Field Office's rather meager cafeteria. Now, it was almost quarter after twelve and I was seated by myself in a vacant conference room on the first floor. I was thinking about how Mason might have known which people to text at the NCAVC back on Monday, when a young agent tapped on the door and leaned his head in.

"Agent Bowers?"

"Yes?"

"Phone call."

I expected it would be word from Ralph or Lien-hua about Brineesha and her baby, but then I realized they would most likely have contacted me through my cell phone.

"Who is it?"

"Says it's Loudon Caribes."

A chill settled into my gut.

"What did you just say?"

He looked at me strangely. "The guy. He said his name is Loudon Caribes. You know him?"

That was one of the aliases Richard Basque had used. *Caribes* was the root word for "cannibal."

"I might."

Of course, just because someone was using that name didn't mean for certain that it was Basque, but there weren't too many people who knew about it and I couldn't think of anybody other than Basque who would call me, claiming to be Loudon.

The young agent looked like he was impatient to get back to his desk. "You want me to tell him you're not available or—"

"No, no." I stood. "Can you trace the call?"

He shrugged. "Sure."

Though the Bureau strives for uniformity, the ability to trace calls and the available technology differs by Field Office. "How long do I need to keep him on the line?"

"Twenty seconds or so, once we patch into it."

That'll work.

There was no phone in this room.

"Where can I take the call?" I asked him.

"You can use my office. Follow me."

We went halfway down the hall and he led me to his desk. He was about to pick up the receiver when I said, "I'll want this recorded as well."

He used his cell to contact the Cyber unit to tell them to record and trace the call; then he picked up the handset, tapped the blinking button, and handed the phone to me. He hesitated for a moment, as if he couldn't decide if he wanted to stay in the room, but finally left and eased the door shut behind him.

I held the phone to my ear. "Hello, Loudon."

"Hello, Patrick." It was Basque's voice "There's something we need to talk about."

# 67

Though I wanted to keep him talking for as long as possible, he was too smart for games and gimmicks, so I just told him, "I'm sorry about your sister."

Yes, Richard was a man that I wanted to find, wanted to bring in, wanted to take down. Yes, he was the person who'd tried to kill Lien-hua and Tessa, but what I told him was true: I did feel sorry that Corrine, an innocent woman, was dead.

"Thank you," he said.

Just hearing his voice brought back a stream of memories, and none of them were good. Bodies. Crime scenes. The look in the eyes of family members when we told them what had happened to their loved ones. The tears. The screams.

But maybe the hardest response of all to see: those blank, disbelieving stares. And then you had to repeat the news and things just got harder from there. I couldn't afford to forget for one second who I was talking with right now or what he had done.

And despite how I felt about speaking to him, I needed to keep him on the line.

"I know you cared about Corrine," I said. "That the two of you were close."

"Yes, we were. From what they're saying on the news, you tried to save her."

I'd done my best to keep my name out of the reports, but it'd leaked out. It seemed like a lot of stuff was leaking to the press lately.

"I tried to." I didn't want to be talking about this. It only reminded me of my failure to get to Corrine in time, my failure to stop Kurt Mason. "Where are you, Richard?"

"I helped him escape from prison."

"I know."

"So that means Corrine's death is also partly my fault. If I hadn't done that, she would still be alive today."

I didn't know how to respond to that. He had a point in a butterfly-effect sort of way, as Tessa might say.

On the other hand, Richard hadn't made the decision to kill Corrine—that was all Mason's doing. So how much responsibility should he really bear for his sister's death?

It wasn't an easy question.

He went on, "I'm guessing you're not the only one listening to this call, are you?"

There was no reason to lie. "No."

"And we're being recorded?"

"Yes."

*Certainly they'll have the call traced by now. Certainly this is long enough. Richard must know that. Something else is up here.*

"I need to talk to you alone," he said. "I have a proposal to make."

"I'm not going to make any deals with you, Richard. Tell me where you are."

"I'll meet you in one hour. Uptown Charlotte."

I looked at the time: 12:19 p.m.

"Where exactly?"

"Be at Independence Square exactly sixty minutes from now."

It was a busy, public place, but certainly he would know we would have backup there, SWAT or HRT as well.

Before I could respond, the call ended.

"Richard? Are you there?"

No reply.

The line was dead.

I rushed into the hallway to locate the agent who'd let me use his phone. I found him running my way from a nearby office suite. "Well?" I asked. "Do we have a location?"

"He's calling from the Bank of America building."

# 68

12:30 p.m.
3 hours until kickoff

The two units who responded found no evidence of Richard Basque at the Bank of America Corporate Center.

The officers stationed outside the building hadn't seen anyone fitting his description enter or leave. Video footage confirmed that.

I was on the second floor of the Field Office with the Cyber unit and they were analyzing the data on the phone trace.

"That doesn't make any sense," the agent who was seated at the computer said. "You're sure it was him on the phone?"

"It was him," I said.

The guy shook his head. "It looks like he must have found a way to reroute the call."

*Yes,* I thought. *That's what it looks like.*

Richard was brilliant and knew his way around computers, but he wasn't a hacker, and as advanced as the Bureau's tracking abilities were, I doubted he would've been able to get past or manipulate them.

"Get this data to the Cyber Division at HQ," I said.

"Ask for Angela Knight. We need to figure out where Basque was when he made that call."

I got on the line with Voss, who was still at police headquarters.

"So what do you propose we do?" he asked.

"I go to Independence Square at one nineteen. I meet him."

It would have been useless for Basque to tell me to come alone. He would've known that, no matter what, we were going to be there ready and waiting.

As much as I anticipated that he would know that, I couldn't shake the thought that he had something in mind. A trap of some kind. A trick he was going to pull.

"We need to be ready for anything," I told Voss, "but if we shut down the square he'll never show. We need a response team there. I want undercover agents on the ground, snipers, a—"

"Hang on, now. Snipers? In Uptown Charlotte?"

"I don't care what strings you have to pull. If you need to have the mayor call FBI Director Wellington, I've got her cell number with me. We have to be ready. There's no telling what Basque has in mind, but I can tell you one thing: He's not just going to turn himself in."

It took some convincing, but finally Voss got on board.

As long as Ingersoll's team was here it made sense to have them, rather than local SWAT, take the lead on this thing, and Voss agreed to contact them.

When we ended the call, my mind was buzzing. On one front, we had the analysis of the mines. On another, we had the search for Mason. And now, additionally, I had a meeting with Richard Basque thrown into the mix.

"Give me a sec," I said to the guys who were analyzing the phone data.

I stepped away from the desk and into the hallway by myself.

The conversation I'd had with Ralph earlier this week came to mind—the one in which we'd discussed how it's impossible to give a hundred percent to both your job and your family.

Well, right now it was just as impossible to give a hundred percent of my focus to only one case.

I tried to sort things out.

*Basque helps Mason escape from prison, and then Mason kills Basque's sister—knowing full well that Basque will come after him when he does.*

Despite myself, I couldn't stop asking why. As futile an exercise as that was, I caught myself trying to guess motives.

*Right now you need to focus on Basque. This is something solid. He knows Mason. Maybe he can lead you to him.*

Richard had told me on the phone that he had a proposal to make. I wasn't about to negotiate with him, but I also wasn't naive enough to think he wanted to meet with me just to unconditionally surrender.

Based on what had happened to Corrine, I imagined that Richard was going to propose something in regard to tracking down Mason.

*Maybe he has information he's willing to share or trade?*

*But trade for what? He has to know there's no way we would ever give him immunity.*

My thoughts circled around each other, spinning back to the first time I apprehended Richard, back in that abandoned slaughterhouse in Milwaukee fourteen years ago, when I was still a homicide detective.

There was a woman lying there, cut very badly, cut in the way only Richard could cut someone. After I cuffed him I tried to save her, but it was too late. The words he spoke as I went over to try to help her came back to me now: "I think we may need an ambulance, don't you, Detective?"

I lied to her.

Told her she was going to be alright.

And unlike Stu Ritterman, who died in my arms on Monday morning, that woman didn't get a chance to share anything with me before she died.

I can still remember standing up, blood dripping from my hands.

Her blood.

Then I turned to Richard.

I lifted him from the concrete where I'd left him while I tried to save her, and I was about to read him his rights when he spoke, his eyes on the woman's fresh corpse: "I guess we won't be needing that ambulance after all."

That did it.

I hit him in the jaw hard enough to send him flying backward onto the ground.

Then I was on him and I hit him again, shattering the bones in the jaw. I was ready to keep going, ready to pull the scalpel out of my leg where he'd stabbed me a few minutes earlier when we were fighting, ready to drive it into his chest or deep into his throat, but then he said those words that I've never forgotten and never will: "It feels good, doesn't it, Detective? It feels really good."

Yes, it did.

That's the thing: Unleashing my anger on him did feel good, and it would have felt good to keep going. It was terrifying to realize that I had cords of darkness in my heart that were just as thick, just as unwieldy, just as lethal as those running through the hearts of the people I tracked.

Since then I've done my best to convince myself that I'm not like him, but in a very real way, I am.

Basque was no more, no less human than I was.

I was like him. Of course I was.

We all are.

In this business you have to catch yourself before you drift too far.

You have to keep the demons at bay.

And now words came to me, words that unsettled me: *You have to keep yourself at bay.*

So, that was the first time I faced off with him.

Then last spring, after he'd been set free in his retrial and had started killing again, I caught up with him at the house he was using near a marsh about an hour from DC. We fought there on the shore, and as we did he nearly drowned me, but at last I was able to get him under the water.

And I held him there.

I could have pulled him to his feet, but I waited until he started convulsing.

And then I waited longer, until the convulsions stopped.

Until he drowned.

Moments later, a car came careening down the bank and I hurriedly dragged him to the shore to get his body out of the way.

I waited. He was gone. It was over.

He was dead.

But in that moment, duty and justice wrestled with each other in my heart, deep questions that have no easy answers, questions about who I was, what I was capable of, who I was choosing to become, and although I could have left him dead, I did not.

I'm still not sure if it was a sign of weakness or of strength, but I went ahead and performed CPR. I brought him back.

I wanted justice to prevail. I just wasn't sure exactly how to help it do so.

*If Basque is partially responsible for Corrine's death, then you are too because you saved his life. If you hadn't, none of this would've happened.*

But then, soon after that, when he escaped and took Tessa, when she was drowning and I had to choose between saving her and killing Basque, I squeezed the trigger and sent him reeling backward into the Potomac.

He didn't have a weapon.

He was ready to turn himself in, but if I'd taken the time to apprehend him, my daughter would have died. I chose to save her. I fired at him.

I had no regrets at the time and I still didn't.

It was hard to figure out how to feel about him contacting me now.

We hadn't known for sure whether or not he was alive.

Now we knew.

We hadn't known how to find him.

Now we did.

And now, finally, I had the chance to end all this and bring him in for good.

I put a call through to Lien-hua and told her about the meeting. She was quiet, and when I'd finished and she didn't respond, I said, "Are you okay with this?"

"What happened out there by the river?"

"What?"

"The Potomac. In April."

"I shot him."

"Yes." She said it as if she were both agreeing with me and disagreeing with me at the same time.

"Tessa was in the car," I said. "Trapped. She was drowning."

"I know. And you shot him."

"I had to get to her. I had to save her. And he was . . ."

"He was what? Threatening you? Coming at you? Trying to kill you?"

*No. He was surrendering. He was going to let me take him in.*

When I said nothing, she continued, "You never told me exactly what happened. Even in the case files it wasn't a hundred percent clear."

I heard a voice in my head: *You promised you wouldn't lie to her. That you would tell her the truth no matter what.*

But I also wanted to protect her and that might mean not letting her know the kinds of things I was actually capable of doing.

It would have been so much easier if Basque had threatened me, if he'd pulled a gun or a knife. It would have made it a lot easier for me to know how to look at myself.

But he had not.

And I'd squeezed the trigger.

"Well?" she asked.

"I had to take the shot," I said simply. "And I have to go and meet with him now."

"You chose Tessa's life above his." My wife wasn't going to let me off the hook.

*Truth or not?*

"Yes. I did."

A long silence ebbed between us.

Too long.

I debated what to say, how to defend my decision, but everything I came up with seemed insufficient.

Finally she spoke, and her response surprised me: "You made the right choice."

"I'm glad you think so."

"But now, you need to bring him in."

"I intend to."

"No. Bring him in, Pat." She seemed to be choosing her words carefully. "Don't do something either of us would regret."

"If I can, yes, I will. I'll bring him in."

"Do what you have to do, but don't let him steal from you the thing you care about most."

"My family?"

"Your integrity."

Then, as I tried to process the implications of what she'd just said, she told me that Brineesha was doing alright, but that the doctors wanted to give her some Pitocin to make her contractions stronger. Before I could pivot back to the topic of Basque, Lien-hua was telling me Debra was calling to check on Brin, and then she was wrapping up the call.

After we'd both said our good-byes, I returned to the conference room, informed the team I was taking off, and left for my car.

*Lien-hua's right, you know. You need to bring him in.*

*Do what you have to do, but don't let him steal from you the thing you care about most: your integrity.*

But was that really what I cared about most?

Or was it my family?

Basque had gone after Lien-hua, tried to kill both her and Tessa, and I would've given up anything, and would still give up anything—my integrity, my honor, my life—to protect them.

I wasn't sure exactly where that left me at the moment, but it did make me feel even more motivated than ever to bring Basque in.

Fourteen years ago it'd felt good to hit him, and earlier this year, it had felt good to shoot him in the chest.

And, honestly, I wasn't sure if that was because I believed in justice or because I was attracted to the darkness.

They were two ends of the spectrum, and somehow when I faced off with Basque, I found myself with my feet in both places at the same time.

That's what I thought of now as I got ready to meet him again.

Yes.

*Bring him in.*

*Don't give in to the demons.*

*Keep them at bay.*

*Keep yourself at bay.*

*Justice.*

*The darkness.*

*Do what has to be done.*

*Okay, I think I will.*

We were going to have a team ready, but still it was foolish to think that Basque was just going to walk up to me on the street and turn himself in. He had something up his sleeve.

So I wanted something up mine.

I put a call through to Professor O'Brien, who hadn't left the UNC Charlotte library yet, and swung by campus while our agents took their positions Uptown at the intersection of Trade and Tryon.

Then I went to assemble with the team before meeting with Richard Basque.

# 69

Kurt Mason arrived back in Charlotte and entered the house in Fourth Ward.

He went online, clicked his way through the firewalls and into the Knoxville Southeast's dispatch office to keep an eye on the arrival of M343's engineer and conductor at the rail yard in Spartanburg.

++++

While I was on my way Uptown, I got word from Ralph: They decided to have the doctors break Brineesha's water. Clear fluid, a good sign. She was dilated six centimeters. Things were moving forward. They expected the baby sometime in the next few hours. And, while I was relieved, I was also distracted by thinking about what was going on right here, right now, in Charlotte.

I parked, put the items I'd picked up from the university in my pocket, and I was walking over to meet with Ingersoll and his team when a call came in from Angela at Cyber. "It sounds like there's an echo on that audio from your conversation with Basque," she said. "Like he might be in a long, narrow room."

"An echo?"

"It's faint, but when I enhance the digital signature, I can catch hold of it."

"Can you analyze the acoustics? Figure out the shape of the room?"

"Not unless I have a baseline of his voice in a known space."

I thought for a moment. "I spoke with him in April, a Friday—it would have been the eleventh or twelfth—in one of their interrogation rooms there at HQ. Pull up the copy of the audio and the room's dimensions."

"Good. I'll see what I can find out."

I convened with Voss, Ingersoll, and two other members of the Hostage Rescue Team in the kitchen of a restaurant just down the block from the intersection where I was going to be meeting with Basque.

While I put on a Kevlar vest, Ingersoll gave me the rundown. "We have three snipers on nearby buildings and four undercover agents—two in nearby restaurants, one dressed as a homeless man, one as a jogger who'll be stretching out nearby. SWAT's on call and two ambulances are around the corner, parked one block away. I'll be across the street in the lobby of a hotel. Stay in radio contact. If you run into any trouble let us know and we will take him out."

"Understood."

I zipped up a light Windbreaker to cover the body armor so I could look as inconspicuous as possible.

Recently, for field ops, the Bureau had switched to wireless mics and receiver patches that you wear discreetly behind your ear.

Ingersoll gave me a set of plastic flex cuffs and an automatic knife, and I put them in my pocket.

After I'd tested my radio patch, I stepped outside into

the sunlight, and at one fifteen I started down the street toward Independence Square.

My senses seemed sharper than normal. I felt the heat of the sun pricking the back of my neck, smelled the scent of coconut sunscreen as a cluster of giggling junior-high girls passed me on the sidewalk, heard snippets of conversations from people talking on their cell phones as they walked by.

It all became clear, as if life were slowing down, my body preparing me to be more ready than I'd ever been to meet with someone.

As I neared the corner, I could see that it was bustling with people: the lunch crowd finding their way to the nearby restaurants, parents out with their kids heading to one of the city's parks or museums, some folks just out enjoying the summer Saturday. I counted twenty-nine people in the close vicinity of the intersection.

"What do we have?" Ingersoll asked from the other end of the radio. "Anything? Any visual?"

"Negative," I said.

*Is Basque really going to meet you here?*

*How is he going to pull that off?*

Arriving at the corner, I scanned the people surrounding me for anyone with Basque's build. He was as tall as I was and muscular, athletic. Even if he were wearing a disguise, he couldn't have hidden his size.

No one fit the bill.

*How did he do that with the cell phone and the Bank of America building? How—*

*Oh.*

An echo.

Yes.

Then I had it, or at least I thought I did.

Yesterday morning when Guido was showing Ralph

and me around Charlotte he'd mentioned that for a news special a reporter had walked through the storm-sewer tunnels to show how vulnerable and easily accessible they are. She'd had phone reception most of the way.

*No, Basque wasn't in the building.*

*He was under it.*

I was evaluating that possibility and its implications when a young man locked eyes with me and started toward me. Early twenties, Caucasian, 1970s sideburns. He looked disoriented, in a daze.

"Someone's coming," I said into my radio. "Hold positions. Do not move."

He lurched forward, his steps choppy and uneven.

*Is he high? Drunk? Drugged?*

I approached him cautiously. "Sir? Are you alright?"

"Are you Patrick?" His voice was as unsteady as his gait.

*He knows your name.*

*Basque sent him.*

He had both of his hands in his pockets. I couldn't tell if he had a weapon.

This was not the time to take unnecessary risks. I drew my gun. "Hands where I can see them. Now."

As soon as I unholstered my weapon, people gasped, screamed. Began to clear the area.

Maybe that was what Basque wanted.

There was no way to tell.

The young man removed his hands.

His left one was empty. In his right he held a flip phone.

"Hold positions," I said into my radio.

He extended his hand to me, offering me the phone. "I have a message for you from Richard."

My heart was hammering. An explosive device? Was this guy a suicide bomber? I tried to decide whether or not to move closer.

He was three meters away.

*A trap?*

*No. Richard contacted you. He wants to meet you.*

*Maybe he wants to kill you after all.*

"Set down the phone," I said. "Do it slowly, then step away."

But before he could comply, he went limp and collapsed onto the pavement.

Holstering my weapon, I rushed toward him. Checked his vitals.

He was breathing. Had a pulse. Strong, steady.

I put a hand beneath his neck to support his head.

The phone he'd been holding had dropped when he fell. Now it rang. I snatched it up. "Richard, what did you do?"

"The nearest manhole southwest on Tryon. Open it, go down the ladder. If anyone follows you I won't give you the antivenom. Lose your radio and your phone. You have five minutes before he dies of respiratory arrest. Go."

I leapt to my feet and scanned the area for the manhole. "Get an ambulance here now," I said into the radio.

As the young man gasped for breath, the undercover agents posing as the homeless man and the jogger hastened to assist him. I ran to the manhole, wrestled the cover off, tossed my own cell phone to the side, and ripped off and discarded the radio patch.

I kept the flip phone.

Ingersoll and one of the agents who'd been stationed in the restaurant across the street were racing toward me.

"Cover this hole behind me," I told them. "Do not follow me or that man will die."

I scrambled down the ladder and landed in ankle-deep water in the storm-sewer system that, according to what Guido had told us the other day, contained three thousand miles' worth of tunnels.

# 70

I drew my weapon again.

Narrow shafts of light angled through the storm grates that appeared sporadically overhead, but still the tunnel was dim compared to the blazing day outside. I used the Maglite that Voss had gotten for me to scrutinize the tunnel, but there was no sign of Basque.

The flip phone worked, but the reception was grainy and I was afraid it was going to fade out all the way. "Where are you?"

"Southeast" . . . *Static* . . . "Go a quarter mile."

*How are you supposed to gauge the distance down here?*

"You said antivenom. Where is it?"

"Go."

I pocketed the flip phone.

Knowing approximately how fast I can run a mile, I checked my watch and took off. In these conditions and with the wounded ankle from my fall in the mine shaft, I might be able to break ninety seconds for a quarter mile, but it was going to be tough.

As I sprinted through the ankle-deep water, gun in one hand, flashlight in the other, I recalled a time when I'd chased Basque through a series of tunnels similar to these in DC, and I wondered if that's why he'd chosen to connect with me this way.

A quick look at my watch: I figured I had another thirty seconds or so of running.

I passed three intersecting tunnels and eventually came to a ladder.

Checked my watch.

The time looked about right.

No other tunnels or access ladders close by.

I tried the flip phone but got no reception.

Quickly evaluating how long it'd taken me to get here, the distance, the direction, and thinking back to the 3-D hologram of Charlotte that I'd studied earlier, I tried to calculate where I was, but after a few seconds when I came up short I didn't spend any extra time pondering things.

*Go up. Check it out.*

After slipping the flashlight and phone into my pockets, I muscled the manhole cover aside and, gun drawn, emerged inside a shielded construction zone for one of the new high-rise condos being put up. The work had paused for the weekend. No one appeared to be present.

As I climbed out, a canvas sheet blocked the view from the street and a tarp that stretched overhead blocked the view from the sky.

When the phone rang again I checked it. Basque's voice came through: "Slide the cover back over the hole."

I did.

"Okay, enter the building."

The half-finished structure that rose before me reminded me in a macabre way of a body with the skin and flesh removed—a steel skeleton rising toward the sky. An appropriate, if unsettling, image, considering who I was here to meet.

Ahead of me, at the far end of what I assumed would be a hallway extending out from the building's main lobby when it was finished, stood a figure, vague in the vacant light, but even from here I could tell that he was well-built.

"Patrick," he said.

I aimed the Glock at his chest. "Hands to the side, Richard." I'd just sprinted a quarter mile as fast as I could and was still catching my breath.

He raised his hands and held them out, palms forward. He was ten meters away.

"Where's the antivenom?" I asked.

"Give me your phone and I'll call it in."

"Use yours."

"I already got rid of it." He indicated the remains of the phone with his foot. "You're wasting time, Pat. Give me the flip phone."

Richard had a history of working with partners, and I had no way of knowing if he had someone hidden nearby right now. This could be an ambush.

I edged closer to him. Saw no one else nearby. At three meters away I slid him the cell phone but didn't take my gun off him. "Make the call."

He picked it up. Tapped in 911. "This is concerning the man who was found on the corner of Trade and Tryon a few minutes go. He's suffering from the venom of a monocled cobra. There are ten vials of antivenom taped to the bottom of the garbage can at the corner of North College and East Fifth Street. You'll probably need all of it."

He closed up the phone.

"Cobra venom?"

"A new interest of mine."

"Will they have time to save him?" I asked. "Do not lie to me."

"It'll be close. They should be able to stabilize him during transport to the hospital. I'm guessing you had ambulances close by before you came to meet with me, just in case."

"We did."

"I'm going to destroy this phone. We can't have anyone interrupting us. When I'm done saying what I need to say, you can take me in if you wish."

I could work with that.

"Go ahead."

He snapped the phone in half, then dropped the pieces and stomped the two halves beneath his heel.

"Do you have any weapons on you?" I asked.

"No."

"I'm going to pat you down."

He complied. I had him turn and face the unfinished wall. As far as I knew he'd never studied hand-to-hand combat or martial arts, but I'd faced off with him before and he could hold his own in a fight. He was resourceful and he was tough, so I was dialed in, focused, as I frisked him.

Clean.

"Hands behind your back."

He hesitated so I drew his hands back for him. Using the plastic flex cuffs Ingersoll had provided me with, I secured Basque's hands, then turned him around to face me.

I felt like punching him hard for payback for envenomating the young man. I barely managed to hold back.

"Are we alone?" I asked him.

"Yes."

Though he was cuffed I kept the Glock out and ready. "Do you know where Mason is?"

"No. But I know how to find him."

"And how is that?"

"I know the alias Mason has been using."

"Danny Everhart. We already have that."

"Not that one. The other one. He'll still be in the area. He wants to be close by when it all goes down."

"When what goes down?"

"What he has planned for this afternoon. Listen, I need the Bureau's resources and you need my information. It's the only way we'll find him. You know Mason: He's good. He'll disappear. We don't have much time."

"We don't have much time before what, Richard? What does he have planned?"

"I can't tell you that, not until we've tracked him down—but if we don't do it in the next few hours, it'll be too late."

*In the mine shaft, Mason told you that he was glad you were alive so you would be around for the climax tonight— not this afternoon.*

*Two events? Is that what we're looking at here?*

"You're not making sense. If you know how to find him, why contact me? Why go through all this, set up this elaborate meeting? Why not just go after him yourself?"

"Like I said, you have resources I need. I tried finding him myself but I couldn't. Neither one of us can catch him in time on our own."

"You keep telling me that we don't have much time. What's his plan?"

"It has to do with the Cathouse Signal. That's all I can say."

"What does that mean—the Cathouse Signal?" But even as I asked him the question I knew he wasn't going to answer me.

And he didn't.

"Is Mason working alone?" I said.

"I don't know. He might have a person in DC."

"How do you even know what he's up to here?"

"We've spoken a couple times since his escape. That's all I can tell you."

I eyed him. "I could take you in right now."

"Yes, but then you won't find him in time."

"So what's this proposal of yours?" I said. "You help me find him? What's in it for you?"

"After we locate him, you leave me alone with him for five minutes, maybe in the back of a police car, in a room while you're going for backup—whatever you come up with. Five minutes, that's all I need. And then after that, you can take me in—or shoot me like you did when we were at the river in April. Your choice."

"You know I can't make a deal like that."

"Think about it. Innocent people are going to die. Do we both get what we want or do we both suffer and let Mason win?"

"You're going to kill him."

"Yes."

"You know I can't stand by and let you kill an unarmed man."

"I was unarmed by the Potomac when you shot me. How is that any different from what I'm proposing?"

Once more I was tempted to punch him, this time just for annoying me.

*You've got Richard now. Bring him in. Move on from there.*

But Mason would still be free, and if Basque was telling the truth—and right now I did believe that he was— more people would die this afternoon.

*You can't do this. If you agree to leave Basque alone with Mason, he'll murder him. You'd be going against everything you've sworn to uphold.*

My conversation with Lien-hua echoed in my mind:

*"Don't let him steal from you the thing you care about most."*

*"My family?"*

*"Your integrity."*

I made my decision and grabbed Basque's arm to take him to the street, where I would find someone, anyone, with a phone and use it to call for a unit, and we would have Basque in custody once and for all.

We could work through things then. Find Mason on our own. Stop whatever it was he had planned.

*But how do you know? Can you be sure you'll find him in time? You don't even have any leads.*

As I started firmly escorting Richard out of the building he said, "Patrick, you won't find Mason without my help. If you take me in now, I won't help you, and I guarantee that by the end of the day you'll wish you had taken me up on my offer."

I kept going. "I'll find Mason."

"Maybe, eventually, but not by three thirty."

Mason mentioned this evening, so, regarding the timing, one of these guys was lying—or we were looking at two separate events.

"Is it at three thirty?" I said. "Or is it tonight?"

He was quiet.

Lien-hua had asked me to promise to bring Basque in rather than the alternative—she wanted me to avoid doing something that either of us would regret.

And letting innocent people die this afternoon would definitely be something to regret.

*Richard is right. You have the opportunity to save people and to get both him and Mason out of the picture.*

Once more, a discussion with my wife came to mind: "What haunts you the most? The pain you've already seen or the pain you will see?"

"The pain I won't be able to stop," I'd told her.

And this was pain I was able to stop.

I couldn't believe I was even considering this.

*But if you do this thing, you'll have both Basque and Mason off the streets. Either get both killers and save innocent people or chance that more might die. Semtex. Two hundred pounds of it. Mason has something big planned.*

*But what about protocol? You'll lose your job if you work with Basque.*

Right now job security was not exactly at the top of my list of concerns.

"How many people are we talking about with what Mason has planned?"

"All I can really tell you is that he's going to make a memorable statement."

"And you won't tell me what it is until we catch him?"

"When we have him, I'll give you what you need to know."

"And I take you in when it's done?"

"Yes. Or kill me. You choose."

I knew my preference there—but I also knew that unless the circumstances required it I had an obligation to something higher than my preferences.

Well, it was a good thing I'd come prepared for something along these lines.

Sirens whined in the distance and I wondered how long it would take Ingersoll and his men to find me. Even without any way of tracing my location, I had the sense that they would be able to track me down.

I unpocketed the case containing the syringe and rubber tubing I'd gotten from Professor O'Brien on my way from the Field Office.

Man, I was tempted to just punch this syringe into

Basque's leg, but when I'd picked it up from O'Brien, he'd told me the injection needed to be in the bloodstream, not just the muscle.

With Basque's hands restrained behind him, the angle wasn't right to get the needle into his vein.

"Stand still." Using the knife Ingersoll had lent me, I freed his hands.

I removed the syringe from the case.

"You're going to drug me?" Basque asked.

"We're going to tag you. Pull up your shirtsleeve."

As he slid his left sleeve up over his elbow he looked at me somewhat uneasily. "What do you mean?"

"You're going to inject this into your arm."

"What is it?"

"Nanobots."

"Nanobots?"

Just the idea of stabbing a needle into a person's arm unsettled me.

Needles.

Man, I hate needles.

"In your vein." I handed him the length of rubber tubing to tie off on his bicep to allow his vein to become more prominent. "We want them in your bloodstream. If you miss the vein I'm taking you in right now."

He tied off the tubing, using his teeth to pull it tight, then positioned the needle against his vein.

"Why am I injecting nanobots into my blood? Are these the kind that send back video images?"

"No. They're the kind that can track where you are. I thought about an ankle bracelet, but I've tried those before and it hasn't always worked out as well as I'd hoped."

"You can get them off."

"It's not easy, but yes. It is possible. Now, go on."

Richard slid the tip of the needle into his arm. "So, you knew all along you might be working with me?"

"I knew all along that I would want to keep tabs on you."

He injected the nanobots.

"So," he said, "these bots, you have some kind of a sensor or GPS tracker to follow me?"

"Something like that." I tapped my pocket where I had the handheld sensor O'Brien had given me. "And this isn't the only one, don't worry. Even if it's damaged or destroyed we'll still be able to find you."

At his lab O'Brien had the only other means of monitoring Basque's movements, but Richard didn't need to know that. "No matter where you go for the next forty-eight hours we'll be able to track you down."

"Forty-eight hours."

"And by then this will all be over."

"Yes." He seemed deep in thought. "It will."

"Get rid of the needle."

He discarded it.

I took out the sensor unit and, after taking a moment to make sure it was working properly, I showed Basque his location on the device. It was overlaid with a street map of the city.

"Alright," I said, "just so you know, if you make any attempt to get away, I'm going to warn you once, and then shoot you dead."

"I believe you. So you're going to give me five minutes with Mason?"

"I can't guarantee you five minutes, but if I get you both in the same room, I'll leave you alone with him. That's the best I can do."

He thought for a moment. "Okay."

*Don't do this, Pat.*

*Yes, you have to.*

The lives of Mason's potential victims—however many that might be—weighed heavily on my mind.

"We need to get out of here," Basque said. "I have a car nearby. We should get moving. I'll tell you what I know when we get there."

"Where are we going?"

"The cemetery."

# 71

1:30 p.m.
2 hours until kickoff

I made Basque drive.

Though I was tempted to keep a gun on him the whole time, that wasn't going to be feasible if we were going to be working together to catch Mason before he pulled off whatever it was he had planned for this afternoon.

But I wasn't going to let down my guard either. Not for an instant.

If Basque ran, I could track him down. And if he tried to attack me, I could always shoot him. I'd done it before.

Basque had an older-model sedan. I wasn't sure of the year, but I guessed that even if it'd had GPS capabilities he would have disabled them.

He took us to a sprawling graveyard not far from Center City. I wasn't sure why he chose this location except that it provided a good vantage point to see if cars were approaching from any direction.

Not bad.

Near one of the mausoleums we got out of the car and

he said, "You wish you'd killed him, don't you? In the mine shaft when he murdered my sister?"

"Yes. Now, we've waited long enough. Tell me the alias Mason is using."

He didn't hesitate. "We're looking for a guy named Leroy Davenport. He'll have a place, something, I don't know—a loft, a condo—somewhere here in Charlotte."

Leroy Davenport: I remembered the name from the list of people who'd accessed the information in the UNC Charlotte's special collections room over the last couple months. "I need to contact the Bureau if I'm going to do a search like that for Davenport's name." I didn't have to remind him that he'd destroyed both of our phones.

"There's an iPad in the trunk."

I retrieved it. "You do know they'll be able to track this if I go online."

"Not this one. I've been using it for the last month. It's untraceable."

I doubted that, not if I had Angela and Lacey working on the trace, but I didn't bring that up.

"Mason told me that seven gods use thirty-eight," I said. "Do you know what that means?"

"No. I've never heard it before."

Though I could certainly have logged in to the Federal Digital Database using my federal ID number, I wasn't about to type that information into this tablet computer in case there was some kind of key-logger program running. The last thing we needed was Richard Basque getting those access codes and sharing them with any friends or associates that he might have.

There was one person I figured I could trust more than anyone else to get me the information I needed without reporting my location.

My wife.

"Is there a video-call app on this iPad?" I asked him. "Skype? Anything like that?"

"Skype."

I tapped at the screen to contact Lien-hua. Still not completely convinced that this wasn't some kind of trap, I had Basque back up from me a few meters and I kept one eye on him as I waited for her to respond.

Momentarily, she accepted the invite and her face came up. "Pat, I've been trying to reach you. Where are you?"

"Hang on. Are you somewhere private?"

"Yeah, I'm good. Hey, I have to—"

"Lien-hua, listen to me. I need you to do some digging for me, but do it discreetly." I detailed what I needed to know about Davenport. "I don't want any red flags coming up about this search, nothing related to Mason."

She looked at me curiously. "What's going on? Does this have anything to do with your meeting with Basque? Is that—are you in some kind of danger?"

"No. I'm fine. Just find out what you can as quickly as you can. We're on a tight time frame here."

"We?"

I paused slightly. "All of us."

She read my equivocation. "Did you meet him? Did you find Basque?"

I was tempted to cover up what was going on, but she would have been able to tell I wasn't being straight with her. Besides, I'd promised not to lie to her, even if I thought it would protect her. "Yes, but I can't get into all that right now."

"Pat, I'm—"

"I can't get into that, Lien-hua."

She took her time assessing things, but finally replied, "Okay, I'll see what I can find out about Davenport, but you need to know something about Brin: It's why I was trying to call you earlier. The doctor is with her now. The baby isn't tolerating labor very well."

"What? What happened?"

"She's in distress. Her heartbeat keeps going down when Brin has a contraction."

"So what do they do about it?"

"They're trying to decide right now whether or not to do a C-section."

I didn't really like talking about this in front of Richard. "Tell Brin she's in my thoughts."

"I will. And I'll let you know about Davenport."

"Good."

We ended the conversation and I quietly prayed that my friend and her baby would be alright.

Richard knew Ralph and Brineesha from our previous encounters, and now he said, "I'm sorry to hear that there's something wrong with the delivery."

He might have been mocking the situation. I couldn't tell. He sounded genuine enough, but I reminded myself not to be blinded, not to lose sight of who he was, of the dozens of people he'd slaughtered, of the fact that he had tried to kill the two people I cared about most.

I didn't address his comment, but just said, "We need to wait to hear from Lien-hua."

He checked his watch. "I hope she's quick."

++++

The wind changed.

It wasn't perfect for what Kurt had in mind, but it was close enough and it would definitely do the trick.

He was at the house monitoring the Knoxville Southeast Railway dispatch office through his laptop. According to the data he was able to pull up, the train engineer and conductor for M343 had checked in at the rail yard ten minutes ago.

++++

Spartanburg, South Carolina

Glenn Ashland watched his conductor, Louis Faulkner, flip through the shipping papers for M343.

A conductor and his engineer have a somewhat strange relationship. The conductor handles all the paperwork. He's also officially in charge of the train, but the engineer is the only one who can run the train.

A person needs to be Federal Railroad Administration certified to move a train. You go to school to become a conductor, but then you have another six months of training to be an engineer.

However, since the conductor is considered the boss, he can order the engineer what to do. When trains stop and pick up or set off cars and engines, the conductor is the one who pulls the pins, gets on the radio, and tells the engineer when to throttle forward.

Glenn had been working as a conductor and then an engineer for twenty years, more than a decade longer than Louis had been a conductor.

Sometimes the relationship created tension, sometimes things were fine. Glenn had always gotten along with Louis well enough.

"We good to go?" Glenn asked him.

"We're still on target to leave at two thirty-five, Old Head."

In the industry the nickname Old Head was an acknowledgment of seniority and also a compliment.

"Good, because I want to get this run over and get back home in time to catch the Braves game tonight."

++++

"How many has it been?" I asked Richard while we waited to hear from my wife.

"How many?"

"How many more victims. How many people have you killed since April, since I—"

"Since you killed me?"

"Since I brought you back."

"I haven't killed anyone. I've been seeing how long I can go in between."

"Why?"

"To test my self-control."

Maybe he was telling me the truth, maybe not. At the moment, though, I couldn't think of anything Richard could gain by lying to me. He would be going back to prison forever when I brought him in, whether there'd been any additional victims or not.

"Do you know why Mason would do this?" I asked him. "Why he would target Corrine after you helped him escape from prison?" I'd almost said, "murder Corrine," but somehow it felt like being that blunt would have dishonored her memory.

"I've been asking myself the same question. The only thing I can come up with: He knew it would hurt me and he's wondering how I'll react." He stared past me toward the skyline. "And he's about to find out."

The breeze brushed past us.

"Richard, why did you start out by killing women who resembled your sister?"

"I've read your books, Patrick. I know how you feel about trying to identify and delineate motives. Are you really asking me to give you the motive that lies behind so much of my past? You, of all people?"

For more than a decade I've been teaching other investigators that motives can't be easily defined, that it's futile to try to summarize complex psychological behavior in a single word or phrase. Hate. Anger. Jealousy. Greed.

Where does one end and another begin?

But still, now, I caught myself wanting to do that, wanting some answers. Some closure.

"Call me curious."

"That lovely wife of yours must be wearing off on you."

"Bring her up again, Richard, and I will make you sorry that you did."

"Ah—that's what I was looking for there: that fierce, protective side of love. You want to know why I killed those women, well, it's because I loved Corrine and I didn't know what to do with that feeling."

"You loved her so you murdered innocent people? You ate them? That doesn't make any sense."

"She had to be the only one."

"The only one?"

"No imitations. No copies. Do you understand?"

I tried to, I really did, but I wasn't able to wrap my mind around what he was saying, to see things from his perspective. Maybe that was a good thing.

There was one more question I'd been wondering about. I couldn't think of a better time than right now to bring it up. "Why did you help Mason escape from prison?"

"I wasn't feeling very magnanimous toward you after our last encounter. As you recall, you shot me. I thought perhaps Mason would go after you, but it looks like he chose someone else."

Yes, he had.

Corrine.

Basque was quiet. "Pat, as long as we're having this little sit-down, tell me why you gave me CPR by the marsh after I'd drowned. Why didn't you just leave me dead?"

*Justice.*

*The darkness.*

*Demons calling to me in the night.*

"Because I was afraid of becoming like you," I told him bluntly.

"You are like me."

He'd claimed that once before and I'd countered it, told him that I wasn't, that I fought the darkness and that's what made us different. Now I didn't reply. As I'd been thinking earlier today: We are, all of us, like him to a certain degree.

But maybe I was more like him than I cared to admit.

*But you did bring him back, Pat.*

*You did—*

A notification came up on the iPad that I had an incoming Skype call.

I tapped the screen and Lien-hua's face came up

"Pat, I found what you need."

"First, how's Brin?"

"They're doing a C-section now. Ralph's in the OR with her. Tessa's in the waiting room. The doctor seems confident the baby will be okay. In the meantime, I have what you wanted on Davenport. It was a little hard to track down, but he rented a place over in Fourth Ward." She gave me the address. "Should I call it in to get a car over there?"

"No. I'll let you know more as soon as I can."

After we'd ended the call, I headed for the car's passenger's door, pulled up a map application on the iPad, and said to Basque, "Alright. Let's go. It doesn't look like it's very far."

++++

Kurt tuned to a live feed of Fan Celebration Day on television.

A news chopper flying overhead provided footage of the thousands of people who were outside the stadium at booths that'd been set up. Even though kickoff was still more than an hour away, hundreds of folks had already entered the stadium so they could get good seats for the upcoming game.

# 72

We parked.

The historic home that Davenport had rented lay across the street—that was, if Davenport was even an alias that Mason was using. This could all be some sort of elaborate ploy.

The neighborhood was quiet.

Still.

I considered leaving Richard in the car, but then realized I could keep a better eye on him if I brought him with me.

"If you let me come in"—he seemed to be reading my thoughts—"I'll help you find him. If you leave me here alone, I'll take off. Then you'll have to split your resources between finding me and finding Mason, and you don't have time for that."

*And maybe this is where you leave the two of them alone in the same room—if Mason's really here.*

"Try anything and I will put you down," I said.

"Understood."

I confirmed that the sensor for tracking him was working; then I left the iPad on the seat, and together we crossed the street toward the house that Kurt Mason was purportedly using.

++++

Kurt heard a knock at the door.

For a moment he tried to figure out if it was just his imagination playing tricks on him, but then he heard it again.

He flicked out the straight razor and, staying toward the back of the room, he peered out the front window.

And saw Patrick Bowers and Richard Basque standing on the front porch of the house.

++++

I knocked again but no one answered. However, through a window, in the recessed shadows of the home, I caught sight of movement at the other end of the living room, so I could tell that someone was here.

"Hello? Mr. Davenport? Kurt?"

Whoever was inside stepped back and vanished into the darkness. Given what I knew, there was no time for second-guessing things.

I unholstered the Glock, then tried the door. Found it locked.

Okay, this might not fly too well with my superiors— but then again, neither would working with Richard Basque.

I stepped back to kick in the door.

*Wait, there might be a trip wire like there was at the apartment. Don't—*

But that's when I heard a door at the back of the house slam shut.

"Get back in the car," I ordered Richard.

I flew around the side of the house and just barely caught sight of Mason hoisting himself over a fence encircling one of the neighboring backyards. I identified myself, shouted for him to stop, but that only spurred him on to move faster, and then he was out of sight.

Sprinting toward the fence, I made short work of it and then scrutinized the area. Someone appeared to be walking to the south of me, near the street, but he disappeared behind a house before I could identify if it was Mason or not.

It was the only person I could see, so I bolted in that direction, but by the time I got there I found it wasn't him. Just a man out walking his dog.

Cursing, I returned to where I'd lost Mason.

Man, I wished I had a radio or a phone to call for backup.

I gauged the layout of neighboring streets, trying to anticipate what direction he might have fled in, but he knew how I thought and he might very well have gone the opposite of what I would anticipate.

*Or, guessing you'd think that, he might not have.*

Enough.

I couldn't read minds.

*Get this neighborhood cordoned off.*

I hurried back to the car to call it in using the iPad.

But found that the sedan was gone.

And so was Richard.

When I glanced toward the house Mason had rented, I saw that the front door had been kicked in.

*Basque must have entered before taking off!*

I saw no landlines leading to Mason's house, but they did go to one of the homes across the street. I ran to the front door, knocked. No one answered.

Well, I wasn't about to waste time going door-to-door to call for some officers.

One kick did it. The lock shattered and the door flew open.

Once inside, I located a phone, punched in 911, and told dispatch to get some cars over here immediately.

While they were confirming the address, I pulled out the sensor to track the nanobots and saw that Basque was already several blocks away and was traveling west.

I couldn't tell for sure if he was still in the vehicle, but he was moving rapidly, so it appeared he wasn't on foot.

I told the dispatcher the last place I'd seen Mason, as well as Basque's exact location and the make, model, and license plate of his car.

*Clear Mason's house. Make sure he wasn't working with anyone.*

I finished the call, angled across the street, and, gun in hand, I entered the residence to confirm that no one was there lying in wait.

# 73

All clear.

No one in the house.

*Eleven minutes average response time,* I kept telling myself, but we were close enough to police headquarters that I figured we could cut that at least in half and, based on the sirens I heard coming this direction, it seemed like that was the case.

Still, Mason had slipped away and Basque was on the move. Richard wanted revenge and I couldn't see him stopping until he'd seen things through to the end. He'd told me that he had more information about Mason's plan. He'd also mentioned three thirty, which gave us just shy of one hour to work with.

And Mason was planning to make a statement.

Basque had mentioned that too.

All part of his story.

*Why did Richard enter the house? Why didn't he chase Mason with you?*

I wasn't sure, but I did know one thing: Until we

could find Mason, Basque was our best bet for stopping whatever he had planned.

And we could track Basque's precise location with the help of those nanobots.

I checked the sensor again to see where he was, then I mentally overlaid a map of the area with what I remembered from driving around the city with Guido yesterday morning.

From what I could tell, Basque's movement stopped at the Charlotte Regional Medical Center, the place I'd gotten my stitches yesterday.

*A hospital? Why would he go there?*

*A blood transfusion to get rid of the nanobots?*

No, I'd asked O'Brien about that and he'd told me it wouldn't work. Besides, it would take way too long, even if Basque somehow had a doctor waiting for him.

*For drugs to try to mask the nanobots' signal?*

That was possible. If so, I wondered how Basque would even be able to guess which ones to use.

I would've called the hospital but I had no phone. Officers were en route. I'd update them in a minute.

A few minutes ago, when I was searching Mason's house, I'd discovered a laptop in the first-floor bedroom. The computer had been smashed in with a decorative stone bookend. Our lab would probably be able to recover data, but that would take time that we did not have.

*Did Basque destroy it or did Mason do it before he fled?*

Earlier, when I first got here and was standing on the front porch, I hadn't heard any sounds from inside the house, but that wasn't definitive. Mason could have still been the one to destroy it.

Sirens outside.

*Okay, deal with the computer in a minute.*

I hurried to the street so I could meet up with the officers as they arrived, and a moment later I saw the flashing lights as one of the cruisers rounded the corner and raced my way.

After identifying myself, I told them where Basque was, then I informed them about the house Davenport had been using and the laptop, and explained that we needed to get the Field Office's Cyber experts and ERT here right away. "Check any cars leaving this neighborhood for Mason."

"Yes, sir."

"I'm going to need your cell phone."

He handed it to me.

This was getting to be a habit.

"And one more thing."

"What's that?"

"Your car."

++++

Glenn waited while Louis finished inspecting the manifest. Then, when he said they were ready to roll, he throttled forward on the route through Charlotte that he'd taken so many times over the years.

++++

As I drove toward the hospital, I checked the scanner and saw that the nanobot signal had stopped transmitting.

I tapped at the sensor's screen; no change.

*What's going on?*

I tried it again.

Nothing.

No signal.

*That doesn't make any sense.*

Using my newly acquired cell phone, I called O'Brien

to see if there was a setting I needed to adjust or recalibrate.

He didn't pick up.

I left a message for him to check Basque's location by using the unit he had on campus; however, I realized it would take precious time for him to get to his equipment.

Time we didn't have.

I ended by telling O'Brien to call me immediately at this number, then I phoned the hospital's security office to make sure they'd gotten word from dispatch to look for Basque.

While I had them on the line, I asked about the young man Basque had envenomated and found out his name was Andy Mitzner and that he was being treated and was currently unconscious but was in stable condition.

Then a thought: *What if that's why Basque went to the hospital? To finish the job he started?*

*Does Mitzner know something? Could they have been working together?*

*Was he a victim here or a partner?*

"Get some officers to Mitzner's room," I told the chief of hospital security, who was on the line with me, a guy named Housman.

"We have an officer stationed there, sir."

"This is Richard Basque we're talking about. One's not going to be enough."

++++

Kurt Mason had barely managed to get out of the neighborhood before the officers arrived.

So, Richard and Patrick were working together. Well, he hadn't seen that one coming.

He'd had just enough time to destroy the laptop back at the house.

The Bureau's computer forensics techs would be able to retrieve data from it eventually, but it would be far too late to stop the dominoes from falling.

Everything was in play. The clock was ticking.

The car he'd been using was still back at the house.

At least he had his phone and could track M343's movement through his cell's Internet connection.

But before anything else, he needed a vehicle.

And then he needed to get out of the city before the authorities tried to evacuate Uptown, or he was going to get stuck in traffic, and that was the last thing he could afford.

++++

A CMPD officer met me at the hospital's front entrance. Housman was with her. The officer was a stout, stern-looking woman; the security chief was wire-thin and had quick, intelligent eyes.

"What do we know?" I asked them.

"Come on." Housman signaled for me to follow him. "It happened in the room where they do MRIs."

# 74

"So what happened, exactly?" I said as the three of us ran down the hall.

"He was here," Housman said in between breaths. "Basque was. We'll show you."

I've had a couple of MRIs in the past, so I knew that the magnet of the machine is always on and you don't want to enter the room unless you're certain you don't have any metal on you. I'd heard stories about oxygen tanks being drawn through the doorway and flying toward the magnet so fast that they exploded on impact.

We met in the lobby just down the hall. Another officer was there, trying to comfort a distraught woman whose hands were trembling. "He made me do it." Her voice faltered. "He made me let him in. He had a butcher knife."

*A butcher knife?*

*Probably from Mason's house.*

*But he couldn't have taken it in the room with him there, so—*

Right now I was much more interested in where Basque was than in what he'd done with the knife.

"A man about my height?" I described his clothes to her. "Dark hair? Athletic build?"

"That's him."

"You're the radiologist?"

She shook her head. "I'm just a tech."

An MRI could last anywhere from ten minutes to several hours—but that was to get accurate images, not simply to be in the presence of the magnet. That would only take a matter of seconds.

*Could the electromagnetic field in the room have short-circuited the nanobots?*

Well, it was enough to fry a cell phone or wipe the magnetic strip on a credit card.

I wasn't sure if the magnet would have pulled the bots right through Basque's body or just fried them where they were in his bloodstream, but either way it could not have felt good.

The MRI tech shuddered. "What he said he would do to me if I didn't help him. I can't even . . ."

Knowing Basque, I could only imagine the kinds of threats he might have made.

I checked the sensor again, found no readings.

Cursed.

*The security cameras.*

"Where's your office?' I asked Housman. "We need to see where and when Basque left this building. Or if maybe he's still here."

On our way to the hospital's security suite we confirmed that Mitzner, the young man who'd been envenomated, was protected.

He was still unconscious.

The security center was outfitted with an array of

eight screens, each showing a half-dozen camera feeds. Cutting-edge.

Yes.

Good.

We had something to work with here.

I gave the staff a description of Basque's sedan and told them the license plate number. "I want to know where he parked, if his car is still here, and where he went after leaving the MRI room."

While the officers and security personnel reviewed the surveillance footage, I sorted through the case. Reviewed where we were at.

Richard Basque was on the run.

Kurt Mason was free and had something big planned for today, something climactic. According to what he'd told me it was coming tonight, but according to what Basque had said, something was supposed to happen this afternoon at three thirty.

Less than thirty-five minutes from now.

Time was ticking.

Mason knew about the mines, he'd researched them at UNC Charlotte's library, apparently while using the name Leroy Davenport.

For the moment I decided to work from the hypothesis that he would've uncovered the same map I did, and I mentally reviewed the location of the sixty-three shafts of the Rudisill–St. Catherine Mine system, including the location of the shaft in that textile mill.

I was reminded of the Semtex and the fragility of that area with all of those shafts and with those tunnels radiating throughout it.

If Basque was right, Mason was going to make a memorable statement.

The more I evaluated things, the more I began to believe that taking out a SWAT or HRT crew as they cleared a mine of explosives wasn't climactic enough for Mason. He would go for something bigger—and, besides, as I'd noted earlier, he wouldn't have known the time we might try to access the mine.

*It's something else.*

The highway?

The railroad?

The stadium?

*It's Fan Celebration Day. Is that what he has planned? He made a delivery there for NVDS. Could he have planted some sort of device?*

*But then how does that fit in with all the work he went through to find the mines?*

No tunnels reached out that far or stretched under the stadium, so he couldn't have—

*Wait a minute.*

There were photos of a rail line at Mason's apartment.

Basque had also mentioned the Cathouse Signal.

Railroad tracks passed right by the stadium.

Cathouse . . . Cathouse . . .

A train signal?

Yes. That fit—the Cathouse. The place where the Panthers play.

*That's it. Mason's going to blow a train as it crosses the Cathouse Signal.*

"Fan Celebration Day," I said to the people with me in the room. "What happens at three thirty?"

"Kickoff," said one of the men. "My brother's there with his kid. Goes every year."

I whipped out the phone I'd gotten from the officer at Mason's house.

"Sir . . ." Housman paused the video on the third

screen from my left. "That's him. In the hall on the south wing. Eight minutes ago."

"See if he leaves the building." I confirmed that it was Basque even as I scrolled on the phone's screen to find what I was looking for. "Listen, a railroad line goes right past the stadium. Do you know which company runs the trains on that track?"

The security team members shook their heads, but the CMPD officer replied, "No, but CSX and Knoxville Southeast Railway have a lot of trains that go through the area."

Okay.

A place to start.

I pulled up Knoxville Southeast Railway's site, called the emergency number, and got patched through to their dispatch center for this region.

The security staff were following the footage as Basque moved from one exterior camera to the next toward the edge of the grounds.

A dispatcher answered.

"There's a track," I said after identifying myself, "one that runs right past the Panthers' stadium here in Charlotte. Do they call it the Cathouse Signal?"

"Yes." She sounded surprised and a little leery. "How did you know that?"

"Are there any passenger trains coming through this afternoon at three thirty?"

"No, sir. Just a freight line. M343."

"What's it carrying?"

"I'd have to check the manifest to—"

"Check it. Hurry."

"Well, the conductor has the most up-to-date shipping papers. I'll radio him, but it'll take a few minutes."

"I'll stay on the line."

On the video footage, the team found Basque's car and images of him leaving this wing, but once he got outside and skirted around the parking lot, he left the view screen and crossed the road toward a strip mall.

"Get out there," I said. "He's on foot. Find him."

"Yes, sir."

Housman stayed with me, while the others took off in search of Basque.

++++

Glenn thought it was a bit unusual for Louis to get a call from dispatch to verify the shipping papers while the train was en route like this, but he just chalked it up to a clerical error or a glitch somewhere in the system. God knows it wouldn't be the first one.

He throttled up from thirty miles an hour to his running speed of fifty and headed toward Charlotte.

++++

"Sir," the woman on the phone told me, "I confirmed the manifest."

"Are there any hazardous materials on that train?"

"Yes, of course. This is a six-thousand-foot train. Nearly every freight train that length is transporting some hazmat cars. It would be unusual if they weren't."

"Look over that list. Are there any chemicals that could . . ." I decided to play it safe. "Listen, can you just stop that train?"

"Sir?"

"Stop the train. Either that or reroute it until we know more of what we're looking at here."

"We can't just order a train to be stopped or diverted to another track."

"Of course you can. That's what a dispatch center is there for."

"Um, you're going to have to talk to my supervisor."

"Put him on."

"Her."

"Her, then." I was losing my patience here. Every second we spent talking, that train was getting closer to the mines that ran right under its tracks. "And hurry," I added.

While I waited on the cell phone, I asked Housman to make a call on the landline.

Right now I didn't have time to waste trying to sort through who to contact, which local authorities might be best to get in touch with and in what order. I decided I could cut through all the red tape with one phone call.

Since 9/11, the Bureau's official capacity has been steadily shifting from law enforcement to counterterrorism. And this would definitely count.

I told Housman the number.

"Who am I calling?"

"The Director of the FBI."

# 75

"What is this I hear about you meeting up with Richard Basque?" Director Wellington asked me sharply.

"Later, Margaret. There's something a lot bigger going down right now."

I was still on hold on the cell phone, waiting for the Knoxville Southeast Railway dispatch office's supervisor to reroute M343.

As quickly as possible, I brought Margaret up to speed.

"But you don't know yet what's on that train?"

"It's carrying hazardous materials. That's all I have at this point. I'm trying to see if they can redirect or stop it."

She thought for a moment. "And how close is this to the textile mill where Ingersoll and his team are?"

"A quarter mile away or so."

"I'll have them inspect the tracks for explosives, any sensors, any detonation materials. In the meantime, we have how many people in harm's way?"

"There's an open-air stadium nearby. They say twenty thousand people are there."

"Alright, I'm going to make a call, see if we should evacuate that stadium."

I didn't always agree with Margaret, but we were on the same page right now.

The tracks crossed under I-277 at the Carson Boulevard exit ramp. The mine extended out under that area. I told her about it. "Everything converges at that point."

"I'll see what I can do."

++++

Margaret Wellington hung up with Patrick Bowers and called the director of the Federal Emergency Management Agency.

She'd worked with FEMA before and, from what she could tell, Director Adler was a sharp guy and he wasn't afraid to stick his neck out if he needed to.

After she'd told him what was going on, he said, "Our number-one priority is getting potential victims to safety in a cautious and defensive manner. In this case our response will depend on the chemical released, the humidity, wind conditions, the size of the spill."

"Think worst-case scenario."

"Start by evacuating everyone within a sixteen-hundred-meter radius."

She hung up and phoned the mayor of Charlotte to have him evacuate that stadium and Uptown Charlotte.

And to shut down I-277.

++++

Kurt Mason was in his newly acquired Lexus SUV, the body of the previous owner stowed in the backseat.

As he found his way out of the city, he used his cell to monitor the train's progress.

It was in signal territory and was running at about fifty miles per hour. He knew that a train that size, going that fast, on a level track would take nearly a mile to stop.

That is, if the air brakes were working properly.

Without the normal braking capability, it would take at least twice that far.

A local radio station was carrying a live feed of the pregame festivities. He tuned in to monitor things as they progressed.

++++

I heard back from the woman in charge of the Knoxville Southeast Railway dispatch office.

"Hello?" She did not sound excited to be on the phone with me. "Who am I speaking with?"

"Patrick Bowers, FBI. Who is this?"

"Deanna Lambert."

"Ms. Lambert, listen to me, there is a very real possibility that your train that's heading for Charlotte—M343—is the target of a potential terrorist attack. We need that train rerouted or stopped."

"Under whose authorization?"

I decided to go straight to the top. "The Director of the FBI."

"I'll need to speak with him."

"Her." I rattled off Margaret's cell number. "In the meantime, e-mail me the manifest. And who can I talk to about the chemicals?"

"That would be Benson."

"Put him on."

I gave her my e-mail address, then used one of the computers on the desk beside me to go online and pull up my account so I could read the file.

Seconds later, the e-mail from Ms. Lambert arrived.

Benson came on the line as I was scanning the document. I didn't recognize most of the chemicals or different hazmat designations. "Talk me though this."

"Well, it lists the contents and location of all the cars on the train. You can tell which ones are hazardous because there's a boxed-in set of asterisks on the left of the manifest for that car. There's always a five-car buffer between any loaded hazmat cars and an engine."

I held the phone against my ear with one hand, used the mouse with the other. I scrolled through the pages. There were dozens of boxed-in sheets. This was not helping.

"Think like a terrorist," I said. "You want to blow this train knowing there are lots of people close by. What chemical would you be hoping to release?"

"I don't know. I couldn't— You really think someone is going to try and blow this train?"

"It's possible. Look at the list. What jumps out at you?"

I checked the time.

3:07 p.m.

"Well, there are a couple boxcars of dynamite. It's also shipping hydrazine, which I'm not too excited about."

"What's hydrazine?"

"It's basically rocket fuel."

*Oh.*

*Perfect.*

"What else?"

"Well, the one thing would be . . . But . . ."

"What are you thinking?"

"Anhydrous ammonia. There are twelve tankers of it."

"Tell me about anhydrous ammonia."

"It's a liquefied compressed gas. 'Anhydrous' just means 'without water.' Its primary use is in fertilizer. Because of the nitrogen content it's also used in power plants and, because it absorbs so much heat—it boils at minus-twenty-eight degrees Fahrenheit—it's also used in refrigeration and as a coolant."

"Is it flammable? Will it explode?"

"It doesn't have a flashpoint, but its upper explosive limit really depends on the vapor concentration in the air. It has a short window of flammability, but, especially in indoor situations where it's being used as a coolant, it might get mixed with oil and that would widen the range. There'll be a deflagration, not an explosion exactly. It'll burn up very fast."

"Alright. Well, that's what we want."

*Good, good, good.*

"But it does create a vapor cloud," he continued. "It's a very strong base, causes severe chemical burns on contact, and, since it's moisture seeking, it'll spread fast."

"So, inhalation," I anticipated where this was going, and it was not a good direction. "Your throat, your lungs—it'll coat them."

"Yes. And your eyes. Corneal burns and blindness. The vapor is lighter than air. Heat, low humidity, wind—they can take a plume up hundreds of feet into the air."

"Let's say the wind carries it toward an open-air stadium. Would it settle in there?"

"A stadium?"

"Yes."

"Well, because of the eddy created as the vapor passes over the upper edge, sure, it would settle in. Is there really a stadium downwind?"

I recalled the breeze in the graveyard.

"There is."

I could picture a vapor cloud curling over the lip of the stadium, then pooling down inside of it. Thousands of people gasping for breath, blinded, panicking, climbing over each other trying to escape.

"But," Benson tried to reassure me, "those pressurized tank cars are reinforced by up to three-quarters of an inch of steel. Most of them have a thermal shield as well and another one-eighth-inch steel jacket covering that. These things do not just spring a leak."

"But what about getting the ammonia in or out? It has to have valves of some kind."

"All the valves and fittings are protected from rollover by a housing on the top of the car."

"For now let's just assume our guy knows what he's doing. What would happen if these twelve cars ruptured and the vapor cloud entered that stadium?"

"Depending on the density of the plume, you could be talking about a life-safety situation."

"Fatal levels of exposure."

"Yes."

*To tens of thousands of people.*

Benson was quiet. "But it won't come to that. Those cars are designed to withstand a derailment."

"Think. If it were possible to puncture the cars."

"It's not."

"But if it were—and we're not just talking about a few tank cars rolling onto their side, but a dozen of them blowing up or potentially dropping hundreds of feet into a network of collapsed mines. Would they rupture?"

"I mean . . ." There was a distinct change in his tone. "With heat impingement . . . Anhydrous ammonia has a direct pressure-to-temperature relationship so as heat goes up, so does the pressure . . . Each of those cars is carrying over thirty thousand gallons of . . . Oh, my God."

I got an incoming call from Margaret and put Benson

on hold. I started to tell her what I knew, but she leapt in. "Ingersoll's men found some sort of pressure-release mechanism. It's welded to the track in several places. The only way to dismantle it is by removing that section of track. And even then we're not sure what might happen— it might be rigged to blow those shafts."

I whipped through what I'd found out from Benson: "Anhydrous ammonia. This train, M343, has twelve tankers of it—over three hundred fifty thousand gallons. It creates a vapor cloud that can be lethal. We have to stop that train."

"I have a call in to the head of the railroad. You're there, Patrick. You know more about this situation than anyone. I want you up in the air, getting real-time eyes on this thing. Where are you?"

"The Charlotte Regional Medical Center."

"Good. They should have a helicopter there. And they'll have a pilot on call or on-site."

I'd landed here yesterday after my confrontation with Mason in the mine. "They do have a landing pad, but—"

"I'll clear things with the hospital. Just get to the pad."

# 76

3:19 p.m.
11 minutes left

Glenn received word from dispatch and tossed the automatic brake valve handle to put the train into emergency status.

Along with the dynamic brakes, he also engaged the head-end device and flipped the switch to get the EOT, or the end-of-train device, to dump air from the rear of the train so there would be continuity in the braking.

Still, it was going to take a while to stop.

++++

By the time I arrived at the landing pad, the on-call pilot was firing up the helicopter. "You must be well connected, my friend," he called over the sound of the rotors. "The order to take you up came straight from the top." I wasn't sure if he was referring to someone from the hospital or to Margaret, and at this point I didn't really care.

I'd ended the call with Benson, but I still had the cell phone with me. However, with the sound of the rotors, I wasn't sure it was going to do me a whole lot of good on the helicopter. "Can we patch in to a landline from the headset, or does it only connect with emergency services?"

"Sure. No problem."

We took off. I set up a conference call with Margaret and the president of Knoxville Southeast Railway, a nervous, twitchy-sounding guy named Albert. I didn't catch his last name.

I told the pilot, "Take us over the stadium."

As we flew across the city, I could see that traffic on I-277 near the overpass had been blocked and the cars were already backed up for nearly half a mile. No vehicles were on the overpass itself. All the roads leading out of Uptown Charlotte were clogged with traffic—and that was just going to get worse as we tried to evacuate the stadium.

I didn't know how Margaret had gotten word out so fast, but then I saw that we were not alone in the sky—a news chopper was hovering above the stadium. Maybe it'd been there to cover Fan Celebration Day or maybe—

"We can't reroute the train," Albert said frantically into my earpiece. "And it's not braking like it should."

"What does that mean?" Margaret asked.

"Something's wrong. It's not going to be able to stop in time."

As we soared near the stadium I could see fans streaming out of it and, considering the possibility of a poisonous vapor cloud spreading across the area, I briefly wondered if it might have been better to have them stay in it.

*No, Pat. They would have been trapped there with the gas.*

I imagined that by now hazmat teams, fire engines, and EMTs would all be on their way.

*We can't reroute the train.*

*We can't stop it in time.*

All the parking spots near the stadium were filled. I'm not a great judge of numbers, but I'd say at least twelve to fifteen thousand people were still inside the stadium itself.

*We need to do something to stop those tankers from rupturing.*

My pilot swiveled the chopper around and I saw M343 approaching from the southwest.

I eyed the track leading in the other direction as it went toward the northeast. "Take us up there," I told the pilot.

He tilted us forward and we shot through the sky.

*There's a pressure mechanism on that track. There's no way to get it off in time.*

*But you have to stop this. You have to!*

"Can we derail the train?" I asked Albert.

His voice was tense, desperate as he replied. "Even if that were an option, we could never get a derailer out there in time."

"A semi on the tracks? Anything like that?"

"That's not going to do it."

But by then I was only half listening. I could see that about three-quarters of a mile from the stadium the tracks branched out into a train yard. M343 was coming up from the opposite direction . . .

*That's crazy, Pat.*

*Maybe. But—*

"There's a rail yard northeast of the stadium," I said to Albert. "I see some engines there with the Knoxville Southeast Railway logo. Is that your train yard?"

"Yes."

"Are there any engineers there?"

"Certainly, but—"

"How soon can we get an engine fired up and on its way out of there?"

"What are you thinking?"

"How soon!"

"Just a matter of minutes if I put the call through, but—"

Margaret interrupted him. "What is it, Patrick? What are you thinking?"

*With that pressure-release mechanism out there, the track is going to blow when an engine crosses over the—*

*But you're talking about several acres of land dropping away and over a quarter of a million gallons of poisonous, liquefied compressed gas escaping a few hundred meters from a stadium filled with—*

Albert muttered, "There's no way we're going to be able to stop that train."

"Then," I said, "we need to blow the track before it gets there."

A pause. "What are you talking about?"

"Send one of those rail yard engines down the track to—"

"What?" he gasped. "Toward M343? A collision course?"

"Yes. Run it across that pressure mechanism so the tracks will blow."

"But M343 will derail when it hits the blown section of track or collides with that other engine," he countered.

"The guy at your dispatch center, Benson, he told me those tanker cars are reinforced, that they're designed to withstand rolling over—but they're not designed to withstand being blown up or dropping into collapsed mine shafts."

"So," Margaret said, "you're thinking we blow the track and just let the cars derail?"

"Yes."

Albert said, "That's insane."

"I'm out of ideas. And we're out of time." I was staring at the stadium. All those people. "What else do you propose?"

"Well, we need to come up with an action plan and—"

Margaret cut in. "There's no time for that. We need to stop M343 before it crosses that section of track. Is there any other way we can do it?"

A blunt silence. I assumed that Albert was processing everything, the implications, the risks. "The engineer will have to jump after he gets it rolling."

"Well, then, tell him to get ready to jump," Margaret said, "because we can't let those hazmat cars blow."

"Alright," Albert agreed at last. "I'll call dispatch and get an engine en route."

# 77

"Say again?" Glenn tapped the button on his radio. "Can you repeat that?"

"We're sending another engine toward you on your line," the dispatcher told him. "You need to jump before you get to the Cathouse Signal."

He knew M343 wasn't braking like it should, but—

He checked, and, to put it lightly, at the speed they were going, it was going to be a rough landing.

But it was better than hitting another engine, derailing, or blowing up.

"Just a little slower," he told Louis, "and then we need to go for it."

++++

I watched as an engine started out of the rail yard and entered the line that paralleled the stadium.

My pilot swiveled the helicopter around, and I could see M343 coming from the other direction. From here I couldn't tell its speed, but it obviously wasn't going to stop in time.

Two men were standing on the sides of the engine as it traveled along the tracks. One leapt off, hit the ground, and rolled. Moments later, the other jumped, hit the ground. And lay still.

++++

As he drove, Kurt Mason had been monitoring the breaking news on the radio.

The news anchor seemed baffled. "It appears there is now another engine on the tracks, heading toward M343. I have no idea what's . . ."

Kurt pulled over and stared at the skyline as he realized what they were trying to do.

++++

We radioed to get paramedics over to help the two men who'd leapt from M343. The engineer who'd started the solo engine in the rail yard had also jumped. He looked fine.

His unmanned engine passed the stadium toward the pressure-release mechanism and then crossed it.

And that's when the tracks blew.

# 78

The initial explosion sent debris flying hundreds of feet into the air and initiated a ripple of other explosions underground, causing a section of earth the size of two football fields to collapse.

As the mineshafts and tunnels of the Saint Catherine Mine blew, they swallowed that unmanned engine and the tracks behind it.

Black, bottomless-looking holes opened up at various places in the fresh wound marring the city as the long-abandoned shafts that had been capped off in the 1900s broke open.

The tracks in front of the engine that had vanished into the earth bowed and rippled as the shock wave rolled through the ground; then M343 hit the fractured section of tracks and its three lead engines derailed. The first two dropped into the rift and exploded, sending a thick, black cloud erupting into the sky.

The coupling of the third engine snapped and the engine plowed off the tracks, causing a pileup of the cars behind it. First, the buffer cars slid sideways, accordion style, as they jumped the tracks one by one. Then the tankers began to derail, colliding with the cars in front of them. Two tank cars smashed sidelong into each other.

One tanker rolled and sheared off the valves inside the protective housing, and immediately a cloud of thick white vapor spewed from it in a quickly expanding plume. The wind caught hold of it and carried it toward the stadium.

More freight cars folded up alongside the anhydrous ammonia tankers, tipping sideways off the track.

The overpass didn't crumble immediately, but seemed to do so in slow motion as its concrete supports shuddered and then cracked apart as the ground under their foundations broke open.

Since traffic had been stopped on both sides of the overpass, no cars were on top of it when it fell, but it smashed down violently onto a couple of M343's freight cars. A huge cloud of dust and debris billowed up from the impact.

Scores of people were trying to get out of the path of the dense vapor cloud. Thousands were covering their mouths as they rushed to get out of the way.

"Take us back to the hospital," I told the pilot soberly. "You're going to be needing this helicopter."

# 79

We landed, I stepped off the chopper, and the pilot immediately took off again to be available to transport victims back here to the hospital.

The wind from the rotors rushed past me, and then, as the sound of the helicopter's motor faded, the whine of emergency-vehicle sirens from all across Charlotte's Uptown filled the void.

Fire-suppression units, paramedics, police.

All en route.

I stood there for a long moment on the landing pad, listening to them.

Within minutes, the first victims would be starting to come in.

My phone vibrated: a text from Ralph: *8 pounds, 7 ounces. 20 inches long. Name: Tryphena. Mom and baby are doing fine.* There was an attached photo of Tryphena in her pink hat.

Tryphena.

Delicate.

Hmm. Eight pounds, seven ounces of delicate.

I wondered if Ralph knew what had just happened in Charlotte. The last I'd heard he was in the OR with Brin, and now, based on his text, it didn't appear he was aware of what was going on here.

I texted him congratulations and asked him to let Lien-hua and Tessa know that I was alright. I ended the message by telling him to turn on the news.

Taking a deep breath, I attempted to relax the tension in my chest, to get rid of the twisted feeling I had in my gut, but it didn't work.

I tried telling myself that we'd stopped this, that we'd acted in time, that we'd avoided the worst possible outcome, but I wasn't happy about the one we'd ended up with.

Undoubtedly, the vapor cloud was much smaller than it would have been if we hadn't taken action. We'd been able to get people out of harm's way, no cars were on the I-277 overpass when it gave way, and no one was on any of the engines when they derailed—although I was concerned about the man I'd seen jump from M343 who'd landed and then lay unmoving by the side of the track.

However, despite what we'd accomplished, Kurt Mason was still free; Richard Basque had slipped through my fingers; and, by agreeing to leave him alone with Mason, I felt like I'd compromised the very thing Lien-hua had exhorted me not to—my integrity.

Additionally, Mason had told me the climax was coming tonight. So if he was telling the truth, there was still something waiting on the horizon.

I walked to the edge of the landing pad and, watching the rising vapor cloud envelop the stadium, I listened to the cacophony of emergency-service vehicles racing to the site.

It was time.

Before things got any worse, I needed to call Margaret and tell her the truth about what had happened earlier today between Basque and me.

# 80

In her office at FBI Headquarters, Director Margaret Wellington listened in silence as Agent Bowers recounted the details of his encounter with Richard Devin Basque earlier that afternoon. "Given the circumstances," he said, "I should have called you."

"And what kind of deal did you make with him to avail yourself of the information he was offering regarding Kurt Mason's location?"

"I told him I would leave him alone with Kurt."

"You were going to leave the two of them alone?"

"That's right. It was a snap decision. And it was the wrong one."

She sorted through what he'd said. "But from what you're telling me, Basque would work only with you, and it's only because of his help that you were able to locate Mason's house, learn about the timing, and prevent what might have been one of the worst train disasters in US history."

"You're saying what? That Basque helped us save people's lives?"

"Not Basque, no, but the chain of events that he was a part of—and that you were a part of—yes."

Patrick was silent.

"These issues will obviously need to be reviewed by the Office of Professional Responsibility. Until then, you're on administrative leave."

"Administrative leave?"

"Yes."

"What about Mason and Basque?"

"Law enforcement down there will take care of that. I want you back in DC."

"When?"

"Tonight. We'll sort things out first thing Monday morning. Be in my office at eight o'clock sharp."

++++

I hung up with Margaret.

That had actually gone better than I'd expected. I'd thought she might ask for my resignation on the spot.

Okay, so administrative leave. I could work with that. I might not have carte blanche regarding the investigation, but it didn't mean my brain was on vacation.

And there were still a few things I needed to take care of.

++++

Margaret hung up and mulled over her next step.

Earlier in the afternoon, she'd discovered that indeed it was National Security Council Representative Pierce Jennings who'd been leaking details to the press. Her people had uncovered phone calls from him to one of Cable Broadcast News's political correspondents before the Bureau had officially released any details about the crimes this week to the press.

Why was he doing it?

Margaret didn't know.

She guessed power or money—in matters like this it was usually one or the other. She could look into that later. Right now she had a lot more to worry about in dealing with the incident in Charlotte than in dealing with Pierce Jennings in DC.

++++

I thought about calling Lien-hua and Tessa to tell them I was coming back to Washington, but opted to just text them instead.

Before leaving the hospital, I stopped by Mitzner's room. He was still unconscious. I told the officers guarding him that the minute he was able to speak, they needed to find out what they could from him about how Basque had envenomated him.

I checked with admitting and learned that the engineer and conductor from M343 were a little banged up from jumping off the train, but they were going to be alright. One of the men had a broken ankle, but that was the worst of it.

The engineer who'd started the engine from the rail yard was fine.

So we had at least a little good news.

Right now there was nothing more for me to do here at the hospital. There wasn't anything for me to do at the site of the wreck, either—it was all up to the fire chief and hazmat crews to evacuate the area and knock down that vapor cloud of anhydrous ammonia. Local and regional law enforcement would take care of security around the stadium.

When I made my way to the hospital's main entrance, the ambulances were starting to arrive with victims suffering the effects of inhaling the cloud of anhydrous ammonia.

The car that Voss had provided me with was still Uptown where I'd left it before my meeting with Basque. Getting into or out of Uptown was going to be nearly impossible.

However, the cruiser I'd borrowed to get to the hospital was here in the parking lot. I could use that for now. They could always pick it up from the airport later, after I'd boarded my plane.

Back at the hotel, I made arrangements to get on the earliest available flight, but it didn't leave Charlotte until after seven thirty, which meant that by the time I flew to DC, landed, and got out of the airport, it would be almost nine o'clock.

I flipped on the news while I packed my things.

They were talking about an anhydrous ammonia leak back in 2002 in Minot, North Dakota, and how it compared to this event today. Back then, emergency services told people to shelter in place—to stay in their houses and shut off their home heating systems to keep the vapor from being drawn indoors. And they told them to go into the bathrooms and, if they could smell the ammonia, to turn on the shower, and to wet washcloths and lay them over their mouths.

Well, that wasn't going to happen with all the people outside for Fan Celebration Day.

That day in North Dakota there'd been one fatality, dozens needed to be treated and nearly twelve thousand people were caught in the path of the vapor cloud.

I prayed that today we would get by without anyone being fatally affected by the anhydrous ammonia spill— the one, that, in a butterfly-effect sort of way, I was responsible for.

++++

Earlier that afternoon when Richard Basque had fled from Patrick, he hadn't known whether or not the MRI magnet would disrupt the nanobot sensors, but it was a chance he'd been willing to take.

He'd been expecting an ankle bracelet. He'd been prepared for that, but Patrick had surprised him.

Given more time he would've liked to research things a bit more in depth, but it looked like it had all worked out in the end.

With all those nanobots in his bloodstream, entering the MRI room had been excruciating——almost like thousands of needles piercing him all at once, trying to get out. It'd hurt like nothing he'd ever experienced before.

But, in the service of avenging his sister's death, it was worth it.

He hadn't found any clues as to Mason's whereabouts in his Fourth Ward home in the brief time he'd been in there while Patrick chased Mason around the back, but based on his previous conversations with him and the story he knew Mason was telling, Richard figured that at this point his best bet would probably be to head to DC.

Patrick had asked him if the climax would be in the afternoon or tonight. The only way he would have asked that question was if Mason had mentioned a timeline to him.

So, now, using the car he'd stolen from a mall parking lot, Richard headed north. No, he hadn't been able to corner Mason in Charlotte, but if he was right in what he was thinking, he would find him in the nation's capital tonight.

++++

I left the hotel and parked at the Charlotte Field Office.

Voss wasn't there—he was on-site over at the stadium,

working with the hazmat incident commander. In fact, almost everyone was gone from the Field Office and there was only a skeleton crew here.

I left the nanobot-tracking sensor, the body armor, the cell phone I'd borrowed from the police officer at the home Mason had rented, Ingersoll's automatic knife, and the Glock, with the agent at the front desk. I made arrangements for one of the agents to pick up the cruiser I was driving to the airport. Since my driver's license and creds were still at the bottom of the mine shaft, I pulled some paperwork together to get me through airport security.

Then, distracted by my thoughts about Mason and Basque, I left for the Charlotte Douglas International Airport to fly back home.

++++

Kurt Mason was impressed.

Yes, the Semtex had exploded. Yes, the mine had collapsed. Yes, the freeway overpass had fallen, and one of the tankers had released some of its contents, but if the news reports were correct, there had been no fatalities.

Patrick had managed to stop M343 before it would have blown as it crossed the pressure sensor.

It was good work, but this had always been about more than just the train wreck and the chemical spill. That was part of it, yes, an important part, but so were the textile plant and the mine. And it was that broader story that mattered more than the number of casualties.

Anonymous people die anonymous deaths every day. But their lives, their deaths, don't always mean anything, unless they're part of something bigger.

However, tonight the people who were going to die would be remembered. Their names were going to live on in posterity after the website went live.

There was still the final act of the story, the one that would tie everything together, the one that, in retrospect, Patrick and his team would see was the place where everything had been heading all along.

And that act would take place tonight at nine thirty in Washington, DC.

# PART V

# The Fourth
# Statue

# 81

6:34 p.m.

Tessa was in the hospital room alone with Brineesha and Tryphena, who lay sleeping in the bassinet beside the bed.

Ralph and Lien-hua had stepped out to make a few calls. Tony, who'd spent the past two hours there, had left to stay the night at his friend's house.

Now, as Tessa watched the news with Brineesha, neither of them said a word.

FBI Director Wellington was giving a news conference about the train wreck in Charlotte. The Director didn't mention names, but Tessa had spoken with Lien-hua before she left the room so she knew about Patrick's role.

She also knew that her dad was flying back tonight. Lien-hua was planning to pick him up from Dulles at nine.

Tessa had tried calling him twice.

He hadn't answered.

Director Wellington finished up by fielding some rather pointed questions from the press about the Bureau's response to the incident.

"Why was the FBI even involved in this?" one reporter asked. "Rather than FEMA?"

"We were in contact with FEMA officials, but counterterrorism is our mission, not theirs. FEMA responds to disasters. We do all we can to stop them."

They asked her about the culpability of the Bureau in regard to her decision to approve the intentional wrecking of a train carrying hazardous materials through a major metropolitan city, and she noted that the wreck had averted a far greater disaster. "This event resulted in no fatalities and, from all available data, that would not be the case if we had not acted when we did to stop M343."

Before closing, she accepted one final question: "You've announced that you're running for Virginia's First District congressional seat next term. How do you think your handling of this situation will impact your political career?"

She replied without hesitation, "There are some things that are more important than a political career. Protecting innocent lives is at the top of that list. Thank you for your time."

Then she stepped away from the podium, the press conference wrapped up, and Brineesha said to Tessa, "I do believe Director Wellington is going to be known for that quote. Whatever her political career ends up being, that statement is going to stick with her."

It wasn't such a bad sentiment to have associated with your name: protecting innocent lives as being more important than a political career.

Tessa was just surprised it'd come from Director Wellington. It sounded more like something Patrick would say.

She tried calling him again.

He didn't pick up.


Lien-hua returned, invited Tessa out for dinner, and they walked down the street to a Thai place near the hospital.

The construction crew that had been there all day was setting up to work into the night. Under the glare of bright work lights, one of them was hooking up the hose of an industrial-strength pressure washer.

To Tessa, it brought back a bad memory.

She'd helped Patrick pressure wash the back deck and the porch earlier in the summer and knew that, depending on the tip you used at the end of the hose and your proximity, you could score concrete with one of those things.

She'd been wearing flip-flops that day and had made the mistake of getting her left foot under the stream for just an instant. The jet of water had ripped through her skin.

Thank God she hadn't had the narrow-stream-tip-thing on there. It probably would've taken off one of her toes. Grossed her out just thinking about it.

*Move past that, girl.*

*You're about to eat supper.*

Tessa and Lien-hua found a booth in the back of the restaurant, just like she'd done with Beck.

*You should be getting used to sitting with your back up against the wall by now.*

As those words rolled through her mind, there seemed to be deeper meaning to them, but at the moment she wasn't quite sure what it was.

After they'd ordered their food, Lien-hua said, "Just so you know, Pat's going to be on administrative leave when he gets back."

"For what? Working with Basque?"

Lien-hua looked at her curiously.

"Brineesha and I have been watching the news."

"They reported about Basque?"

"I pieced a few things together."

"Well, yes. Your dad is on leave for working with Richard Basque."

They were both quiet. As the only two women to survive being abducted by that man, they shared a deep, harrowing connection with each other—but it was something neither of them liked to bring up or talk about.

Tessa took a sip of her root beer. "But no one died in the train wreck and, from what they're saying, that wouldn't have been the case if they hadn't acted—if Patrick hadn't acted."

"That's true. Hundreds of people—thousands, actually—were at risk of losing their lives."

"That should count for something, right?"

Lien-hua seemed to be balancing out how to reply. "Things don't always count for what they should."

"So, basically, for Patrick, today both rocked and sucked at the same time."

"I think that's not a bad way of putting things."

The food came. The two of them ate in relative silence, and finally Tessa said, "I haven't called Beck yet, by the way. I don't know if I'm going to."

"Well, if you are, I'd suggest you do so before your dad gets home."

"Why's that?"

"Pat's going to have a lot on his mind." Lien-hua left it at that.

"Yeah." Tessa wasn't sure that really answered her question, but it didn't seem like the right time to probe. "I guess he will." Then she asked, "Is my dad going to be okay?"

Lien-hua didn't answer right away. "Yes. He will. He'll be okay."

# 82

While Lien-hua stepped away from the table to use the restroom, Tessa took out her cell phone and stared at it.

Despite her reluctance to talk on the phone, she needed to actually talk to Beck—not just text him—if she was going to find any closure on this.

A sigh.

A decision.

And then, at last, she went ahead and tapped in his number.

Three rings later he answered. "Hello?"

"Hey, it's Tessa."

"Tessa?"

"Yeah. Don't hang up."

"How did you get this number?"

"That doesn't matter." But as soon as she'd said those words, she realized that they might not serve to get this conversation off on the right foot. "I got it off Lien-hua's phone. Listen, can we talk? I mean, face-to-face?"

"You can't call me, Tessa."

"I just want to straighten things out. The way they ended last night, the way . . . Well, if you'll meet with me just this once, then you never have to talk to me again. Just don't blow me off. Please don't blow me off."

A pause. "I'm on an assignment."

"Until when? When do you get off?"

"I won't be done until nine or ten tonight."

"That's fine." She really did not want to wait until tomorrow. "That'll work."

"Where will you be?"

"I'm not sure if I'll be at home or at the hospital."

"It might be better if we didn't meet at your house."

"Um, yeah. Okay."

"I'll text you when I'm done here. You can let me know where you want to get together."

"Okay. I'll see you soon."

"I'll see you soon, Tessa."

++++

It took Kurt Mason two stops before he found a grocery store that carried balloons with the message on them that he was looking for.

He purchased one and jumped back on the highway, then, once he was on his way, he called ahead to his person in DC. "I'm going to be needing you after all."

"And then you'll bring her home?"

"Yes."

"When do you need me there?"

"Nine thirty."

"And then all this will be over?"

"Yes. Then all this will be over."

# 83

I spent the flight deep in thought.

I ran through what had happened today: dropping Ralph off at the airport this morning, the briefing at the Field Office, the research with Professor O'Brien, meeting with Richard Basque . . . almost catching Mason at the house.

Almost.

And then the flurry of activity as we tried to stop the train to avert a catastrophic anhydrous ammonia spill.

We almost succeeded there too.

Almost.

That seemed to be the refrain for the day.

*You almost caught Mason, almost caught Basque, almost stopped the train before it derailed.*

*Yeah, and you almost kept your promise to Lien-hua about upholding your integrity—but then you chose to work with Basque, agreed to leave him alone with Mason.*

I told myself that there was a good reason for it—saving people's lives.

But maybe I was just trying to justify my choice—which was something I've never been very good at.

*How much of your integrity are you willing to give up in your quest to save others?*

All of it, I suppose, based on the choices I'd made earlier today.

In addition to the case, I had some unfinished personal business, including telling Sherry Ritterman the truth about what her husband had said to me right before he died: the message that he was sorry about Iris.

And also, I felt like I'd left things unresolved with Tessa.

Before leaving DC, I'd explained to her that I was going to be leaving someone to watch over her and she'd told me, "You're gonna owe me big-time for this."

Yes, she was eighteen and she was a pretty self-reliant girl, but still, I felt responsible for her and couldn't help but want to do all I could to make sure she was safe.

Now as I thought about her, I recalled the day when she first told me she was going to refer to me as her father.

"Okay, I'm going to officially call you Dad from here on out."

"I'd like that."

"Not my stepdad—although I reserve the right to still call you Patrick."

"Fair enough."

"But this job of being a dad comes with a lot of responsibility."

"Yes, I know."

"So if I ever get married—which I actually doubt, because every guy I go out with ends up being a total loser, but if I do—you'll walk down the aisle with me?"

"Yes."

"And you'll be there for me if I ever get malaria or scurvy or something?"

"Malaria or scurvy?"

"I'm just saying."

"I'll be there no matter what. If you need me, I don't care where I am in the world, you need me, you call me, and I'll be on the next flight. You have my word."

I stared out the window at the clouds.

I wanted things to be cool with her.

*Take some time. Sort things out when you get home.*

The clouds were billowing into ominous thunderheads that somehow served to shift my attention back to the case.

Currently, we had no leads on Mason or Basque and I knew that more suffering was on its way unless we could come up with something soon.

So, administrative leave or not, I wasn't going to rest until that situation was resolved.

*Now seven gods use thirty-eight.*

*What does that mean?*

*To Mason everything is significant; it's all part of the story he's telling.*

*Every detail matters.*

Every.

Detail.

Matters.

The case appeared to be all about the train, but I've been in this business long enough to know that when something seems obvious you should be very careful—all too often there's a deeper truth that's running under the surface and things aren't what they at first appear to be.

He told me the climax would be tonight. I just had to figure out what that was going to be.

# 84

Kurt Mason arrived in DC and drove through the industrial district to the abandoned building on 669 Pine Street, where he'd kept his captive locked in the basement since last Sunday afternoon.

He'd chained her ankle to the bed, but had left enough food and water for her to survive for ten days. There was plenty of air. It was warm enough. She wasn't in any danger of dying of hypothermia.

He wasn't interested in torturing her or making her suffer. He'd even left a television and a stack of DVDs down there to help her pass the time. No, he just wanted to make sure she wasn't going to go anywhere.

After confirming that no one else was in the vicinity, he entered the building and knocked on the door.

He heard her crying.

Okay.

She was still alive.

Good enough.

He was the only one who knew she was here.

If anything happened to him she would be left there, locked up. Secure. Until she ran out of food and water.

And life.

He returned to the SUV and left for the place where the climax was going to occur.

++++

9:01 p.m.

After we touched down, I found Lien-hua waiting for me at the curb in her Infiniti Q60 Coupe.

She informed me that Brin was hoping we could swing by tonight so I could see Tryphena before visiting hours ended at ten.

At this time of day it would normally be about a thirty-five-minute drive to the hospital. However, with Lien-hua behind the wheel, we would probably be talking more along the lines of twenty-five.

My cell was still at the bottom of that Rudisill mine shaft, so I borrowed my wife's to call Sherry Ritterman.

"This is Patrick Bowers. Yes, listen; I'm sorry to be calling at this time of night. I need to . . . Well, I'm wondering if we could meet? . . . No, we haven't caught Mason. It's . . . Well, if we could talk in person? . . . Tomorrow afternoon should be fine. Yes, thanks. Two o'clock at your house? Alright."

Then I phoned my daughter to clear the air.

# 85

After her dinner with Lien-hua, Tessa had gone to a coffee shop nearby and ordered a no-whip, soy-mocha-latte-thing that Patrick would never have approved of. She was trying to concentrate on the novel she had with her, *Silence*, by Shūsaku Endō, but was distracted by waiting for a text from Beck that he was ready to meet.

She found herself rereading the same paragraph for the third time when her phone rang. Lien-hua's ringtone, but when she answered, it was Patrick on the other end.

A bit of small talk, then he said, "So, I know it's been a weird week, having someone assigned to watch you and everything."

"Yeah."

"Now that I'm back we'll reevaluate that. I . . . um, well, I get some time off while they sort through how many laws I broke working with Richard Basque."

"Time off, huh? Shooting for a little positive spin there?"

"You got me. In any case, since I'll be around, it doesn't look like we'll be needing anyone to protect you."

"Right." She couldn't help but feel a little conflicted about that.

*Well, Beck's already working on another assignment anyway.*

"Good," she said. "So, are you heading home right away?"

"Brineesha wants us to swing by the hospital. She really wants me to see her new baby. Are you still there?"

"I'm at a coffee shop, but it's pretty close. I can come back and meet you there, or I can see you at home. Whatever's best."

She got a notification on her phone: a text from Beck. He was done and could meet her anytime.

"Up to you," Patrick said.

"I'll let you know. I need to think for a sec. I'll text you."

"Okay."

End call.

She texted Beck back with the address of the coffee shop and he replied that he wasn't far and would be right over.

++++

Richard didn't know all the details of Mason's plan, but he knew enough, so when he didn't find what he was looking for at St. Mary's, he moved on to the next hospital on his list.

Tanner Medical Center.

++++

Sometimes it's best to go back to the beginning when you're trying to piece a case together, to set all your assumptions aside and look at things with fresh eyes, as if you were viewing them for the first time.

I thought of what Lien-hua had said to me at the hospital on Monday: that we needed to take into account the personal narrative the offender was working from, the posing, the meaning that lay beneath the appearance of the crime.

*The truth that lies beneath the appearances . . .*

Jerome Cole was last seen on Sunday evening leaving his friend's place at a few minutes after eight, but the security archives were accessed almost two hours earlier. No, it didn't make sense that Jerome would have been the one to do that.

But if not him, who?

Mason? But how did he access them?

What was I missing here?

I flipped open my laptop and, as Lien-hua wove through traffic, I used her phone as a hot spot and went online, then I logged in to the Federal Digital Database and began to sort through the personnel files to see if I could figure out who might've had access to that information.

# 86

The streetlights outside the coffee shop blinked on as darkness eased down across the city.

Tessa was texting Melody, letting her know about the meeting she had coming up with Beck and, in between texts, was watching out the window, putting on her best I'm-not-really-waiting-for-a-guy face.

Then she saw him heading her way on the sidewalk.

After a short internal debate, she grabbed her things and went to talk with him outside, where it would be a little more private than here in a coffee shop with a bunch of other people around inadvertently eavesdropping.

She caught up with him beneath the yellowish, hazy glow cast down from the vapor streetlight above him.

"Hi," she said.

"Hey." He fumbled to put his hands into his pockets, trying to look nonchalant. Wasn't working. "So, how are Mrs. Hawkins and the baby?"

"They're good. They named her Tryphena. I like it. It's pretty."

"Yes." Then, "It's crazy about Charlotte and your dad—he's okay?"

"He's fine. Yeah. He's good."

"Was he near the stadium when it happened?"

"I guess you could say he was in the general vicinity."

This conversation drifted into a silence that felt even more awkward than the first time when they were talking in the living room at home.

"So," she said, "you had an assignment today?"

"Paperwork. You were right, what you said last night about me having to spend my life filling it out. Sometimes it seems like that's all I do."

"Yeah."

Traffic coursed past them on the street nearby.

*Okay, just do this thing.*

She took a deep breath and dove right in. "So listen. I'm not usually forward like that—like kissing you last night. I usually just sit around waiting for the guy to make the first move, but I was . . . Look, I don't care that you're a few years older than me. I feel like we had something—okay?—chemistry, whatever. And I'm sorry I ruined it. I hope I didn't get you into trouble. That's why I wanted to meet. So I could apologize. I'm sorry."

He said nothing.

She wanted him to say something—anything—but he remained silent. "Okay," she said at last. "It's your turn now. You get to respond to what I just said."

He hesitated. He was obviously searching for the right words. "You know that superpower you told me you wished you had?"

"To not be invisible to you."

"Well, you don't have to wish for that."

"What do you mean? Why do you say that?"

"You're anything but invisible to me. From the first time I met you I haven't been able to stop thinking about you."

She stared at him dumbfounded. "But then . . . Why did you . . . ?"

"Pull away when you kissed me?"

"Was it just a professional-duty thing?"

"Well, there is that. And we can't ignore the fact that there's also an age issue here."

"Seriously, that's not a big deal. You can't—"

"Would your dad be okay with me seeing you?"

"I'm old enough to decide who I want to hang out with."

"I didn't mean it that way. But if it matters to him, then it should matter to us."

She had the sense that he was right, but she didn't want to admit that he was. Patrick would almost certainly not approve of her seeing Beck, and bringing it up to him might very well end things with this guy before they even got started.

"I want to get to know you better," he said, "but since we met while I was on duty protecting you, I feel like, well . . ."

"You need to talk to my dad."

"I kind of do. Yes."

She was about to counter that, but then the impact of what he was saying struck her.

*He really wants to see you. To get to know you. He does. He likes you.*

"So," Beck said, "is he still in Charlotte?"

"Who? Patrick?"

"Yeah."

"No, he just flew in. He's on his way to the hospital to see Brineesha and Tryphena."

Beck checked the time. "Maybe tomorrow we could connect and I could talk to him."

She'd kind of been hoping he would ask to go and talk with Patrick right away, but it probably wouldn't be ideal trying to chat there at the hospital when her dad was just hoping to see Brineesha and Tryphena.

"Sure," she said. "Tomorrow. That would be good. What are you going to tell him?"

Beck stared at her in the gentle glow of the streetlight. "That I think his daughter is pretty amazing. That I'd like to get to know her better." The way he looked at her seemed to somehow disarm her and fill her with courage at the same time. "And then I'll tell him why I asked to be reassigned today."

"What do you mean? It wasn't because you didn't want to see me?"

"Just the opposite. I did want to see you, but not while I was getting paid to do it."

She thought, thought, thought, then—

*Screw it.*

She did not want to wait until tomorrow.

"Follow me." She indicated toward her car. "You can talk to my dad tonight."

# 87

Since Brin had misplaced her cell phone before coming to the hospital, Ralph left his by her side, but he turned off the ringer so it wouldn't disturb her. She unplugged the room phone.

One of the nurses told him that it was time to give Tryphena a bath.

"I'll come along," Ralph said. "You can review it for me. It's been a few years."

"Of course."

Then he kissed his wife on the forehead. "We'll be back in a little bit, dear."

"Don't be too long. You know Pat and Lien-hua are on their way over."

++++

Kurt Mason passed the construction area across the street from the hospital and then cruised to a stop in the parking lot.

He didn't want to attract any undue attention, so he photographed the complex while still sitting in the SUV.

Tonight, after everything was done, he would post the pictures and go live with his site.

++++

As Lien-hua drove, I took into account what we knew about the case.

"Talk this through with me," I said to her. "Mason, he's always telling stories that relate to history or literature. So what's the story he's telling here?"

"Seven gods use thirty-eight . . . I know Angela and Lacey are looking into historical references he might have drawn from, but beyond that . . . I don't know. The team didn't find anything related to Native American myths or folklore, did they?"

"No. And Mason told me it wasn't what I would think. There's something else going on here."

"Well," Lien-hua said, "he left clues to lead you to Charlotte—the stolen Colonial-era weapons, the Meck Dec mnemonic, the Latin text message . . . He evidently wanted you to go down there."

"Yes, but based on what he said when I arrived in the mine, I don't think he expected me quite so soon."

I recalled the photos in the bedroom of his apartment, visualized them: the ones I recognized, the ones I didn't.

He used a textile warehouse.

And a mine shaft.

And he blew up the railroad bed.

All three.

*Three statues.*

Every detail matters.

*And a fourth.*

Ice ran through me, found its way to the base of my spine.

"It's the statues," I said half to myself.

*Yes, the ones on Independence Square, the place the Meck Dec had been signed. That was the key. That was—*

"What statues?" Lien-hua asked.

*No, please—*

"What are you thinking, Pat?"

"It all fits, in a twisted way, it all fits together. He's retelling the story of Charlotte. That's what he always does, he's . . ."

*No, no, no.*

I snatched up her phone.

*That's why Mason told you that the future ends tomorrow evening, Pat. That's why he told you to tell Ralph—*

"Pat, don't shut me out. What is it?"

I was punching in Ralph's cell number. "The four statues at the corner of Trade and Tryon. One represents industry—it's a textile-mill worker. One is transportation—that's a man with a hammer to lay railroad tracks. The third is a gold miner—and Mason used them all: the gold mine, the railroad tracks, the textile mill. But all those statues are facing the final one, the fourth one—"

The phone rang. I waited for Ralph to pick up.

"What's the fourth statue?" Lien-hua asked.

*Love stories—that's what he tells.*

*The tragic consequences of love.*

*But also death.*

*Love and death.*

"It's the one representing the future: a woman holding up her baby." I felt a harsh lump rise in my throat as I said the words.

"Oh." I could tell she was tracking right with me. "Brineesha and Tryphena. That's the story. Tragedy. Love. Death."

"The future ends tonight." I couldn't keep the dread out of my voice. "A mother and her child. Dying to complete the tale."

I waited for my friend to answer.

*Pick up, Ralph. Come on!*

Mason's story had unity and cohesion; it was every-thing he went for. It even had an ending that I hadn't seen coming.

Until now.

*Until too late—*

No, it wasn't too late. Mason couldn't have gotten up here by now.

*Unless he—*

The call went to voicemail.

"Ralph," I exclaimed, "it's Pat. Get to the room with Brineesha and Tryphena. I think Mason's coming after them."

I hung up and immediately called the hospital to have them get security over to Brineesha's room.

"How far to the hospital?" I asked Lien-hua.

"Six minutes." She punched the gas, swept past a car going ten miles over the speed limit, then whipped us back into our lane. "Make that five."

++++

Officer Desmond Smythe got the call to check in on someone named Brineesha Hawkins in the family birthing wing.

Other end of the hospital.

Great.

He sighed.

And, munching on his bag of chips, started ambling down the hall.

++++

Ralph watched as the nurse talked him through giving his daughter a bath.

"So, you already have one child?" she asked him.

"A boy. Yeah. But he's twelve. It's been a while."

"Well." She squeezed some water out of the sponge. "I'm sure it'll all come back to you. Don't be nervous. There's nothing to worry about. Your little girl is going to be just fine."

# 88

Kurt made sure that he had both the insulin and the sedative with him.

He would either introduce the insulin into Brineesha's IV, if she had one, or he would inject it into her arm.

There were several advantages to insulin: common, easy to acquire, it could be delivered intravenously.

When the nurses found that she was unresponsive, they wouldn't know why and wouldn't immediately think to check her blood-sugar levels. In the case of a woman who'd just given birth, they would probably think at first that she might have thrown a blood clot and they would send off for some blood work, stat.

By the time they figured out what was wrong with the victim, it would be too late.

The insulin would drop her blood sugar and, eventually, when it got low enough, she would slip into a coma that would ultimately prove fatal.

It was a relatively quiet, painless way to go.

He had something much different planned for the child.

He retrieved the pink CONGRATULATIONS! balloon he'd bought at the grocery store on the way up here from

Charlotte. There was a stork on it with a baby in a sling that it carried in its beak.

Perfect.

Balloon in hand, he entered the hospital and headed to the family birthing wing.

"I'm here to visit my sister-in-law," he told the nurse at the work desk. "She just had a baby today."

She glanced at the balloon. "Name?"

"Brineesha Hawkins."

"Room 114."

"Thank you."

"Tell her congratulations."

"I'll be sure to do that."

He passed through the hall. He'd made it this far, but now he needed to get into her room unnoticed.

From his research, he knew that new residents start at hospitals in July, so the nurses and doctors on duty would still not necessarily know everyone. Really, if there was ever a time of year to get in and out without raising suspicion, this was it.

Once Kurt was out of sight down the hallway, he found a doctor who looked about his size. The man was entering a patient's room and Kurt followed closely behind, flicking out his straight razor as he did.

++++

Lien-hua wove us through traffic.

Moments ago, I'd phoned the police dispatcher and told them what was going on. "There's already an officer on-site at the hospital," he assured me. "We're having him look in on Ms. Hawkins."

I tried Brin's room phone, but no one answered.

After I hung up, I processed this.

Was Mason working alone?

Debra had discovered that the security archives had been accessed Sunday evening. But we still didn't know who had accessed them.

I had a thought.

Maybe it was nothing.

Maybe not.

"You didn't receive a text," I said to Lien-hua.

"When?"

"Monday morning. Right before the attack."

"No, only the people there did." Then she caught on to what I was thinking. "Ah, but how did Mason know?"

"Right. You were supposed to be at the NCAVC with me and Ralph. Your physical therapy appointment was only set up a couple days before, remember? On Friday afternoon."

She caught on. "He had someone there. Someone who knew my schedule." Her voice was hushed. "Did we ever check Cole's phone to see incoming calls?"

"Yes. Mason wouldn't have used that phone . . ."

I stared at the cell. Thought about what we knew, what we didn't know.

Who could have accessed those security archives? Jerome?

*No, no, no, the timing didn't work.*

"Think motives, Lien-hua. Why would anyone help Mason? Why would anyone give him the security-camera locations or the cell numbers so he could text the staff?"

"Fear."

"Of what?"

"Losing something precious. Or someone precious." Then she said, "So, what did Mason tell you exactly? About seven gods?"

"He said, 'Now seven gods use thirty-eight.' "

"Why would seven gods use thirty-eight *now*? What happens now?"

"He told me it's not what I would think."

"Maybe it's not gods like we typically think of them."

*Don't discount anything.*

Meck Dec.

I am back.

The alternate spelling of the name of that mine: Rudisil.

All phone spellings—

"You're right," I muttered. "It's not. There was a photo at the apartment building, the address we were trying to track down: 669."

"But that hasn't brought anything up."

"Seven gods use . . ." I muttered.

*No, wait—*

*Oh.*

Who would have all the staff members' cell numbers? Who would know who was on duty? Debra had checked on the—

I stared at the number pad on the phone, the letters, the combinations:

```
7-gods-use-38
7-4637-873-38
```

I called the number.

Nothing.

*But it was never the numbers, always the message. Always what it spelled.*

I muttered aloud what I was thinking and right away Lien-hua suggested I plug the numbers into the site that calculates words from phone numbers. "Maybe it spells something else."

I'd already pulled up the site. I scrolled through the words and almost immediately found what we needed:

7463-787338
Pine-Street

"That's it," I said. "Pine Street."

"That's what it spells?"

"Yes. It was never about phone numbers. It was always about the codes, about the spellings . . . It's an address: 669 Pine Street."

"Why 669?"

"Because it spells N-O-W on a phone."

"Everything matters," she said.

"Exactly. There's a Pine Street over by the industrial district."

*Debra didn't find out who'd accessed the security archives.*

No.

Of course she didn't—

"You mentioned yesterday that Debra's been working on this nonstop?" I said.

"Yes."

*Her daughter Allie is nine . . . Debra said she was at camp, said she was at her dad's . . .*

"I need to talk to her. You said she called earlier to check on Brin, so her number's on your phone?"

"Should be."

I scrolled through her contacts, found it. First, I called dispatch and told them to get a car to 669 Pine Street to search the place, then I gave them the number to text when they had.

I tried Debra Guirret but she didn't pick up. I left a voicemail for her to call me. Then I texted her as well.

++++

Kurt was careful not to wake the patient while he dragged the doctor's body into the bathroom.

The arms of the lab coat were a little too short but he snugged them up his forearms so no one would notice.

He snapped a photo of the dead doctor and then, bringing the man's clipboard with him and leaving the balloon behind in the room, he passed into the hallway toward room 114.

# 89

Kurt entered Brineesha's room, eased the door shut behind him, and approached the bed. She did have an IV, which made sense, considering she'd had a C-section that afternoon.

"Good evening, Mrs. Hawkins." He held the dead doctor's clipboard in front of him and flipped through the papers as if he were consulting them.

"Hello," she said. "Who are you?"

He tapped the name badge on the lab coat. "Dr. Preet." Then he acted as if he were reading from the page. "It says here on your charts that I'm supposed to give you something to help you sleep." He reached for her IV bag.

"Where's Dr. Harber?"

"I'm doing rounds tonight. He asked me to check in on you."

Brineesha's face grew pale and Kurt realized his mistake. "Oh. Dr. Harber isn't a *he*, huh?"

Brineesha Hawkins opened her mouth to cry out but he swiftly covered it with his hand.

It didn't look like he would be able to go with the IV idea after all. No, he needed to deliver the insulin right away. Well, the subcutaneous overdose was much faster anyway.

But first he needed to calm her down.

Administering the sedative one-handed wasn't easy, but he managed to jam the needle into the base of her neck and depress the plunger.

As she faded out, he removed his hand from her mouth and gave her the insulin.

*There, now*—

"Kurt." It was a man's voice. Someone behind him near the doorway. "Turn around slowly."

Kurt Mason knew that voice.

He held his hands to the side and turned.

Richard Basque stood before him, a scalpel in his hand.

"I'm glad to see you, Richard," Kurt said. "I was hoping you'd make it here for the climax."

++++

"So," the nurse told Ralph, "we're going to keep her here under the baby warmer for a few minutes. Make sure she keeps her temperature up."

"And you'll bring her back to the room?"

"Absolutely." She slipped the pink hat onto Tryphena's head.

Ralph headed to the lobby to get a Mountain Dew and meet Pat and Lien-hua, who were on their way over from the airport.

As he did, he passed a break room for the doctors on the birthing wing. The door was ajar.

He stopped in his tracks.

He recognized it even though he'd never been here before. He'd seen it in a photograph—in one of the pictures hanging up in the bedroom of the apartment Kurt Mason had rented in Charlotte.

The photos were all of Mason's research sites. Locations for—

Ralph spun and sprinted down the hallway toward his wife's room.

++++

Officer Desmond Smythe was at the end of the hall when he saw a huge man barreling through the hall toward him. "Hey!" he yelled. "Stop right there!"

But the man didn't stop.

He tossed open the door to room 114.

Desmond drew his weapon and ran as fast as he could toward the room.

++++

Ralph knelt at his wife's side.

No one else was in the room.

He tried to wake her but she was unresponsive. He punched the nurse's call button just as the door behind him banged open and a police officer burst into the room, gun drawn.

"Step away from her!" the guy yelled.

"I'm a federal agent," Ralph shouted. "This is my wife. I'm reaching into my pocket. I'm going to show you my creds. Now lower your weapon."

++++

Lien-hua brought the car to a skidding stop in front of the family birthing center wing doors. I handed her cell phone to her and leapt out of the car—and saw Tessa and Beck Danner waiting nearby.

"Hey, Dad," Tessa said, "I—"

"Not a good time." I turned to Beck. "Go back to your car. Stay with her. I'll explain everything later."

Neither argued. They could tell something big was up. "Yes, sir," Beck said.

The two of them left for the car while Lien-hua and I rushed inside the hospital, to get to Brin's room.

++++

Richard Basque led Mason down the stairwell toward the morgue.

A fitting place for this man to meet his end.

"You killed Corrine," Richard said. "Why?"

"Your story is part of mine and her story is part of yours. It wouldn't have been complete if you weren't here at the end. There'll be a much bigger audience this way. Without you, the climax wouldn't be nearly as memorable."

"Well, then, let's make this memorable."

++++

By the time we got to Brin's room, Ralph was outside the door shouting for doctors to get over there *now!*

"Where's Tryphena?" I asked him hurriedly.

"End of the hall. Fourth room on the left. She's in the warming room."

"Stay here with Brin," I told him and Lien-hua. Then I took off to get Tryphena.

I was halfway to the room when the fire alarms went off.

# 90

The doors in the wing began to close automatically to contain the fire, and emergency lighting went on, throbbing red lights set at regular intervals down the hall.

Maybe there was a fire.

Maybe not.

When I arrived at the warming room, I found a nurse unconscious on the floor. Other than that, the room was empty.

Tryphena was gone.

I shook the nurse's shoulder and was able to revive her. "What happened?" I asked urgently.

"I don't know. Someone hit me from behind."

"Where's the baby that was in here? Tryphena Hawkins?"

"I . . . She's gone? Is she gone?"

Another nurse appeared at the doorway and while she bent to help the woman who'd been attacked, I returned to the hall to sort things through.

Patients were already filing into the hallways.

In a matter of moments these halls would be filled with doctors, nurses, patients.

There was no smoke.

In modern birthing wards there are plenty of measures

in place to stop baby theft, including systems that give each child something that looks like a miniature GPS-tracking ankle bracelet.

Crime prevention 101: If a child who's wearing one is brought within a certain distance of an exterior door, an alarm will sound and the door will automatically lock. So to get the baby out of the ward you'd need to remove the device, or, if you couldn't get it off, figure out a way to make sure the doors didn't lock you in when you tried to leave.

But a fire alarm would override that, of course, since you can't lock people in a hospital during a fire.

If I were trying to get a baby out of here, that's what I would've done: pulled the fire alarm. It would also create confusion and everyone would be trying to leave the building—which is exactly what you would want.

*So where's Tryphena?*

We could check the security footage, but that would take time.

I studied the hall, thought of what I knew of the floor plan of the hospital from being here in the past.

There weren't many ways out of this wing. Just two intersecting hallways, a stairwell that led down to the morgue and up to the other floors, but—

*The morgue. There's another exit through there—where they bring the bodies in. And the hall also leads to the parking garage.*

I saw Ralph hurrying my way. "Where's Tryphena?"

"She's gone, but—"

"Gone? What!"

"Call security, have them review the footage. Whoever took her can't have made it far."

"My phone's in Brin's room."

He shouted to a police officer who was close behind

him, and the guy left immediately to contact security and check footage from this wing.

Ralph was still coming toward me. I asked him how Brin was.

"Unconscious. Docs are with her. Lien-hua too." He was focused. Intense. Ready for action. "We need to find my daughter."

I ran to the stairwell. When I opened the door I saw it there on the floor: a hospital band had been slit through and discarded. I snatched it up. Tryphena's name was on it.

"Over here, Ralph!" I descended the steps, taking them two at a time, and banged open the basement door.

Ralph was right behind me.

The hall split off in two directions. By the looks of it, one hallway led to administrative offices and the parking garage, the other went past the morgue.

There didn't appear to be any patient rooms on this level and the emergency lighting was less substantial than it had been on the first floor. Dim red lights glowed to illuminate the hallway, while the fire alarm continued to cycle in the background.

Ralph unholstered his weapon. "You go right. I've got left."

"Good."

The hallway stretched before me, hospital-white and throbbing in the crimson, pulsing light.

Red like blood. White like bones.

Blood and bones.

I clicked on my Maglite and directed it in front of me as I sprinted down the hall, wondering if I'd been right about Pine Street, if the officers would get there in time, if—

I could only hope they—

I came to the morgue.

The door was closed but I whipped it open.

And found Richard Basque leaning over the autopsy table. There was a rolling gurney situated between us. I couldn't see what he was doing, but I could hear wet, rough coughing sounds coming from the table.

Someone was lying there.

From here it looked like he was wearing a physician's lab coat.

"Step back, Richard."

Basque turned and looked at me. He held a scalpel in one hand. Blood covered the bottom of his face and dripped from his lips.

Just like the first time I'd apprehended him.

A scalpel in his hand.

Blood.

A victim.

Full circle.

I had no gun—my SIG was in that mine shaft; the Glock was back in Charlotte.

Oh, well.

I would use my hands.

I pocketed the flashlight.

When Basque faced me, whoever was on the table rolled off the other side and landed heavily on the floor.

Then rose unsteadily to his feet.

Kurt Mason.

His abdomen had been sliced open, exposing a loop of intestines. It reminded me of my gruesome dream earlier in the week of a woman whose stomach had been torn open. His chest had been cut into as well. I had no idea how Mason was even able to stand with the extent of his injuries.

He snatched a bone saw off the counter next to him.

*How did Basque do that to him without restraining*

*him? Drug him? Knock him out? How did he get Mason to lie still for—*

"You promised to leave me alone with him," Basque said to me. He licked some of the blood off his upper lip.

"You've had plenty of time." Then I called to Mason, "What did you do to Brineesha?"

"You can't save her."

"What did you give her!"

++++

Ralph Hawkins found nothing on his end of the hallway or in the parking garage.

He hastened back to the stairwell and saw that the wing Pat had gone down was empty.

*Pat's in one of the rooms.*

He dashed forward to find out which one.

# 91

"I'm not going to tell you." Mason sounded firm but weak. "But it's too late for her."

"I know about Pine Street," I said.

"What?"

"Allie. I know who took Tryphena, and—"

"I—" He coughed and winced in pain, holding one hand against his open stomach to push back in parts of himself that were bulging out and unlooping in glistening, gruesome folds.

Richard said, "It looks like Brineesha and the baby die in the final act."

"You knew to come here." I felt my hands tighten into fists. "You knew Kurt was going after them."

"Of course. Patrick, don't forget who I am. I would've killed that little girl and eaten her myself if I'd had the chance. You know that."

Mason coughed and doubled over in pain.

He wasn't going to last long.

I went at Basque but he grabbed the rolling gurney and shot it toward me. As I leapt aside, he made his way to the door and escaped into the hallway. I debated for a second whether I should chase him or stay here with Mason to try to find out what he knew, but he was profoundly injured and he wasn't going anywhere.

Entering the hall, I shouted for Ralph, who I now saw sprinting toward me.

Basque had flared in the opposite direction, toward the loading area where they move corpses into and out of the building. He was too far away for Ralph to get a shot.

"I've got him!" I yelled. "Mason's in the autopsy room. He's dying. Get him to tell you what he gave Brin!"

"And Tryphena?"

"He didn't take her." I thought I knew who had, and, if I was right, we could still save her. "We'll find her!"

I swung open the door and saw Basque running across the parking lot toward a brightly lit construction area across the street, maybe fifty meters away.

I bolted after him.

# 92

Ralph entered the autopsy room, tossed aside the gurney that was partially blocking the doorway, and approached Kurt Mason, who was leaning against the counter, a bone saw in his hand.

"What did you give my wife?" Ralph said.

"It's too late. The story's over. No one will ever find Allie."

"Allie?"

Then he raised the saw and drew it violently against his exposed intestines, ripping out a long, bleeding clump of viscera that flopped heavily onto the floor beside his feet.

Before Kurt could collapse, Ralph grabbed the man who had killed six of his people earlier this week and had targeted his family tonight, and considered what he would need to do to save his wife.

++++

Tessa was standing outside with Beck, wondering whether or not there really was a fire in the hospital, when she saw a woman hurrying out one of the doors, carrying a crying baby.

With the fire alarm blaring, there were a lot of people

exiting, but this woman's urgency caught Tessa's attention.

When she repositioned the child in her arms, Tessa saw the pink hat the baby was wearing.

*It's the one Brineesha knitted!*

She gasped. "That's Tryphena."

"What?" Beck said.

"Hey!" Tessa yelled to the woman. "Come back here!"

But that only served to spur her on, and she hurried faster toward a nearby car, opened the door, slid inside, fired up the engine, and started toward the street.

"Stop her!" Tessa cried to Beck. "She's got Tryphena!" He raced across the grass to cut her off before she could make it out of the lot and onto the road that led toward the highway.

++++

As I chased Basque I thought of all the times we'd faced each other in the past and his words to me: "It feels good, doesn't it?"

Yes, it felt good to taste the darkness.

Yes, but one thing was going to feel even better.

Ending this.

He went at one of the construction workers, but the guy leapt out of the way, letting go of the industrial-strength pressure washer he'd been using. The hose shot backward, twisting and heaving through the air like a giant, spitting viper, until the handle reengaged and the hose dropped solidly to the pavement.

The generator was loud, and although I shouted for Basque to stop, I doubted he could hear me. He went for the hose and aimed the nozzle at the man who'd been using it only a moment earlier.

They were about four meters apart.

*No!*

Basque squeezed the trigger and a fierce, cable-tight stream of water cut through the air and hit the man's shoulder. The force torqued him to the side and drove him backward.

He fell and groped along the ground to get out of the path of the water. I tried not to think about what the coarse jet would have done to him if he were any closer to Basque, or if Richard had aimed it at the guy's stomach. With that much pressure it could have bored right through him.

I faced Basque and closed the space between us until I was less than two meters away.

The sound of the generator drowned out everything else, but that was okay. We'd said all that needed to be said.

The time for talk was over.

*If you go any closer and he aims that at you, it could—*
*This ends now.*

I went at him.

He directed the nozzle at my abdomen and squeezed the trigger. I spun, the jet sliced across the back of my wrist, tearing off my skin and leaving a streak of ragged red behind.

But I made it to him. Tackled him.

Somehow he managed to hold on to the hose, and as we landed, he was quick and rolled to the side, and I found myself on my back with him on top of me.

I'd almost forgotten how fiercely strong he was, and he held me in place while he triggered the water and blasted it just to the side of my face, moving it toward my left eyeball.

For the moment I was able to hold his arm at bay, but that wasn't going to work for long.

I remembered when I was fighting him in the marsh in April, when it looked like he was going to drown me. That night I was able to get out my knife and stab him in the jaw.

Tonight I had no knife.

No gun.

But I did have the Maglite.

While I struggled with one hand to keep him from drilling that column of water through my face, I used my other to tug the flashlight out of my pocket. I swung it up, flicked it on, and directed its beam within inches of his eyes.

As he flinched and squeezed his eyes shut, his grip on me loosened. I dropped the flashlight, grabbed his wrist and wrenched it backward, but he didn't stop squeezing the nozzle, and as we rolled again the stiff jet of water ripped across the front of his neck, stripping right through the skin and muscle.

A hot spray of blood shot from his throat, and though I lurched to the side, I wasn't able to stop it from splattering across my own face and neck.

As Basque struggled to breathe, his hand fell away from the trigger and the hose writhed backward briefly until the trigger locked in place and the water stopped shooting out and the hose fell lifelessly to the ground.

I pushed myself to my feet and looked at Richard.

The harsh stream had ripped through his external carotid artery. He was choking, bleeding out, drowning in his own blood.

As I stood there, I thought of death, of life, of justice and darkness and of how they all affect us. I thought of funerals and clarity, of integrity and choices about who we will become. We all have the same inclination for the darkness. We all need to keep ourselves at bay.

Behind me, someone shut off the generator and when he did, I could hear Basque gasping for his last few wet, useless breaths.

Then his body quivered.

And then it stopped.

He lay there unmoving, the blood pooling out of his shredded neck.

I could hardly believe that after all this time it was really over, that after all this time he was finally dead.

I thought that maybe his death would bring me some sort of satisfaction, but it didn't.

However, it did give me a sense of closure.

No, I'm not like him. He lived to see others die. I would die to see others live.

The construction worker Basque had attacked a few moments earlier was on the ground, holding his shoulder.

"You okay?" I asked.

"Yeah." He was staring at Basque's corpse, then looked at the blood splashed across my clothes, at the red streak where the water had scored the back of my hand. "You?"

"I will be."

I heard a car horn and when I glanced past him, I saw Beck rushing to position himself in front of a sedan that was about to exit the parking lot. He had his weapon drawn, and even from here I could hear him shouting for the driver to stop and put her hands on the ceiling.

The car screeched to a halt less than a meter from him.

As I started toward them, the woman exited the car.

It was Agent Debra Guirret, the woman who had served as the receptionist at the NCAVC building.

And she was holding a baby.

# 93

I could see things ending badly here, very badly.

I sprinted toward them.

"He took my daughter!" she cried. "He told me he'd kill her unless I did as he said. Please, he took my Allie!"

"Just calm down, ma'am," Beck said.

The baby she was holding was wailing. I recognized the pink hat. Tryphena.

To my left, Ralph was shouldering his way through the crowd of people who'd gathered outside, crossing the parking lot toward us.

"Debra," I called, "give Ralph back his daughter. Allie is going to be okay."

"Where's Mason?"

"It's over." Ralph shouted. "He's gone. He's dead."

"No!" A terrible look shadowed her face and I was afraid she might do something desperate.

"Debra," I said, "your daughter is going to be alright."

She shook her head. "You don't understand."

"No, I do. You love Allie. You'd do anything for her. Mason just asked you for the location of the camera and the work schedules. You didn't know anything about the explosives, did you?"

"No, I . . ." She trembled. "I had no idea it would . . .

I mean . . . And he said he wouldn't just kill her, but that he would . . . She's only nine."

She began reaching for her weapon.

"No!" Beck shouted.

Debra paused. She was weeping, repeating the name of her daughter over and over. "Allie, Allie, I'm sorry."

She was losing it.

Things were spiraling off sideways fast.

"Take it easy, Debra," I said. "It's— "

She cut me off: "But Mason is the only one who knows where she is. He's the only one. He said he would lock her up and leave her to die."

Beck still had his gun trained on her. He hadn't even flinched when the car was speeding toward him. Still hadn't.

On the one hand, with Tryphena there, I wanted him to lower his weapon, but I knew Debra was armed. She was despairing and maybe suicidal and I didn't know where things were going to go from here. He needed to keep that weapon out.

"Check your phone," I said to her.

"What?"

"Check your phone for a message."

Slowly, Ralph approached Debra. "I'm coming for Tryphena. Don't do anything to hurt her. I'm—"

"Stop!" she screeched.

He did.

My heart was still pounding hard and harsh from chasing Basque, from fighting him, and I tried unsuccessfully to calm myself, to catch my breath.

"Check your phone," I repeated. "Please. Before anyone gets hurt."

*Did the text go through? Was there enough time?*

I hoped so. Prayed there was.

Holding Tryphena to one side, Debra drew her cell phone out of her pocket and checked her messages. "How did . . . ?" she said disbelievingly. "Is this a trick?"

*Oh, thank God.*

"No. It's not a trick."

She stared at me. "So Allie's okay?"

I anticipated what the text message had been. "She's with the police now."

"But how did you—?"

"It was an address: 669 Pine Street. I called dispatch on the way to the hospital. I gave them your number."

Ralph held out his hands and Debra was trembling as she handed over his daughter.

"Get down," Beck commanded. Debra knelt and held her hands out. I promptly relieved her of her weapon and Beck cuffed her. He was on top of things. Professional. He impressed me and I was glad he'd been here watching Tessa this week.

Until we could get a police cruiser here, Beck kept an eye on Debra, although moments later when the dispatcher put Allie on the line, he held the phone to Debra's ear so she could talk to her daughter.

I took a breath.

So, the girl was okay.

Tryphena was safe.

I thought that Ralph being out here was a good sign. "So, what do we know about Brineesha?"

"They're treating her, giving her something called D50. She's gonna be alright. Mason gave her an overdose of insulin."

"How did you get him to tell you that?"

"I found a couple syringes in the lab coat he was wearing. They were empty, but I used to be an Army Ranger."

"You used to . . . ? Oh. You know how to get people to talk."

"When necessary. Yes. Let's just say I got him to open up."

I didn't ask him to elaborate. I wasn't quite sure I wanted to know the details.

An officer from the hospital arrived, and as we handed Debra over into his custody, Tessa found her way to Beck's side. "Not bad work there, Agent Danner. You ran right in front of that car. You didn't even hesitate."

"I'm not paid to hesitate, ma'am."

"Did you just come up with that line or have you been waiting to use it?"

"It just came to me."

Then he took her in his arms and kissed her.

And she kissed him back.

Hmm.

Well.

How about that.

This was a night full of surprises.

Ralph was staring across the street at Basque's body. "So, he's dead?"

"Yes."

He watched one of the guys move the hose away from Basque and he pieced things together: "I guess you could say the pressure got to him."

I looked at him. "Did you really just say that?"

A slight smirk.

"You've been watching too many Bruce Willis movies, my friend."

"You can never watch too many of those."

I glanced down. I was a mess—drenched from the water, splattered with blood. I patted my side. "Can you believe it? I think my stitches ripped out again."

"Imagine that."

Then he wrapped his mammoth arms around his tiny daughter to hold her. To love her. To protect her from the world.

And we went back inside the hospital to check on our wives.

# 94

The next day
1:55 p.m.

I knocked on Sherry Ritterman's front door.

There were still a few loose ends that we were wrapping up, a few questions that we were working on answering, but Brin and Tryphena were okay, and Debra's daughter, Allie, was fine. Debra was being questioned. Mason and Basque were dead. And I had a promise to keep.

Sherry opened the door and invited me in. I'd decided earlier that it would probably be best if I just said what I needed to say without entering her home. It would've just made it harder for her to ask me to leave afterward.

So I politely declined her invitation to come in and we stood there looking at each other from opposite sides of the doorway. Cool air from inside her home seeped out and curled around me.

"I heard about Mason," she said. "I'm glad it's over. I'm glad you got him. But Debra?"

"People will take extreme measures to protect the ones they love."

"Yes. That they will."

Then neither of us spoke.

"So," she said, "what did you need to tell me, Patrick?"

I took a small breath. "Sherry, last Monday when we were at the hospital and we were talking about when Stu died, I . . . well I told you what he'd said before he passed away."

"That he loves me. That he's always loved me."

"Well, that wasn't what he said. In truth, he told me something else."

She looked at me quizzically. "What do you mean?"

"Actually, he apologized."

"What are you talking about?"

"He said he wanted me to tell you that he was sorry. That he was sorry about Iris."

"Iris." I couldn't read her tone. "He said he was sorry about her?"

"Yes."

A tremor caught hold of her and she leaned one hand against the doorframe to steady herself. "Why didn't you tell me this earlier?"

*I was trying to protect you.*

"I should have. I'm sorry. I was afraid it would hurt you."

I had the inclination to lay a hand on her shoulder to try to comfort her, but thought better of it.

She began to cry, soft, tender tears that I wished I could wipe away.

*See? All you did was bring back harsh memories, Pat.*

*You shouldn't have said anything. You shouldn't have told her.*

*No, the truth is the one thing no one needs to be protected from. Remember?*

Well, maybe sometimes that's not the case.

Sherry wiped at the tears but didn't manage to get them all. "I was pregnant last winter." Her voice was quiet. "We didn't tell anyone. I wanted to have the baby and Stu told me he wasn't ready. He . . . Well, if it was a girl, I was going to name her Iris."

She let the words hang in the air.

I couldn't tell whether or not she wanted me to respond.

*It wasn't just Stu's way of apologizing; it was his way of saying that he loved Sherry. Both her and their baby.*

I was really struggling here, trying to find a way to help be part of the solution rather than adding any more pain to what Sherry was already feeling.

*Remember, when people are hurting they don't always need answers, sometimes they just need companionship. Just someone to listen.*

I wasn't the right person for that.

"My daughter," I said at last. "Her mother made the same decision, I mean—it's a long story. I don't know if it would help . . . but maybe you could call Tessa. When you're ready. If you need someone to talk to."

She looked unsure, but took a moment to write down my daughter's number. "Thank you." Then she hastily stepped back to close the door. "I'll have to see."

++++

Four hours later

Brineesha had recovered from the insulin overdose, but considering what she'd been through, the C-section, and the difficulties of the delivery, the doctors wanted to keep her admitted for another twenty-four hours.

She'd just finished nursing Tryphena and was now cuddling her.

Ralph, Lien-hua, and I were in the room. Tessa and

Tony had left a couple of minutes ago to get something to eat from the cafeteria.

Brin said, "There's one thing I still don't understand: How did Mason plan everything when he didn't know when Tryphena would be born? I mean, I was past due."

"It wasn't your due date that determined the timing," I replied, "it was the shipment of the anhydrous ammonia."

Ralph nodded. "He could have come after you and Tryphena anytime. Thank God we stopped him."

"Yes," Brin said. "Thank God."

Kurt had apparently been planning to post pictures of this whole thing, share his story with the world. Ralph found a website link on his cell phone, but Mason had died before he could post it.

Well, too bad for him.

"And Debra?" Brin said. "How did you know she was involved?"

"I didn't know it for sure," I admitted. "But she told me Allie was at her dad's house but she mentioned to Lien-hua that she was at camp. Also, she didn't identify who accessed the security-camera locations because she was the one who did it and she wasn't about to implicate herself. Finally, as the receptionist, she knew everyone's time schedules and who was going to be at work on Monday."

"So based on that, you guessed it was her?"

"I *hypothesized* it was."

She eyed me skeptically. "Sounds to me like you were going with your gut there, Pat. At least a little."

"Maybe a little."

"At last," Ralph said. "We've been waiting a long time to hear you say that."

"I can only imagine."

"Now that that's cleared up," he said, "I understand you have a meeting with Margaret tomorrow—isn't that right, Agent Powers?"

"Yup."

"I already put in the good word for you."

"Thank you." I had my phone out and was tapping at the screen distractedly. "There."

"There, what?"

I showed him the picture I'd taken of him wearing the dainty white gloves at the Mint Museum. I'd just posted it to the official NCAVC site. "This is for the Agent Powers comments."

"Okay, you need to delete that now."

I shook my head. "I'm not really sure how to."

"Oh yes, you are."

While we were going back and forth, Tessa and Tony returned and Tony asked almost reverently if he could hold his sister.

"Come on," I said to Lien-hua and Tessa. "Let's give them a little family time. There's a coffee shop nearby, right?"

"Yeah," Tessa said. "Not too far."

On the way to the car, she leaned close and said, "So, you haven't said anything yet, and I need to know what you're thinking. Are you weirded out that I kissed Beck last night?"

"He's a handsome-enough guy. Seems to be brave, professional, courteous. Good at his job. I think if I were you I would have kissed him too."

"You know, there's something very wrong with that statement."

"That's probably true."

"But you're cool if I hang out with him?"

"As long as it's okay with your mother."

Lien-hua winked at Tessa. "Don't get me in the middle of this."

"I saw that," I said.

"What?"

"That little winky deal there."

"Something in my eye."

"Uh-huh."

"You know, Tessa," I said. "I hope things work out with you and Beck. I really do. It's about time you ended up getting the guy."

"I'll say it is."

And then we went out for coffee.

As a family.

# Epilogue

Eleven days later

"Well, I think that's the last of it."

I set down the box of books I'd carried to Tessa's third-floor residence-hall room. No more stitches, but my side was still pretty sore, as was my forearm where I'd been injured during my fight with Basque. However, I didn't want my daughter to worry, so I didn't let on that it was hurting. "I think maybe I should buy you an e-reader. Save a couple trees."

"Actually, studies show the effects of the production of e-readers on deforestation isn't what—"

"I was kidding."

"Oh. Well, anyway, I like the feel of a real book in my hands. Call me old-fashioned."

"That's not exactly the first image that pops into my mind when I think of you."

"Oh. What is?"

"A raven spreading her wings."

She nodded, satisfied. "Now, see, that was a good answer."

++++

Tessa liked it when her dad called her Raven, always had.

She looked around her room.

Okay, so it was a mess.

Hopefully, she'd be able to clean up a little before her new roommate got here.

She knew her dad's side was still bothering him, but she let him pretend like it wasn't hurting. It was important to let guys do that sort of thing once in a while. Helped with their egos.

A lot had happened in the past week and a half.

Agent Guirret was facing some serious charges, but Ralph and Brineesha weren't pressing kidnapping charges.

Patrick's meeting with Director Wellington had gone better than he'd expected. The Office of Professional Responsibility had taken all of the circumstances involving his work with Basque into consideration and, evidently, the Director had even gone to bat for him.

In the end, he received an official reprimand.

Oh, well.

It wasn't his first.

Wouldn't be his last.

Some guy named Pierce Jennings was in the news. He'd lost his position at the National Security Council after he'd been discovered leaking information to the press. Not a huge deal, but Patrick seemed to find it satisfying.

Director Wellington's comment about how protecting innocent lives was more important than politics had gone viral. It might very well prove to be the best thing that could have happened to her political career.

Tessa had a feeling that a woman with her drive and ambition wouldn't stop at just a seat in Congress, but would eye the White House.

Imagine that—Margaret Wellington for president.

*Well, stranger things have happened.*
*Actually, maybe not.*

++++

Tessa seemed deep in thought.

I broke the silence. "I guess this is one of those things a dad is supposed to do, huh? Saying good-bye to his daughter at college?"

"It's there in the job description somewhere."

"Next to the stuff about coming to your side if you have malaria or scurvy?"

"Sounds about right."

A moment eased past us.

"There's something I wanted to tell you," I said.

"What's that?"

"You're not fungible, Tessa."

"Fungible?"

"It means you're irreplaceable. To be fungible means—"

"No, I know what it means, it's just not exactly a Patrick-word."

"I've been saving it up for a special occasion."

"Like a fine wine."

"Like a fine wine."

"Well, thank you, Dad. No one has ever told me I'm not fungible before."

"You're welcome."

She walked toward the window that overlooked campus. "So, I spoke with Mrs. Ritterman yesterday. She called me."

"I hope I didn't put you in too awkward of a position."

"No. It's fine. Anyway, she told me about Iris, about her abortion."

I waited. I could tell there was more. Tessa needlessly repositioned a box, then said, "Really, I didn't know what to say, you know? I finally just told her my story. I mean, there's no way I could speak for her baby, but hearing that I wasn't mad at my mom anymore seemed to help."

"Thanks for doing that."

"Yeah."

We were both quiet.

And that was okay.

"I have a present for you," I told her.

"A present?"

I unholstered my banged-up SIG.

"I thought that was at the bottom of the mine shaft down there in Charlotte?" she said.

"Yeah, well, after they retrieved it, I had it sent up here." I handed it to her. "I want you to have it."

"You're giving me a gun? On a college campus?"

"It doesn't work anymore. It got too damaged when I dropped it. I just thought it'd make a good souvenir for someone studying criminal science. It's not dangerous. I mean, basically, it's worthless, but—"

"It's not worthless."

"What do you mean?"

"It's full of your stories."

"I guess it is. And some of yours too."

"Yeah. True." She accepted it. "Seriously, that is very cool of you and I will get in a ton of trouble if anyone finds it."

"Do you want me to keep it at home?"

"Naw. I'll be discreet. I'm pretty good at keeping secrets when I need to."

She put the SIG on a shelf where it would be out of sight from her resident assistant.

"We've been through a lot," I said.

"Yeah. But I'm glad things turned out how they did. I mean, with you being my dad."

"Maybe I'll be teaching you someday at the Academy."

"Maybe you will."

"I love you, Tessa."

"I love you too, Patrick."

I gave her a kiss on the forehead and she gave me a hug that spoke volumes.

We were interrupted by a knock at the door.

A girl who looked about Tessa's age bopped into the room, carrying a paper bag from a fast-food joint.

"Hey!" she chirped. "I'm Giselle. Oh—love your hair!" She gently touched the dark blue streak in my daughter's hair. "You must be Tessa—I only say that because I met our RA and she said you were already here and—" Something out the window caught her attention and she glanced outside. "Awesome view of campus—wow! I mean, are you *kidding me*?!" Then, almost instantaneously, Giselle flipped her attention back to us again and offered me her hand. "And you are?"

"Patrick." I shook her hand. "I'm Tessa's dad."

"Honored to meet you." A slight nod and bow. She held up the bag of fast food. "Fat Pig Barbecue! I only brought two pulled-pork sandwiches, though. I wasn't thinking anyone else—"

"I was just leaving."

"Don't mean to run you off or anything. Oh, these sandwiches are *amazing*." She smiled at my daughter. "I'm super stoked. We're gonna have such a *sweet* year!"

Giselle plopped down at the desk and pulled out two pork sandwiches from her bag.

I patted Tessa's shoulder. "Well, I'll let you two alone to get to know each other."

"Awesome!" Giselle said cheerily. "Nice to meet you!"

"Nice to meet you too, Giselle." Then I said to my daughter, "Good-bye, Tessa. I'll text you."

"You can call me." She was staring uneasily at the pulled-pork sandwich Giselle was holding out to her. "I mean once in a while. Just to say hi."

"I will. I promise."

As I left I heard Giselle say, "I hope you're hungry, sis, 'cause Fat Pig Barbecue rules!"

Lien-hua had said good-bye to Tessa before our last trip up to the room and was waiting for me beside her coupe.

"So, how was it?" she asked.

"Harder than I thought it would be."

"You gave her the SIG?"

"Yeah. Not your typical dad/daughter gift."

"You're not a typical dad/daughter."

"I guess we're not," I said. "You know, I never really saw myself as being a dad."

"And I never saw myself as being a mom."

"Life is full of surprises."

"That it is." She gestured toward the door. "Ready to go?"

I let my eyes linger on the dorm and I thought of the last couple weeks, all that had happened, all that had led us to this moment.

You strive for justice, you move toward the light when you can, and you shake off the darkness that clings to you from living on this fractured planet of lost dreams and sharp heartache.

Because it's also a place that hope calls home.

Justice wrestles with the darkness and we are, each of us, caught up in the fight. We strive for the first, but have a weakness for the second and between them is a chasm that spans all of our souls.

"Pat? Are you okay?"

"Yeah. Let's go home."

Lien-hua took her place behind the wheel. "I think we make a good team, Agent Bowers."

"I think so too, Agent Bowers."

"So." She fired up the car. "Basque is out of the picture at last."

While it was true that Mason was gone as well, Basque was the one who'd plagued me the longest, who'd haunted me ever since my early days as a detective.

"He is," I said.

"And you start back at work on Monday."

"I do."

"So, what does the knight do now that the dragon is dead?"

"Hmm . . . That's an interesting way to put it."

*He wipes the blood off his sword and stands ready, because there are more dragons lurking out there in the hills.*

More dragons.

Lurking in the hills.

Yes, there are.

"I think, before anything else, he takes a break and spends the night at home alone with his wife."

"I think I like that plan."

*Yeah, and then when he wakes up tomorrow, the fight will go on again.*

Yes, it will.

And that's just fine by me.

# ACKNOWLEDGMENTS

Special thanks to A. J. Hartley, Cecil Stokes, the Mint Museum, Reed's Gold Mine, Marilyn Schuster, Liesl Huhn, Wayne Smith, Ryan Vernon, Scott Francis, Pam Johnson, Dr. Eva Pickler, Heather Knudtsen, Shawn Scullin, Dr. Clay Runnels, Darren Barkett, Dr. Todd Huhn, Trinity Huhn, Brent Howard, Susanna Einstein, Scott Boyd, Matt Walker, Dr. Ray Hunter, Simon Gervais, Shane Bowman, Tom Mendenhall, Maria David, Major Tim Danchess, Jeffrey Boggs, Paul Worley, the Charlotte Chamber of Commerce, Joseph Courtemanche, and Derek Pacifico.